The tombs were carved from ice, names and inscriptions embedded at their bases, final statements on their lives from family members who had outlived them. This was a place of no consolation, the true end of life for victims of accident or neglect or pure malice, only their bodies ensured of immortality on this bitterest and bleakest of worlds. Even the poorest of families were able to have their truedead brought here by virtue of communal funds, but this was scant consolation for the end of their very existence.

The sled began to slow again, and its snorts turned into something that resembled distressed barks. It refused a further nutrient stick. Shivaun checked the fuel bag, examining one of the sticks minutely. She took a knife from her belt pack and slit it open. White flakes spilled out of it.

'What is it?' Imrani asked.

'Polymer shreds. Waste material. The sled can't digest it.'

He frowned. 'I don't get it.'

Shivaun was slicing open the other sticks in the bag. They were the same. The flakes slowly spiralled down to the ground, little plastic snow flurries.

'The feed bag's been doctored,' she said. 'They don't want us to make it.'

Mortal Remains

or
Heirs of the Noosphere

Christopher Evans

VISTA

First published in Great Britain 1995
by Victor Gollancz

This Vista edition published 1996
Vista is an imprint of the Cassell Group
Wellington House, 125 Strand, London WC2R 0BB

A catalogue record for this book is
available from the British Library.

ISBN 0 575 60043 8

Printed and bound in Great Britain
by Cox & Wyman Ltd, Reading, Berks

96 97 98 99   10 9 8 7 6 5 4 3 2 1

For Richard Evans and Rog Peyton.
Two stalwarts.

All religions, nearly all philosophies, and even a part of science testify to the unwearying, heroic effort of mankind desperately denying its own contingency.

– Jacques Monod: *Chance and Necessity*

Let the good times roll.

– Ancient folksong

Part One

BLUE MOON

One

The houses breathed quietly in the dawnlight, leathery domes exhaling steam plumes into the chill morning air. Tired though she was after working all night in the city, Marea kept to the gravity trail, passing neat houses with their clusters of flowering oxygenia, her cloak tightly wrapped about her head and shoulders.

The sky was turning rose-gold with the approach of dawn. High on the horizon, she saw a streak of light which she first took to be a shooting star; but it did not vanish as she stared at it.

Their house stood apart from the others in a tree-fringed hollow. It opened a sleepy eye as she approached, then its doormouth parted, enveloping her in warm living air. As soon as she was inside, her cloak slid from her shoulders and scuttled over to the heart to bask in its warmth.

Marea found her husbands in the living chamber, both in a state of agitation. Yuri lay feverish on his bunk, his blanket cowering on the floor as if it had been hurled there in rage or delirium. Salih was fussing over him, trying to dab his brow with a damp cloth.

Marea hastened to the bedside. Yuri's eyes were closed, though she was sure he was conscious. Their console squatted unheeded in one corner, its big bulbous optic showing the weather forecast for the Tharsis region.

'Has he been like this all night?' she asked Salih.

He nodded anxiously, touching the womb-sac at his side. Salih was eight months pregnant, and Yuri's various sicknesses had grown ever more demanding each week that passed.

'Have you called the doctor?'

'I spoke to him myself!' Yuri cried, raising himself from his pillow. 'He was rude, unprofessional!'

He sank back down again. His face shone with sweat, and his eyes were glazed. They closed again.

'The doctor said there was nothing physically wrong with him,' Salih announced sheepishly. 'He said it was transference, sympathetic pregnancy pains.'

Which was what they had known all along. And yet Salih continued to behave as if he was actively causing Yuri's ailments.

'Did he recommend anything?' Marea asked, barely controlling her impatience.

'Bindweed tea,' Salih replied. 'As a sedative and restorant.' He fiddled with the attachment joining the polymer umbilical to his navel. 'We're out of it. I didn't like to leave him.'

Marea gave a great sigh, then turned and went out, calling for her cloak. It was dozing, but it stirred reluctantly, loping over to her and clambering up on her shoulders. The doormouth opened at her command.

Outside, the sun was just rising over the rim of the canyon. The streak in the sky was still visible, broader, brighter now.

Their horse was about to foal and could not be ridden. Marea went around to the back of the house where their tractor sat, its scandium flanks and balloon wheels coated with a season's rusty dust. She wiped clean the sunsensors with a gloved hand, climbed up into the driver's seat and punched the ignition. Nothing. She tried again. To her surprise, the engine began to hum, then whined into life.

Grinning, Marea put the tractor into gear and headed off. The grin belied her irritation. Really, both her husbands were infuriating at times. Yuri was temperamental and demanding, while Salih was a caring and domesticated man who unfortunately lacked initiative. They tended the crops in their plantation while Marea pursued her career in the city. Two standard years into their marriage and she continued to debate the wisdom of the contract, as she had done from the start. Both Salih and Yuri had been persistent suitors, and in the end she had just given in. Now there was to be a child, and it might have been triplets or quads if she hadn't stood firm. Not that the Marineris Valley was overpopulated – she simply hadn't wanted the responsibility of more than one child, and damn the social stigma. Neither of her husbands knew that the egg which she had donated had come not from her own womb but from the ovum bank in Bellona.

Of course it was unforgivable: a deceit and a betrayal of both men. But the truth was she could not envisage a permanent life with them, and leaving would be far easier if any child of theirs was no flesh of hers. There were times when she despised herself for even thinking this. Really, both Salih and Yuri deserved a better wife.

She drove the tractor off the gravity trail, her weariness lifting a little with the diminished tug on her flesh and bones. She followed the rough track which wound gradually upwards through oxygenia scrub and crater plantations of omicorn that shone lemon and lime against the ochre earth.

As the sun warmed the land, the frost around the houses' vent holes melted away; water began to trickle in irrigation channels. To the south, vapours rose from the squat towers and pyramids of Bellona as the city stirred with the morning. The bright streak in the sky was more like a flaming meteor.

'What do you suppose that is?' she said aloud to her cloak.

The creature twitched on her shoulders but made no other response. It had no language, no intelligence really, just the instincts and capacities for which it had been fashioned.

'You can get down,' she told it, beginning to feel warm.

The cloak slithered off her shoulders and curled up on the passenger seat, its pointed snout buried under black-furred paws, slitted grey eyes closed.

At the very edge of the plantation she found the craterpool where the bindweed grew. The canyon walls reared up directly ahead of her, blotched with blue-green aquavines whose pods exploded like gunfire each spring, sending torrents of water down the slopes to irrigate the valley.

Suckerflies were darting over the icy surface of the water, so Marea approached cautiously and cut a handful of the tall bindweeds at the pool's edge. She sliced off the best of the leaves and put them in her pouch.

A distant sound like a terrible shrieking carried to her ears.

She looked up and saw the flaming meteor – huge now, and plunging directly towards the ground. The tortured sounds grew louder, and Marea saw that it was not a meteor but a mothership, irreparably damaged, blistered and blazing with friction heat, screaming in agony.

Her cloak began to mewl in alarm. It scuttled out of its seat and darted for cover under the tractor.

Marea stood transfixed. The ship was big, its serpentine head opening out into a bulging mottled body of fins and tendrils and a ragged, charred hole where the vent ducts should have been. Its neck reared and twisted, and the shrieking sounds continued, awesomely loud.

All Marea could do was stand and watch. At the very last moment before the ship disappeared from sight behind a jagged elbow of the canyon, she thought she saw an emergency pod eject from its head and go spiralling down. Then there was a huge explosion which sent her reeling.

As she lay there, tangled among the bindweed, fragments of the ship's polymer hull began to rain down on her, drifts of fibre and organic coolant, shards of bulwark chitin and bone.

She scrambled to her feet. A cloud of dust was rising from the side canyon known as Snake Vale. Without a moment's hesitation, Marea hurried off towards it.

The mothership had come down close to where Snake Vale joined the canyon proper. There was little left of it. As the dust settled, Marea saw that the head and neck were just a gory mass of charred tissue and splintered bone. There was no hope of finding any of the crew alive. Even the heat-resistant hull had burned away, and only the ship's broken ceramic ribs and spine remained of the superstructure.

She approached the wreckage with caution. The heat was intense, oils and other secretions sizzling on twisted metal plates, greasy smoke rising up into the pink sky. Then the ship lurched, and Marea leapt back in terror, thinking it was about to rear up. But it was only the foreribs collapsing as the great beast settled further in its death.

Marea scanned the surrounding slopes. Wreckage was strewn everywhere, bloody flesh and plastic littering the aquavines. Then she saw it. Halfway up one of the slopes the emergency pod was flashing whitely in the dawn.

Marea scrambled up the slope, stumbling through the woody vinestems which hugged the ground like coiled rope. She was puffing like a house by the time she reached the pod.

There was a dark spot at the centre of the pod, and when she touched it the pod flipped open. Inside the small compartment nestled an egg.

It was no bigger than a baby's head, a perfect fleshy oval swirled with purple and red veins. A womb. Marea instinctively searched for the umbilical, intending to connect it to the navel implant which she had had put in in case Salih proved unequal to the pregnancy. But the womb had no umbilical.

Gently, she lifted it out. It was warm to the touch, and she felt as if the life inside was snuggling in her arms, relieved to have escaped a death that Marea knew someone had planned for it.

She clutched the womb to her breast and fled back to the tractor. Soon other people from the surrounding plantations and from Bellona itself would come to investigate the crash. She had to get the child away to safety, hide it in case the people who wished it harm should find it.

Her cloak came out from under the tractor to greet her, its broad furry tail sweeping the dust in pleasure.

'Look what I've got,' she said to it. 'A baby.'

She climbed into the tractor and opened the storage bin behind her seat. The cloak loped after her, curious and puzzled.

'We're going to look after it,' Marea told her pet. 'But you mustn't tell anyone. Not even Yuri and Salih.'

She wrapped the womb in an emergency thermal blanket. It fitted perfectly in the bin. She closed the lid and locked the latches.

'Not a word,' she reminded the cloak, who was peering into her face, eyes wide with uncomprehending inquisitiveness. 'This is a secret between the two of us.'

She swivelled around in her seat and started up the tractor. As she moved off, she realized that she had lost the pouch containing the bindweed. She gave the engine full throttle.

*

The room was white, and there was a window opposite with a pale blind drawn on it. For some time I knew nothing, registered nothing, apart from this. Then gradually I became aware that I was lying in a bed, groggy and weak, unable even to raise my head.

Time passed, and I did nothing except stare at the featureless ceiling and walls. It was an effort to keep my eyes open, to do anything except register my shallow breathing. It was slow and delicate, like drawn-out whispers, or sighs.

Then at length I became aware of a movement nearby. A woman's face loomed in front of my eyes.

She was fair-haired and olive-skinned, with strong, attractive features. Only by looking at her did it register on me that I was a man. She smiled down at me. I was seized with terror.

I felt her hand behind my head, lifting me up. I tried to scream, but couldn't. I wanted her away from me, was terrified without reason at the sight of her.

She was holding a cup to my lips.

Somehow she made me drink. The water went down my throat like a cool balm. I hadn't realized how parched I was.

Some of my terror must have registered in my eyes, because she stroked the side of my face with her fingers.

'It's all right,' she whispered. 'Just rest. You're going to be fine.'

Her voice was gentle, encouraging, and I sensed that it was important to her I did recover. But this did nothing to reassure me. I was certain she meant me harm.

She lowered my head to the pillow. And then she was gone.

Marea met Tunde at the terminus on the outskirts of Bellona. His shuttle, a crystalline spirogyrator, landed on time but he was delayed at customs. There was a heavy security presence everywhere, helmeted politia toting pulse-pistols and stopping people at random for questioning. Marea had to show her identity disk, and its information was double-checked with a console before the officer was satisfied.

When Tunde finally emerged, his big dark face broke into a broad grin at the sight of her. They embraced one another.

Though they had met strictly through business and saw one another only infrequently, they had become good friends.

'What's going on here?' he asked her. 'You at war or something?'

Marea shrugged. 'There's some security flap. As usual, no one's told anyone what's happening.'

Marea had a company gravlev waiting outside the terminus, a compact but racy two-seater into which Tunde's frame barely fitted. He was tall for a Venusian, and might have passed as a native of Mars.

'How long's it been?' he asked her.

'Nearly a year.'

'That long? You're looking as good as ever.'

'You're only saying that because you know I'm married.'

He grinned again. 'How are they both?'

'We're soon to be parents.'

'Really? How many?'

'Just the one.'

He adjusted his seatbelt. 'Very frugal of you. No instant family, eh?'

'I persuaded them against it.'

He eyed her. 'This some sort of ideological statement?'

Little did he know.

'Maybe it is.'

He didn't follow this up. 'Boy or girl?'

'We decided to leave it in the lap of the gods.'

She drove off, merging with the city-bound traffic.

'How's your trio?' she asked presently.

'Blooming,' he replied. 'Eight years old now. They keep Yolande and me occupied, I can tell you. You should come and visit us sometime.'

'Venus? I've never even made Olympus Mons.'

'You'd like it. Richer air, plenty of water.'

'Bioforms oozing out of the slime everywhere.'

He chuckled. 'Something like that. Who's carrying the baby?'

'Salih. We were going to draw lots, but he insisted.'

He gave an exaggerated sigh. 'You've broken my heart. I was hoping you'd pack them in and run away with me.'

She pulled out to avoid a decipede that had halted and was

retching in the inside lane. 'You'd never leave Yolande and the kids, and you know it. Uh oh.'

The traffic was slowing, piling up as they approached a toll gate. Once again, armed politia were checking IDs and baggage.

It was half an hour before they were through. Tunde always travelled light, his attaché case containing a single change of clothing and his comlink. He kept another wardrobe in the company apartments, so regular were his visits to Mars. An officious female officer insisted on checking every detail of his business. While Marea simmered with irritation, Tunde remained implacably courteous and cooperative. Finally they were waved on.

'I could have hit her,' Marea said as soon as they were clear.

'Wrong move. You get their backs up and they'll find ways of delaying you longer. Relentless courtesy, that's the answer. It unnerves them, and they can't wait to be rid of you. What are they worried about, anyway? Found a nest of Augmenters or something?'

Marea kept her eyes on the road.

They lunched in the company dome, overlooking the extractor pens. Some of the great beasts were dozing in the midafternoon warmth while others continued to munch their quota of ground rock.

Tunde had slept through the interplanetary leg of his flight and was ready to get on with business. His company, Vesta Variations, supplied hers with custom-grown bioforms – everything from surveyor hounds to armour-plated borers. Marea left him with the line managers who were better equipped to explain the difficulties their extractors were experiencing with the gastro-smelting of certain lanthanide ores currently in great demand. There were limits to even her tolerance, and the attraction of watching behemoths excrete gleaming nodules of neodymium had long waned.

Marea had been on duty since dawn that morning, and her work was over for the day. But she had arranged to have dinner with Tunde in Bellona that evening – he was on a short visit, and she wanted to make the most of him – so she went to the recreation dome and sat in a masseur for an hour. Afterwards she checked her locker to ensure that the womb remained safe inside the holdall where she had hidden it.

As before, the womb was warm to the touch and apparently quite vital. For three days she had hoarded it and pondered over its self-sustaining nature. She could only guess at how developed it was: five months, perhaps, in comparison with an ordinary umbilical womb. How did the embryo obtain oxygen and food for its development? She had never seen anything like it, but she daren't make any enquiries for fear of arousing suspicion.

Two colleagues were coming down the corridor. She hastily returned the womb to the locker. Ever since the crash at Snake Vale there had been politia everywhere, conducting searches in the city and countryside alike. There was no official explanation, but Marea was positive it had to be connected with the womb; they knew it had survived, and they wanted it. What for? She hadn't the faintest notion. All she knew was that she had to protect it, keep it safe.

She asked a console beside the levelator to call home. Presently its optic flashed into life, showing Salih seated at the kitchen table.

'How is he?' she asked immediately.

'Bilious,' Salih replied, looking pained. 'But the fever's passed.'

'Tell him to go out for a walk. Get some air.'

'He was asking for bindweed tea.'

'Why doesn't he get it himself?'

Salih appeared taken aback. 'What are you so angry about, Marea?'

'Nothing.' She was impatient with the trivialities of their relationship – especially with Tunde in town. 'I'm going to be late. I have to take a client to dinner.'

'What time will you be back?'

She suppressed a sigh. 'When you see me.'

She heard Yuri's voice, demonstrative and wheedling. Salih gave him his attention for a moment, then turned back to Marea.

'Yuri was wondering if you'd bring him home some dispepsin, if it's not too much trouble.'

Salih's tone was perfectly reasonable, but to Marea it was like an accusation, a moral obligation.

'Can't you get it from the store?'

'He prefers the brand they sell in Omnimed.'

'Don't count on it,' she said. 'End call.'

The optic went grey. When Marea did not move or speak, it shuffled over to its usual place in an alcove.

She took the gravlev back into town and sat in a park. The city busied itself around her, workers boarding serpentines, cleaners munching debris from disposall chutes. Lights came on in window slits, holograms shimmered into life, green beetles emerged from flagstone cracks and crawled over her boots, denizens of the city's nooks and crannies with agendas wholly *un*human.

A passing console stopped to announce a public vote on the question of funding for an experimental centre where children would be gathered together on a daily basis to learn from tutors rather than getting their education at home. Marea listened briefly to the summary of the issues, then voted against the proposal. She paged the news. Most of it was routine Martian affairs with no mention of the womb, though one item from the Uranian ecosphere featured the grisly suicide of a woman who had inexplicably gone berserk in her compartment in Umbriel East, mutilating her living chamber before hurling herself out of the window. It was hard to credit, unnerving to dwell upon. Imagine going mad. Imagine killing yourself. The whole thing was disgustingly primitive.

Across the square was one of the city's shrines, a tiered dome of roserock and mirrored plass topped by a silver needle jutting to the heavens. Inside there were several levels ringed with booths. Bored-looking intercessors patrolled the balconies or sat with visitors at whorlwood tables in the central concourse.

Marea entered a booth on the second level, locking the door behind her and sitting down at the Noosphere interface. It comprised a white neural hood laced with biocircuitry that coiled into the prayer terminal with its hand sockets and touchpad controls.

She pulled the hood down and focused on the icon, a swirling kaleidoscopic crystal. She tried to empty her mind, to concentrate wholly on herself and her identity as Marea Elodaris, twenty-six standard years old, a native of Bellona City on Mars, shipment facilitator for Marineris Metal Conglomerates. She filled her mind with as much of the pure essence of herself as she could. And she felt the Noosphere begin to stir, to reach out the warm dark folds of its vast communality towards her.

As always, she sensed Takti, her maternal grandmother, most strongly. She was a wry and mischievous woman who had raised her after her parents emigrated to Ganymede with their new quins when she was two years old. Her grandmother had died and been absorbed into the Noosphere five years before, and she greeted Marea with her customary warmth and pleasure. But there were others, too – great-grandparents and their ancestors on both sides of the family, much of her whole lineage stretching right back to the distant days when the Solar System was first settled and the Noosphere established. Most she had never known except through the Noosphere, but they had become friends and counsellors to her, confidants who offered their own wisdom and that of the billions who had entered the Noosphere on death. They spoke to her not in words but in a flood of moods and emotions that enriched her own understanding and calmed the anxieties of the physical life which they had now transcended.

There were people who communed with the Noosphere every day, some for days on end, but Marea was not one of them. She rationed her visits, fearful of the dependency that often characterized the Devout. Today, however, she was in pressing need of her ancestors' guidance. As the multiplicity of their personalities jostled in her mind, she opened herself fully, reliving the morning of the mothership's death fall and everything that had flowed from it. What was she to do with the womb? Was the security clampdown in the valley connected with it?

She expected a calm and calming response from Takti and the host, and was taken aback when they responded with unease and even agitation. They confirmed with urgency that to possess the womb was to be in great danger. The womb *was* important, though her ancestors could not make clear to her *why*. There was a faction in the physical world that wished to

acquire it and would stop at nothing to do so. Her very life
might be in danger. Yet to surrender the womb to the authorities would also be to draw unwelcome attention to herself
and court a different kind of danger. The responsibility was
not hers. She must relieve herself of it.

Marea raised the hood, breaking the connection. The entire
emotional tone of the response had startled her, even though it
had merely confirmed her own suspicions. And she was not
simply shocked, but also irritated. Takti, whose presence
always overpowered that of all the others, seemed almost
disapproving in her unease. Marea felt a little like a precocious
child being scolded by censorious parents for being too forward. She left the booth and hurried out of the shrine, avoiding
the eyes of any intercessors.

Almost an hour had passed since she had entered the booth:
time often sped by when she communed with the Noosphere.
She drove back to the recreation dome.

With some trepidation she approached her locker, certain
she would find it empty, ransacked or surrounded by politia
who would arrest her on sight. But the womb was in the
holdall, warm and alive. Closing up the bag, she heaved it over
her shoulder, shut the locker and left.

As she was heading down the corridor, a console paged her.
Its optic winked on to show Tunde.

'Marea,' he said, 'I'm sorry, but I'm not going to be able to
make dinner.'

She did not try to hide her disappointment.

'We've got a real problem with the extractors. One of them's
died, and I'm trying to arrange immediate freight back to
Venus.'

'Where are you?'

'At the terminus. I may be here all night.' He shrugged
helplessly. 'The wheels of bureaucracy . . .'

'Damn.' The holdall was heavy in her hands. She did not
know what to do with it, or with herself. 'Have you eaten?'
she asked.

He shook his head.

'I'll come over. Be with you in half an hour.'

She ended the call before he had the chance to protest.

The terminus was on the far side of the city, an octagon of interconnected runways and control tower mushrooms. Tunde was sitting outside a sterile room in one of the off-planet warehouses.

'You look terminally bored,' Marea said to him.

The pun was feeble. His only response was to shake his head wearily.

'How long have you been here?'

'Hours. I'm waiting for customs to OK the carcass.'

Through the door window, Marea could see a trio of customs people inspecting the dead extractor. It was a calf rather than fully grown, but it filled the chamber. It had been laid on a huge slab, its ample belly lasered open to reveal the organoceramic digestive tract. Fortunately the blood had been drained from the beast, and Marea was just about able to bear the sight of undigested ore in its stomach and lumps of slag in a slit portion of the lower intestine. One of the officials was running a bioscanner over the innards.

'They're checking it for bugs,' Tunde said. 'They'll only let it through when they're satisfied it's clean.'

'Do you have to wait here?'

'I stayed on hand in case anything cropped up.'

'Come on. Let's go and eat.'

In fact eating was the last thing on her mind, but she was restless and wanted to get as far away as possible from any sort of officialdom.

They rode the levelator up to the restaurant.

'What's in the bag?' Tunde enquired.

'Don't ask.'

He scrutinized her with a mixture of interest and suspicion.

'It's not a bomb,' she said defensively.

He smiled. 'You say the nicest things.'

The restaurant had a surprisingly varied menu, and Tunde insisted she try the *oolaga* soup, a regional Venusian speciality. Marea dutifully spooned her way through the dish, thinking as she did so that she preferred protein spirals when they didn't wriggle in the mouth.

Tunde showed her holos of his son and two daughters at play in the Lavinia theme park. Neither of them personally knew one another's families, but that was part of the fun. They bantered and flirted with one another as was their custom, though this had a serious edge. If she had met Tunde before she married, and if he had been a free man ... well, it was foolish to speculate, really. They had met one another too late and had to settle for the kind of close friendship that neither of them could allow to slide into something more intimate for fear of ruining everything.

Marea sipped her frostwine. It was then Tunde told her that this was to be his last visit to Mars for the foreseeable future.

'I'm moving from product development to home sales.' He sounded apologetic. 'It's a sideways move. Sideways and slightly downwards, I suppose, but I asked for it. The kids are growing up, and I'm missing a lot of them with all this travelling.'

It made sense: he had always doted on his children.

'I'll miss you,' she said.

'Likewise.' He stared at her across the table, suddenly very serious. 'What's up, Marea? You look worried half to death.'

'I'm hoping I can keep the *oolaga* down.'

He didn't smile, just kept staring at her.

It was all she needed – a show of real concern. She proceeded to pour out the whole story, as she had done to the Noosphere but now bringing it right up to date. Tunde listened without comment until she stopped talking.

'And it's here?' he said. 'In the bag under the table?'

She nodded, checking for the umpteenth time that no one nearby was listening to them.

'Has anyone else checked it out?'

She shook her head.

'I still don't understand why you think someone wants to harm it.'

'I can't explain it. It's an overpowering feeling, a certainty. My ancestors felt the same, don't forget. I've got to get rid of it, Tunde, but make sure it's safe with whoever it's passed on to.'

Tunde looked out the window as an interworld sicklewing took off along a runway, phosphor-nodules twinkling in the dark.

'I think I may know someone,' he said.

Marea had been half hoping for this; at the same time she knew what a wrench it would be to surrender the womb to anyone else.

'Who?' she said.

'Someone on Venus.'

'You'd sneak it back there?'

'I'd have to. And it would take the heat off you, wouldn't it?'

'But how? They're searching everyone and everything. You'd never get it through customs.'

He winked at her. 'Maybe *I* won't have to carry it.'

A light speared into my eyes, making me close them instantly. I did not dare open them again; I merely lay there, too limp to move. My insides felt as if they had been liquefied.

I could hear sounds, someone talking, but it was distant, muffled. I tried to concentrate and listen without opening my eyes, without letting them know I was awake. But it was like being under water; I couldn't make out anything. All I knew was that there were two different voices.

Presently they diminished and drifted away as I sank down again.

It was past midnight by the time they returned to the freight terminal. The customs people had gone, leaving behind a console which informed them that the extractor was cleared for export on condition that its insides were sealed for transit. A plasm-welder had been provided for this purpose.

'Excellent,' Tunde said.

He dismissed the console. When it was gone, he picked up the welding torch and turned to Marea.

'Give me the womb. We'll put it somewhere where no one'll find it.'

Marea felt as if he had somehow seized the initiative from her. He was confident, assertive and wouldn't say what he intended to do with the womb beyond showing it to a trusted colleague who would be in a better position to establish where it had come from and what it contained. Marea wanted more, but Tunde insisted she simply had to trust him; the more she knew, the more danger she would be in.

She knew she really had no choice. The womb did not belong to her, and she could not guarantee its safekeeping.

Tunde switched on the welder. She realized what he intended with a combination of delight and disgust.

'It'll be perfectly safe,' he assured her. 'Packaged, protected, hidden from prying eyes.'

'I'm not sure I like the idea, Tunde.'

'It's the only way. Otherwise it'll show on the bioform registers.'

Gently she removed the womb from the holdall. She wanted to keep it for herself. But that would be foolishness, madness, not to mention a continuing betrayal of both her husbands.

Tunde was waiting. With great reluctance, and an even greater sense of ceremony, she handed over the womb. He tucked it under his arm as if it were a ball.

'I'll need you to stand watch outside,' he said softly, 'to make sure we're not disturbed.'

Again she hesitated. Then she turned and went outside.

After it was over Tunde took her to the chamber he had rented for the night at the terminus. Though they both knew that this was perhaps the last time they would see one another in the flesh, there was some final barrier of reticence which neither of them was quite willing to breach. Instead they spent the night talking as a dust storm blew up outside. When dawn finally broke and it was time for Marea to leave, Tunde kissed her chastely on the cheek and wished her every happiness in the future.

'Keep it safe, won't you?' she whispered urgently.

He nodded. 'I promise.'

'Will you let me know what's happened to it?'

'Count on it.'

Marea drove home slowly through the storm, grit blasting her windscreen and tinkling in the exhaust outlets. She stuck to the gravity trails to minimize the effects of the cross-winds.

The storm had died away by the time she turned up the main track towards home. The houses were venting dust from their insides while parasol trees unfurled their silver leaves to the morning.

As she descended into the hollow, she saw her own house collapsed like a punctured ball. Yuri lay face down in the gaping doormouth.

She leapt out of the gravlev and raced over to him. There was frozen blood in his nostrils and ears, and his body was quite cold. A metal dart was embedded in the base of his skull.

She found Salih in the bedchamber, sitting in an armchair cradling the womb. His eyes were open, and relief washed through her. Then she saw the puncture in his neck where the dart had gone in.

The womb-sac was below room temperature, but alive. Marea unplugged the umbilical from Salih's navel. Tears were streaming down her cheeks. She slit the belly of her tunic and slotted the valve into place. Within seconds she felt her body responding to the foetus's demands, dormant hormones surging into her bloodstream, a rush of vital fluids that made her giddy.

She teetered outside. None of their neighbours had noticed anything. Of course houses did sometimes implode, she knew that, but this was no accident of nature. Whoever had engineered it must have come stealthily during the night, under cover of the storm. They had *assassinated* both her husbands.

She cradled the womb in both hands, awash with a confusion of emotions and glandular secretions. Blood drained from her head, and she dropped to her knees.

Something touched her shoulder, startling her. It was her cloak, cowering, wagging its tail uncertainly. She put an arm around its shoulders, crying, letting it nuzzle her neck.

Above, in the pink sky, she saw a rising streak of light slanting straight to the heavens. Tunde's ship, she prayed, carrying him safely with the womb to the shrouded landmasses of Venus.

'There, there,' she said, patting both the cloak and the womb as she watched it depart.

I surfaced again from sleep, and found myself in the same place as before. The white room.

I still had no strength and could only lie there, sluggish in thought. This time I realized that I was thirsty, my mouth dry. But no one came to give me a drink. Stillness and silence surrounded me.

Slowly I breathed, drawing in air, hissing it out through my nostrils. The air had no smell, or else it was the smell of sterility. I couldn't tell where the light was coming from, but at least it didn't hurt my eyes any more.

When I mustered the effort, I found that I was able to look down. A white sheet covered me to the neck. At first it was weightless, but even as the thought registered I began to feel that it was wrapping itself around me, tightening, restricting. Panic swelled up in me again. I laboured for air, weakly gasping. But it was useless; I couldn't even move. As I sank down into darkness I was certain I was dying.

Two

'. . . chances are,' Metin was saying, 'he's down in the docking bays checking out the merchandise. You know Pavel – always an eye for a bargain.' Metin looked up from his wristlink optic. 'We didn't know you were coming in on this flight.'

'I had to return early. I need to see him.'

'I've bleeped him. He'll call in soon enough.'

They stood in the crowded concourse of the transit station, interplanetary passengers milling about or riding slidewalks to terminals.

'Anything else we can do for you in the meantime?' Metin asked.

Tunde gazed out through a portal, where the chrome and ebonite strut of a docking bay bisected the downy white of Venus. Hesperus was one of the larger Venusian transit stations, a regular stopping-off point for Tunde on his travels. He knew its staff – and its comforts – well.

'Is Ushanna here?'

Metin checked his comlink again, a studied frown creasing his forehead. He was short and plump, a physique rarely chosen.

'She finished her term a couple of months back. But we've got a new girl. Jaslynn. Very pretty, same sort of type. Accommodating, you know?'

Tunde stepped aside to let a group of Martian tourists pass. The hubbub of the crowd was regularly interrupted by flight announcements and passengers being paged.

'How old is she?' he asked.

'Twenty-two, it says here. I hear she's one of our best.'

He peered at Tunde expectantly. Tunde shrugged in acquiescence.

'Delta fifty-five. She's free at the moment.' Metin winked. 'I'll call ahead, make sure she's ready and waiting.'

Tunde was already striding away; he could only take so much of the smaller man's fake and sleazy camaraderie.

He found an empty levelator pod next to one of the main viewports where passengers were thronging to watch a cargoship unfurl its solar wings like a gigantic black butterfly. It made Tunde feel giddy, so he averted his eyes and entered the enclosed pod gratefully. He murmured his destination, and the pod put on a Chrysian pastorale to swamp the sound of Flight Central giving details of shuttles and baggage handling. For once Tunde did not object to the music. He felt a little deflated, grubby in more than one sense.

Delta sector's hermetic salmon-pink corridors provided a sticky intimacy that was perfectly appropriate for a red-light district. A woman with zigzagged black hair – probably Tritonian – took Tunde's place in the pod as he emerged.

She winked at him as she passed, looking dishevelled and sated. 'That feels a whole lot better, I can tell you.'

The pod whisked her away. Tunde saw that the doormouth to cubicle fifty-five was already open, the woman waiting there for him.

She was tall and dark-skinned, dressed in a black stripsuit, gold hair cut short like Ushanna's. Not a double of her by any stretch of the imagination, but striking enough in her own way.

'Hello,' she said. A wide-mouthed smile. 'You're Tunde, yes?'

He merely nodded.

'I'm Jaslynn. Good to meet you.'

He let her usher him inside. The cubicle was dominated by a big contour bed which began to fluff itself on sight of him. It was dark flesh-pink, the same colour as the room. The colour he'd specified when he'd first started making use of the facilities here and had his profile put on record.

'Drink?' Jaslynn said brightly, going over to the cocktail waiter.

'No thanks. Are you new here?'

'My second month,' she said, stroking the squatting waiter's lumpen head. 'You're one of our regulars, right? OK with you if I have something?'

'Go ahead. Can I see your medical?'

The waiter dished her out a petrol-blue liquor in a spiral glass. With her free hand she produced her medical certificate from a hidden pocket of her suit.

Tunde took the disk and thumbed its vocal. According to Pavel the whores were checked every ten days. She was clean.

'You want to see mine?' he asked.

She shook her head, smiling again. 'Metin knows you. That's fine with me. Want to get on with it?'

Her pupils were dilated, as if she were avid for him. 'Sure.'

She set the drink down, came over and began stroking him, nuzzling his face with her mouth. The liquor on her breath was minty, strong.

'Anything special you like?' she asked as she peeled his shirt from his shoulders. 'Metin says whatever you want – as long as you leave me in one piece.'

She gave a laugh that was a come-on – complicit, completely decadent, yet at the same time with a hint of nervousness, as if she was afraid he *would* want to go beyond the usual limits. She had a strong, sensual face which promised every sort of lewdness. She wouldn't stop him from doing whatever he wanted. Tunde was already aroused.

'What do you suggest?' he said.

'We've got something new since you were here last. Languor.'

'Languor?'

'It slows things down. Stretches them out. Makes the pleasure last, you know?' Her hands were everywhere, expertly stripping him. 'You'll never want it to end.'

Now her head began to slide down his chest, his naked belly.

He pulled her up. 'Tell me why you do this,' he said.

It was out before he knew it: he hadn't meant to ask.

She barely blinked. 'I do it for fun. For the sheer pleasure of it. Down on Venus I'm the daughter of a high priest in the Church of Moral Purity. Sex only within sanctified monogamous marriage. I'm positively virginal. Then I come here and let men do whatever they want with me – '

There was no expression on her face. Tunde sighed, then grabbed her wrists and dragged her over to the bed. He pushed her down, pinioning her, then began to peel each strip of the suit away. The panels made a satisfying tearing sound as the bed spread itself to accommodate them. Everywhere she was as ample, as full-bodied, as he required. She was laughing, urging him on with hoarse whispered obscenities.

Tunde knew it would be over in minutes – perhaps even seconds. But as he entered her, she reached over and picked up something from the bedside table. She put it to his mouth.

It was a small thing, like a tiny black snail.

'Languor,' she said, parting his lips, pressing it into his mouth, her fingers crushing the shell against his tongue.

The shell dissolved instantly, and a fragrant penetrating vapour swamped his senses, blotting everything out. Then, when the black mist receded, he found himself moving slowly within her – infinitely slowly, his ferocious desire paused to such an extent that he was able to relish its urgency, each sensation stretched out, flesh within flesh, the only kind of contact that made him feel as if he was truly alive.

He could hear Jaslynn moaning in pleasure as she moved beneath him. At the back of his mind he remained lucid, but outside, within the cubicle, he was hazily, contentedly drowning in extended desire. She was gripping his arms, writhing beneath him in rhythm with the bed, mouth open, neck arched. He surrendered completely to pure sensation, let it go on and on, this passion, hunger, rage, revenge . . .

. . . and then the drug abruptly released him, and he surged out again into real time, surged into her with a huge groan as she cried 'Yes! Yes!' and thrust herself hard against him.

He slumped across her and did not move for a long while. Neither did she. Eventually the silence was broken by the console announcing a call.

Jaslynn answered it, and Pavel's vulpine face filled the screen. He spoke directly to Tunde.

'Give you enough time, did I?' A coarse chuckle. 'Metin tells me you have something urgent.'

Tunde's wits were dull with the drug. He sat up slowly.

'I need to talk to you. Somewhere very private.'

'My office. Fifteen minutes, OK?'

Tunde tried to blink his dazedness away. 'All right.'

'Give you what you wanted, did she?'

The question was asked with only academic interest. Jaslynn lay on her belly among the tatters of her stripsuit, ignoring both of them. Tunde wanted to tell him to mind his own damn business, but that was precisely what he was doing.

Tunde rose and stumbled into the latheratory. Jaslynn had his clothes laid out on the bed when he emerged, pressed and fragrant: she had put them in the laundrovat while he was bathing.

'I hope you'll come again,' she said, pressing herself against him as he made to leave. 'You were wonderful. The best I've had.'

He wanted to shake her at that moment, to shake the real person out. He turned and fled.

Outside a pod was open. It whisked him through the tunnels to the central sector of the station. Metin was waiting at the other end to escort him through.

Pavel's office was a cluttered windowless chamber tucked between freight blisters and plasmachinery workshops at the very centre of the satellite. He was a creature of the nooks and crannies of the station, carrying out his dubious or wholly illegal activities while managing to evade the notice of the customs officials who ostensibly controlled everything on Hesperus. A big-boned man with shifty green eyes, he squatted in a bucket seat surrounded by cartons and crates of his latest booty.

Tunde accepted a seat opposite him, then waited while he and Metin inspected a handful of Callistan gemstones that had been hidden in a consignment of antique vases. The gemstones, naturally luminous, shone pale rose and ice-blue in the dim light that Pavel favoured in his 'office'. An ancient titanium drinks dispenser stood in one corner next to a squat mechanical cleaner that scouted the floor for dirt or insects with its trumpet-shaped nozzle.

'So,' Pavel said without looking up from his palm, 'what have you got for me?'

'Something very special,' Tunde replied.

Pavel put a pear-shaped stone between his teeth and bit on it. The stone broke.

Pavel spat the piece into his hand.

'What the hell is this?'

Metin spread his pudgy arms helplessly; he knew nothing about it.

Pavel's face was dark with anger. He swatted furiously at a suckerfly that had found its way into the room, then screamed at the cleaner to deal with it. The machine went into overdrive, raising its trumpet and scurrying about the room chasing the fly. Pavel sat rigid, watching it, until the fly was sucked down into its chrome-plated belly.

Pavel returned his attention to the fake gemstones.

'I paid good credit for these,' he said. 'I think we need to have an earnest discussion with our friend Wai Ling. Her ship left yet?'

The question was addressed to Metin, who spoke to his wristlink. A curved section of the chamber wall blinked into transparency. Tunde saw a mothership suspended in space, a cetacoid with its vast black fins wafting in the solar wind. A thick feedline looped from its mouth to the end of a docking strut so that it resembled a gargantuan fish caught on a line. Tunde had done a lot of fishing in Venus's fertile seas as a child, before his whole world turned sour.

'It's not due out for thirty-five minutes,' Metin announced.

'Fetch her,' Pavel said. 'Make sure there's no fuss or damage, get my meaning?'

Metin merely grinned and hurried away without further ado, giving the cleaner a perfunctory kick in its ribbed backside as he went.

Pavel set the jewels aside. 'Get us some coffees, will you?' he said to Tunde. 'Make mine an Ishtaran spiced.'

Tunde went over to the machine and punched up two. He was still a little woozy from the drug. While Pavel ordered some pastries over his comlink, the dispenser bleeped and rumbled, then delivered.

The drinks were in flimsy white cups. Pavel took his from Tunde.

'So,' he said, 'let's hear what you've got.'

Tunde settled himself on a crate.

'I don't think you've ever handled anything quite like this before,' he said. 'I got it in Bellona.'

Pavel arched an eyebrow. 'And?'

'It's with the freight. On its way to Venus by now. Akna terminus. Biological. Very hot.'

Pavel blew on his coffee. 'From Bellona, you said. Haven't they had a big clampdown there?'

Tunde nodded.

'Connected with this *merchandise* of yours?'

'I can't be certain, but I'd bet on it.'

Pavel blanked the window. 'So let's hear it.'

Tunde shifted on his perch. 'Are we safe here?'

'Fucking count on it. EMR opaque. Think I'd use it if it wasn't?'

Pavel liked to think of himself as a big wheel, though really he was strictly small-time, hidebound by his own narrow horizons. Not that Tunde underestimated his capacity for violence if he was thwarted. He was about to speak when the door pulsed open and a woman entered with a tray of cakes. It was Jaslynn.

She wore a crisp emerald and gold Transolar flight attendant's tunic, obviously Pavel's idea of a joke. She set the tray down on the table holding the gemstones, showing not a flicker of recognition for Tunde. Her eyes looked through him and her smile was merely one of professional courtesy. Pavel laughed, while Tunde fought the urge to speak to her, to make real human contact. She departed without a word.

When she was gone, Pavel said, 'Suit you, did she?'

'She was fine,' Tunde said, 'but you overdid it with the daughter of the archbishop and the Church of Moral Purity, or whatever it was.'

'You want perfection, you pay premium rates.'

'Where did she come from?'

'How the fuck should I know?'

He knew, all right. 'Is she a volunteer or a crim?'

Pavel bit into a starcherry fancy, cream and puff pastry coating his upper lip. 'Maybe she's a fugitive killer, or maybe she's saving for a total body reconstruct. Maybe she needs the credits to pay for her great-granddaddy's funeral passage. Does it matter?'

Pavel had little personal interest in the individuals he acquired for his business, or more likely he simply preferred to pretend so to discourage inquisitiveness. Strictly speaking, prostitution was illegal but tolerated provided health standards were maintained and the men and women who offered their services did so without coercion. The job was, in any case, vicarious, whores being supplied with psycosmetic drugs which temporarily imprinted fake personalities over their normal consciousnesses. Pavel was adept at offering psychoprofiles which closely matched his customers' needs so that their fantasies were thoroughly served. The whores themselves retained no memory of their activities once the drugs were withdrawn or substituted.

'I take it she wasn't under the influence just now,' Tunde said.

Pavel crammed the rest of the pastry into his mouth. 'I wouldn't know,' he said. 'She doubles up as one of my personal assistants. The more she works, the more she gets paid. I've never asked her if she does it on autopilot.'

Tunde wondered how personal an assistant she was.

'Isn't it supposed to be dangerous to go straight from one persona to another?'

A flash of irritation crossed Pavel's sharp features. 'I didn't say she did, did I? What d'you think I'm running here? She needs the credits and wants the work. I don't make them do anything they don't ask for. Now, what is it you've got for me?'

Suddenly he was impatient, and Tunde realized he'd better get on with it. He had known Pavel for several years, ever since he began sneaking valuable items from various worlds to Hesperus under the guise of his legitimate business. Mostly it had been minor stuff – exotic perfumes, speciality drugs, objets d'art – but this was something of a different order.

'A womb,' he said.

Pavel's only reaction was to take a draught of his coffee.

Tunde hurried on, telling him the whole story of Marea and the womb. He knew he was betraying a friendship that he had always valued, betraying a closeness that he might have cultivated if he'd been honest with her; but he was desperate. It was Vesta who had suggested the transfer to a desk job, almost certainly because they were becoming suspicious of his activities on each interplanetary trip. Smuggling – it seemed absurd to dignify his activities with such a quaint and romantic word – was a short-term game for the courier, and this was probably his last chance to make some real money from it.

Pavel heard him out in silence, slowly crushing the cup in his fist. Finally he spoke.

'And it's down on Venus?'

Tunde nodded.

'Stupid move. We could have arranged it here.'

'Not with freight that size. It's company property, automatically routed on. Customs would have become suspicious if I'd tried to hold it up.'

Pavel seemed unconvinced. 'How much?'

'What?'

'Don't be fucking coy. It's the only question worth asking. How much do you want for it?'

I came bursting out of a hot dark tunnel. The woman was standing over me, dabbing something moist and cool on my forehead. This time there was no fear, but I felt feverish.

I heard a low noise escape from my throat, and I realized that I had tried to speak and almost succeeded. A second attempt yielded nothing.

The woman pressed a sponge to my mouth, and cool water trickled into it. I swallowed greedily. My whole body felt as if it was on fire.

She swabbed my forehead again, pressed more water into my mouth. Her face was serious, absorbed in the task, as if it was the most important thing in the world. A shock of blonde hair fell across one temple, but her eyebrows were dark. A surge of sheer physical attraction overtook me then. I would have embraced her and kissed her on the lips had I been able. But I couldn't move.

This reaction was as unexpected as it was inappropriate, and it was swiftly followed by a deep sense of embarrassment. I felt my cheeks flush hot. The woman noticed nothing.

She stripped the sheet off me and proceeded to sponge my whole body. I was naked, dark-haired, skin paler than hers. My body was that of a man in his prime.

'Don't excite yourself,' she murmured. 'It takes time. You're going to be all right, I promise you.'

It was said with such conviction that I believed it immediately. Relief washed through me. Then I was sinking down again. I caught a last glimpse of her profile before I slipped away.

Tunde took an open-topped roadrunner from the terminus, letting the soft rain patter on his head. After forty-eight hours on Hesperus it felt wonderful to smell the egg and gunpowder air, feel its warmth and wetness, see the unbroken cloud shutting out the void beyond. Interplanetary travel had always continued to unnerve him, no matter how many trips he made, its expanses inducing vertigo, a feeling that he might fall forward, ever outward and downwards into its infinite nothingness. Only beneath the enveloping atmosphere of his home-world did he feel truly safe.

He rode the main causeway that led west across the lagoons and shallows, weaving past crowded serpentines and puffers trailing gouts of steam. Beyond the bustling traffic umbrella trees and palmbrush shimmered grey-green between quicksilver stretches of water. A leviathan was wallowing in a mere-meadow near a farmstead, its great coils entangled in water-vine, oxygen farts bursting from nodes along its flanks.

Another causeway joined his own, then split again, was joined by others as he approached the thickly settled shores of Nephthys. Swampland gave way to emerald pasture, wedges of farmland, domed settlements clustered beside streams and rivers that tumbled down from mottled mountains.

Nephthys City braided the steep arc of a bay and was home to a quarter of a million people. Tunde had been born in the slums hugging the coastal swamps but now lived in a select mountainside estate with a splendid view out over the ocean. At this height the view was picturesque, the waterfront squalor unnoticeable.

Yolande was entertaining guests when he arrived.

'I wasn't expecting you,' was the first thing she said on catching sight of him. 'You didn't call.'

A statuesque and elegant woman, she was busy dishing out sweetmeats to her guests. They were the kind of guests she always invited: poised and well-heeled, dressed in fashionable slipstreams whose fabrics slowly shifted across their bodies, changing colour constantly. Tunde recognized most of them, though there were none he knew well.

'I got an early flight,' he said. 'I thought I'd surprise you.'

'You certainly did that.'

His palm was moist on the handle of his shoulderbag.

'Are the children here?'

'They'll be out shortly. Do you think you could possibly give me a hand with the drinks?'

It was the current vogue to serve one's guests personally rather than use a menial; and Yolande was nothing if not fashionable.

'Give me a few minutes,' he said.

He went off to his room before she could say anything further. Once inside, he locked the door and opened the shoulderbag on the bed. The womb was safe, and he was amazed that he had managed to get it out of the terminus so easily. At the last moment he had decided to hide the womb not in the belly of the extractor but deep within a funnel-shaped earvent so that it could be removed without having to cut open the beast. An official who was a regular customer for his smuggled goods had arranged for him to inspect the beast alone, and it had been a simple matter of using a long pair of forceps to retrieve the womb and carrying it through in his hand luggage. But he'd never sweated so much in his life . . .

The womb was loosely swaddled in a white wrap. Tunde could feel its warmth through the fabric. He zipped up the bag again, resisting the urge to pore over it and ponder its uniqueness. To him it was going to be a means of escape, and he couldn't afford to consider it as anything more than an item of barter. He stashed it in a cabinet under the window and had the cabinet give him a new lock code with twenty-four-hour confidentiality. That would be time enough.

Yolande's guests had congregated on the balcony, drinks and titbits already provided. Yolande cast him a fleeting critical glance, then announced that the children were ready to entertain. She had given them the grand names of Maximinian, Corisabel and Esmeraldine, and it was a constant source of irritation to her that he always referred to them as Max, Cori and Esme. The three of them now came cartwheeling out of the house and proceeded to perform a series of leaps, rolls and pirouettes to a bolero by a popular Venusian composer whose work Tunde hated.

The children were dressed in white, their movements expertly choreographed by the instructor Yolande had employed six months ago. Gymnastics was her latest passion, and her guests were suitably appreciative, applauding politely at the end of each routine while Yolande luxuriated in reflected glory.

As ever, Tunde found it sickening. Ever since the trio were born, Yolande had sought to mould them into creatures of her own design. First it had been enhancer drugs to boost their intelligence; then gene manipulation to maximize their physical development. As they grew older, she had insisted on corrective surgery to straighten a crooked nose, tuck in protruding ears, ensure a perfect set of teeth. And constantly there were the tutors and experts who attended the children, teaching them deportment, conversational skills, the psychology of interpersonal relationships. And he a powerless spectator to the whole thing.

Max was now poised on the shoulders of Cori and Esme. Suddenly the three of them vaulted backwards off the lip of the balcony. Tunde saw them arcing down through the water of the swimming pool on the level below, their white tunics trailing away to leave three perfect naked dark bodies that rose together at the centre of the blue water, arms raised and clasped together in triumph.

The applause was genuine and doubtless sincere, but Tunde found it no less tawdry for that. Yolande was a daughter of one of the oldest and richest families on Venus, and the people she invited to the house also tended to be of old and privileged stock; yet their appetites were vulgar in his eyes, the children too often served up for them as entertainment fodder.

He slipped away and went to the bathroom for a shower. He was lathering himself with a sponge when the creature extended a tentacle down towards his groin. It took a moment to register what was happening. Either Yolande or one of the children must have taught it some sexual tricks. And he was aroused; he had always had an active libido, especially when he contemplated Yolande's ensnarement of him. He achieved a swift, passionless release from his frustrations.

'You're disgusting, do you know that?'

Yolande had come in. Shame flooded through him, but it was such a familiar emotion it had lost its edge. He peeled the flaccid creature from his body and let it slither to the tiled floor.

'I'm a nobody dragged up from the slums, remember?'

It was what she was always telling him. She didn't rise to it.

'We have guests. You haven't said hello to any of them. Or to your children.'

'They scarcely know I'm here. What difference does it make?'

'I want you out there, doing your part.'

He reached for his robe, and it wrapped itself around him. 'I'm tired. I've been travelling for the last thirty-six hours. You expect me to show consideration to your guests when you never show me any whatsoever?'

Tunde was aware that they were about to embark on another of their many pointless arguments. In one sense he enjoyed them because they made little networks of lines form around Yolande's eyes, the only sign of her true age.

This time, however, she didn't stand and fight.

'I want you out there,' she said, then turned and left.

He went into his room, dried himself, then dressed in a drab olive torsal that was certain to cut a pointed contrast to that of everyone else. His life had descended to such pettinesses, and had been like this ever since the children were born – since the moment they were conceived, in fact.

From his window he saw Cori chatting with a bronzed

muscular man. Though he could hear nothing, it was clear that
her conversation was not childlike, that she was holding her
own, eight years old, with someone who was four or five or
even ten times her age. You never knew with Yolande's circle.
He had not realized that Yolande herself was in her seventies
until she had told him after the children were born. It wouldn't
have bothered him in the slightest had he known from the
beginning, but she had presented it as a deliberate deceit.

That was what had started it: that and the fact that Yolande
had made it plain to him that she no longer had any use for
him once she was pregnant. She had plucked him out of
obscurity, she liked to say, spotted him one day when a boat
of hers made an emergency stop at the wharves for feeding
after a day's pleasure cruising. She'd whisked him away to her
rich home and showed him the life he could lead if he would
marry her. And he had readily agreed, because he found her
beautiful and because she genuinely seemed to want him – and
because he saw it as an escape from the sordidness of his life,
from the filth and squalor of the waterfront, from a sprawling,
squawling family to whom he was just another face, another
mouth to feed. And everything had been fine at first; Yolande
had been hungry for his passion and physicality – but only, he
was later to realize, for him to provide her with children. Once
she had conceived, he had become . . . not exactly disposable,
but an ornament, irrelevant to the real purpose of her future
life.

It had taken him some time to understand it. If she'd never
had any true feeling for him, why hadn't she chosen a different
husband or simply purchased his sperm? He would have
accepted a reasonable price. But the old families of Venus
didn't do things that way, and there had been a vogue for
downcaste lovers among her class at the time. Of course, he
was blissfully unaware of this. The codes by which Yolande
and her ilk lived were different from his, and she would not
agree to a divorce, not yet, not until the children were old
enough. And if *he* had divorced *her*, he would have lost
everything, including the children. They were the only reason
he had stayed. Yolande's wealth was secondary, and none of it
had ever been his. She had always insisted he lived solely off

the money he earned himself. That was why he had got himself
involved with Pavel, in the hope of making a big killing one
day so that he would be financially independent of her.

Steeling himself, Tunde went outside. It was warm and dry
on the balcony, the blue-tinted weatherdome keeping away the
drizzle. The children were naked in front of the guests –
Yolande liked to display them in every sense of the word.
Tunde knew there was no point in objecting. She would only
mock him for his quaint morality and accuse him of hypocrisy.
It was not beyond her to tell everyone what he had been doing
in the shower, let the children hear as well. She had no shame.

Before he could begin the unrewarding chore of making
small talk with Yolande's guests, Max and Esme came to his
side.

'We didn't know you were back,' Max said, peering up into
his face. 'You look troubled, Father. Is something the matter?'

'He and Mother have had another argument,' Esme said. 'I
can tell.'

'I don't think the two of them are well matched,' Max
observed. 'It's a great shame.'

He might have been listening to adults; they were very
knowing, and they spoke matter-of-factly, almost without
reference to his actual presence.

'Did you see our display?' Esme asked.

Tunde nodded. 'It was very impressive. Those hours in the
gym have obviously paid dividends.'

'We only do it because Mother wants,' Max said.

This was unexpected. 'Isn't it fun?'

'Oh, of course. But we'll be glad when we're old enough to
make our own choices.'

Before he could say anything to this, Cori came over and
hugged him around the waist; she was the most affectionate of
the three. Tunde crouched and put his big arms around all of
them, but they looked self-conscious, perhaps afraid he might
do something grossly paternal in front of their guests.

'What have you brought us?' Esme asked.

With a shock, Tunde realized that he had completely forgotten to get them presents this trip. They had come to expect it,

but he had left Mars in too much of a rush and been too preoccupied with getting the womb safely to Venus.

'He hasn't,' Max said emphatically.

'My trip was called short,' Tunde said. 'I had to come back in a hurry.'

'That's perfectly all right,' Cori said. 'We're old enough not to expect presents *every* trip.'

Which only made it worse. He could see the disappointment, even resentment, on their faces. Eight years old, going on twenty-eight. They were almost interchangeable in the way they spoke and behaved, children already gone beyond a childhood they had never truly experienced. Only someone as rich as Yolande could have got away with such blatant gene-tampering to create them anew: there were strict laws against it. Tunde had loved them dearly from the moment they were born, but increasingly that love had become more and more academic, unsustained by a similar spontaneity of feeling from them. He had lost the battle for them.

'I bet Father's got a lover on Mars,' Esme said.

'Maybe he's got more than one,' Max added.

'You're embarrassed!' Cori remarked with glee.

And he was, but not for the reasons they supposed. He was embarrassed for them, and embarrassed for Marea who had deserved better treatment. She was as fine a woman as he was ever likely to meet, but their friendship was based on a lie – *his* lie – that he was happily married with a perfect family. Yet in a sense the children *were* perfect – perfect products of their highly refined upbringing. But how could you be a real father to offspring who were always patronizing you?

'Don't worry, Father,' Cori was saying, 'we're only teasing.' She squeezed his arm. 'Anyway, you're an adult and you can do as you please. If I were grown up, I bet I'd be attracted to you.'

'You'd sleep with your own father?' Esme said. 'That's overbounds.'

'I was speaking hypothetically, micro-brain.'

'Don't you call me micro-brain, you . . . you *mutoid*.'

'I'd rather be mutoid than—'

'All right!' Tunde said angrily. 'That's enough!'

He had spoken loudly, and heads turned. It was Max who finally broke the silence.

'Well,' he said with great confidence, 'that's *one* way of announcing your presence.'

I found myself sitting up in bed, a bowl of something on a tray in front of me. I had no memory of waking or sitting up. I had no memory of anything but the dreams and my previous awakenings. My head felt bloated, as if my brain was pressing against the inside of my skull.

The woman was sitting at my bedside, holding a spoon.

She smiled at me, then she dipped the spoon into the bowl and raised it to my mouth.

'Come on,' she said gently.

Without taking my eyes off her face, I opened my mouth. She put the spoon into it.

It was some kind of soup, salty, only luke-warm, yet it burned as it went down my throat.

I was propped up against the pillows, limp, mute. The woman fed more soup into my mouth, using a napkin to swab my lips and chin. I began to sense the soup filling my stomach, its warmth percolating through me.

I discovered that I could move my head a little. My hands were spread out on my lap. Clean, perfect, ordinary hands. By concentrating hard I found that I was able, just able, to twitch a finger.

'You're doing well,' the woman remarked softly.

'Who are you?'

The words came out unbidden. I was startled by the sound of my own voice. It was neither familiar nor strange.

She smiled – with her eyes as well as her lips.

'You can call me Nina,' she told me.

Dawn was breaking in a grey haze as Tunde left the house. He had heard Yolande rising half an hour before and seen a light burning in the garden shrine as he stole away. She communed regularly with her ancestors, and he had often wondered how much they had influenced her obsession with programming her children's lives.

Tunde left in great sadness, aware that he was unlikely ever to see any of his family again, whatever the outcome. He had looked in on the children before he departed and found them curled up in bed together, as innocent and as young as any ordinary eight-year-olds. That had been the most painful moment, gazing down at Cori who lay with her little finger tucked in a corner of her mouth, wanting to kiss her, to hug all three, but unable to risk waking them.

He took the padded mere-horse from the stables, stroking its mottled flanks and holding its muzzle to keep it quiet until he was a safe distance from the house. It had been his wedding gift to Yolande, and she went riding daily with her cronies in the coastal swamps. Taking it back was not just a practical act. Tunde climbed into the saddle and strapped the shoulderbag at his belly before riding slowly away, out through the weather-dome and into the drizzle.

Morning mist shrouded the lower slopes of the city and veiled the lake; the city's pastel houselamps were fuzzy patches in the gloom. Offworld visitors found Venus intolerably drab with its sulphurous mists and lowering rainclouds, but to Tunde it was the very breath of life. He rode unhurriedly, knowing he had set off in plenty of time.

On the higher slopes the houses were elaborate labyrinthine affairs, ribbed domes and knuckled towers, tentacular corridors leading to the polyps of outbuildings, hazy under their weatherdomes, surrounded by ample well-tended gardens. But as he descended buildings grew smaller, mere blisters huddled together as if for warmth, their breathing often raucous, decrepit walls streaked with algae or blotched with tenement-rot. Most were still slumbering, and the only sign of life Tunde passed was a streetcleaner busy slurping gutter litter through its several writhing mouths.

It was some years since he had last visited the waterfront. He had not kept in touch with his family there when he married Yolande, deliberately shutting himself off from that world, knowing the two could never mix. There was no going back now, even if he had wanted to. But he felt at home in the old surroundings, the looming broadbacked warehouses that wafted the stink of fish; the huts and hovels that had multiplied around them; the twisting thoroughfares crowded with workers and pleasure-seekers, riotous with bargaining and bartering while a multitude of boats bobbed at busy wharves in the leaden water – trawlers, leisure craft, dredgers with their weed-matted snouts. At this hour, though, the waterfront was deserted except for a few crews readying their fishers at the end of the wharves. Tunde felt like a ghost, abandoned by the living.

He followed the road to the isolated cove where he had arranged his rendezvous with Pavel. It was an old haunt of his childhood, a place of rampant reeds and leprous waterplants, hemmed in by blisterbushes, visited by few.

The place had scarcely changed in almost twenty years. Beneath the water on the shoreline outlet arteries from an illicit fabricatory inland still pulsed murky organics into the water. A riot of malformed growth matted the shoreline: bloodrushes with their spiked crimson heads, bilecreeper whose bloated bladders reeked of vomit. Strange creatures scuttled over the rocks or lurked in the stagnant shallows. This was the place where he had fished as a child and caught many marvels.

He dismounted and led the horse into one of the derelict warehouses fronting the water. The air was stale, the building long dead, its walls slick with rust-coloured growths. He tethered the horse, removed a long package from the saddlebag, unstrapped the shoulderbag containing the womb and carried both along the wharf, treading carefully to avoid the lake-spiders and squirtcrabs that darted across it. He was wearing thick leatherene boots, but everything that lived here was unpredictable . . .

He went to the edge of the wharf, where the water was clear of vegetation, and found a suitable spot to sit. Unwrapping the package, he took out a segmented fishing rod. With great care and deliberation, he began to fit it together.

Not long afterwards he was ready. But while he had been assembling the rod an uneasy feeling had grown that someone was watching him. He caught a movement at the edge of his eye, and turned his head.

A short figure was standing near the warehouse.

It was Cori.

Propping the rod between two rocks, Tunde hurried over to her. She was dressed in a hood and cape, her boots mud-splattered.

'I followed you,' she said. 'What are you doing here, Father?'

He scooped her up in his arms.

'You're running away, aren't you?'

'Did you come on your own?'

She nodded vigorously.

'On foot?'

'It was easy to follow you. You rode so slowly.'

'Do you realize how dangerous that was?'

'I want to come with you. Please, Father, can I?'

This was completely unexpected. He enfolded her in his arms, relishing her presence.

'I know you aren't happy with Mother. She can have Es and Maxim. I'll come with you.'

Tunde felt a confusion of emotions – relief, even joy, and great concern for her safety.

'Do they know?' he asked. 'Esme and Max?'

'They don't know you've run away. Or that I came after you. Why are you fishing here?'

He looked into her dark, serious eyes. 'There's something I have to do,' he said. 'Something that might be very dangerous. You can't stay here.'

But at that very moment, he heard the distant whine of an approaching gravlev.

He hurried her into the warehouse and bundled her on to the horse.

'Don't come out of here on any account,' he said urgently. 'If anything bad happens, I want your promise that you'll ride home as fast as you can.'

'What's going to happen?'

'I don't know. It may be nothing. When it's safe I'll call for you, but you must stay hidden here till then.'

'What is it you have to do?'

'I'll explain everything later. There really is no time now. Will you promise?'

Like the other two, Cori would rarely do things on trust,

without a good reason. There always had to be a debate. But she surprised him by bobbing her head under her hood.

'Good,' he said. 'Stay here until I call you.'

'I will.'

'I love you very much.'

There were tears in her eyes. 'Please don't die.'

Tunde went outside and returned to his rod. The line dangled into the closed petals of a flashlily, a big chrome-yellow flower that phosphoresced softly on its bed of warty leaves. He saw the gravlev come over the ridgeroad and settle a short distance from the wharf.

It was a big black and silver Nagatech with mirrored windows that sealed and secured its occupants from the outside world. Its door irised open and Pavel himself clambered out.

Tunde did not move. He held the line steady and waited.

Pavel scanned the surroundings, then began walking towards him. The other door of the car opened and Metin got out.

Tunde eyed the dunes behind the car and the sky overhead. There was no sign of anyone else. It was as he had hoped: though Pavel always liked to boast, his was essentially a two-man operation, furtive and small-scale. The authorities of Hesperus probably left him alone because his activities were usually too petty to concern them. Which didn't mean that Tunde was about to underestimate him.

Pavel was carrying a small black case. He was grimacing as he approached Tunde.

Still Tunde remained seated.

'It was supposed to be just me and you,' he remarked.

'Come on,' Pavel said. 'It's only Metin. Think I'd meet you here on my own?'

He looked distinctly uncomfortable, constantly searching the ground around his booted feet and retreating hastily from anything that moved.

'Why'd you pick this place?' he went on. 'Fucking hell's kitchen. Stinks worse than anywhere I've been on this dungheap.'

Tunde had picked it precisely because Pavel was a biophobe. He hoped it would give him an edge.

Metin was now following him along the wharf, chewing gum and popping bubbles as he came.

'Didn't you trust me?' Tunde said.

Pavel dodged a brownish splatter that was twitching.

'I made the trip down, didn't I, like you asked? Have you got it?'

Tunde resisted the urge to confirm it. 'I want to see the money.'

Pavel stood a short distance from him. He set the case down and flipped it open. It was packed with credit notes.

'It's all there,' he said. 'Fifty thousand solars, like you asked. Take it.'

He pushed it towards Tunde with his foot. Still holding the rod, Tunde reached out with his free hand and grabbed it. He removed a credit note and held it up to the light. The stylized sun hologram in the plastic spiralled around, rainbow-hued: it was genuine.

'Where is it?' Pavel said.

Tunde pointed to the flashlily. 'It's in there.'

'In the water?' Pavel said incredulously. 'You put it in the fucking water? For crissakes, why?'

'It isn't in the water. It's in the flower.'

Pavel looked appalled. 'There's monsters in there, you cretin.'

'It's quite safe. I put it in a waterproof bag. Nothing's going to touch it.'

'It'll suffocate.'

Tunde shook his head.

'Get it the hell out.'

While they had been talking, Metin had been moving towards them. Tunde closed the case and picked it up with one hand.

'There's a problem,' he said, backing away to the very edge of the wharf. 'The moment I hand it over to you, I'm disposable.'

Pavel contrived to appear surprised. 'What are you giving me? Why should I do that? We've always dealt straight with one another.'

'But I'm not going to be any use to you any longer, am I?

And I think this womb is so important you'd prefer to cover your tracks.'

Pavel crushed a purple spider under his boot with considerable disgust. Tunde was now holding the rod out over the water.

'This is stupid,' Pavel said. 'If you drop that rod in the water, you can be sure I'll fucking kill you.'

'The womb's no use to me,' Tunde said. 'You can have it. But I have to be sure you'll let me get away safely.'

Pavel shook his head. 'I'm disappointed in you, Tunde. This is really stupid.'

'Maybe. But that's the way I want it.'

Metin moved forward, chewing furiously. He was holding a stub-gun.

'I know you can simply shoot me,' Tunde said; there was a quaver in his voice. 'But I'll make sure the rod goes into the water and takes the womb with it. There's things in there that'd make a meal of it in seconds.'

Tunde could see the fury in Pavel's eyes. He was barely controlling himself.

'What do you want, Tunde?'

'I want you to go back to the car and wait. I'll follow, reeling out the line. When I'm a safe distance, I'll drop it and be on my way.'

'I think maybe we should just fucking shoot you,' Pavel said.

Tunde's mouth went dry. 'Don't underestimate how desperate I am,' he managed to say. 'It's all or nothing for me. The same for you. You can have the womb. It's a good price, and you know it. I'm only asking that you let me get away. You'll never see or hear from me again.'

Metin was eager to kill him, Tunde was certain. But Pavel was less hasty, more calculating. He took the gun off Metin.

'How do I know it's even in there? Why the fuck should I swallow *any* of this?'

'It's there,' Tunde said.

Very gently, he twitched the line. The flashlily's petals opened slowly, flattening themselves. The womb could clearly been seen, wrapped in a transparent film.

Pavel raised the stub-gun and fired.

The energy bolt seared through the rod close to the handgrip, the force of the blast sending Tunde spinning back so that he fell to his knees on the wharf's edge, the case flying from his hand.

The rod had spun away and dropped into the shallows. The flashlily was folding up again, enveloping the womb.

'You stupid fucker,' Pavel said, standing over him with the gun. 'Think we're going to play your games?' He turned to Metin. 'Go and get it.'

Metin was less than thrilled at the prospect. The rod and line were already drifting out towards the lily.

'It's alive in there,' he said.

'Use his boots, for crissake. It'll only take a few seconds.'

Metin chewed it over; he still wasn't convinced.

'Why don't you send him out for it?'

Pavel sighed. 'And then what's to stop him dumping it in the water? Do like I say. Move it!'

Metin came forward and tugged Tunde's long boots from his feet. They fitted easily over his own footwear, stretching right up to his groin. He looked at Tunde with pure malice.

'Get the hell on with it,' Pavel said.

Metin clambered down over the rocks, then, very tentatively, he waded into the shallows.

The line had drifted out and was caught in the lily leaves. Metin would have to go right to the plant itself to retrieve the womb. He moved slowly, with extreme caution, pushing his way through slimy weed, the water rising higher with each step. Pavel divided his attention between watching him and keeping the stub-gun trained on Tunde.

The water was at Metin's thighs by the time he reached the lily. He delicately manoeuvred himself past the leaves, keeping his hands high, then reached in and touched the flower.

Its petals opened. Metin grabbed the womb and lifted it out. As he did so, two long green flails arced up from the water and swiped him across the face.

He screamed and staggered back, the womb spilling from his hands. It hit the water but bobbed to the surface. Metin, already retreating in terror, made a grab for it but missed.

'You fucker!' Pavel said in fury, levelling the stub-gun at Tunde's face.

There was a thunderous sound behind them as Cori spurred the horse out of the warehouse, padded feet pounding on stone.

Pavel jerked his head around. Tunde lashed out with his foot, hitting him hard on the knee. He toppled over, the gun rolling off the edge of the wharf and clattering on the rocks below. Tunde leapt up, but Pavel just lay there, clutching his leg.

Tunde managed to grab the reins and halt the horse. Metin was thrashing about in the shallows, yelling with terror and pain. He had recovered the womb and was holding it aloft. A crimson crown-leech was stuck to his head.

Pavel sat crouched and unmoving. Tunde realized that he was afraid of him, that he had no stomach for violence when the odds were equal. Tunde retrieved the case and clambered into the saddle, wrapping his arms around Cori.

'I think Metin needs some help,' Tunde said to Pavel. He swung the horse around and urged it along the wharf.

Cori clung on tight. Glancing back, Tunde saw Pavel stumbling in over the rocks towards Metin. He had recovered the stub-gun, and he began to blast the water around the short man, furiously swearing and hopping about as he did so while Metin continued to cry out in pain and disgust. Pavel snatched the womb from his hands as he teetered out of the water, festooned with leeches and waterweed.

Tunde reined in the horse at the gravlev. The driver's door was open, the engine on idle. Hastily he bundled Cori into the passenger seat then climbed behind the wheel. He activated the engine, shouted 'Drive!', and the car moved swiftly off. He caught a final glimpse of Pavel crouched over the womb while Metin frantically stripped off his infested clothes.

Tunde steered the car down the rough track towards the causeway.

'Did I do well, Father?' Cori asked.

'Your timing was perfect. You were a life-saver.'

She beamed. 'You see, sometimes it pays not to follow your parents' advice. You're not going to take me home, are you?'

'Not if you don't want me to.'

'I don't. I'm coming with you.'

They turned on to the causeway, heading away from Nephthys. Tunde switched the car to automatic and slotted the case into a baggage niche. With fifty thousand solars they would be able to start anew somewhere, find a quiet corner where neither Yolande nor anyone else would ever find them. Of course it wouldn't be easy; but at least it would be a real life.

After a short time, Cori said, 'You've lost your boots.'

'Better than losing my marbles.'

It was a weak joke, but she laughed. 'Where are we going?'

A big sunbird, carnelian and gold, rose from the dunescrub along the shore and soared over their heads like an apparition, a blessing. Cori's eyes widened with delight.

'Let's just follow it,' Tunde said, 'and see where it takes us.'

Three

Her Graciousness Bezile Reeta Miushme-Adewoyin, High Arbiter of Melisande and the continent of Aphrodite, shifted her stocky frame in her favourite fur chair as her secretary went through her list of duties for the day. In addition to the daily analysis of current public opinion on issues arising, there was a meeting with a quartet of High Intercessors from Hyperion district, a dedicatory service for the new shrine on Abelard, a luncheon with civic leaders, beneficence visits to a poor quarter, and a sermon on the transubstantiation of the psyche to be recorded for public transmission. Last but far from least, she was giving the final rites of passage to Hidukei, an old friend who had finally decided to take death.

Bezile gave a distracted sigh and contemplated the model Noosphere suspended on her desk, an ebony globe laced with spiderwebs of ivory and gold.

'And the Phalarope meeting?' she said.

Luis spread his hands. 'It may still be possible. If the sermon can be written, we might be able to record it while you're travelling between engagements.'

'I'll do it on the hoof,' Bezile told him. 'Make the necessary arrangements.'

Luis picked up his compad and rose. But he did not immediately leave.

'Was there something else?'

He fiddled with the pad. 'It's probably nothing. But there was a call. From a man who refused to identify himself. He claimed he had something very important he wished to pass on to you. For an appropriate price, he said.'

'What sort of something?'

'A biological object of great curiosity and importance. And even sanctity, he claimed.'

She eyed him. 'Is there anything in it?'

Luis looked pained that they even had to discuss it: he was a fastidious man. 'We don't have much to go on – it was an audio call. But he's an offworlder with a transplanetary accent. Voice-pattern analysis suggests he was telling the truth and that he believes in the worth of what he has. Apparently it comes from Mars.'

Bezile felt a mild quickening of interest. She spun the globe on its zeegee plinth so that its intricate patterns blurred. 'What is he proposing?'

'He wants to talk to you. In confidence. I believe his idea is to arrange a meeting so that you can see what he has. He's asking two million solars.'

'Preposterous!'

'That's what we thought. He's certainly a criminal type, that was plain from the modulations. We explained that you couldn't possibly accommodate him. He seems quite confident he can sell the object to other interested parties if we refuse him. He intends to make a further call later today to receive our final answer.'

Bezile fell into a meditation. From Mars. The man claimed to have something from Mars. She'd heard the rumours that something important had been lost, perhaps destroyed, there. No one seemed to know exactly what, except that it might have originated from the Noosphere itself. Could there be a connection? Of course it was perfectly possible that the man was simply a charlatan, trading on such rumours. But it was not something she could pass by without finding out more.

'Make sure he has a line through to us,' she said. 'We'll listen to what he has to say. And have it fully monitored. Inform the expediters' office. Tell them I want Shivaun.'

Luis nodded. She waved a beringed hand to indicate that he was dismissed.

The morning passed swiftly, Bezile maintaining her hectic schedule by a combination of brisk efficiency and brute psychological force. The Hyperian intercessors were worried about a certain decline in the use of the Noosphere in their region: she promised a sermon on that express subject, to be backed up by a team of mediators who would canvass citizens in their doormouths. The Abelard shrine was opened with due ceremony, and she was able to slip away before the speeches became too interminable. She managed to complete her sermon while on her way to lunch, her roller trundling through Melisande's teeming streets while she spoke extempore about the virtues of making peace with oneself in this world before entering the next.

Lunch was a tolerable pork-of-vine pie, and it passed without any pressing municipal problem to delay her. She was doling out alms in a seedy backstreet when the call came through.

She announced her apologies to the poor who were clustered around the alms wagon, but reassured them that her staff would be perfectly able to meet their needs. Then she retreated into her roller.

Luis was speaking urgently into the roller's console, his brow amply furrowed with anxiety. 'She's on her way, I assure you. Please wait.'

'You're giving me the runaround,' the voice was answering back. 'Maybe you don't realize what the hell I'm holding here. I haven't got any more time to waste.'

Bezile took the mouthpiece from him.

'My, my,' she said into it. 'We are an impatient one.'

'Who's this?'

'I gather you were wishing to speak to me.'

'You the Graciousness? Adewoyin?'

'*Miushme*-Adewoyin. And you are?'

There was a brief pause, then: 'You sure it's you?'

Bezile gave an irritable sigh. 'Does it not sound like me? Why should I pretend?'

A further pause. 'Yeah, OK, I needed to be sure. Listen, I think I've got something of interest to you.'

She did not dignify this with any response.

'Something hot. Very hot. Well, warm to the touch, anyway.' A snigger. 'Alive, get my drift?'

Bezile motioned for Luis to leave the vehicle. Not without consternation, he departed.

'You still there?' the voice at the other end was saying.

'What is it exactly?' Bezile demanded.

'Something I think you'll want to get your hands on.'

'That's impossible to judge until I know what it is.'

Yet another silence. 'Are we safe? On this line?'

'You would not have been given it otherwise.'

'Yeah. OK.' She heard an intake of breath. 'It's a real live embryo sac, know what I mean? A uterus.'

Bezile put her slender fingers on the domed head of the console: its blank optic was mother-of-pearl.

'I can't see what possible interest that is to me,' she said.

'It's got no cord, that's why. No parent, nothing. We're talking advanced biotec here, the kind of thing only the higher-ups would know about. Never seen anything like it before.'

The console began to purr as she stroked it. 'I see. And how did you come by this . . . *uterus*?'

'By way of Mars. A friend of a friend. It was rescued from the corpse of a mothership. I paid good money for it.'

'But not as much as you require from me.'

'Two million's a good price. There's others that'd pay more.'

'Then why not approach them?'

'What is this? You telling me you're not interested?'

'I'm telling you nothing of the sort. I don't know you, or know anything about this merchandise you're offering. I have only your word that such an *object* exists. Two million is a great deal of money.'

There was a muffled exchange with someone else at the other end. Then: 'The Noocracy can afford it. I need a quick sale, no fooling around. There's people I reckon would kill to have it.'

And you among them, Bezile thought. He really did sound a most unsavoury type.

Luis popped his head through the door and whispered in her ear. The man was calling from a public booth in an outlying township. He had been identified as Pavel Regio Maltazar, a small-time entrepreneur based on Hesperus Station with a string of minor convictions for larceny and procuring. He had an associate with him who was almost certainly Metin Emile Develski, a known confederate and minor criminal. His pad showed holograms of both, undistinguished faces with the crabbed features and wary eyes of the petty criminal. Luis informed her that an expediter and several politia were already in position around the booth, and both men could be picked up immediately if wished.

Bezile smiled and slowly shook her head.

'Are you in the vicinity of Melisande?' she enquired innocently.

'There or thereabouts,' Maltazar replied. 'Maybe you've even got this call traced by now. But what I'm offering isn't with me, so if you try anything you'll never get your fucking hands on it.'

Bezile recoiled ostentatiously at the vulgarity.

'What an extraordinary suggestion!' she said. 'You must realize, though, that I can't possibly take any of this on your word alone.'

'Who's asking? Your console take replics?'

'Of course.'

'Then I'll fax you one of what I've got. Call you back in an hour. I'll be wanting an answer, don't forget.'

The line went dead.

Bezile replaced the mouthpiece, then waited as a digestive rumbling began to issue from the throat of the console. A brief glow suffused its flattened facial façade before its belly yawed open.

Bezile reached inside and withdrew the object.

It was warm from transmission, accentuating the impression of a real living thing. Bezile found it rather grotesque, as indeed she did everything connected with the messy and distracting business of reproduction. She had avoided anything remotely connected with insemination throughout her seventy-five years, and fully intended to continue to do so. But there was no doubt that the uterus was indeed unusual, quite unlike the common run of growth-bags.

Luis was still standing in the doorway, patiently awaiting instructions.

'Make sure they're followed,' Bezile told him. 'Is Shivaun in charge?'

Luis checked his pad and nodded. Shivaun was an

experienced operator whom Bezile used regularly: she was both efficient and discreet.

'I want you to contact her,' Bezile told Luis. 'She's to meet us at Hidukei's. Arrange for the money to be available.'

Luis was predictably aghast at the idea that they would actually stump up the money, but she shooed him away without further explanation.

Bezile was in good heart as she and her entourage set off for Hidukei's home. Evening had drawn on, and the jumbled polymorphous habitations of the city, the largest on Venus, were beginning to glow with soft pastels while people hurried homewards through the rain. Beyond the city the volcanic slopes of Daphnis and Chloe rose in the twilit distance, their peaks forever lost in the clouds. Hidukei was an old gene-master, and Bezile was confident he would be able to tell her what she needed to know about the uterus.

Hidukei lived in an elaborate mansion which soared above the candelabra plantations on the lower slopes of Pelleas. The air was resinous here, everything cloaked in warmsnow from the cloudlets whose shifting forms could sometimes be glimpsed in the lower atmosphere; they metabolized sulphurous compounds and excreted them as polymer sleets which the candelabras collected in their bowled suction flowers.

Hidukei's house was perched like an ice crown on a frosted pillar high above the trees. The milky resins the candelabras produced were harvested and used as building materials, lightweight but strong, which could be moulded into fanciful shapes. Bezile rode a levelator upwards, adjusting her ceremonial robes and studying her forthright middle-aged countenance in the mirror until she was satisfied she had achieved the right expression of serene and compassionate authority.

The old man and his extensive family were gathered on the balcony at the front of the house. Bezile was greeted with extreme courtesy and ushered into his presence. He sat, blackrobed, in his death chair surrounded by the youngest members of his family.

Hidukei had made the decision to enter the Noosphere in his ninety-second year, eight years before he was legally obliged to. Since then he had undergone formal thanatosis which had removed the anti-ageing codons that were everyone's birth-right. This was not essential, but his family had always been strictly orthodox in their interpretation of the rites of passage. Over the past year he had gently decayed into a wizened and white-haired old man, though mentally his functions were undiminished.

For days on end preceding, there would have been many reunions and confessionals, private moments of profound emotion between himself and his descendants as he squared outstanding accounts and ensured that his passage into the world of pure mentality was free from unresolved family conflicts. And today there would have been a celebration tinged with sadness as his lineage bid him their final farewells.

Everyone was naturally very nervous, except for Hidukei himself. He greeted Bezile warmly, taking her hand in his own withered fingers and kissing it. He had aged considerably since she had last seen him, but she was used to that. This was perhaps the part of her duties that she enjoyed most, ensuring that those whose time had come were granted a secure place in the afterlife.

She asked the family for a few moments alone with her charge, and they promptly filed away into the house. The moment had arrived for Hidukei to admit any outstanding conflicts or sins and so finally free himself from the bonds of physicality; and she, in return, as his death attendant, would request a small favour which he would grant so that his last corporal act was charitable.

She leaned close and whispered, in the informal manner which she reserved for those penitents she knew personally: 'Well, old man, it's your chosen time. Are you fully prepared?'

He looked up at her from the enveloping black folds of the death chair. 'Indeed I am.'

His voice was strong and forthright. In his prime he had been head of Artimatas-Franklyn Multiplasm, a planet-wide corporation that supplied bioforms to every sector of society. She had first met him when she was a fledgling sub-arbiter, and their friendship had survived the inevitable occasional conflicts between business and spirituality, the sacred and the profane.

'Do you have anything to confess?' she asked.

'Only that my ambition sometimes outweighed my humanity. For that I ask the forgiveness of this world.'

'It is granted. Nothing more?'

He chuckled. 'I think that covers a multitude of sins.'

Bezile winked at him. 'You old rascal. Now I must ask my favour of you.'

'Ask.'

From under her voluminous gilded robe, Bezile produced the replic. She held it out in front of him and proceeded to explain the circumstances by which she had obtained it.

Hidukei's eyes were now yellow and rheumy, but he gave the uterus a keen scrutiny. When she had finished talking he asked for a closer look. She put it into his hands.

With the sedulous precision of the truly aged, he turned the replic in his withered hands, holding it so close to his face that he might have sniffed it had it any smell.

'My favour is this,' Bezile said. 'I would like to know who the makers might be of such a curiosity.'

Hidukei was still peering minutely at the womb. 'This thing really exists?' he said.

'I have every reason to believe so.'

'It appears to have its own food stores,' he said, indicating paler nodules beneath its veined surface. 'And active semi-permeable membranes for gas exchange. As your informant surmised, whatever's inside might well be self-sustaining.'

'But is it a human uterus?'

'It certainly has every appearance of being so.'

'Where does it come from?'

He was silent for a while. 'Certainly not from the production lines of any biotec corporation on Venus. It's either illegal – some sort of monstrosity – or from a much more *elevated* source.'

It was as much a question as a suggestion.

'Do you mean the Noosphere?'

His reply was slow in coming. 'It's not beyond the bounds of possibility. But it gives every appearance of being Augmented.'

He knew as well as she did that while optimal modifications to the human phenotype had always been permitted, public opinion at large was against the idea of radical changes to the genotype for fear of creating new species of human being. And the Noosphere always reflected the views of the majority through its servants. Augmentation was a heresy. Wars had been fought to rid the Noospace of their kind.

'Of course,' Hidukei went on, 'it might simply be some sort of elaborate joke. At my expense, perhaps?'

For once her capacity to see the droll side of things had deserted her.

'No,' she said. 'I don't believe it is.'

A contemplative nod. 'And you really have no idea where it came from?'

She shook her head.

He sat back and closed his eyes for a moment. The effort of talking had obviously drained him; he had truly come to his end. But she wasn't quite finished with him. She checked again to ensure that they were alone, truly alone. Uncertainty was not a familiar emotion to her.

'Could it possibly be . . . *unofficial?*'

Wrinkles multiplied as he smiled. 'Do you mean the Advocates? Our glorious unpredictable Julius and Orela? It's possible. It's impossible to say.'

His eyes closed again. She realized this was the best she was going to get and that if she delayed any longer he might abjectly die before she could translate him to the Noosphere, something that would be catastrophic for everyone concerned.

The family were watching from the mansion, faces framed in its many windows, generations in waiting. At her summons, they filed out as efficiently as they had gone in. While each of them queued to give Hidukei a final parting kiss, she delivered a short oration praising his achievements in life and assuring his flock that he would be warmly welcomed by the many ancestors who had preceded him.

Everyone now clustered around the death chair, the younger children hoisted up in their parents' arms so they would have a view. With perfect timing, a drizzle of warmsnow began to fall and the children peered skywards in the hope of glimpsing a cloudlet. But no ripples of movement were discernible in the paleness.

Bezile stepped forward.

'We enter life naked,' she intoned, 'and thus we go naked into the afterlife.'

She reached down and with a deft tug removed the robe from Hidukei's body. True age had shrunk the flesh on him so that it was hard to imagine that the substance of the man still remained in such a crumpled sack of sinew and bone.

'Farewell,' she said, pulling the neural hood down over his head.

She pressed her thumb into the fovea at the centre of the hood. His eyes were open again, but the light in them died and they closed as Hidukei's psyche was withdrawn from his body and channelled along the powerline which led to his own private shrine, from there to be translated across space to the Noosphere where he would join his ancestors and the billions of others who had gone before him.

The snow began falling more heavily. Bezile waited until the tall needle atop the shrine came alive with a brief magnesium light as Hidukei's mental essence was translated heavenwards, then she activated the chair.

The chair's black folds closed in over the corpse, enveloping it completely. There was a low humming, and after long moments the chair unfurled itself again. All that remained of Hidukei was a small pile of greyish dust.

One of Hidukei's family handed Bezile an urn and a death spoon. As she transferred the ashes to the urn, she ceremonially announced that Hidukei had now joined the Noosphere and would be in eternal communion with them whenever they needed his wisdom or comfort.

Three of his surviving wives and one of their husbands immediately began wailing. They were soon joined by others. This again was another tradition of Hidukei's particular orthodoxy, one which Bezile privately did not care for. When her own time came – and that would not be till the end of her full term – she hoped that her relations would spare themselves such excesses; but it was a personal rather than moral issue. Her task was done, and the manifest outpouring of grief made it easier for her to slip away with a minimum of fuss.

The snowfall slackened as she made her way back down the

hillside to the roller. Luis was waiting for her, anxiety personified.

'He called,' he announced. 'He wanted to know your decision.'

'Did you explain that I had a pressing private engagement of the most spiritual nature?'

'As you instructed. I managed to persuade him to call one more time. He says it will be in the next hour.'

Which meant that he was eager to offload the womb to them. Eager and possibly desperate.

'Have we been able to raise the money?'

'Not without grave difficulty.' He produced a metal case, flipping it open to reveal the notes packed inside. 'Awkward questions were asked, a strain put on certain loyalties.'

She merely laughed. 'You're such a worrier.'

He bristled. 'It's my duty to advise you against this course of action.'

'Come, come,' she said soothingly. 'Do you think I actually have any intention of handing over two million solars to a pair of petty thieves?'

Now he was flustered. 'I don't understand . . . exactly what it is you intend.'

'Is Shivaun here?'

Luis turned and motioned to one of the staff. A figure stepped forward.

Shivaun was a slim but muscular woman with handsome features and sapphire eyes. She wore the deep purple expediter's tunic, her dark hair tied back, emphasizing her forthright air. She was forty-five, in prime physical condition. Flesh of my flesh, Bezile thought proudly with an inward smile.

'Thank you for coming so promptly, my dear,' she said. 'Join me in the roller. We have things to discuss.'

Luis stood rooted with confusion. 'It would be helpful,' he began, 'if I were informed of your . . . proposal.'

'I propose that we proceed immediately to Phalarope,' she told him. 'I take it we can still be in time for the meeting?'

With a studied show of forbearance, he checked his pad. 'Yes.'

'Then let us go. Do you think I would flog myself through

such a day of toil, only then to deprive myself of one of my few recreations?'

I surfaced briefly out of a fog of dreams. The room was dimly lit, a rectangle of light at the open door.

I was lying with my head to one side. The woman – Nina – was standing in the doorway with two others. At first I thought they were twins, but then I saw it was a young man and woman, he dark, she fair.

All three were dressed in white. All three were looking in my direction. I tried to read their expressions but I couldn't focus. They began talking, but the words were a drone. Then sleep swallowed me up again.

Melisande was a city that shone brighter by night than by day. Its buildings phosphoresced and scintillated in the drizzly darkness while brollied citizens emerged to find their pleasures in nightsports, stimstores, under awnings in street cafés awash with holograms advertising mood-mellowers and the delights of offworld excursions. By day the oppressive equatorial heat and dampness limited activities to the essentials, but night brought cooling breezes that enlivened everyone.

Phalarope was a swampy district on the eastern outskirts of the city, famous for its racetracks. Bezile had liked to gamble on the races ever since her youth, but she was prudent enough not to risk stakes that might jeopardize her status as an arbiter. The distraction of the womb was more than mildly irritating, despite its undoubted importance, the more so when Maltazar called again as they were arriving at the stadium.

Bezile was brusque. 'The money is available,' she told him. 'But I must take delivery tonight.'

'That's impossible,' he protested.

'Then find another buyer. I have no intention of doing any further bargaining with you.'

A muffled silence at the other end. Then: 'You've got the money, you said.'

'It's all in notes. Old ones, untraceable. That's the usual arrangement, I understand.'

More hesitation. 'Do you want me to meet you?'

'I should have thought that would be vital to the transaction.'

'Where are you?'

'I'm at the Phalarope stadium. For the races. Do you know it?'

Another sullen pause. 'I've heard of it.'

'What better place to make the exchange than in the middle of a crowd? I'm wearing my robes. I should be easy to spot.'

'You've got the money with you?'

'In a case.'

'I don't like the sound of it.'

'That is unfortunate. I shall be here until midnight, no later.'

She was certain she could hear him cursing under his breath. There were three hours to midnight. Bezile stifled a yawn: it had been a hard day, and it was far from over.

'I'll call you with further instructions,' he told her.

He hung up. Bezile contemplated the maw of the handset, then turned to Luis. 'Did you get that?'

'I think this is very dangerous,' he said earnestly. 'These are not the sort of people we should be trifling with. We could lose everything.'

'Rather exciting, though, you have to admit. Such cloak and daggery. Who'd have believed that people really do act in this way?' She turned to Shivaun. 'I think you had better go and prepare yourself.'

Without a word, the expediter rose and slipped out of the roller.

Bezile had a private box high in the south stand of the stadium. The meeting was well under way, the crowd busy roaring their approval or derision for the bayhounds who were pursuing a marsh-hare around the outer watercourse, its flippers thrashing madly as it raced for the sanctuary of the finishing enclosure. Bezile's box was insulated from the raucousness, but she sometimes donned civilian clothes and went down among the crowd with its sweat and swearing and general disorder. You had to beware of pickpockets, though; they'd strip you of everything including your dignity given half a chance. But it was worth the risk, each adventure an antidote to the stifling gentility of her public life.

The box was already occupied by Shivaun, who was donning

a biofibre wraparound of Bezile's image. It fitted her perfectly, and Bezile's private irony was delicious: only up close was the illusion obvious in the grainy skin tones. With a certain sense of excitement, Bezile took off her rings and handed them over to her clone-daughter.

Of course Shivaun knew nothing of her true maternity, and Bezile had had every one of her brood-daughters prenatally modified so that none would resemble her *too* closely. Besides, her own cosmetic ageing, done for the gravitas of her office, set her apart from the youthful norm. Bezile had always taken a close but professional interest in Shivaun's career, using her for assignments that required discretion and absolute loyalty. And Shivaun had never failed her: of the seven of her daughters, she was the best of them, the only one who had truly fulfilled her potential.

Bezile felt a distinct thrill to be involved in such skulduggery: normally she led a very sheltered life. Her only regret was that she could play no active part herself from now on.

Donning a drab cowled cloak, she surrendered her robes and went down into the crowd. The long-suffering Luis hovered at her side, ready to enter her bets, intolerably nervous at the thought of losing the two million. She occupied him with a complicated accumulator, then lost herself in the crowd, preferring to be alone with her comlink.

The main focus of her interest that evening was the rhinocerhorse races. She liked nothing better than to watch the bulky flat-footed beasts charge their way down the swamp track, buffeting and banging at one another with their blunt horns and noseplates. She had backed an outsider for the first race and was delighted when it came in, its jockey bruised and bleeding but triumphant. The second race was about to get under way when Maltazar called.

'I'm here,' he announced without preamble.

Her wrist optic remained resolutely grey.

'At the stadium?' she said.

'Where else?'

'Excellent,' she replied, peering up at the box. Shivaun stood framed in the window in her regalia, and she was confident Maltazar could see her and would assume it was her. Shivaun also had her link open so she could monitor everything that was said.

'Here's the way we'll work it,' Maltazar went on. 'I want you to come down to the paddock nearest the North Gate. Got that? The North Gate. You come alone. Anonymous. Get rid of the robes. Civilian dress, otherwise you don't see me. Bring the money with you. And no funny business!'

He cut the contact.

Bezile saw Shivaun moving away from the window. Really, this was terribly exciting!

Drably garbed but still ample, her daughter presently appeared and began to descend an aisle. Bezile indulged herself in a little vanity at the sight of her image: big-framed and matronly, she was quite a striking woman. It did not surprise her when a few individuals in the crowd began to recognize her, despite the workaday guise. She was soon surrounded by a small group of admirers and suppliants.

The man came on line again: 'You've got an audience. The deal's off.'

'Don't be ridiculous. Am I to be blamed if my face is well known? Do you wish to draw even more attention to me by dragging this out?'

It was a gamble. There was a long silence. Then:

'Go to the cash booth next to the hound pens.'

Bezile instructed Shivaun to switch on her eye contacts. Her optic showed her pushing through the crowd towards the booth. People kept coming up to her, kissing her ring, pleading for some favour or redress. Shivaun played the part to perfection, uttering soothing words but moving relentlessly on. Even those who touched her did not seem to register the disguise: it was as if her very presence overwhelmed any trifling details of unreality.

Punters were clustered around the booth, the hounds were baying in their pens, and suddenly two men thrust themselves upon her. Bezile saw them wrench the case from Shivaun's hand, then push a bag into her arms before attempting to flee.

But Shivaun reacted swiftly, as she was trained to do. An expert in unarmed combat, she leapt forward, knocking one man down with a well-aimed kick. Several officials burst out of the crowd and bundled the second man to the muddy earth. In a matter of seconds, both were securely in custody.

Bezile blanked the optic; she had seen enough. The second race was starting and she watched it, yelling for her horse which won by two good lengths. Only then did she begin to make her way through the crowd to her box.

Luis, more lathered than the horses, greeted her with abject relief. He had her robes waiting for her and a silver mug of warm vine-milk. Her fur chair travelled most places with her; she settled herself comfortably in it.

Presently, the miscreants were brought before her. The squatter of the two was covered with mud and dung, while Maltazar limped heavily on one leg. Shivaun, restored to her familiar form, stood guard over them along with three politia officers. Bezile silvered the windows on the box to ensure privacy.

One of the officers handed the money case to Luis, who proceeded to check its contents minutely. Shivaun was holding the bag. Bezile stroked the arms of her chair, and it gave off a low growl of contentment. Despite the injury to his leg, Maltazar stood before her in an attitude of surly defiance. Bezile ignored him, and instructed Shivaun to open the bag.

The egg-shaped object inside was wrapped in a grubby cloth. It proved to be nothing more than a lump of grey spongestone.

Bezile turned her gaze to Maltazar. 'Where is it?'

'Go to hell.'

She smiled. 'That is something that should be concerning you more than me at the moment, my good man.'

The third race was announced. Bezile pointedly delayed the interrogation while she watched it. She was on a run of luck, but unfortunately the mount she had backed unseated its rider even as it crossed the finishing line. It was promptly disqualified. This did not improve her mood.

'We face something of a dilemma here,' she informed Maltazar and his confederate. 'You promised me something but you have failed to deliver. Let me tell you now that I am not a charitable woman, despite my station. You both have criminal records. I think I shall have you erased.'

Maltazar cloaked his initial surprise with a dismissive expression. 'You can't do that.'

'Unfortunately for you, I can. And shall unless you tell me where the womb is.'

'Erasure's only allowed for capital offences,' Maltazar insisted.

'Which makes it wholly appropriate in your case. We have evidence of your implication in at least two murders. And, of course, there is the missing *object*. A living thing, you said. A thing of considerable biological importance. Unless it is recovered, I shall personally see to it that you receive the maximum possible sentence for the wanton destruction of a human life form.'

She saw him swallow. 'You're bluffing.'

'You may rest assured I am not. As you can imagine, my offices have considerable resources at their disposal. I regard this as a matter of the highest criminality. I hope you understand what I am saying. There will be no mercy.'

'Pavel, tell her,' the plump man said.

Thoroughly coated with ripe rhino excreta, he looked both miserable and terrified. Erasure meant a total, irreversible mind-blank. Death in the most brutal mental sense.

'It was a fair deal,' Maltazar insisted. 'You had no intention of paying up, did you? I had to protect my investment.'

'Investment? What a quaint choice of word. You wanted to take the money and run, without delivering anything. That is what irks me. Is there no honour amongst thieves?'

Beyond the silvered box, the crowd were cheering as another race commenced. Maltazar maintained an attitude of defiance.

'I think we need waste our time no further here,' Bezile said to Shivaun. 'It's obvious they never had what they claimed. You may take them away. Have them stupefied ready for despatch.'

The officers took hold of both men. Bezile unsilvered the window, as if to give her full attention to the race. As Maltazar was bustled towards the door, he said, 'All right.'

Bezile turned to face him.

'You've got to give me something,' he said. 'Some payment.'

'You're no longer in a position to bargain with me.'

'I contacted you in good faith.'

'Good faith has been rather absent in this entire enterprise, wouldn't you say?'

'I'll take a tenth of my original price.'

She laughed. 'I have no evidence you have anything to offer.'

'You had the replic.'

'And far more convincing it was, too, than this ball of stone. Do you expect me to believe in something that has no actual substance?'

He regarded her with open loathing. 'You've made a career of it, haven't you?'

It was a good riposte, she conceded to herself.

'Am I to take it that I'm talking to a Mortalist?'

'I don't need the dead to tell me how to lead my life.'

'The present situation appears to contradict that in all respects.'

'You owe me! If you want the goods, then you've got to pay.'

Bezile flexed her fingers on the arms of the chair, hard enough so that its purr was interrupted by a grunt of discomfort. She always enjoyed a good verbal tussle, especially when she knew she had the upper hand.

'I'm prepared to give you a token payment as a sign of good faith. Shall we say ten thousand?'

'That's less than I paid for it!'

'I assure you I don't intend to drain our coffers by one solar more. That is my final offer. You can have the money and free passage to – let us see – one of the Uranian moons, perhaps. A few years' indented service contract as a clinical trialist of psycosmetics might be appropriate. I gather there's a very good sanatory in Miranda Prime.'

'This is outrageous!'

'It might be worse. Would you prefer somewhere hotter? Sol-side on Mercury, perhaps? There are plenty of positions available and a shortage of able bodies.' She was enjoying herself again. 'We'll hold the money in interest, along with a reasonable pension. Enough to keep you both comfortable for a decade or so after your term.' Her casual tone changed to one of deadly seriousness: 'I want you to understand that you really have no choice in the matter. And all of this only applies when I have the object here in front of me and have verified its worth.'

She gave him her most relentless stare. He blustered a little more, but she was obdurate. His accomplice, still terrified, began to urge him to accept.

'I'll come out of this worse off than I went in,' he complained.

'You'll come out of it alive. In complete possession of your faculties. I'm also prepared, as a special gesture of goodwill, to have your records wiped clean. In five years' time you can begin again as citizens of good standing. Such a bargain! What is five years against immediate, absolute death?' She allowed a pause. 'Where is it?'

'It's in one of the feeder bins,' the other man blurted. 'At the slayhound pens.'

'What? You've put it in the dogfood?'

'It's wedged just inside the hopper,' Maltazar told her. 'You couldn't budge it unless you knew what you were looking for.'

Bezile let a silence extend.

'It's the truth!' Maltazar's accomplice insisted.

'Go down and see,' Bezile ordered Shivaun.

They waited, Bezile studying her wristlink while Luis confirmed that none of the money had been lost. She told him to count out ten thousand solars in hundred solar notes. She seldom used money herself, though she fully understood why it remained the favourite medium of exchange amongst underclass types such as Maltazar, who would prefer not to leave a record of his transactions through skin scrapes or retina scans. Not that either man was going to get a single solar.

Bezile instructed the officers to take both men away and clean them up. She suggested that Luis accompany them. He obviously felt that so menial a task was beneath him, but she knew he would do as she wanted. And she wanted him temporarily out of the way.

Alone, Bezile opened her wristlink. She saw Shivaun recover the bag from the pen. On Bezile's instructions, she opened the bag and displayed it. It seemed to be the genuine article, and Shivaun confirmed that it was warm and alive. She instructed

Shivaun to take it straight to her private office and say nothing to anyone.

When Luis returned with both men, Bezile announced that nothing had been found.

Maltazar immediately began to protest. 'You're crazy! I put it there myself.'

'The bins were searched thoroughly,' Bezile said calmly. 'There was no sign of it.'

'Take me down there!' Maltazar insisted. 'I'll find it.'

Bezile gave a weary sigh.

'You've got to believe me!' Maltazar insisted. 'It's there! Let me go down!'

Bezile allowed two of the officers to escort Maltazar to the pens. It was worth going through the tedious formalities for the sake of appearances. The other man remained under guard.

While they waited, Luis murmured, 'Have you got it?'

'It wasn't there.'

Plainly he was unsure whether or not to believe her. He was a devoted servant of the Noosphere, but far too highly strung to rest easy in the knowledge that they had indeed acquired the artifact. Besides, there were so many factions these days; one never knew whom one could really trust.

'Then we went through all that for nothing,' he said.

It was half a question. She merely shrugged. Then she instructed him to replace the ten thousand solars in the case.

'Pavel put it in there,' Maltazar's accomplice assured her. 'I was with him.'

She could hear the sheer terror in his voice. She spread her hands. 'What can I do? Let us pray it hasn't been fed to the dogs. For your sake.'

He looked crushed, and she felt the faintest twinge of remorse for using him so. It was something she would have to try to make amends for when she next communed with the Noosphere. Not that she really intended to have them erased. She'd pass them over to the judicators, and they'd probably get off with a short course of corrective psychosurgery and a year's community drone service in the Swamplands.

When Maltazar was brought back, he was flustered and furious.

'Somebody must have stolen it,' he argued. 'I swear it was there!'

Bezile snapped the money case shut.

'I think,' she said to both men, 'that concludes our business. Take them away.'

Stridently protesting, both were bundled out. At this point Bezile heard that her rhinocerhorse had been reinstated and that a slayhound she had backed had come in on the last race at fifteen to one.

She gave Luis a generous smile. It really had been a most satisfactory day.

I was staring at a plate that held a dark brown mash. As if I had suddenly woken from a trance. I had no memory of what had gone before.

'Are you all right?' Nina asked.

She was sitting beside the bed. Her hair was tied back. It made her look . . . I searched for the word. Custodial.

'I think I blanked out,' I said.

She was holding the spoon, had obviously been feeding me.

'A fugue,' she said.

'A what?'

'Drifting in and out. It happens.'

I felt stupid and helpless. I had the vaguest memory of something, but I couldn't grasp it.

'Were we talking a moment ago?'

She nodded.

A surge of anger and frustration. 'I can't remember any of it.'

'It wasn't important.'

'I can't even remember you bringing this food.'

She didn't seem surprised. 'Try not to get upset about it. It'll get better.'

'Will it? How the hell do you know it will?'

I couldn't help the anger: it came unbidden, a generalized fury at my whole condition. It was hard to get my thoughts in order.

'What's going on?' I demanded. 'This is a hospital, right? What happened to me?'

She didn't reply straight away, then said finally, 'Do you remember anything?'

I tried to think. There was nothing.

'It's a blank.'

'Nothing at all?'

'I told you!' I said fiercely.

She was eager to calm me. 'It's normal. I give you my word. It was the same for me.'

This took me by surprise. I stared at her. 'You went through this?'

She nodded.

'Tell me.'

'Everything you're experiencing – the hot flushes, the mood swings, the memory loss – it happened to me.'

'You're a patient here, too?'

She put a hand to my forehead. I must have been feverish, because her palm felt cool.

'I'm a little further along the road to recovery than you,' she said.

She appeared perfectly healthy. If she was a patient, why was she feeding me?

'Do we know one another?' I asked.

'Not until now,' she said.

I blinked, and everything shifted again. I was lying flat once more, drowsy, fighting sleep. I knew we had talked further, but whatever time had elapsed had vanished. I heard footsteps receding, the door open and close.

And then only silence.

Four

Shivaun's flyer was a big octopoid transporter which did the run between the inner planets and the Jovian worlds, ferrying supplies to the settled moons and bringing back ice to Venus. Normally it carried no crew or passengers, but it was fully primed for her when she transferred from the shuttle, announcing that the run to Ganymede was one of its regular trips.

Shivaun settled herself in the cramped skulldeck, placing her bulky luggage in the compartment niche below the arc of the lensport. She put her dutybag on the empty seat beside her, securing it under the restraining web.

The ship gave full flight details while the skulldeck filled with a muted rumbling. In the digestive heart of the craft, organic fission of stored solar hydrogen generated tailfin energy emissions that accelerated the ship at a constant one G to the midpoint of the voyage, reverse thrust being applied thereafter. With no passengers on board, the ships were capable of fifty per cent lightspeed at G-forces that would pulverize ordinary protoplasm; but this was to be a more leisurely flight.

'Excuse me for asking,' the flyer remarked in its brisk female voice, 'but who's the other lifeform on board?'

'My luggage,' Shivaun said curtly.

'Oh?'

'Nothing you need to know about.'

Shivaun asked the seat to go into leanback. She adjusted her webbing, pulled down an optic stalk.

'*The New Crusaders* is on band fifty-one,' the flyer informed her. 'Are you a fan?'

'Not particularly.' It was a popular space opera, one of the many set during the expulsion of the Augmenters from the Settled Worlds generations before. She'd never seen it.

She selected some meditative imagery, monochrome fractals blossoming endlessly. The status optics on the control console told her that the flyer had already broken orbit; the damped yet pervasive roar of biofission filled the cabin as star patterns and the gunmetal snowflake of Veneris Station swam across the lensport.

'It's rather nice to have a passenger on board,' the flyer informed her.

'Really?'

'Normally I travel alone. It does get rather lonely at times.'

Shivaun said nothing to this. It was just her luck to get a loquacious ship, and one that thought it was fully human. Of course the controlling neural networks were modelled on the brain cortex, and sometimes brain tissue from the truedead was used; but she did not for one moment believe that ships had truly human feelings.

'I've been running this route for eight years. Back and forth like a yoyo, whatever that is. Never a single hitch. Not that you'd know it from any thanks I've got—'

'Listen.'

'Yes?'

'I'm going to take a nap. Wake me when we're there. Clear?'

There was a pause, followed by a noise almost like someone clearing their throat.

'Perfectly,' said the flyer, sounding hurt.

Shivaun slept, as she always did, without dreaming. When the flyer woke her the Jovian system was already in sight, two of its four moons visible in their eco-orbits around their shining bronze parent. Jupiter itself was blotched with light from the photoplasms that swam in its atmosphere, enormous amoeboids that ingested hard radiation and re-emitted it in the visible and infrared to sustain the biospheres of Ganymede, Callisto and Europa. They blazed like miniature polymorphous suns.

Ganymede loomed, its sallow ocean interspersed with green island continents of reedmat. Shivaun had the flyer notify the Prime Arbiter's office in Lysithea of their arrival. A private shuttle would be sent up for her, customs conveniently bypassed.

She went aft into the narrow gangway, had the flyer put on double-G and did thirty minutes of exercises in pure oxygen to loosen herself up. When she returned to the skulldeck, she was hungry.

'What have you got to eat?' she asked the flyer.

Rather primly, the flyer gave her its menu; it was still sulking from the earlier rebuff. Ships always carried foodstuffs in case of emergency, and Shivaun ordered Mercurian peppers stuffed with spiced sausageplant; it was the hottest meal she had ever eaten, and she swallowed two tubes of iced water before the fires were cooled. A spidery shuttle appeared and began matching orbit with them. She gathered up her luggage and went down to the airvalve.

'I hope you had a pleasant trip,' the flyer said pointedly.

'Very pleasant,' she told it. 'You have my compliments.'

'You didn't even ask me my name.'

'My apologies. Do you have one?'

'I have a technical specification.'

Shivaun withheld a smile. 'That's not the same, is it? Would you like me to name you?'

The flyer made a surprised sound. 'That would be most considerate of you. Do you have something in mind?'

Shivaun thought about it, then said: 'Pandora.'

The flyer practically purred. 'I rather like the sound of it. Wasn't she an ancient goddess who unlocked a box that released all the wisdom of the world?'

'Not in the version I was taught,' Shivaun replied. 'She was a siren who was warned never to speak. Then one day she opened her mouth and all the horrors of creation poured out of it.'

The transfer to the shuttle and the flight down to Ganymede went smoothly. Shivaun was in uniform, and the shuttle's crew was courteous but noncommittal. Everyone knew what sort of jobs offworld expediters were called in for.

An official from Venzano's office was waiting for her at the terminus, which sat in the bole of a big gravitree, its flat branchways radiating out from the centre. A wide-footed hopper carried them across the open reedmat towards Lysithea with an effortless series of long arcing leaps. The reedmat was strong enough under Ganymede's low gravity to support hunters who stalked snakefish with knives and pneumatic spears. The people here were carnivorous, having none of the Inner Planets' moral qualms about eating dead meat.

The hopper carried them to the shore of Lysithea, finally slumping in the shadowed undergrowth as the gravity fields of the trees on the island continent reached full strength. The trees were massive, their drooping boughs many-branched, hollowed boles providing homes for the city's people. They carved stairways in the fibrous bark, used the boughs as thoroughfares, built sturdy vine bridges to cross from one arboreal to another. Pollen flour for breadmaking was harvested from blossoms, fruits and nuts were abundant and the heart-shaped leathery leaves could be fashioned into clothing, carpets or wide-brimmed hats to protect against the urine rain of the primeapes who inhabited the uppermost tiers. The apes were also hunted for food.

Shivaun and her escort climbed a spiral stairway. There was a refreshing coolness under the shade of the trees, Jupiter's brassy light scintillating through layers of foliage. Power lianas snaked along ridged bark, clothes were being aired on silkspinner webs and a noisy family squatted in a doormouth, the children feeding raw fish to an amphibian roaster while their three parents conducted a vehement argument in the local argot, theatrically slapping one another about the arms and head. The roasters, a fixture in almost every home, could cook a whole snakefish in their fiery innards within minutes and regurgitate it ready to eat; at night their constant croaking kept the uninitiated awake. Shivaun had visited Ganymede before, and she knew its inhabitants to be extravagant and libertine, prey to customs which offworlders often found repulsive. As tree dwellers, they had only one pervasive sanction: no fire.

They reached a terminus where a roller was waiting. It wove expertly along a main branchway, dodging local psyclists precariously perched on their eyeless mounts. Their psycles, smaller two-wheeled relatives of rollers, were reputedly steered by sheer force of will, though Shivaun was sure that this was simply a local joke to highlight the fact that road manners were practically nonexistent.

The Prime Arbiter's treehouse occupied the entire bole of a gravitree that stood alone in a clearing. Its elegant corridors and stairways held elaborate decorations carved from the living wood. Shivaun was taken directly to Venzano's office, where she found the Arbiter and his staff watching a large optic. As Prime Arbiter, Venzano was the most senior representative of the Noocracy outside the Noosphere itself. He was slumped in a chair, gnawing on his thumb, intent on the display.

It was the Advocates themselves who stood at the centre of the optic, Julius swarthy and intense, Orela a fair-skinned beauty who on this occasion wore her hair in a flame-coloured cascade. Both were dressed in their scarlet and grey robes. They were on a goodwill visit to Tenebra on Nereid, where there had been an outbreak of a mysterious new affliction that had caused over a dozen hitherto ordinary citizens to descend into a frenzied madness, destroying their surroundings or attacking those around them before succumbing to death either by suicide or a seizure. There was no apparent connection between the victims, and similar cases had been reported on Iapetus and Titania. The networks were calling the syndrome the Dementia, and no one had any idea as to its cause.

Julius and Orela were addressing a huge crowd in the centre of the crystalline city. They spoke together, promising that special medicant teams would be assembled to respond swiftly so that sufferers could be sedated before they injured themselves or others. Extra resources would be marshalled to investigate the cause of the ailment and provide a cure.

As ever, the Advocates were quietly dramatic and persuasive, punctuating their words from the diamond balcony with small gestures which managed to be at once intimate and all-encompassing, as if they were addressing not a crowd but every individual who was watching the broadcast. Shivaun studied the sallow Venzano. His expression was thoughtful but guarded. It was rumoured that relations between the Prime Arbiter and the Advocates had been strained in recent years.

As Advocates, Julius and Orela were the exemplars of the Noosphere, the conscience and authority of the whole of humanity, the mouthpieces of its wishes as expressed through public votes or private communion in shrines. No one in the room moved or spoke until the broadcast was complete. It ended with Julius and Orela going down among the crowd to receive their heartfelt gratitude. As the image faded, Venzano turned and acknowledged Shivaun's presence. He asked the rest of his staff to leave.

'Safe journey?' was the first thing he said to her when they were alone.

Shivaun nodded. 'Everything went smoothly, Your Graciousness.'

'You have it with you?'

She nodded again, hefting the bag and placing it on the desk before him.

He opened it and removed the object. For a long time there was silence as he turned it slowly in his hands.

He had her repeat the story of how Bezile had acquired it. She did so fully. Still he continued to inspect the womb, running his fingers along its veins and arteries, placing his hands flat against its surface as if to test its warmth or weight, even putting an ear to it.

At long last he said, 'You did well.'

Again she merely nodded. She had only done her duty.

'My people here will have a good look at it,' he continued. 'This will take several days. Then you can carry my answer back to Bezile. In the meantime, I suggest you relax, enjoy some rest and recreation.'

'I have official duties to attend to,' she said. She produced a letter of authorization. 'Here, and on Pluto.'

He did not bother to voice the letter. 'That was just a pretext so we could get you here with a minimum of fuss.'

'Nevertheless, it would be suitable if I executed them.'

He almost winced. 'If you so wish . . .'

'I understand this entire matter is very sensitive.'

'Indeed it is.'

'My presence here might be remarked upon if I were not to carry out my work.'

'Of course. Of course.' He cleared his throat. 'You have an . . . *itinerary*?'

'There are two subjects to be dealt with here on Ganymede. The first is believed to be hiding in this very city.'

'Indeed? Then that is convenient at least.'

'I believe the High Arbiter of Aphrodite sent you full notification.'

'Bezile?' He was distracted by the womb. 'Oh, yes, no doubt. Well, you have my complete sanction, that goes without saying. Will you need any assistance?'

'Where circumstances permit, I prefer to work alone.'

'Then I'll leave you to make the arrangements. Perhaps it should be done with more than the usual *discretion*, given the circumstances. We don't want to draw unnecessary attention to ourselves, do we?'

She was faintly insulted by the suggestion that she would act otherwise. 'Rest assured I shall not prejudice your good offices. Will that be all?'

'What? Oh, yes.' He rang for one of his staff to take her to her quarters, his eyes avidly on the womb.

She showered and changed, using make-up and hydrodermics to elaborate her lithe, muscular body into something far more buxom and voluptuous. A rainbowsheen wig and a waterveil dress completed the transformation.

She spent half an hour perfecting her Callistan accent with a pedantic elocution console before leaving her quarters and hailing a slither. A convincing accent wasn't particularly necessary for the assignment, but she liked to feel properly prepared in case of emergency.

She told the slither she wanted The Rink, a popular club out on the northern coastal waters of the city. Traffic was sparse, and they made good time. A major branchway of a coastal arboreal curved downwards and out across the reedmats, Jupiter sinking huge and molten into the sea on the western horizon. Scarecrows were calling raucously from twilit shallows as the slither pulled up at a silverslide floe. On top of it stood the ribbed dome of The Rink.

Inside, the chamber was already crowded with skaters, the mirrored floor writhing and undulating beneath them as they happily collided with one another in their bright padded suits. According to her most recent information, The Rink was a

favourite haunt of her subject, one Raoul Nestorine Forster, a
fugitive for the past two years.

She sent her coat and shoulderbag off to the cloakroom and
walked brazenly to a broad curving bar at the back of the
chamber. It was serving all manner of concoctions to minimize
inhibitions and maximize the fun. Scroungedogs loped expertly
between the skaters, ready to open their huge maws for anyone
who wished to throw up. Social puking was yet another highly
rated aspect of Ganymedan culture which defeated the esteem
of most outsiders.

Shivaun cradled a firewine at the bar and surveyed the rink.
Two men began talking to her, and she she did nothing to
discourage the impression that she was easy prey to their
attentions. But her eyes remained active. She had studied
Forster's file minutely before leaving Melisande, and she was
confident she would recognize him even if he was disguised.
Her eyes held retina scans which would signal when she had
found him. But, of course, she would have to get up close first.

She let both men buy her a drink, then another, slipping
away in between to visit the cloakroom and swallow a capsule
that would catalyse the alcohol into glucose. One of the men
summoned skates and suits. They kitted up, and the three of
them went on to the rink.

Shivaun found it a crude sport, with its bunching and
buffeting, its clasping of bodies, its sweating and fevered
breaths and dizzying twists and turns. But she laughed uninhibitedly, letting herself be flung from one skater to another,
pawed and mauled and thrust ever onwards while the music,
hectic Callistan boleros, spiralled and swirled and the rink
buckled and writhed and the dogs ran slavering between their
feet. The rink was responsive to pressure changes caused by
the skaters themselves, wobbling and weaving according to
their movements.

A side effect of the capsule she had swallowed was uncontrollable flatulence, and this only served to make her more
popular with the crowd. She found herself in the arms of a
man with a swarthy face and black hair sculpted flat to his
scalp. He looked nothing like Forster, but pinpricks of light
flashed at the back of her eyes and she knew she had her man.

The ebb and flow of the rink carried her away again almost immediately, but not before she had planted an open-mouthed kiss on his cheek. He was dressed in crimson and lavender and would be easy to find.

When the music ended, she left the rink and returned to the bar. Her two suitors from earlier soon appeared at her side, both obviously intent on a threesome. But she was busy tracking Forster with her gaze. He seemed to have a huge appetite for the dance, pausing only briefly to snatch a drink from the menials orbiting the edges of the rink, gulping it down and then rejoining the mêlée. She knew he had been a drunkard throughout his long life and had had his liver reconstituted several times.

Her suitors were becoming tiresome, a positive distraction. One of them suggested that they slip away together. Shivaun slid a hand down to his groin and squeezed, hard. He gave a strangled yelp and teetered back, staring at her in astonishment, seeing the fierceness in her face, the fearlessness and disdain. The other man saw it too. She moved through the crowd. They did not follow.

On the rink once more, she made a beeline for Forster. The undulations of the floor were less pronounced, doubtless because the skaters were much drunker and less able to stand up. Forster was in the loose embrace of another woman, but Shivaun elbowed her expertly aside and caught hold of him.

Forster was already very drunk, his lips moist, eyes glazed.

'Hello,' she said, nuzzling against him, pretending that she was just the same. She let out a huge belch. 'I think maybe I'm going to puke.'

He liked his women blowzy and coarse, she knew that from his profile. Before absconding he had been a professor of moral philosophy and thanatology at Themis University on Ishtar, but had devoted his 'retirement' to far less elevated pursuits.

'Throw up here often?' he said with a snigger.

'Only in the right company,' she retorted.

They swirled around together for a spell. He was wilting, so her timing was perfect. His face gleamed with sweat, and she could feel the heat of his hands through her waterveil.

'I don't think I've seen you here before,' he remarked.

'I come and go,' she told him.

'You live round here?'

'What is this – the first degree?'

He laughed and said, 'At least let's hear a name.'

'Delphine.' She manoeuvred him towards the edge. 'Shit, I think I need to sit down.'

He joined her at a table, ordering more drinks. She had a spectral, colours swirling in a fluted glass.

'That stuff will blow your head off,' he told her.

She took a big enough gulp to let a trickle of it run down her chin. She wiped it away with the back of her hand. He grasped the hand across the table and licked it.

She laughed. 'That your party trick?'

'I've got others.'

'Want to get out of here?'

He seemed surprised and not a little suspicious of the suggestion. 'Are you in a hurry?'

She made light of it. 'I follow my instincts. You only get one life, that's what I say.'

She deliberately didn't look at him, taking a slow draught of her spectral, annoyed with herself for pushing him too fast. On the edge of her vision, she saw him raise his glass and drain it.

'How about another?' he said.

She belched. 'Sure. Why not?'

He dragged her back on to the rink for a few more dances. He was so drunk she practically had to hold him upright. He was slobbering against her, and she wondered if he was going to pass out and ruin it. But then he said, 'I think you'd better take me home.'

She got him out of his skates, summoned her coat and shoulderbag and helped him outside. There was a couple waiting ahead of them at the slither stand, but a two-seater came down the branchway and they boarded it, leaving Shivaun alone with her charge. He had fallen asleep against her and she knew she could finish it easily and efficiently, without him even knowing. But that wasn't her way. She liked to play things by the code, ensure they passed on in full awareness of the fact.

Europa was up, its silver disc broken by the trees. Flashmoths twinkled and flittered in the darkness. A voice behind her said, 'Well, look who it is.'

The two men who had been flirting with her earlier came out of the shadows. They had obviously been waiting for her.

Shivaun didn't give them a chance to say anything further. She darted up, chopping the closest of the two across the windpipe with the back of her hand.

The first man staggered back, croaking and gurgling; the second fled. Shivaun saw a psycle coming down a moonlit branchway, a high-spirited quartet clutched together on its back. Forster was slumped, still asleep, where she had left him. She slapped his cheek to wake him as the psycle pulled up and its passengers clambered off.

'This vehicle yours?' she asked them.

'For hire,' the psycle announced. It extracted payment from the four with its tongue.

She managed to get Forster into the front saddle. The controls were a set of nodules along the creature's scrawny neck. She had no idea how to use them.

'Autopilot,' Forster blurted. 'Full speed ahead!' He murmured his address, then slumped again.

The psycle spun around and set off at an alarming pace back up the branchway. Shivaun had to cling on tight while at the same time holding on to Forster to make sure he didn't slip from the saddle. There was a constant raucous hissing as the creature sucked in air through flapped nostrils and vented it through its rear end.

As before, there was little traffic on the branchways, but despite this the psycle contrived two near-misses, one with a coach-roller full of sleepy tourists, another with an enormous roaster that had settled itself for the evening across an intersection and fled with feral steamy barks as the psycle's rear wheel nipped one of its toes on the turn. Shivaun had to admit that it was an exhilarating ride.

Forster's house was on an outlying archipelago of Kuiper rock, part of a relatively new settlement of drab boxy inorganics, obviously thrown up in haste as temporary housing for Lysithea's ever-growing population. Only the shortage of dry land constrained growth, and stony asteroids were constantly being imported to provide more terra firma for Ganymede and its sister worlds.

The psycle extended a rough tongue to her open palm, sampling skin. Gruff-voiced, it announced a satisfactory credit transfer. Shivaun watched it depart, white-walled wheels softly glowing in the night. It disappeared swiftly into the arboreal.

The single chamber inside Forster's house was windowless and hermetic, the air stale. It was crammed with shelves of books, some of them reading books. Shivaun examined the shelf above the bed while Forster stumbled over to a cocktail cabinet. She punched title buttons at random, heard them announce themselves as *The Rhetoric of Longevity*, *The Commensurate Mind*, *Implications of Immortality*.

Forster poured himself something golden from a scalloped bottle.

'You want one?' he asked. 'Aphrodisian. Works even better when you're drunk.'

She shook her head, shoulderbag clutched to her side, surveying the chamber. It was neat, ordered, cheerless. An academic's bolthole all right, a place for lodging rather than living.

'What's with the books?' she asked.

'Eh? Ah, those.' He shrugged. 'It's a hobby of mine.'

He swallowed the drink down in one. She saw him straighten and regard her with renewed, lurid interest. She smiled provocatively at him.

'My God,' he said, 'I do believe I'm positively bursting with desire.'

She let him wrestle her on to the bed, then slipped her hand into her shoulderbag and pulled out the needle. It was already primed. As he searched for the straps on her waterveil, she slid it into the back of his neck.

He went limp beneath her, eyes wide open. The narcotic was a motor inhibitor that paralysed while leaving him otherwise alert.

She looked down at him and said, 'It's time, Mr Forster.'

She could see the fear, the dawning realization, rising in his eyes. She got off the bed, went over to the cocktail cabinet and mixed up an antalcohol. Cradling his head in one arm, she held it to his mouth. Tears were oozing out of his eyes. He gulped it down like a child taking medicine.

She laid him back on the pillow and held him gently while she waited for the antalcohol to work. Really it made no difference whether he was drunk or sober, but she liked her clients to be clear-headed, fully aware of what was happening to them.

When she was satisfied that he had sobered up, she said softly, 'You absconded from your homeworld one standard month before your terminal day, Mr Forster. You are now one hundred and two years old, is that not correct? That's two more years than your permitted span.'

The drug rendered him incapable of saying anything. She preferred it that way; it avoided the tiresome arguments, the pleading, the abject fear when they realized that she would not be swayed from carrying out the termination.

'Your family back on Venus have been most concerned about your welfare, Mr Forster. I'm afraid they're rather shamed by your actions – you understand the stigma, I'm sure. They asked me to tell you that they love you and want nothing more than for you to take your rightful place in the Noosphere with your ancestors.'

She heard the liquid flow as he voided himself in terror. It *was* degrading, she had to admit, which was why she always tried to ensure that terminations were carried out in private, preferably in a person's own home.

'There's nothing to fear,' she said. 'Only your body will die.'

She could feel him trembling as his terror blunted the effect of the narcotic. Shivaun was aware that her words were inadequate for someone like him; he had probably spent most of his lifetime considering the philosophy of death. But no amount of knowledge could protect against the naked horror that some felt at the prospect. Yet her duties had their rituals, their verbal obligations.

'Consider your future: immortal, and in the company of those who have gone before you – parents, grandparents, aunts and uncles, even your son, Maldwin, who I believe took an early death. A reunion, Mr Forster, with those you've loved and who have gone on to the ultimate stage of existence.'

He started to tremble, tears running freely.

'Calm yourself,' she told him. 'It won't hurt.'

She took the shades from her shoulderbag. As she was doing so, Forster began a sluggish flailing which dislodged one of the books above the bed. It fell open on the floor, the pink SUMMARY light winking on.

– must reject the claims of the Immortalists, who would rob us of our human souls should they ever find the means to extend human life indefinitely. Similarly, the Augmenters would adapt us to the varied demands of the cosmos at the very expense of our humanity, turning us into creatures who would be alien in both psyche and physiology to *Homo sapiens sapiens*—

Shivaun returned to the bed and gently held Forster down. 'Listen,' she whispered to him. 'Listen.'

– through the Noosphere we preserve the essential mind and spirit of every individual that is or was a part of humanity. The realm of the Noosphere is the true Afterlife dreamt of by our ancient forebears—

'There, there,' she said, stroking his head and smiling down at him, feeling that as an intellectual he should appreciate this fortuitous valediction. She fitted the shades over his eyes. They moulded themselves around his temples, biodisplays on the mirrorlenses giving her a status report. Everything was in order, the storage nodule along the ridge of the shades winking as it readied itself to receive his psyche.

Forster made one last attempt to deny his fate, a weak spastic twitching as the narcotic began to wear off. Shivaun put one hand flat on his chest and with her other hand pressed a thumb into the recess in the temple of the shades. The ridge phosphoresced for an instant, then died. Shivaun felt Forster's palpitating heart stop in the same instant. He went still beneath her.

The status line showed that the transfer was complete, Forster's psyche now contained in the shades' biocircuitry. She removed the shades and folded them into a case. Forster's eyes remained open, staring blindly at the star-filled skylight in the ceiling. She closed them, then tidied his clothes and straightened his limbs.

'Our ancestors dreamt of Heaven or Nirvana,' the book was telling her, 'a place to which the righteous and the pure might aspire. We have made our own—'

Shivaun snapped the book shut and returned it to the shelf.

The house had gone into privacy mode on their arrival, and she was not surprised to find the doormouth locked. Deliberately she began heaving hard on its lip, and the house began an ululating alarm.

It was twenty minutes before the stewards arrived. They burst in, two of them, both men, wielding pulse-pistols and quietsticks. They found her sitting calmly on the edge of the bed, her identification at the ready.

They checked the disk, regarded the dead Forster, looked at her with a certain respect and, she knew, fear. She carried full authorization. The details of her termination would be put on record, making her visit official, authentic.

'Anything we can do?' one of them asked her guardedly.

'I'll arrange translation and notification,' she told them. 'There's only the body for disposal. I presume I can leave that to you?'

The man nodded.

'Then I simply require a lift back to the Prime Arbiter's office.'

Their eagerness to oblige her belied their unease. She knew that politia officers everywhere often had to deal with the messy consequences of violence or accidents, but they rarely encountered fully dead bodies. The conversation was restrained as they drove along the city's branchways. Shivaun found herself mindlessly counting the pendulamps that swayed gently in the darkness in the breeze of the night.

On arriving at Venzano's, she used a shrine to transfer Forster's psyche from the shades directly into the Noosphere. His relatives would be informed of the translation and advised that he was now accessible to them through communion. No doubt they would throw a deathday party to make the news public.

There was a call from home, but she had no time to play it. She took the tapeworm from the console and put it in her luggage.

She left a message for the sleeping Venzano, telling him that she was going on to Ananke where the second of her clients, a former zeeballer who had captained Venus, was reputedly hiding in an illegal stimstore, hiring out his memories of many successful Worlds Cup campaigns over a forty-year career. But as the hopper carried her out of the city, she directed it to take her straight to the terminus. A pilgrimage ship was docking at Amalthea within the hour, and she had already booked passage.

Flocks of whirligigs spiralled up from their roosts among the upper branches of the trees as the shuttle rose through Jupiter's huge cinnamon dawn. It was a scheduled flight, and she was not in uniform. The scattering of other passengers paid her no heed.

Amalthea Station was a honeycomb of docking bays and transit tunnels, its innards hollowed out by rock-eaters many generations before. The pilgrimage ship was already boarding, a stately cetacoid with a huge tailfin that gleamed like graphite. Attached to its belly was the fat capsule of an automated ferry, doubtless loading coffins into the hold. Shivaun always carried more than one set of travel permits, and she presented those which identified her in a private capacity as a mourner visiting the grave of a departed. The bored official at the gate waved her through after a cursory scan.

She had a seat alone at the rear of the passenger chamber, with plenty of legroom. After securing her luggage, she activated the privacy hood and swiftly fell into a deep sleep. When she woke, they were already out past the orbit of Uranus, eleven hours into the voyage with another thirty to go.

Ship time was midafternoon, but she ordered a substantial breakfast of scrambled veg, wolfing it down with two big mugs of fragrant Melisandean tea. Then she slipped the tapeworm into the midriff of her seat interface.

It was blonde-haired Cibylle who filled the optic, three children in her arms, two of them Shivaun's own by Kovec, one of three men she and Cibylle had married. Cibylle had opted for childcare, raising her own year-old triplets along with Shivaun's pair of three-year-olds. She had by far the strongest parental instincts of the five of them.

'Greetings from the slough of despond,' Cibylle began in her hearty manner. 'I don't know where you are, but I hope all's well and that you're taking care of yourself. The little ones are missing you, and everyone sends their love.'

There was a pause, and the children went coy, burrowing their faces in Cibylle's breast. They were responding to a prerecorded hologram of Shivaun which she knew would be making funny faces at them.

Cibylle then related an anecdote about their neighbours, a monogamous couple who had scandalized local opinion by keeping a merecat as a pet in their compartment. Left alone one evening, the cat had gnawed through the compartment's main water artery, flooding their own kitchen below.

'I woke to these awful spluttering sounds,' Cibylle told her. 'The food processor and the launderer were in a terrible state of distress. We had to call the intestors out in the middle of the night, and they ended up having to tranquillize half the appliances! You should have seen the mess!'

More gossip followed, about incidents dating back further than the three days Shivaun had been gone. Shivaun let them wash over her, watching the children, who seemed lulled by the very sound of Cibylle's voice. When they had first married Cibylle had been a voxbox, providing summaries of local issues for citizens during public votes; now it was all domestic trifles.

'I hope you'll be back before too long,' she went on. 'I'm coping, but I think a holiday would be nice, don't you?'

She hoisted the children into a more comfortable position, effortlessly encompassing them in her broad arms.

'The others are out. Vy and Kovec have got a new commission. One of the big mansions up on Palleas. They've been over there the past two days.'

She proceeded to give Shivaun the details. The two men ran a thriving interior decor business, specializing in hand-reared furniture and custom wallcoverings. Cibylle had aspirations to wealth and a bigger habitation for their growing brood.

'I hope you'll find time to call,' Shivaun heard Cibylle say presently. 'Don't worry, I'm not nagging. I understand the difficulties in your line of work. It's just sometimes I miss a bit of *adult* company, you know?'

One of the children began to giggle, while another flexed its fingers at her. No doubt her hologram was giving them her friendly monster facial: it was one of her best.

Cibylle registered it too, with a kind of weary tolerance. Then she became serious. 'I wasn't going to mention it because I know you've probably got other things on your mind, but you might as well know.' She unloaded the children into the playpen beside her; the pen fluffed its walls and nuzzled them. 'Imrani's gone AWOL again.' A big meaningful sigh. 'The last time I saw him was the day before you left, and he hasn't been seen since. No message anywhere, nothing. Wouldn't surprise me if he's gone off on some impromptu tour.'

Imrani worked in the Organ Supply Department of Melisande General; he was a talented tissue fabricator, but he also liked to moonlight as a pipe player with various bands in the city. It was Shivaun who had persuaded the others to let him join their marriage contract only two years before: at twenty-three, he was considerably younger than the rest of them. Cibylle had never approved.

'I know you're fond of him,' she was saying, 'but I think we're going to have to consider his position when our contract comes up for renewal. He just hasn't been assuming his share of the responsibilities. You know what he's like. Always off on some spur-of-the-moment thing.'

For no obvious reason, Letty, one of Shivaun's children, began to cry.

'I'm going to have to go,' Cibylle said. 'I hope you're taking care of yourself. Don't let them work you too hard or do anything too *unpleasant*. And get in touch when you have a moment. Bye.'

Her smiling face faded to grey as the optic blanked. Shivaun took the worm out of the slot and put it away. It was an unspoken rule among her partners that they never discussed her specific duties, yet Cibylle was always making indirect reference to them, like a child who knows a swearword and is forever skirting the boundaries of actually saying it.

She recorded a brief return message filled with local Ganymedean colour and making no reference to anything specific in Cibylle's. Then, against her instincts, she put in a call to Niome, her daughter by a previous marriage who lived on Triton, six hours' call-time distant. It was several years since they had last spoken and Shivaun kept the message brief, informing her that she was en route to Charon in order to pay her respects to Niome's two departed brood-brothers. Niome lived and worked in one of the big nomadic ménages favoured by Tritonians, her own five children being raised communally. So far the Dementia had not reached there. With luck, Niome would have time to return her call before she reached Pluto.

An atmosphere of doleful sobriety prevailed in the passenger chamber, few people talking, many enveloped in privacy hoods networked to the ship's shrine. This was unsurprising, given the nature of the voyage. Shivaun scrolled through the optic channels. Normally she favoured educatories, but she was possessed by an unfamiliar sense of the fragility of things, the thinness of the barrier between herself and the vastness beyond the ship's hide. The worlds of the Solar System, where the human race scuttled like ants on boulders, were no more than a wisp of smoke in a radiation-soaked void. There were so many ways in which its blind imperatives could deal out death, heedlessly, in the spasm of a heartbeat.

She found herself watching an episode of *Lords of the Nether*, another space opera. One of the lords had gone back into the past to become queen of a tribe of Amazonals who rode fire-breathing dragons into battle against the hideous hordes of Ampyrea, whose eyes flashed lightning bolts. She entered the interactive mode, became the queen herself. She slaughtered thousands and reduced their citadels to rubble and cinders.

When it was over, her frustration remained. She disliked inactivity, the tedium of passenger travel, any sense that she was not in full control of her life. She paged a flight attendant, inputted Bezile's authorization letter, then asked for the use of a lifecraft for a 'recreational flight'.

Somewhat to her surprise, the request was granted. She went down to the bays and found one of the lozenge-shaped craft already primed for her. She clambered aboard and overrode its controls, opting for full manual. She gave it maximum acceleration out of the bay.

For the next few hours, Shivaun indulged herself in feints and skirmishes with the pilgrimage ship itself, darting at it, spiralling around it, testing the lifecraft's capacities to the full. She was an excellent pilot, having served a five-year stint as a ferry operator in the Equatorial Rifts on Mercury before she became an expediter. She had restrained the impulse to take control of the transporter during the first leg of her journey out from Venus; but now, awash with adrenalin, it was sheer bliss to express herself.

Only when the pilgrimage ship began to page her did she reluctantly return to it. The lifecraft spontaneously thanked her for the exercise as she was leaving the bay.

She went straight to the recreation deck and played an hour's solo scootball before finally returning to the passenger chamber. She slept again, and when she awoke the overhead display showed a fantailed craft intersecting their flight path. This was the Chiron ferry, bringing the last batch of pilgrims to join them.

At length the ferry docked, and there was a series of asthmatic exchanges as airvalves opened and closed. She had her seat dilate its viewer and direct its gaze so that she could see the ferry as it drifted away again, tail rising and falling as it began to pick up speed for the return to the small and isolated outpost whose few inhabitants were always outnumbered by travellers going elsewhere.

Presently the new passengers entered the chamber. One of them was an olive-skinned man with black hair over his chin and cheeks. He was carrying a struggling bioform that looked like a leathery sac attached to a pile of long bent sticks. The chitinous legs clicked together in agitation as he tried to hold it securely and manoeuvre his way down the aisle.

With some effort he managed to subdue the creature before finally slumping in the seat beside Shivaun. He folded its legs up beneath it and massaged its stubby neck until its head dropped into its body and its eyes closed.

'What's that on your chin?' Shivaun asked.

The man fingered his thick stubble. He grinned at her. 'I had my chin repilated while I was waiting for the ferry. It's a beard.'

'I know what it's called.'

'There was a big craze on body hair. That, and tattoos.' He looked contrite. 'I had one of those, too.'

She did not hide her disapproval. In a quieter voice she said: 'Any problems?'

He was continuing to fold the creature's legs under its bloated belly and did not appear to hear her.

'Imrani,' she said. 'Have you got it?'

He nodded. 'It's safe.'

'With you?'

He patted the sac. 'Right here.'

She activated the privacy hood. Then she made him put the creature aside before stripping him. They made fast and furious love in the cramped seat, Shivaun astride him, riding him uninhibitedly.

When it was over, Imrani gazed up at her from behind his beard like a man dazed. She knew he enjoyed her sexual rapaciousness, but it never ceased to amaze him.

'Where is it?' she asked.

He reached down and hauled up the creature. There was a wide curving flap in its backside. Imrani prised it open with his fingers.

Inside was the womb.

I woke from the dream like erupting from a nightmare. My heart was pulsating in my chest, my body filmed with hot sweat.

A faint light came from somewhere unidentifiable. Around me the room was dim and silent. It held only the bed.

I realized I was moving my head without difficulty. I could flex my fingers, too, and my feet. I could shift my arms and legs.

I ran my hands over my body. I couldn't detect any damage, any dressings or scars. I felt my face. It seemed normal. The hair on my head had been cropped to a stubble.

Slowly I sat up on my elbows. Then I pushed my hands

down and heaved myself to a sitting position. I still felt groggy, light-headed, but the dreams were beginning to unnerve me. I didn't want to let myself slip straight back down into them.

Though I was sluggish, everything seemed to be functioning. I swung my legs down. It felt as if I had never done this before. I inched myself forward, letting my legs and feet slowly take the weight. They were weak, but they supported me as I pushed myself upright.

Blood swam in front of my eyes. I had to hold on hard to the bed until my vision cleared. I took a step forward. Then another, flattening both hands against the wall.

Like something ancient and decrepit, I began to edge my way towards the window. I knew I wasn't old, but I doddered along like an invalid.

A pulse was throbbing in my head by the time I reached the window. A plain white blind enveloped it. I searched for its edges, for a purchase. The blood-rush hit me again, and I gripped the sill. It seemed to yield under my fingers.

When the mist receded, the blind was up.

The window looked out over a lake that shone silver in the darkness. It was backdropped by a curving line of hills under a clear night sky. The stars were brilliant.

Nothing moved on the lake, and no lights were shining. The entire scene was completely tranquil. It made no register on my memory. How I had come here, and why, remained a blank.

I must have gone into another fugue, because I felt as if I had been staring at the lake for some time even as it began to tilt away from me. I tried to grab the window sill, but my legs had gone and I blacked out before I hit the floor.

Five

'What do you think?' Imrani asked Shivaun.

He had split open his shirt and bared his chest to her. A purple and gold spider was hologrammed around his right nipple.

'Couldn't resist it,' he told Shivaun. 'Woman who did it said it was a steelweb, only found on Oberon. It moves when I do, see?' He tried to ripple a pectoral. 'See? It twitched.'

Shivaun was staring at him with what he took to be weary affection. Imrani widened his eyes. 'There was nothing else to do there except wait.'

Shivaun reached up and tentatively touched the beard, prodding it with her finger. 'Any other alterations I should know about? Did they give you a tail or a third eye?'

'Strictly cosmetic stuff, I promise.'

'Doesn't exactly make you look inconspicuous, does it?'

'On Chiron it's nothing special.'

'I hate it.'

Truth was, he didn't much like the feel of the hair on his chin himself; he'd had it done on a whim, and had only kept it to surprise her.

'They've got it sprouting everywhere. Armpits, chest, genitalia. Eyebrows and nostrils as bushy as you like. Rings and tufts wherever you want them.'

She shook her head. 'It'll have to go.'

He fastened his shirt. 'You're the boss.'

She asked her seat to order a depilant. One of the flight attendants delivered it soon afterwards on a silver tray. It was a creamy gel which he had to smear over his cheeks. It smelt spicy and tingled on his skin. When he wiped it off, his chin was smooth again.

'You did a good job,' Shivaun said. 'Venzano took it for the real thing.'

When she'd delivered the womb to the recuperatory and told him she wanted as exact a copy as possible, he'd worked through the night to get it done because she wanted it urgently. Of course in Emergency he was used to rush jobs – limb rejuvs, organ replacements, you name it – but this was the first time he'd had to concoct something without a tissue sample, without even knowing exactly what was inside it. Shivaun had sworn him to secrecy, warned him not to harm an atom of the original.

'It was fun,' he said. 'I don't often get to freelance. Or work blind.'

The original was opaque to every scanner at his disposal, and the biosynthesizer had complained bitterly at the lack of detail on internal structure. He'd had to override the usual systems analysis and build the thing from scratch while at the same time ensuring that no details of what he was doing were lodged in its long-term memory. He'd used undifferentiated tissue throughout, making the cell nuclei radiation sinks to preserve its opacity. Then, on Shivaun's instructions, he'd booked a tourist flight to Triton, only switching instead to the pilgrimage ship after his sojourn on Chiron.

'I'm not sure the pipes were such a good idea,' Shivaun said.

'They were perfect!' Imrani responded with mock outrage. He stroked the sac. 'I've been tranquillizing them to keep them quiet, poor things. It's not every day a musical instrument gets a womb stuffed up its rear.'

Shivaun was stern. 'This is no game, Imrani, you know that, don't you?'

'That's about all I know.'

She hadn't explained anything, telling him only that she really didn't want to involve him in the first place but that time was short and there was no alternative. He'd trusted her completely, done everything she'd asked. He said as much. Still she was quiet.

'You going to tell me?' he persisted.

'Later.'

Imrani pouted.

'Don't be offended,' she said.

'I'm not.'

'It isn't that I don't trust you. It's just that you're better off not knowing until we get there.'

'Pluto?'

'Be patient.'

He didn't press it; sooner or later he'd know. In fact, the mystery was a large part of the excitement. The shadowy side of Shivaun was one of the things that had attracted him to her in the first place. To be with her out here in space, and he only a youth really – well, he'd always craved adventure, never stayed long in one place, yet had never travelled off Venus before. His friends had warned him that he was mad to involve himself with an expediter twice his age, but the past two years had been terrific and he'd never had one regret.

'Cibylle called,' Shivaun said. 'She thinks you've sneaked off on another unofficial tour.'

'I never could do anything right in her eyes. What did you tell her?'

'Nothing. As far as she's concerned, I haven't seen you.'

'I think she'll be happier with just Kovec and Vy.'

She didn't respond to this; he felt as if she was looking straight through him.

'You did say we wouldn't be going back in a hurry.'

She nodded. 'I was thinking of the children.'

It was typical of him to have overlooked this; he'd never fathered any himself.

'Cibylle'll take good care of them.' He tried to read her face. 'How long *are* we going to be gone, anyway?'

She smiled and raised a hand to his cheek. She ran a fingernail along its smooth surface. There was always a slight edge of menace about even her simplest affections. That was part of the attraction, he supposed.

'We've stolen something,' she reminded him. 'Something that's important to some very powerful people. Nobody is even sure what it is, but everyone who knows about it wants it. With luck, your duplicate will keep them fooled for a day or two, buying us time. Without luck, they'll already be on our trail. If they have to kill us to get it back, you can be certain they will.'

Her ice-blue eyes were fierce. Imrani gave a little burst of laughter.

'OK, I'm scared.'

'You need to take this seriously.'

'I do.'

He had been stroking the pipes so hard that one of its eyes had half-risen from its socket, bleary yet quizzical. He smoothed it down again, felt it settle.

'Can we snack?' he said. 'I'm peckish.'

They ordered a light meal, unblanking the privacy hood. Imrani studied the other passengers, sober and solemn, scarcely a murmur of conversation between them.

'Are we going where they're going?' he asked.

Shivaun's glance was pure exasperation, but something told him he'd hit the mark.

So it was Charon. Cemetery world. He thought of asking if they could stop off at Pluto to sample the pleasuredomes of Orpheus. But decided against it.

He transpared a window, peered out at empty space. A star-dusted blackness that didn't alter after ten minutes, thirty. He readily agreed when Shivaun suggested he went off for a sim-swim in the water pod on the recreation deck. It was his first experience of a pod, which created the excellent illusion that he was floating alone in the warm shallow waters of a Venusian lake, its shores fringed with silver sand and palmbush. He did an hour's steady crawl and emerged feeling fully toned.

Shivaun was wrestling with the bagpipes when he returned to his seat. He took it from her and fed the sac the meal he'd laced with tranquillizer. A flight attendant appeared and asked him if he cared to play something suitable for the rest of the passengers, something *soothing* or *reverential*.

'Sorry,' he said. 'No can do. She's in no condition for playing, see?'

The attendant focused its optic on the instrument. 'Unwell?' it enquired politely.

'Pregnant,' Imrani replied.

When the attendant had gone, Shivaun said, 'You shouldn't have drawn attention to it.'

'If I'd tried to play it, I'd have certainly drawn some attention.'

'You don't need to tell anyone anything they don't need to know.'

She sat straight-backed in her seat, jaw set hard.

'You're tense, aren't you?' he said.

'I've told you, this isn't a game.'

'Want a neck rub?'

She sighed. Her console started blinking.

It was a call from Triton. A man's face came up on the screen.

'Hello,' he said to Shivaun when she identified herself. He was a husband of her daughter, Niome, who had gone for a ten-day walkabout in the Poseidon Desert, common practice there, the man assured her, a chance to be alone for a while. But it meant she couldn't be contacted. Did Shivaun want her message passed on when she returned?

Shivaun blanked the call abruptly, without voicing a reply.

Imrani hadn't known about any children other than those with Cybille until now.

'She's your eldest?' he asked.

'The same age as you.'

It sounded like a challenge. He did an exaggerated wince, as if she had sworn at him. 'Anything I should know?'

'If it was any of your business, I'd tell you.'

'My, my,' he said, 'you *are* irritable.'

He spent the rest of the voyage dozing or trawling the entertainment channels. Space travel had always seemed romantic to him, but now he knew it as dull, dull, dull.

Gill-mask clamped to his nose, he was locked in dread combat with a huge and hairless underwater wrestler when Shivaun wrenched him unceremoniously back into real space time. The ship was going into orbit around Charon.

Shivaun made him give the bagpipes another dose of tranquillizer sufficient to knock it out for forty-eight hours. Imrani packed the creature neatly into his flightbag, concertinaing its legs with great care. With all the indignities it had suffered, it would probably never play properly again.

Pluto's moon was the only major inhabited satellite where there was no customs, and a shuttle carried the passengers down promptly to its drab surface, everyone donning bulky warmsuits comprising armour-like panels lined with bodycoddle and elastic thermal polymers for manoeuvrability. The suits were luminous fruity colours, each one having a bulbous space in its midriff for carrying luggage: Imrani stored the pipes inside while Shivaun packed away the womb with her luggage. Big-visored recycling hoods enveloped their heads. Imrani laughed at their reflections in the suiting room mirror, he a study in shocking strawberry to Shivaun's electric lime. An intercom informed them that the ridged soles of their boots incorporated cryobacteria that could digest the moon's rock ice, supplementing the suit's air with extra oxygen, cycling hydrogen to thermal nodules throughout its layered skin where additional heat was generated through biofusion. The temperature outside was only twenty degrees above absolute zero.

Charon Prime, the main settlement on the moon, was a regular array of dark angular modules that sat in a frozen crater sea like a black snowflake. It was lit by pale blue stalk-lamps which gave it an eerie, dolorous air and turned the surrounding ice the colour of steel. Around and beyond it rose rippled ice ridges, while above the great crescent of Pluto arched like a luminous bridge across the star-fierce blackness. There were dark-suited politia everywhere, at checkpoints, in bulky slidecars on the ice. They were armed.

'There's one thing I want to know,' Imrani said jauntily across the suit radio to Shivaun. 'What do people around here do for *fun*?'

Conspicuously, Shivaun did not reply.

Few people ever came to Charon except to visit the Valleys of the Dead, and the routine for such pilgrimages was well established. The flight attendants were on hand to escort the passengers across the runway to the terminus so that they could practise walking in their warmsuits. Imrani had one pratfall before finding that slow, loping strides with arms outstretched was best for steady balanced movement in the low gravity. Beneath their feet the scarred and pockmarked ice was as hard as any rock.

Inside the terminus building, the passengers were divided into two groups: those bringing dead relatives to be laid to rest, and those visiting the already entombed. Imrani followed Shivaun into a wide-windowed room where aides were waiting with colour-coded maps of the valleys, which radiated out from the ceremonial centre of Acheron at their heart. Each valley had a different zone number, and the pilgrims would be marshalled into appropriate groups before being taken to the omnibuses that waited beyond the frosted plass window, slow-moving beasts whose stately progress meant that they still had several hours' travel ahead of them. Little puffs of steam jetted from the buses' nostrils, and their warty hides were rimed with bright carbon monoxide frost.

Imrani fell in behind Shivaun as they shuffled along at the end of a queue towards one of the transit points. Shivaun warned him to say nothing unless he was directly addressed and to keep his answers to a minimum even then. He was to agree with everything she said.

When it was her turn to face the official at the desk, Shivaun showed her identity disk and asked for a private two-seater sled.

The official looked out at her through his visor, a heavy-featured man with a prominent brow.

'What's the nature of your visit?' he asked.

'I'm here to see my first husband. He was entombed here eighteen years ago.'

Imrani knew nothing about any previous husband of hers, let alone one that had died. She told the official his name – Rajandre – and the entombment coordinates. He checked it on his console, then said, 'There's a bus going to that sector. You can join the others.'

Shivaun shook her head inside her helmet. 'I have additional business. Official business. I need a sled to take me and my companion to Acheron.'

The official didn't move or speak. Imrani started to feel nervous. He tried a winning smile as the man scrutinized him, then realized it was wasted inside his warmsuit.

The man slotted Shivaun's disk into his console. The unseen optic below the desk splashed shifting colours across his visor, a privacy murmur blotting out the disk's commentary.

Finally he looked up. He instructed Shivaun to eyeball the retina scanner.

'You're an expediter,' he said.

'Do we get the sled?'

'And your companion?'

'A spouse. He's just sightseeing.'

Imrani had to step forward and have his eyeballs light-probed.

'We don't get many expediters here,' the man said to Shivaun. 'Especially all the way from Venus.'

'As I said, I have a husband buried here. That's the only reason I volunteered.'

'Subject?'

'I'm not required to reveal that. You can make an official request to any arbiter's office. Without delay to me.'

Imrani didn't like this. The man was one of those officials who wasn't about to let go.

'I can't say we welcome them,' he said. 'Our population's small and hard to hold on to as it is. Life isn't cheap here.'

Shivaun gave a patient sigh. 'I have the greatest respect for human life, I can assure you. I believe it should be lived to the full. But we each have our legitimate term. You've voiced the documentation. You know I'm merely carrying out the law.'

Still he would not budge; he just sat there.

'There's only one person here I know who's over the limit. Elydia. Elydia Chan-Vetterlein.'

Shivaun retrieved her authorization disk; she said nothing.

'She's a good woman. One of the best we have.'

'Then you have my sincerest regrets. She's one hundred and twelve years old.'

'You've come a long way for her.'

'As I've told you, I also wanted to visit my husband. High Arbiter Miushme-Adewoyin of Melisande was most under-standing in giving me the commission.'

Now there was a distinct note of irritation in Shivaun's voice. Imrani felt uncomfortable in more senses than one: the bagpipes were twitching in their sleep against his belly. He wondered if they were dreaming, if they were capable of dreaming. He did not turn around, but he was sure that everyone in the building was watching them, waiting for them.

'That means nothing to me,' the man was saying to Shivaun. 'Here we believe in live and let live. There aren't that many of us, and we take care of our own. Maybe I'll just have you sent straight back—'

In one swift movement Shivaun reached out, grabbed his arm with both hands and pulled him across the desk. She held him fast, putting pressure against his elbow. Imrani wondered if she could break it even through his suit.

'That would be particularly stupid,' she told the man, their visors touching. 'I've been more than polite, and I've no more time for your games. You've delayed us long enough.'

Her voice was fierce across the comlink. This time Imrani *did* glance around. The rest of the pilgrims were already filing through the airlocks to the buses: no one was paying them the slightest bit of attention. No one, that is, except for another official who was standing nearby watching them. She came over to the desk. There was a fat-barrelled pistol in a belt holster, but she did not get it out.

'What's going on here?' she said.

'Who're you?' Shivaun asked angrily.

'Gwilever. Transit Coordinator. Is there a problem?'

Shivaun explained, not releasing the man. She had the flat of one hand against his elbow, the other tugging his wrist in the opposite direction.

The woman checked the details on the console. 'I presume you intend to carry out your duties immediately,' she said.

'That is my usual practice,' Shivaun told her.

'Then we need delay you no further. A sled will be provided for your use.'

Ten minutes later, Shivaun and Imrani were jetting out of the city on the broad bowed back of the sled, a low-slung creature whose thermal snout and ground-pads melted a thin layer of ice as it scooted along, powered by nutrient sticks which Imrani had been instructed to feed into its maw at regular intervals. The maw was a cartilaginous slit at the centre of the steering ridge. It dilated when the sled was hungry.

In the low-gravity near-vacuum, they made good speed, Pluto's sweeping arc providing sufficient light for Imrani to see the granite-coloured ridges that stretched in all directions, hollows filled with ammonia ice and methane snow. The bleakness of the scene entranced Imrani, who had known nothing but the muggy dampness of the Venusian lowlands. The far-distant sun was a mere dot of light at their backs, but the stars were so bright he couldn't resist enthusing about them, knowing that he was behaving like a typical tourist. Shivaun steered the sled, saying little. But Imrani was not one to be daunted by silences.

'Who is this Lydia woman, anyway?' he asked.

'Elydia,' Shivaun corrected him. 'Elydia Chan-Vetterlein. She put my husband to rest when I brought him here.'

Imrani hazarded a guess: 'Was he Niome's father?'

A pause. 'Yes.'

He waited for her to say more. When she didn't, he asked: 'What happened? How did he die?'

He'd never had much tact, he knew that; but they were lovers, husband and wife: surely she would tell him.

'He drowned in a boating accident on a lake. A stupid paddler took in too much water and sank. Niome was lucky to survive. Her two brood-brothers also drowned. We only recovered Raj's body.'

So it had been a family catastrophe. He tried to imagine the grief. It was beyond him. Bad enough the three had died. Even worse with youngsters involved. And they'd never found the children's corpses. He couldn't help thinking of them rotting at the bottom of the lake, lives snuffed out before they'd scarcely begun. It was horrible. The very word 'corpse' was enough to make him shiver. In all his time at the recuperatory, he'd managed to avoid ever seeing a dead body.

'It must have been appalling,' he said.

'It wasn't one of my better moments. But eighteen years is a long time. Elydia was in her late eighties even then.'

He thought about it. 'But you weren't an expediter.'

'You remembered,' she said drily. 'I told her I planned to

become one. I even joked that I might come back to get her if she overstayed her welcome.'

'And now you have.'

'It gives me a reason to be here. I told Bezile I wanted to visit my huband's tomb *and* terminate Elydia Chan-Vetterlein. She's been on the wanted list for some time. People here are hard to get at.'

'And you're really going to terminate her?'

She kept staring straight ahead, gloved hands tight on the steering horns.

'You're not, are you?' he persisted.

Silence.

'I think maybe you're going to show her the womb.'

Shivaun would not give him the satisfaction of a reply.

They travelled on across rugged cratered plains and shallow scree-filled valleys. Here and there Imrani saw rocks streaked with luminous green thermoss, an attempt to provide the moon with year-round warmth and light from plantlife – an attempt that had failed. Even the hardiest of biodesigned species fared poorly on this bleak world. There was no other sign of life.

Imrani's breathing filled the dome of his hood. They skirted a crystalline sea, then passed a ridge where the planet's tenuous wind had sculpted methane snow into frozen waves, like huge breakers about to crash down on them. Imrani couldn't contain himself.

'Just think of it,' he said, 'here we are at the very edge of the Solar System. Out there' – he pointed to the heavens – 'is the space between the stars, going on and on. All that lies between us and the universe is the skin of this suit. Isn't that amazing!'

They were obviously travelling a well-worn path: he could see the bus tracks ridged into the ice. On either side low ice hills began to heighten and Shivaun remarked that they were entering the valley zone. The sled had a snorting fit and began to slow. Imrani fed it another nutrient stick.

The tracks in the ice thickened as the slopes rose more sheerly on either side of them. Their flanks were carved with stairways and contoured ledges where the shining dead were entombed. There were hundreds, thousands of them, arranged in every conceivable pose from the statuesque to the informal.

Some clutched favoured objects while others were surrounded by replics of their dearest – parents, children, lovers. The replics did not shine like the truedead; they were merely solid holos.

Imrani drank it in with his eyes. The tombs were carved from ice, names and inscriptions embedded at their bases, final statements on their lives from family members who had outlived them. Like most people, Imrani could not read, but Shivaun told him the inscriptions vocalized if you went close. She recited some of those she remembered – descriptions of their dying along with expressions of utmost grief from their relatives. This was a place of no consolation, the true end of life for victims of accident or neglect or pure malice, only their bodies ensured of immortality on this bitterest and bleakest of worlds. Even the poorest of families were able to have their truedead brought here by virtue of communal funds, but this was scant consolation for the end of their very existence.

The sled began to slow again, and its snorts turned into something that resembled distressed barks. It refused a further nutrient stick. Shivaun checked the fuel bag, examining one of the sticks minutely. She took a knife from her belt pack and slit it open. White flakes spilled out of it.

'What is it?' Imrani asked.

'Polymer shreds. Waste material. The sled can't digest it.'

He frowned. 'I don't get it.'

Shivaun was slicing open the other sticks in the bag. They were the same. The flakes slowly spiralled down to the ground, little plastic snow flurries.

'The feed bag's been doctored,' she said. 'They don't want us to make it.'

The sled came to a dead stop, its broad back palpitating. Imrani waited for Shivaun to do something. The sled heaved, and a murky detritus gushed out of its snout, instantly crystallizing into a ragged ochre bloom on the ice.

It was a few moments before the enormity of it dawned on him. Here anything that lived was considered precious because life was so marginal; yet the three of them, sled included, had been set up to die, out where there was no one to help them.

'Are you carrying any food?' Shivaun asked.

'Food?'

'Anything we can feed the sled.'

Imrani shook his head helplessly.

She checked the pockets of her suit. He did likewise. There was nothing.

'We're going to have to feed it the bagpipes,' Shivaun said.

'What?'

'You heard.'

'It's my instrument!'

'Do you want to die, Imrani? Do you?'

He didn't know what to say. 'But it's sick. What if it doesn't want to eat?'

'You got any better suggestions?'

He had none.

'Just stand there,' Shivaun said. 'Don't do anything. Brace yourself. Try not to fall over.'

He didn't have a clue what she was talking about. Then she stepped forward and twisted the release dial on his belt.

The chest plates swung open. A great gout of ice crystals plumed from his belly, but he felt nothing except a void. Shivaun was already reaching inside, rummaging around, then wrenching the pipes out.

The pipes began a violent twitching while Shivaun reversed his belt dial. Slowly, slowly, his chest plates closed, creaking against the frost that rimed them. Then he felt the searing cold at his belly, radiating up like a wave across his chest so that he gasped with the shock of it. His head and limbs were sealed off from the impact, but this was only small relief. Shivaun dropped the pipes and steadied him with both hands on his arms.

His suit filled with a rush of warm air as its self-adjusting system compensated. Within thirty seconds the cold was gone and he could breathe normally again.

'Are you all right?' Shivaun asked.

'I – I think so.' He felt a warming at his belly, no sense of permanent damage. He told Shivaun as much.

'Thank hell for that.'

The pipes lay frozen. Dead. Shivaun raised her booted foot

and brought it down on the creature. It shattered as if it were glass, keratin and cartilage skittering across the ice.

He helped Shivaun retrieve chunks of gristle and snap them into bite-sized pieces. Though the pipes had been nothing special as instruments went, the manner of their dying made him feel like a butcher. He stood squeamishly aside, holding a jagged fragment of leg, while Shivaun stuffed piece after piece of the sac into the sled's maw. As if she was dumping garbage down a disposall.

The sled lay slumped on the ice and did not respond. Shivaun stroked its ear slits and pressed her visor against its throat, making soothing noises; but though it swallowed automatically, it did not move to her entreaties. She crammed another frozen fragment into its maw, whispering further entreaties.

There was no movement, nothing. Above them, Pluto's upcurving slash was like a grimace, a leer. Imrani felt helpless, doomed. The sled gave a lurch, then another. At the third attempt, it raised itself from the ice.

'Get on board,' Shivaun yelled to him.

He was clambering up after her when she suddenly jolted, then pitched backwards into him, sending them both plummeting down on to the ice.

He rolled over beside her. She was lying face down, but he could see a splatter of darkness inside her visor. It took him a moment to realize that it was blood. She did not move or speak when he shook her. The status panel on the chest of her suit was flashing orange into the ice: life-support was failing.

He scrambled to his feet in alarm. Something hit him in the shoulder, and he felt a piercing cold pain as he fell.

A small dark cylinder was sticking out of the skin of his suit. He made to pull it out, then stopped himself. His own suit went to yellow alert, then announced it was sealing the puncture. He saw another dart sticking out of the back of Shivaun's neck. The flower of blood in her visor had crystallized, entirely blotting out her face.

They were needle-gun darts. Someone had shot at them.

Shivaun's suit light deepened to blood-orange.

His entire body was palpitating with fear, but he managed

to lie without moving, only turning his head inside the hood to scan the ledges of the dead.

Nothing moved on the ice galleries: the shining corpses stared down at him from both sides, encased in their ice tombs, frozen for ever. It was the perfect hiding place for any assassin.

He turned his head the other way. Shivaun's light had gone red. It flashed for a while, then shone steady.

Life support had failed: it was over for her.

For a moment he couldn't accept it. Then he began to blubber. It didn't seem possible that she was dead. He'd imagined this journey to Pluto as the start of a new life for them, not an end; he'd imagined them spending at least the next twenty years together, having children, travelling. How would he survive without her? He was crying as much from fear as sorrow, he knew. What could he do now? Whoever had shot at them was still out there somewhere. He had to fight down his panic, try to think clearly.

His shoulder ached badly from the wound, but he was no longer losing heat or air. The pulsing alert light was yellow, meaning that the immediate emergency had passed. He did his best to ignore the possibility that the dart might be poisoned. His chances were slim even if it wasn't.

Imrani knew that if he made any obvious movement he would be targeted again. On an inspiration, he surreptitiously used his belt controls to override the automatic alarm, boosting the status light to orange, and then to red. To all appearances, he was also now dead.

Again he scanned the ledges, looking for a sign of movement, of something living.

There was nothing.

The sled had slumped once more, then Imrani saw its long throat ripple as it disgorged another mass of plastic fibre on to the ice. Its hooded eyes opened briefly, nostrils pulsing with distress.

There was a movement beyond the beast.

It was the merest glint of light, quickly gone, but as he strained his eyes he saw a dark shape moving down an ice stairway.

The figure mounted a sled that had been lying dormant at the bottom of the ridge. The sled began to move towards them.

Imrani watched it from where he lay, suit light shining red on his chest, the only camouflage he had. He felt a mixture of terror and something that might have been relief. When he was sure that no other riders were following, he slipped his hand across the ice to retrieve the fragment of leg from the pipes. He tucked it securely under his glove.

It seemed an age before the rider finally drew up. Its suit was the steel-grey of the officials at the terminus. Imrani watched the figure dismount and lope forward. It was a woman. The needle-gun was in her hand.

Imrani had gradually edged his feet around until they were braced against the sled's flank. He had never done anything violent in his life, and his entire body was trembling with adrenalin. As the woman approached Shivaun, he sprang forward, raising the broken pipe like a dagger.

She began to turn as he arched towards her like a zeeballer. But it was too late. They collided, and Imrani felt the pipe scrape across her chest plate, then slide under it into the webbing at the armpit.

They both landed in a tangle on the ice. Imrani managed to roll away, yelling with pain as the dart in his shoulder went in deeper. The suit began a vocal alarm, warning him in a shrill sexless whisper that he was bleeding and losing air pressure.

He managed to scramble to his feet, his ears filled with the gasp and rush of his breathing. But the woman was also rising, suit winking orange, the needle-gun gripped in her hand. Imrani had no weapon left, nothing in arm's reach.

His attacker began to level the pistol at him, then wavered. Imrani saw something hanging from her armpit – something long and jagged: a frozen stalactite of blood.

The figure made a half-step, then fell forward as the suit's light went scarlet. She hit the ice face on, bounced and rolled over once, twice. Then lay still.

Imrani did not move. His suit had gone quiet, the puncture sealed again. The needle-gun lay on the ice, too close to the gloved hand for him to be incautious. A small plume of pale vapour rose from the helmet, then stopped. Red light pulsed from the suit's chest, as scarlet as Shivaun's had been. He waited until the light was steady. Only then did he move forward.

He kicked the pistol out of reach. Skirting the fallen figure, he reached down carefully and picked it up.

The visor was frosted over on the inside. Imrani smashed the butt of the pistol again and again against the plass, crying with rage and sorrow. Finally it starred, and he broke the visor open. The whole head was rimed with frost, the eyes open. He recognized the woman as the official at the terminus who had arranged for them to be provided with the sled.

He went over to Shivaun, knelt beside her. He was trying to think clearly, to fight his grief. His suit began to fret again. He told it to be quiet, then activated Shivaun's belt dial and his own a second later.

As her plates opened, he reached inside and grabbed the womb, pulling it out and cramming it into his own abdominal cavity. Again he twisted the dial on his belt. Again the plates slowly closed up and he felt the burning cold. The womb was unlikely to have survived the passage, but it was all he could do. He closed Shivaun up while his temperature returned to normal, feeling as if he had actually cut her open, as if he had committed some grotesque form of disembowelling.

The assassin's sled was sitting placidly on the ice close by. In the low gravity it was a simple matter to load Shivaun's body across its back. Their own sled had revived a little, so Imrani tethered the two together, determined not to abandon either of them, piling the woman's body into its back seat. Then he led both creatures off.

The pain from his shoulder wound had returned, and it intensified as he limped along. The valley began to narrow, the massed ranks of corpses crowding in on both sides with their radiant faces and jewel-like eyes. They looked more alive than the living, this one crouching to pat his pet familigator, that one in wedding robes with three holo husbands, another a whole family group clustered around the replic of a shrine. Imrani was light-headed, babbling words of encouragement to the sleds, hoping that soon they would come in sight of some habitation, some real living humans. He began to drift in and out of true awareness, found himself sobbing, jabbering non-sense, pleading with the stars to help him. His strength was ebbing fast, and still the valley went on, its galleries unending. A coldness was spreading down his arm. He thought he saw lights in the distance; they began to waver, then spiralled around as he pitched forward on to the ice.

Some time later he surfaced briefly and felt himself being lifted up. Something passed in front of his eyes – something big yet stooped, like an animal yet purposeful, almost human. A dull terror seized him at the white flash of its saucerous eyes. Then it was gone, and he sank down into blissful oblivion.

I was sitting at the window, the aftertaste of a warm drink in my mouth. Nina had brought it earlier, I knew, but now she was gone. I had lost not only the last few minutes but also some previous episodes of wakefulness. I was aware I had experienced them, but they were like ghost memories, without detail.

The inward-curving hills were tree-covered under a blue sky. My window was recessed so I didn't have a large field of view, but it was a pleasant sight, the lake a perfect blue. A few dark birds were flying across it. I didn't know what they were. I didn't know the names of any birds or trees or flowers. I knew nothing except for the fact that I was alive.

I caught my reflection in the glass. I was a youngish man, dark-haired. The face looked all right as far as I could tell, everything in proportion, nothing out of place. But my cropped hair made me look like a victim of something. Imprisonment or disease.

The hills outside were a just-minted green. There was no wind, no cloud. No other sign of life apart from the birds. I couldn't even see the rest of the hospital building.

I had an urge to smell the air. After some effort, I managed to stand up. It wasn't easy, but I felt stronger than I'd done before. The thick glass was set into the frame with no obvious mechanism for opening it.

Very carefully, keeping one hand flat against the wall, I walked to the door. It had no handle, was sealed at its edges. I looked around the room. Everything was white, even the loose gown I was wearing. There was none of the paraphernalia of a hospital room. I didn't know exactly what I expected to see, but at least I could register *absences*.

Already I was tiring. I managed to stumble back to the bed, to sit down on it. I wondered if they were putting something in my food to make me sleep. I wondered if I was a patient or a prisoner.

Then I was at the window again. I must have suffered another fugue while getting there. I was feeling around the frame, the underside of the sill. My finger touched something, depressed it.

In an instant the scene beyond the window changed. The sky went from blue to black and the sun went out. The lake waters turned to iron, the hills changed from verdant to bone-white.

In place of the sun there hung a huge blue moon.

Part Two

BEYOND THE PALE

Six

'Nathan?'

I turned from the window. Nina had come into the room. The young man and woman were with her. They wore white as before.

'Nathan,' she said again, approaching me. 'Are you all right?'

'Is that my name?'

The word meant nothing. The sound was meaningless to me.

'It's the name we gave you,' the young woman said.

'It was chosen at random,' her companion added. 'It has no special significance.'

They both spoke in soft, measured voices. They were brown-skinned, almond-eyed, both fair-featured, in the prime of late youth. Clearly not twins, but a pair nevertheless.

I wondered how long I had been standing at the window.

'Where is this?' I said.

The view remained as before: ivory hills framing a steel lake. The huge luminous blue disc hung in the black sky, wreathed with white cloud. I could see pale landmasses beneath.

'It's the Moon,' Nina said. 'We're on the Moon.'

I felt completely disorientated. The girl and boy spoke quietly to one another. I stared out again. The view seemed to shimmer, to dissolve, but I blinked and it was back.

I made to say something, but for a moment my voice wouldn't work.

I pointed. 'That's Earth?'

Nina nodded. I knew only that I should have been there, not here.

'Who am I?'

'We don't know your real name.'

This was the boy. He spoke offhandedly, as if it were not especially important. I felt another pulse of rage and frustration. It came without conscious thought.

'What do you mean?'

My anger must have shown, because Nina laid a hand on my arm. 'Perhaps you ought to sit down.'

'I don't want to sit down! What's going on? What am I doing here?'

They led me back to the bed. I was too weak to argue or resist. When I was settled, Nina said:

'We – both of us – are reanimates.'

A tide of weariness was flushing through me. 'What is that supposed to mean?'

'We were dead. More or less, anyway. We're now alive again.'

I couldn't take this in. 'Are these ours? Our children?'

'Perhaps you'll allow us to explain.'

It was the girl. She was elfin-faced, perfectly proportioned. In her blue eyes was a serious adult look.

'First we should introduce ourselves,' she said brightly. 'My name is Chloe.'

'And I'm Lucian,' the boy added.

'We don't know your real name because there are no records of your life. You're from Earth's past. A sleeper, reanimated.'

For a brief moment I seemed to slip away. Then I was back. 'This is senseless to me,' I said.

'You must be patient,' said the girl. 'There is much to explain. Lucian and I are servants of the Noosphere.'

The word shocked me. The *Noosphere*. A word from my strange fevered dreams. It was *real*? The dreams were real?

My reaction had a physical effect. I sank back as if drugged, and when I surfaced again I was lying flat, staring vaguely at images that seemed to float in front of me, three-dimensional but insubstantial. It was only through a haze that I could listen and see. Chloe and Lucian talked in turns, one following seamlessly on from the other. They talked in a flat factual way, as if everything they were telling me was commonplace. They talked like adults telling a child an instructive story.

I saw the view from my window again, then the perspective

abruptly tilted and zoomed back, everything dwindling rapidly until an entire world hung in the blackness of space – a bone-white world laced with intricate webs of silver and gold. The Moon was the Noosphere I had seen on Bezile's desk – a moon transformed, Chloe and Lucian were telling me, by advanced methods into the nerve centre of the human species. Then the scene shifted, and workers in hooded suits were clambering over what looked like a dusty mausoleum carved out of the bedrock, a cavernous vault holding a rank of dark broken coffins. During a recent reconstruction, I was informed, a cryogenic chamber had been unearthed, buried at a site that possibly dated back to the earliest times of planetary colonization. Nina and I had been taken out of our tombs and our bodies subjected to repair and regrowth. The process of revival had been long and complicated, even with the sophisticated techniques of biosynthesis, but now we were both whole again.

The images receded. I drifted back into some semblance of normal consciousness.

'Do you expect me to swallow this?' I said.

'It's the truth.'

This was Nina. On her face was a kind of contained anxiety, as if she desperately wanted me to believe it.

'I don't remember being entombed,' I said. 'I don't remember any of it.'

'You have no memory,' the boy – Lucian – said. 'It's quite likely it no longer exists.'

'What do you mean?'

'Much of your body was quite severely decayed, including parts of the cerebral cortex.'

'We can reconstitute a brain,' said Chloe, 'but we can't necessarily recover the memories that were stored in it.'

I looked at my hands. They were perfect, even down to the fingernails.

'I can't remember anything either,' Nina told me. She must have seen my distress because she closed her hand around mine. The emotional effect was far more powerful than I had anticipated, a surge of comfort at her touch.

After a while I asked, 'Are there others?'

'Only the two of us. We were the only ones who survived.'

Chloe and Lucian were talking together again; I couldn't hear their words. They were plainly of this world, whatever it was. My very weakness was proof that something drastic had happened to me, but to accept that I had been rebuilt cell by cell from some pile of mortifying flesh ... there was no adequate response I could give.

'You know nothing about us?' I said at length.

'Nothing,' Chloe said. 'I'm sorry.'

I swam away once more, as if my consciousness was fragile, still convalescent. It must have only been for a moment, because nothing had changed when I resurfaced.

'The dreams,' I said. 'I've been having some very strange dreams ...'

'We can talk about them later,' Chloe said. 'You must take it a little at a time. You mustn't overwhelm yourself.'

Nina was stroking my hand. I studied the line of her chin and long-necked throat.

'Were you revived before me?'

'There was less deterioration,' Lucian said. 'She was more fortunate.'

'Don't you remember anything?'

She met my gaze. There was still anxiety in her eyes. 'Nothing at all. I'm as blank as you, Nathan.'

'That's not my name.'

She flinched at the venom in my voice.

'I'm sorry,' I said. 'This isn't easy.'

'Don't I know it.'

I felt her grip relaxing, and now it was I who held on. It must have been far more difficult for her, being the first to revive, waiting for me to recover too, no doubt desperate for some companionship of her own kind yet unable to say too much too soon.

'We had to proceed very slowly and carefully,' Lucian was saying. 'Normal cell regeneration poses no problems, but loss of brain tissue is much more problematical.'

He had a brisker, more disinterested manner than Chloe, as if only the facts were pertinent.

'We do our best to restore the original neural networks as accurately as possible to maximize the potential for memory retrieval. The success of the procedure depends on the existing loss of cortical tissue. In both your cases, we did not have high hopes.'

'Are you doctors?'

'Not ourselves personally,' Lucian said. 'But you were given the best attention we could provide.'

'We hoped you would remember who you were,' Chloe said. 'Believe us, we're as disappointed as you must be. It would have been interesting to have your recollections of the distant past.'

For a split second I flashed away and saw myself as a walking corpse, blackened and festering. I lurched back to reality and hoped that the spasm of fear I felt had not shown.

'I remember nothing,' I said flatly. I looked at Nina.

'It's the same for me,' she insisted.

'You've got a name,' I pointed out.

'Given, like yours. Nina and Nathan.' She shrugged. 'It's as good as anything.'

'You recovered faster than me.'

'Only because I had a head start. Otherwise there's no difference between us. I only know what I've learned since I was restored.'

'Then your experiment has failed,' I said to Chloe and Lucian. 'You've rebuilt us, but all you've got are two empty vessels.'

Chloe was anxious to reassure me. 'Please don't misunderstand us. We revived you because you weren't dead. Your chambers were functioning, if imperfectly. You still survived.'

'We have a duty to preserve life,' Lucian said. 'What was our alternative – to leave you to rot? Consider yourself fortunate. Is not your very existence – or should we say, *re*-existence – a miracle of a sort in itself? To be alive after so long a period of death—'

'How long?'

'It's impossible to say, alas. We have no knowledge of when you were entombed. Very little documentary evidence survived the great upheavals that followed the settlement of the worlds of the Noospace. Your missing memories are small things compared to the vanished histories of entire peoples and places.'

'And yet,' said Chloe, 'it's quite obvious that you have some sense of self, no matter how absent the facts may be. Is that not so?'

I couldn't deny this. Or at least I couldn't deny the anger I felt at my predicament. Mine and Nina's.

'Did they find us together?' I asked her.

She nodded. 'You two were the only bodies which were viable. The rest were quite mortified.'

'We've preserved what tissue remained, of course,' said Lucian. 'Ancient genetic material is always potentially valuable.'

'But there are no plans to build any more monsters like us.'

They barely managed to mask their distaste, and even Nina gave me a disapproving look. Was I being ungrateful? Perhaps I was, but this at least was a sign of my selfhood; it seemed unlikely they had programmed that into me.

'Are Nina and I related?'

Chloe shook her head. 'There's no genetic connection. You both arise from quite separate ur-populations.'

'And there's nothing to tell whether we knew one another?'

'Nothing. The chamber had been breached. Everything was in an advanced state of corrosion and decay when we found it.'

'Corrosion? Here on the Moon?'

Chloe smiled. 'You see, you remember some things, even if you don't realize it.'

'What do you mean?'

'In your time, the Moon was probably airless. But it has had an atmosphere ever since the Noosphere was established here.'

How long had I been asleep? Hundreds of years? More? It seemed futile even to speculate. When you could remember nothing, how could you weigh one fact against another? How could you decide what was important? Remarkable? Insignificant? Did I know that the Moon had once been airless? I felt as if I knew nothing. Yet I could speak, use words, understand meanings.

I must have mumbled something, because Lucian said:

'We've been *acclimatizing* you. We've endeavoured to supply both of you with the necessary understanding to familiarize yourself with your new surroundings. This was essential, since you now live in our world.'

'But you shouldn't try to rush the process,' Chloe said. 'Your nervous system is still adjusting, and there will be lapses, minor confusions, fluctuations in homeostasis.'

So they were to be expected – the mood swings, the fugues. There was some relief in that.

'Are the dreams part of it?'

'Part of your adjustment, yes,' said Chloe. 'They'll play a vital role in your recovery.'

This intrigued me; I wanted to ask more. But I had started to feel cold, and then an uncontrollable shivering overtook me, my teeth vibrating so much that I couldn't speak. Nina began to tuck the bedclothes around me, leaning over me and whispering that it was a perfectly normal part of the process of recovery. She was so close I could smell her body heat, and I warmed to it.

This time I knew I was sinking down to sleep. The last thing I felt was her hand on my forehead. Like a benediction.

'Uprise! Uprise! Uprise!'

Marea lurched from sleep to find the alarm cock squatting on her chest. She swiped at it and it fluttered away, squawking, leaving a foul odour behind.

She closed her eyes and counted to twenty before finally heaving herself up in her bunk. The bird was rooting about among the debris under one of the bunks while still burbling: 'Rise and mine, rise and mine.' She flung a boot at it but it hopped away, farting. It was mangy and flatulent, used to maltreatment from the cons.

As ever, the air inside the long-hut was stale with bodily odours. The tiredness remained, as it always did, a core of permanent exhaustion that no amount of sleep could cure. Belatedly, Marea realized that the rest of the hut was empty, the others gone.

'What time is it?' she asked the bird.

'Thirty after Jove-down.'

'You let me oversleep!'

'Special dispensation, special dispensation.'

She wondered why, then stopped herself, refusing to fan the slightest ember of hope.

Her suit was folded neatly on her bunk as a pillow. Yawning, she slipped it on, forcing her legs through the thick padded layers, zipping it up to the neck. She retrieved her boots, and then her cloak crawled out from under the bunk and wrapped itself around her neck. She stroked its muzzle, its patchy fur. It was malnourished but never complained, gently purring against her neck.

Hastily evacuated, the long-hut looked ransacked, its cluttered surfaces coated with mustardy dust. The foetid smell of the place – the cast-off boots, unwashed clothes, the permanent stink of exhaustion – scarcely registered on her now. Though she did not feel like eating, she paused at the dispenser to cram a meal cracker in her mouth, slurping it down with tepid water from a nipple. She fed a few morsels to the cloak. Within seconds, the cracker was swelling in her belly, banishing hunger for a few hours.

She put her masked hood on, adjusted the oculars and checked the air supply. At her command, the airvalve inhaled, and she went out through it, the alarm cock muttering: 'Alone again ork, alone again ork,' as she went.

Jupiter had dropped over the sooty horizon, its amber glow silhouetting the rugged hills. The sun was up on the opposite side of the black sky, shrunken and distant, its light smeared by high-level haze. Haemus labour camp was four long-huts arranged cross-wise on a dusty plateau surrounded by russet plains, darker crusted lakes and bright lava flows. In theory, the habitats were air-conditioned, but the huts were so old and decrepit their lungs barely recycled gases, let alone cleansed them. The mining teams worked Jove-nights to avoid the heat and radiation.

A few trundlers were already moving off down the escarpment to the mining ridges; others were loading their teams. Vargo, Marea's overseer, sat on his three-wheeled trike, gloved hands spread wide on its curving horns, supervising everything. He motioned to her, and she went over and stood there while he shouted at a laggardly group of inmates. Even with her suitcom thumbed down, his every word could be heard. He liked the sound of his own voice, did Vargo.

His oculars were usually adjusted to nearsight so that his scarred milky eye was magnified. Without turning, he said, 'Enjoy the extra half-hour?'

'What did I do to deserve it?'

'Special job for you today. You've got ten minutes before your transport arrives. Maybe you want to get over to the postroom while you can. There's a fax for you.'

A fax. Again she tried not to feel hopeful. In the year since she had been transported to Io she'd had no communication with anyone offworld. And faxes were only allowed under special consideration.

He gave her the number, reciting it from memory. She didn't linger, scampering off across to the administrative cluster at the centre of the huts. The postroom was one of the smaller blisters. Marea punched in her identification, gave the floor manager the fax number and the airvalve opened.

She tore her hood off the instant she was inside. A large optic winked into life, filled with the image of a red-haired woman holding a baby in her arms. Marea immediately knew that the child was her daughter. Or, rather, Salih and Yuri's daughter. She had heard nothing of the baby since her arrest and exile.

'Hello,' said the woman. 'I'm Lynith, and you must be Marea. They asked me to call to let you know how Rashmi's getting on. As you can see, she's fine.'

She held out the child in the white swathe of a snuggle. It was plump, healthy – Yuri's child, she saw immediately. Well, both men had insisted they leave the paternity to chance, but Salih—

Salih was dead. And Yuri. And now the child had a foster-mother. At least they had given her the name she and her husbands had chosen beforehand. It was a small consolation.

Marea stepped close and looked into its bright-cheeked, blue-eyed face. The fax was interactive, the child redolent of milk and clean linen. Marea wanted to pick her up, hold her, but that luxury was not available.

There were the noises of children in the background. She looked at Lynith, freckled with a kindly, tolerant face.

'Tell me about yourself,' she said.

'I've got five other fosterlings and six of my own,' Lynith responded. 'We're in Ares City, four of us and the children. We run a production company, doing historical reconstructions on Channel Eight Eighty. Maybe you've seen some of them? *The Fall of the Romulan Empire, The Great Exodus, The Triumph of the Afterlife*?'

Marea smiled. It was clear that the child had been put into the care of good solid citizens.

'How does she sleep?' she asked.

'Like a baby,' Lynith replied. And then laughed to hear herself say it. 'She's no trouble at all. You should be proud of her. She feeds well, too.'

'Do you know where I am?'

There was a moment's pause, while the program contemplated its reply.

'You're on Io.'

'I've been here almost a year,' she said. She wanted to say: 'Unsentenced', but knew she couldn't.

Lynith's holo looked uncomfortable. 'We're not supposed to talk about that.'

'Of course not. I didn't mean to embarrass you. It was good of you to fax me.'

'They asked me to. Don't worry, we're taking good care of her. She'll come to no harm. I'm seventy-two, and this batch are the third generation I've raised. A lot have stayed with us, acting in our productions. Maybe Rashmi will, too.' Her voice took on a confidential tone. 'In fact, we're thinking of using her as the infant Orela in *The Lives of the Advocates*. She might end up a celebrity.'

The pager announced that there were only thirty seconds remaining. Marea looked at the child one last time, now certain she would never see it again.

'I have to go,' she said. 'Thank you for letting me see her.'

'It was a pleasure,' Lynith replied. 'You take care out there.'

Marea made to turn away, but found she didn't want to

move. She stared at the child until the images winked out as the optic blanked.

Outside, Vargo was still perched on his trike, and she could hear Andreas's voice on the comlink. He was the base governor, a stern man seldom seen in the flesh.

The fax had left her feeling hollowed out rather than comforted, and she longed for the seclusion of a shrine, the comforts of communion with her ancestors. But there were no shrines for the cons on Io. That was part of the punishment.

On the ridge was a small caterpillar, its plump flanks dusty from the climb up the escarpment. A paddler lay upturned in its cargo space, webbed feet pointing to the sky. Two figures were sitting in the driving chamber, both of them men.

Vargo pointed a gloved hand. 'That's your transport,' he told her. 'Get aboard.'

'Where am I going?'

'We've got a feral.'

'A feral?'

'It was hiding out in one of the old tunnels over at Juno. We didn't even know it was there. Escaped a couple of hours ago. Fried a few and left a few more in the shaft with first-degree burns before flying off.'

'A dragon?'

'What else? You've been assigned to the swat team.' He reached into the trike's holdall and pulled out a stun-rod.

'This is for me?' she said.

'Your chance for glory. Make a killing.'

So *that* was why she'd had the favours, the extra half-hour, the fax. A sop before sending her out on something *really* dangerous.

The telescopic rod had a cone-shaped discharger at its business end; a twist grip controlled the power.

'I've never used one of these before,' she said. 'I don't know anything about hunting.'

'You've seen the briefings. We think it's hiding out near the lakelands around Cinnabar Ridge. Those two'll show you the ropes.'

'Why me? I've nearly done my year's term. They can't hold me any longer without sentencing.'

'Orders. I don't ask. Look on the positive side. It's a break from the tunnels.'

'A chance to get fried, you mean. Is it adult?'

'Adolescent, we think.'

And so at its most unpredictable, she thought.

'A big one?'

'Biggish, by all accounts.'

'Don't try to sugar it.'

He set the rod to maximum. 'We'll track you from here, keep an eye on your progress.'

'It isn't fair! I've been expecting my release date any day.'

Vargo shrugged. 'Luck of the draw. Maybe there'll be something when you get back.'

She scrutinized him on zoom. His eyes told her nothing.

'Don't do anything stupid,' he said emphatically. 'I want you back in one piece.'

'I didn't know you cared.'

One of the men yelled at her: 'You coming, or are we going to sit here till our back ends freeze?'

She went across and clambered into the seat behind them. The shorter of the two grunted at her, and that was the extent of the greeting. She didn't know either of them.

'Remember what I said!' Vargo called as they moved off.

The caterpillar accelerated gradually, raising a low dust cloud as they descended the escarpment to the plain. Periodically Marea wiped her gloved hand across her oculars to clear them, and then her cloak would raise its snout from her throat to peer out. On the riddled umber slopes to the west the mining teams were marshalling the dragons, driving the flightless ore-burrowers into the tunnels to excavate the mineral-rich rocks for export to fabricatories throughout the Solar System. At this distance, the creatures looked like lizards with vestigial wings, their herders even more diminutive. All the workers were criminals, most serving sentences of between one and ten years. Some – the murderers – were here for life.

The two men in front continued to ignore her, driving the caterpillar onwards, one of them swearing constantly under his breath, saying what a shit-hole the moon was, what a fucking outrage it was that they had been consigned to it. The shorter man, who was steering, chewed gum under his mask, popping bubbles occasionally as if to punctuate his companion's invective. Around them stretched a broken tan and olive plain fragmented with jutting saffron rhombs of sulphur and ruddy patches of thiolichens. Distant geysers jetted sulphur dioxide crystals high into the black sky; the crystals refracted the light so that the hazy sun was bracketed by spectral crescent mock suns.

Within an hour they were approaching Cinnabar Ridge, an outcrop of vermilion rocks rising from thinly crusted terrain which Marea knew was treacherous. They had seen nothing along the way apart from a monitor bird, drifting high on vapour plumes. It tracked them, swooping down from time to time to radio its overview, reporting no sightings of the beast.

They pulled up on the shore of a lava lake, a tract of liquid sulphur the colour of old gold, crusted here and there with solid patches like floating islands. Elsewhere the lake was simmering, boiling into the near vacuum.

Her cloak was restless, shuffling about her shoulders and peeking out through the visor.

'You want to go walkabout?' she asked it.

'What?' said the voice of the taller man across the suitcom. She had left the channel open.

'Nothing. I was talking to my cloak.'

'Fucking cons and their pets,' she heard him mutter.

The monitor bird came in from a long circuit of the ridge.

'Nothing,' it screeched, jetting pale exhaust from its ragged black wings then swooping down over the lake.

'You sure?' shouted the taller man after it.

The bird, its optics linked to monitors back at the base, continued its flight without replying.

She manoeuvred the cloak around, then swiftly unzipped the shoulder flaps of her mask. The cloak slithered out with a puff of misty air and ran across to the lake shore.

Marea sealed her mask before the chill penetrated, enjoying the brief thrill of exposure. Sniffing around, the cloak found a stunted brown patch of lavaflowers and began to crop them. It could survive outside for an hour or so, and the exercise and grazing would do it good.

'Well,' came the taller man's voice, 'you just going to stand there?'

He and his companion were unloading the paddler from the trailer.

'Are we going out on the lake?' Marea said.

'Why the hell else do you think we brought this bowl of blubber along?'

In fact, he stood back and let Marea and the shorter man do the lifting. The paddler was oval, dimpled, the bulbous mouth-engine at the rear. They turned it over and dropped it in the shallows. Immediately it began sucking lake liquid – it was hard not to think of it as 'water' – into its maw, inflating the bladders around its edges. The taller man hoisted a harpoon gun and clambered delicately on board while the shorter man held the paddler still in the shallows.

'Get aboard,' he said to her. 'Think we got all day?'

Her cloak was now stalking the monitor bird, which had settled nearby; the bird flew away as it pounced. When it saw Marea getting on board, it scampered across and leapt in just as the shorter man kick-started the boat by stamping his heel sharply into one of its ribs. Marea was hurled back as it shot out across the lake, fins furiously pumping.

Both men were suitably amused at her fall.

'You steer,' the taller man told her, leaving Marea in the stern seat while he and his companion climbed into the prow.

They headed straight out across the lake, the paddler settling down to a steady pace, jetting liquid from gills below the engine sacs, flippers moving in an effortless rhythm. The taller man had his harpoon gun at the ready, while his companion had produced a long-bladed knife. Marea wondered where it had come from, since it was not the type of weapon which would have been issued for the job. But then these two were hardly a reputable pair, even by the standards of Io.

Around them, the lake seethed and bubbled, vapours rising like shreds of mist. Marea negotiated the ragged islands where the sulphur had crystallized by using the pressure of her palm on the paddler's Eustachian ridge. At first they bumped a few islands, to the annoyance of the men, but she soon got used to it.

On some of the floating islands there were patches of withered vegetation, and on one of them she thought she glimpsed a pale creature darting through a smear of feathery scrub. Like all the Settled Worlds, Io had been liberally seeded with a variety of organisms to assist the exploitation of its mineralogy, but those that survived the hostile conditions rarely bred true so that mutations were the norm rather than the exception. Most were sickly or useless specimens that did not survive long, but occasionally the moon threw up something unpredictable and dangerous. The ore-burrowers were a terrestrial modification of trans-Gallilean fliers, their wings deliberately stunted and their propulsion systems diverted through the lungs so that the creatures could mine ore by heat-blasting. They were bred to be docile and obedient; they were also supposed to be unable to fly.

The taller man continued an intermittent tirade about their status, conditions of work and general treatment as enforced labourers; Marea fingered the volume on the suitcom down to minimum, wondering what crimes the two of them had originally committed. Her cloak crawled up into her lap as she steered the paddler into the shadows of the ridge. Banded deposits rose up in shades of orange and brown; on zoom they were a kaleidoscope of scintillations.

There was no sign of anything. The sun gilded the vaporous lake, giving an illusion of tranquillity. She offered her cloak a lungful of air from her back-up sac; it gulped at the nozzle like a feeding infant. She heard the monitor bird saying 'All clear', but the second word was cut short even as a big shadow passed fleetingly over them.

Her cloak darted under the seat, but when Marea looked up there was nothing in the sky.

'What the hell was that?' the taller man said.

Both of them were standing, peering around. The shadow had vanished over the water towards the ridge. Marea scanned the sky, but nothing appeared. Nothing at all.

Presently the two men settled back. Marea wondered if she should say something. Maybe it had been a vapour plume, temporarily blotting out the sun. Maybe the monitor bird had flown off to scout beyond the ridge.

Despite her urging, her cloak refused to come out from under the seat.

'Something frightened it,' she said. 'I think we should head back to shore.'

But then the shorter man was standing again, pointing.

'Look at that. Is it me, or is it a nest?'

On an island directly ahead of them was a pile of dried vegetation. And at its centre was a smooth mound.

'It's an egg,' the taller man shouted in triumph. 'It's a fucking dragon's egg.'

'I think we should get out of here,' Marea said.

'You kidding? You a moron or something? Any idea how much those things fetch on the open market? Get this tub over there.'

She didn't move. 'Who's the moron? This is a prison world, in case you've forgotten. You planning on selling it to Andreas, maybe?'

He stuck the explosive end of the harpoon gun in her face. 'You listen to me. We're taking it, got that? What we do with it is our business.'

She pushed the barrel aside. 'This is stupid. If there's an egg, then the dragon's around here somewhere.'

'All the more reason not to waste time arguing. Now get this tub to the island.'

She looked at the other man. 'What do you say?'

He chomped on his gum, melodramatically fingering the blade of his knife. 'I think you'd better do exactly what he tells you.'

She told the paddler to slow, then brought it alongside the shore of the island.

'Right,' the taller man said. 'Metin, go get it.'

The shorter man looked nonplussed. 'Me? Why me?'

'Think I'd trust her?' He had levelled the harpoon gun at her chest. 'Be quick about it.'

Not without reluctance, the shorter man clambered uncertainly out of the boat, gingerly testing his feet on the thin surface of the island. When he was sure it would support his weight, he hurried across to the nest.

'Hell's teeth,' Marea heard him say as he peered inside. 'It's a big one.'

And then he was hoisting it out, cradling it against his chest. It filled his arms, mottled green and crimson, a wrinkled leathery thing. Marea's cloak scuttled up her leg, vibrating in alarm.

Marea could tell that he was grinning under his mask as he hurried towards the paddler. Then the shadow descended again, and something huge loomed over them. There was a bronze blur, and as it lifted she saw the man's head had gone. Blood was fountaining from his neck, vaporizing into a dark cloud.

The egg fell from his arms and rolled away. The dragon soared up, and Marea was certain the head was clutched in its claws. The paddler, already panicked, began to flee across the lake as the headless body crumpled.

Both she and the other man were flung headlong. The creature was huge, no mere adolescent but a fully grown mother who would protect its unborn infant with all the ferocity it could muster. Marea glimpsed it veering over the ridge. It was at least twenty times the length of the paddler, fully developed wings sprouting from its leathery gold-green hide, exhaust pluming from their web sacs.

The paddler was furiously weaving past the islands in its fright. Marea clung on hard to her seat. Then the dragon swooped down again, heading not towards them but the island where it had made its nest. It landed, was lost from sight behind a swirl of lake vapour.

The other man was crouched in the prow, still gripping the harpoon gun.

'Did you see it?' he said. 'Did you fucking see the size of it?'

Marea resisted the temptation to say she had warned him; she was too frightened and nauseated to speak.

'Think it'll come after us?' he said. There was a quaver in his voice. When she made no reply, he said, 'I'm talking to you!'

She stroked her cloak, trying to calm it. 'Maybe it'll be satisfied if it's got the egg.'

He stared at her, eyes black with fear behind his oculars. Then he turned towards the ridge.

Shortly afterwards the lake vapour cleared momentarily, and they could see the nest island.

The dragon was gone.

They both scanned the skies, but there was no sign of it. The paddler continued hurrying towards the distant shore. It was a far better navigator, even in panic, when left to itself.

Now that they were away from the ridge, they had a clearer field of vision. All that could be seen were distant vapour plumes, the sun shining smudgily in the blackness, a dusting of brighter stars. Her cloak twitched in her lap, claws scratching at her knees.

The man was standing, harpoon gun raised. 'I can't believe the size of it. A fucking monster. Took his head clean off.'

She was revolted by the memory. She had never known death until she found the womb and brought about the destruction of both her husbands. Now it seemed to stalk her.

The man pivoted around, watching the sky.

'What's your name?' she asked him, because suddenly it seemed important to know.

'What the hell difference does it make?'

She practically screamed at him: 'Tell me!'

'Pavel.' He had to swallow to say it. He didn't ask her hers.

The shore was approaching rapidly. Marea began to think that perhaps they would make it to dry land. Then the lake erupted in front of them.

The dragon reared out of it.

Its wedge-shaped head coiled up from the lake until it was looming over them, drooling dark slime from the lake bottom. It began venting smoky hydrocarbon gases from its nostrils while its wings broke surface, sweeping out to hold it in position. Very slowly the lids on its triangular eyes opened. It stared down at them with a gaze the colour of fire.

The man had turned and frozen at the sight; the harpoon gun slipped from his hands and fell to the bottom of the boat. Marea managed to retrieve her stun-rod, but she knew it would be useless against a creature of this size.

Slowly the dragon's jaw opened wider and wider. She saw the jagged arrays of flinty teeth, the cavern of its huge throat.

It was almost as if it was yawning, could dispose of them so effortlessly that even their killing bored it.

The man leapt from the boat, diving into the lake. Furiously he began to try to swim away, sinking and rising, sinking and rising, as if he had never swum before but was propelled on by sheer terror.

Languidly the dragon turned its head in his direction. Its jaws snapped together, and two jets of flame roared from its nostrils. The lake liquid exploded, boiling even more furiously, buffeting the paddler. But the vapours cleared quickly, the lake subsiding to its usual simmer. If anything remained of the man, it did not surface.

The dragon swung its head back towards Marea, bringing its snout so close she might have smelt its swamp breath had she not been masked. The slitted pupils of the eyes began to dilate as its jaws yawned open. Marea saw its marbled tongue quivering in its maw. She was certain it intended to eat her.

She felt a scrabbling movement along her body, and then the cloak leapt on to the dragon's snout and clung on. Marea managed to react immediately, activating the stun-rod and ramming it into the creature's mouth.

The dragon reared back in surprise. Marea saw her cloak scramble along its nose ridge to claw at its eye. She dived for the harpoon gun, snatching it up. The dragon reared again, flicking its head wildly and finally dislodging the cloak, which went spiralling into the lake. She was positive she could hear it roaring as the head came veering towards her again, jaws opening wide.

She fired. The explosive dart went straight down the creature's gullet.

It kept coming. Then its eyes burst apart an instant before its entire head exploded.

The blast flung her over the edge of the paddler. She clung on to one of the bladders as the boat pitched and swayed. The debris of the beast began to fall down around her like clotted rain.

Summoning all her strength, she finally managed to clamber back into the paddler. The last few fragments of the beast were sinking towards the bottom of the lake. Purple patches of blood frothed on its surface.

Had she been able to, Marea might have vomited, but she was limp with exhaustion and fright. She sat there for a long while, trembling inside her suit. Then something crawled over the side of the boat. It was her cloak, and it slithered into her lap, shaking lake sulphur from its pelt, splattering her oculars.

She cradled and stroked it, feeding it air, crying and laughing at the same time. Only gradually did its quivering subside.

'My hero,' she told it. 'What a wonder you are!'

The paddler was in shock and would not move at her command. She prodded one of its ribs with her toe, gave it a gentle kick, then kicked harder. Suddenly it shot across the lake, moving at a furious pace, crashing straight through any crusts in its path until they hit the shallows. And even then it kept going, though it was not designed for movement on dry land, careering up the shore until finally it stumbled, catapulting Marea into a drift of sulphur dioxide snow.

She sat up, unhurt inside her suit, the cloak clutched around her neck.

Vargo was sitting on his trike nearby. He held a rifle in his hands.

'We lost the monitor bird,' he told her. 'I thought I'd better come and investigate.'

'You're too late. It's over.'

He holstered the rifle, then clambered off the trike and walked over to her. Gently he lifted her up.

'You OK?'

Marea began to sob.

Vargo held her, letting her cry until eventually she stopped.

'The other two,' she said. 'It took them. They're both dead.'

She told him the whole story, sparing no details. Then she cried again.

Vargo took something from one of his suit pouches and pressed it into her hand. It looked like a small cube of bark.

'In your mouth,' he ordered. 'Chew on it slowly.'

'What is it?'

'It'll make you feel better.'

She did as he instructed, opening the mouthpiece on her mask and pushing the cube inside.

It was fibrous, grainy, bitter-tasting. But within seconds she felt a great liberating tide of calm washing through her, blunting her terror.

'What is it?' she asked again.

'Somalin.'

Somalin was a psycosmetic drug used as a tranquillizer and mood-enhancer. It was rare, costly. Unheard of on Io.

'Where did you get it?'

'Emergency rations,' he said, straight-voiced.

She turned the pulpy mass around in her mouth. Her mind was lucid, but the calmness was like a delirium.

'Will you collect their bodies?' she asked. Tears were running down her face again.

'Listen.' He was holding her firmly by the arms. 'If it's any consolation, they wouldn't have lasted much longer anyway.'

'What do you mean?'

'They were terminal cases. They didn't know it, but their time was up.'

He waited. She couldn't speak.

'You understand what I'm saying? They were due for blanking.'

She swayed in his arms. He held her upright.

'I'm telling you this to make you feel better. You're not supposed to know.'

'Who were they?'

'Does it matter?'

'I want to know!' Even her anger sounded remote.

'They weren't from our sector. Shipped in yesterday from Pele for the job. That's about all I know.'

She was afraid to ask him what she was certain he did know. He led her through the snow to the trike.

'They didn't expect any of us to come back, did they?'

'What makes you say that?'

'It was a full-grown beast. With an egg to protect. Somebody must have known that. We weren't even properly armed.'

She was pretty sure Vargo had had no part in it himself. He

was a con, like her, and had been on Io for six years, earning his position of responsibility by being tough but reliable.

'You may be right,' he conceded. 'But you got through, didn't you?'

'They didn't though, did they? The dragon took them, decapitated one and incinerated the other. Did they deserve that?'

He gave an angry sigh. 'What the hell did you do, anyway? It must have been more than just carving up your husbands.'

That was the official story, the public reason for her arrest. She tried to tell him what had really happened but began to splutter, as she always did. Some kind of block had been implanted after her arrest to prevent her from revealing anything. She couldn't even mention anything connected with her arrest, not the womb, nothing. They'd come the same day of Yuri and Salih's killing, taking her while she lay barely conscious in the ruins of the house. When she'd woken she was already in transit to Io.

Vargo helped her mount the trike. She slouched against him, holding on to his waist harness. He gunned the trike, and they headed off back towards Haemus.

Marea closed her eyes for a while, relaxing into the rhythm of the ride, the trike's padded wheels cushioning them against the bumpy terrain. Her cloak was asleep, she felt pleasantly woozy and also a little randy, relishing Vargo's bulk in front of her.

There were all sorts of rumours about Vargo. According to camp gossip, he had lost the sight in his eye at a fumarole explosion five years before and would have to live with it; biological refits were not part of the medical aid for criminal labour on Io, even those like Vargo who had achieved overseer status. It didn't seem to bother him in the slightest, a fact which Marea found admirable. But there was much more to him than this. He was said to be a madman, a God-worshipper, a renegade politia commander.

'Tell me,' she said, 'is it true you killed one of your brothers?'

The words were out before she knew it. Without the somalin, she would never have had the courage to ask him.

'Nope,' he said. 'I killed my *only* brother.'

'It's true?'

He murmured something to the trike. Then: 'I chopped him up and fed him into the disposall.'

'You're kidding me.'

'I used the kitchen mincer. I planned it very carefully.'

He sounded perfectly serious. She didn't have the wit to consider whether he was simply stringing her along.

'Why?' she asked.

'He was intimate with my wife.'

Intimate. It was an archaic way of expressing it.

'He was her lover?'

'Among us, that's a great sin.'

'You're a Deist?'

He gave a small laugh. 'That's what others call us.'

'You believe in a creator? A God?'

'How else did we get here?'

'You don't believe in the Noosphere?'

She felt him shake his head. 'It's not a question of that. We have a stronger belief in something else. Something beyond death.'

'Heaven?'

'If you like.'

There were many different sects, she knew, most of them small in number and scattered throughout the Settled Worlds. They only used the shrines for public votes, holding to the view that ancestor communion was heresy.

'So what happens when you reach the end of your time?'

'We take proper death.'

So it was true. He *was* a madman, in a way. At least it seemed like insanity to her.

'And is that the end of it?' she said. 'The end of everything?'

He turned his head. 'What is this? An interrogation?'

'I'm interested. I'd like to know.'

'Death isn't the end,' he said reluctantly. 'The immortal soul lives on, at one with the Creative Spirit, for ever.' He sounded a little embarrassed, unused to expressing his creed. 'It's how I was brought up.'

She found it hard to imagine having such beliefs, taking

death at your century without the certain knowledge of an afterlife. She must have asked something, because he said:

'We believe in serial marriages, in monogamy. Among us adultery is punishable by death.'

'Is that why you killed him?'

He was silent for a while, skirting the edge of a blood-black swamp of plastic sulphur.

'I did it out of revenge,' he said. 'Because she wanted him, not me.'

It was difficult to muster her thoughts, but equally hard not to be garrulous. 'You loved her? Your wife?'

Another mirthless laugh. 'Why else would I have killed him?'

They rode on in silence for a while, crossing a flat expanse of sulphur flowers. A mineral meadow of golds and oranges and browns. Probably stank to high heaven.

'They also say you were a politia commander.'

He made no response to this; didn't deny it.

'Based on Ceres?'

The trike began a cautionary burbling.

'I covered the whole belt,' Vargo told her. 'Mars sometimes, too. Thirty-one years. Anything else you want to know?'

'Did you get the maximum sentence?'

'What do you think? It was premeditated.'

'They were going to blank you?'

'There's nothing they'd have liked better. Me, too, in some ways. Then I thought about it. Decided to take the killer's option instead.'

The maximum sentence for capital crimes was brain erasure, but murderers were sometimes given a choice: they could opt for a life sentence on Io instead.

The trike was burbling more loudly, and Vargo slowed it.

'Do you think you'll ever get out?' Marea asked.

'Nope,' he replied. 'I expect to die here.'

Ahead of them a small piebald geyser had erupted. Others joined it, filling the air with a peppered snow that slowly drifted down. Through the haze she could see the base perched on its plateau in the near distance.

They got off the trike and watched the eruptions run their course. The sight of Haemus had a sobering effect on Marea.

She knew she could not put off any longer what she had to ask.

'What about me?' she said at last.

He turned to look at her. Both of his oculars were misted by the snow. 'You?'

'You know what I mean, Vargo. My sentence has come through, hasn't it?'

He didn't say anything.

'Well?' she said. 'It's the same as the other two, isn't it?'

'I heard this morning. There was no point in telling you until now.'

'Blanking?' She couldn't believe she was saying the word.

Again he was silent.

'When?'

'There'll be time to put your affairs in order. You'll be given access to a shrine when we get back.'

'Damn the shrine!'

She stalked off, but did not go far. She tried to imagine having her mind snuffed out for ever, having her body taken over by someone else or being dismembered for servo-organism parts. An end to everything. Truedeath.

Vargo came up beside her. 'I'm really sorry, Marea.'

'No killer's option?'

'Not this time.'

'Can I appeal?'

'Andreas told me it won't even be considered.'

The womb had come unbidden into her hands. And they were going to kill her for possessing it. She would die without even knowing who wanted her dead, or why.

It was too much. She was numb with the deaths of the two men, and now she faced her own extinction. Both facts ran counter to everything she'd been taught to believe about the sanctity of human life.

'Do you know how they do it?' she asked him.

'It depends.'

'I've heard they incinerate you. Or bury you alive. Or—'

He grabbed hold of her. 'It's nothing like that. However they do it, it'll be painless. Believe me, it's better not to think about it.'

The effects of the drug had worn off, and she was awash with a cold panic.

'When?' she asked again.

'Six days,' he replied.

Seven

I woke to darkness. For a long time I was caught up in the imagery of the dream – it was almost as if I had experienced it myself. I was certain I had never before had such vivid dreams, dreams that carried sensations of smell, touch and taste as well as sights and sounds.

Someone was lying beside me.

Nina.

She appeared to be asleep, but when I stirred she said: 'Nathan?'

I was silent.

'Are you awake?'

'I'm awake.'

She sat up on one elbow. She was clothed. 'They let me stay. I asked. I hope you don't mind.'

The blinds on the window were open, but it was dark outside. A lunar darkness.

'I can't believe this,' I said.

'Until you recovered,' she said, 'I thought I might be mad.'

'Do you dream?'

'All the time. I know we both do. They told me.'

'The same dreams?'

'Yes. I think so.'

'Tell me what you've dreamt. Marea and the falling ship?'

She nodded.

'Tunde on Venus?'

'I never thought he'd make it.'

'The woman Bezile? And Shivaun?'

'Imrani, too. And now Marea again. On that hellhole.'

It was my turn to sit up. 'You were with her?'

'I was inside her head. That's how it seemed. Seeing everything through her eyes. And then I woke. You, too?'

I took hold of her wrist, because I needed extra confirmation that she was real. 'I have to be sure about this. I need to know whether we're both dreaming exactly the same thing.'

We talked for a long time, discussing each episode in great detail. There were no significant differences between our dreams, nothing Nina knew or had witnessed that I had not. We had both inhabited the same characters, lived through the same experiences as they.

It was clear that Nina was as relieved as I was to hear that our dreams tallied. I felt a sense of liberation, as if I had finally released myself from a burdensome secret. Yet many questions remained.

'Have they told you why we're being fed this stuff?'

'Only that it's part of the process of adjustment.'

'The stories are unfinished. There's obviously more to come.'

'Next time we dream.'

We lay in silence for a while. There were no sounds from beyond the door. Nothing.

'It must be the middle of the night,' I remarked. 'Assuming that means anything here.'

She stifled a yawn. 'What do you think they'll do with us?'

I thought about it. 'We must be curiosities to them. Maybe they want to see how we react to the dreams. How we *acclimatize*.'

'What do you make of them?'

'Chloe and Lucian?'

'They talk like adults. It's disconcerting.'

'They seem considerate enough, in their way. It's a different world here.'

The dreams had given us some idea of that. But vivid though they were, they were by their nature second-hand. I felt a generalized frustration bubbling up.

'I hate this,' I said. 'Not knowing anything.'

The anger had come again, though it was accompanied by a wave of weariness. 'I hate being an invalid. Weak.'

She put her arm across my chest. 'At least we're alive. We're in pretty good condition considering we've both been practically dead for hundreds of years or more.'

It was so ridiculous we both started laughing. I could just make out her face in the gloom: it was alive with animation, with sheer uncomplicated humanity. I reached over and kissed her on the cheek.

She seemed surprised. 'What was that for?'

'I wanted to see how you tasted.'

We both lay back again. I was fighting my tiredness. I could feel myself drifting down.

After a while I said, 'Nina?'

There was no answer. She was already asleep.

Tunde took breakfast out on the balcony. The morning air was ripe, a steady breeze blowing down from the Atlas Mountains. Adele's mansion overlooked the great network of ravines, and Tunde watched a pair of juvenile fliers cavort in play, bright frilled creatures like giant fish that chased one another, riding the updraughts, dipping and diving and coiling around each other, scarlet and gold and sapphire blue. Overhead, a parent drifted by, keeping a watchful eye on them. Finally the smaller of the two juveniles darted down to take refuge in one of the hatcheries that pockmarked the cliffs. The jutting launchpads often held all manner of craft from great tentacled interplanetary vessels to tiny shuttles fashioned entirely from inorganics, but it was the young creatures Tunde liked best, the ones that engaged in uninhibited fun. Soon enough they would have to learn that most of their lives would be drudgery, not play.

Saturn was already half up over the horizon, a bronze blur in the atmospheric haze. Titan reminded him of Venus, its air rich with organics, its comforting murkiness shutting out the expanses beyond. The morning was warm, promising a hot day.

Tunde went downstairs and found Adele scanning the news reports on the kaleidoptic in the main living chamber. The Uranian moons were under quarantine because of the spread of the Dementia. Fresh batches of cases had been reported in Antaeus City itself, and there was to be a statutory vote on whether stabilized sufferers should be committed to the No-osphere before the disease progressed to total insanity.

'It's looking serious,' Adele said.

She was dressed enticingly in blue. Tunde kissed the back of her neck. 'I don't think they know how to stop it.'

'Mmm. You can't stop something until you know what's causing it.'

No infective agent had yet been identified, and it was hard to see any pattern to how the illness was spread except that so far it was confined to the Outer Worlds and that young children seemed immune.

One of the optics showed a victim of the sickness on the rampage in a shopping mall on Oberon-Nine. He was puncturing window blisters with a hedge pruner, smashing through displays of crystalware, sending soft furnishings scurrying in fright as he flashed the terrified creature's jaws open and shut, raving all the while. Then he noticed the optic that was recording him. The last thing they saw was a close-up of his smeared face and bulging eyes before the picture went blank.

'Not a pretty sight,' Adele remarked.

'Did you see his teeth?' Tunde said with patent distaste. 'They were broken. There was blood all over his lips.'

Julius and Orela came on view. They were shown greeting a plagueship bringing more victims to their orbital Sanctuary, then walking the wards with medicants, ministering to the patients. Most lay drugged and motionless on padded rockers, only their dishevelled state revealing what was wrong. Both Advocates touched hands and stroked brows as they went by, as if intent on countering the popular superstition that the sickness could only be spread by direct human contact. Orela even took a distressed woman in her arms and kissed her forehead before settling her gently back in her rocker.

'Well,' Tunde said, 'at least they're setting a proper example.'

The Advocates had boosted their popularity by establishing the Sanctuary, a derelict habitation now in distant Earth-orbit that had been reconstituted as an isolation centre for Dementia victims. The commentary informed them that the best biotecs had been assembled from throughout the Settled Worlds to study the victims; teams were working day and night to find a cure.

'It's comforting,' Adele said, 'but the people are very scared.'

'With good reason. Who wants to go mad?'

'We'll find a cure.'

'You sound confident.'

'We've never failed in the past.'

Adele was a remote nurse, working mainly for the recuperatory in Antaeus. She had not actually had any direct dealings with Dementia victims but kept abreast of every development.

Julius and Orela were still captured on the optic. Both looked remarkably youthful considering that they were well beyond their centuries. They were reminding everyone of the need to act clear-headedly to help combat the crisis.

'Have you voted yet?' Adele asked.

Tunde paged a zeeball result: Nephthys had been seconded 20–35–12 in the three-way with Chryse and Paladin on Iapetus.

'Fowote?'

It was the name he had adopted. He blanked the score. 'I'll do it later.'

'Don't forget. You missed the last compulsory. They'll have you mucking out the city intestinals for default.'

'Don't I know it.'

The console announced that there was a call for Adele from her first husband, Morgen.

Even though Morgen knew of him, Tunde instinctively moved out of the screen's line of sight before Adele took the call. Lately he had grown nervous, feeling that the refuge he had found for the past year would not last.

Morgen was a dark-haired man in his sixties whom Adele had married fifteen years before. He was one of the directors of Transect, a corporation that specialized in the fabrication of interplanetary motherships. Titan, with its rich source of organics, was one of the prime centres of ship building in the Settled Worlds; its hatcheries were rivalled only by those of Aphrodite on Venus.

'Are you alone?' was the first thing Morgen said to Adele.

'Alone?'

'Isn't Fowote with you?'

Adele turned towards him, making a show of searching the chambers. Tunde shook his head vigorously.

'No,' she said to the optic. 'He's around somewhere. Probably watching your little beastlings perform. Is something wrong?'

'No, nothing,' he said. 'Nothing at all. I'd like you to come over. Bring our three.'

Adele was surprised. 'Why?'

'I want to see you, that's all. It's been a month or more, hasn't it?'

'More.'

'Make it about noon. We'll eat in the office arbour. I know you like it there.'

'Just the five of us?'

'There's a family matter I want to discuss. Don't be late.'

He blanked the optic without further comment.

Adele turned to Tunde. 'Why didn't you want him to know you were here?'

Tunde shrugged. 'Call it instinct. I thought he wanted to talk to you alone.'

'Don't give me that.'

'Where's Cori?'

'Out in the garden having her lessons with my three. Don't change the subject. What's going on, Fo?'

Every mention of the name was a reminder of what a fraud he was. He had bought fake identities for himself and Cori through a contact at Ishtar Transit who owed him a favour, along with passage to Titan. Adele was a fellow Venusian from a similar background to his whom he had met on the flight out: she had been visiting relatives in the Swamplands. They had struck up an immediate rapport, Tunde posing as a mediator on a year's sabbatical. Though still married, Adele and Morgen had been living apart for some years, and when Tunde proposed a one-year live-in contract, she had immediately accepted. Their marriage had proved surprisingly successful, physically satisfying to them both and free of suspicion. Until now.

'Maybe you ought to ask Morgen,' he said to her. 'He's the one who sounded cagey.'

'He hasn't seen me or the children in the flesh for a while. What's so suspicious about a family gathering?'

'Nothing. Forget it.'

But she obviously wouldn't; she was a direct woman, emphatic in all she did. Today she was wearing sapphire cosmetics and an indigo thrall whose tight folds emphasized her ampleness. Her uncomplicated attitude towards sex had done much to restore his self-esteem; but though straightforward, she was not lacking in shrewdness.

'Is it because he didn't invite you and Cori?'

'We've never met. Why should he?'

'You've never met because you never wanted to.' Her eyes appraised him, and eventually she said, 'Are you planning on leaving, Fo?'

She had him. He decided there was no point in trying to lie.

'It may be time. We're coming to the end of the year.'

'And you don't want to extend the contract?'

'It's not that. I have to get back. To my duties.'

She smiled and shook her head. 'You're not a mediator. I've never believed that. Not from the start.'

'No?' He checked that the aural was off on the console; it was. 'Then what am I?'

'It doesn't matter to me. Perhaps that added to the fascination. Your deceit.'

She really was a desirable woman, and at that moment it pained him to think that she had known him to be a fraud from the start. He sighed. 'What can I say? I had good reasons. And I didn't lie to you about anything else.'

'We've been good together. Good for one another. Can you deny it?'

'No. I won't deny it.'

'But you're in some sort of trouble.'

'I may be. If I stay here any longer.'

'Isn't it time you told me about it?'

'That's one thing I daren't do. It dates back to before I met you. In the best possible way, it's none of your business.'

She considered. 'There must be something I can do to help.'

'You're better off out of it. You and the children.'

He knew where to hit her; she immediately became guarded.

Ultimately she was a pragmatist who would do anything to protect her offspring.

'Are we in danger?'

'No, I don't think so. Not if you carry on exactly as you intended to today. It may be nothing anyway. But when you get back from Morgen's we'll probably be gone.'

'Cori, too?'

'I wouldn't go anywhere without her.'

Adele rose, approached him. 'This is so abrupt, Fo. You gave me no warning.'

He had to swallow. 'I wouldn't leave if there was any other alternative, I promise you.'

'Can't you tell me *anything* about it?'

His only response was silence.

Her eyes were moist, but he knew she wouldn't make an emotional issue out of it. That wasn't her way.

He put his arms around her waist. 'I'm really sorry. Apart from anything else, I'm almost out of money.'

'I'd subsidize you for another year or two. I've got enough for us both.'

'I know you would. But it isn't a question of whether I want to stay. There's no alternative.'

She looked rueful. 'It's been fun.'

'Sure has.'

He drew her to him, kissed her lips. She was always responsive, her appetite matching his.

'You want to *extend* this farewell?' she suggested mischievously.

He had to force his desire down. 'There's nothing I'd like better, but any delay increases the risk.'

She drew back. 'Will I hear from you?'

'I don't even know where I'm going to be.'

She put a turquoise fingernail to his chin. 'I'm going to miss you.'

'It works both ways. I'll never forget you, Adele.'

'You'd better not!'

She gave him a huge kiss, and then, suddenly businesslike, announced that she was going to take a long dip in the pulsator before she left.

As she rode the stairway upwards, Tunde said, 'A last favour. Can I borrow one of the strollers?'

'Feel free. Take the Psyche. She's got the fastest turn of speed.'

Then the stairway carried her out of sight.

Tunde stood there for a little while, staring around at the spacious light-filled curves of the mansion. He had been perfectly content living in her home, a secure place for himself and for Cori, with considerable luxuries. And Morgen had seemed to accept his reclusiveness – until now. As a fugitive, Tunde had learned to be suspicious of everyone and everything. It was Morgen's insistence that Adele bring only their three children that had clinched his feeling that something was afoot.

He went out through the mansion's throatway into the garden.

Cori loved it here, he knew. The garden was extensive, filled with feathertrees, spiral cacti and stretches of glaucous lawn. Cori was sitting with the other children around a tutor that was patiently explaining the fundamentals of gravity control, its optic illustrating the point with a cutaway hologram of a gravity trail. Cori wasn't paying much attention; she was curling her bare feet together and trying to catch a jumpjack that was flipping around her on the grass.

Tunde crouched beside her and whispered, 'I might test you on this later.'

She shrugged. 'I did it at primary.' Her voice took on a stilted pedantic drone: 'Concentrated nuclear matter is laid down in swathes to a density corresponding to standard gravitational pull. Such matter is produced in the lower intestinal tracts of fluxors as a byproduct of energy generation in power plantations. The process involves the biofusion of baryonic matter blah blah blah.' She squinted up at him. 'See?'

'I'm impressed with your memory,' he told her. 'But do you understand it?'

She gave him a look as if to say: Don't insult me.

'Want to go shopping?' he asked.

'Yes, please!'

Adele's three children – two boys and a girl – were four years younger, but Cori had been happy in their company, had

enjoyed being the older sister. She had insisted on keeping her
true name, though she had readily agreed to the rest of his
deception, seeing it as an adult game and playing her part to
perfection. In fact, they had told no other lies, and had become
a real part of Adele's family. It had been good for Cori, good
for him.

'Listen,' he said quietly. 'How would you feel if I said we're
going to have to leave?'

She captured the jumpjack and held it up to him in her
cupped hands. Its tiny triangular head poked out, forked pink
tongue flashing. Though he had told Adele that both he and
Cori would be going, it had occurred to him that he should
take nothing for granted.

'Would you want to stay, or come with me?'

'Come with you, of course,' she said, as if it had been the
stupidest question in the world. Then she said, 'Ouch!' as the
jumpjack nipped her finger and hopped away through the
grass.

He took her inside to her room and told her to pack any
belongings she might want to take with her. She did not
question him, but he felt obliged to make it clear that they
might be fugitives again. This she also seemed to accept.
Though their lives had been more settled, even carefree, in the
past year he'd always continued to behave as if it was a
temporary arrangement, and he suspected she had too. Cori
was shrewd beyond her years.

He waited until Adele and her children had left, then drove
the stroller around to the side of the house where a thick stand
of hydratia screened them from view but allowed them to see
the main driveway to the entrance. Bees droned in the azure
flowers, and the heat lay heavy on them, even with the vehicle
fully venting. Tunde instructed it to stay on idle.

'Why are we waiting here?' Cori wanted to know.

'There's something I need to check. Be patient.'

They did not have long to wait. Presently a big ground car
rolled up and several figures got out. Though they were not in
uniform, Tunde was sure they were politia: they were discreetly
armed with quellsticks. Quietly they surged through the garden
towards the mansion, going in through different portals. Tunde

drove the stroller off at speed down the secluded side road that coiled away from the house towards the main highway.

It was an hour's drive to Antaeus, but Tunde only went halfway, pulling over at a service umbilical where a passenger blimp had just tethered. The blimp was taking tourists on the scenic flight to the city, and Tunde bought passage for both himself and Cori. He instructed the stroller to take the long route home via the Atlas Chasms, a route that would take the best part of a day even at maximum speed; should any politia decide to track down the vehicle they would have a high time following it through tunnels, over bridges, up and down mountain roads where flocks of fledgling ships were a major hazard in addition to the precipitous bends.

The blimp was full with a gaggle of Mercurian tourists who were expressive in their appreciation of every spectacle. They skirted the shores of the Hercules Sea, where surfers rode the breakers on pneumatic floatfish; they sailed over the Argentine Delta, where hordes of newly hatched shuttles grazed on silverleaf that shone like white fire; they circled the Great Shrine of Oldengland, reputedly built by one of the architects of the Noosphere from the skeletons and ceramic superstructures of decrepit ships who had come to die in the bone-strewn marshlands that surrounded it. The shrine was a marvel of many-tusked domes and ribbed balustrades, much of it open to the air. Despite himself, Tunde was as impressed as the other passengers; he had always meant to take Cori on a day trip there but had never got around to it.

He bought frost fountains for the two of them, trying to make a holiday of it. Presently Antaeus hove into view, a compact metropolis of fluted towers and sinuous segmented habitats that formed whorls and spirals around leafy open spaces. After landing, he took Cori to a gastrodome overlooking the Oline Falls; they shared a bowl of fruit mélange while watching the fiery torrent cascade down to extinction in the Hercules River far below. Cori, subdued until now, began to perk up as he let her lead him around the shopping arteries and indulged her by buying her a picture book about the Seventy Wonders of Old Earth.

His mind was elsewhere: he was thinking of Marea. She had

been increasingly in his thoughts over the past month, and a few days ago he had taken the risk and put a transplanetary call through to her abode, only to be informed when he returned for the reply that the number was no longer operational, her house no longer extant, and could he please identify himself? He had cut the connection immediately, grateful that he was using a public booth. But that was probably how the authorities had traced him to Titan; either that, or Morgen had suspected something and got in touch with them.

Later, by dint of the most delicate investigation in one of the library files Adele kept on the prematurely deceased, he discovered that both her husbands were dead; but her own fate was unrecorded. It was ominous. And now they were after him, had been probably ever since he'd taken the womb from her.

A pager in the atrium was reminding everyone not to forget the public vote. This was another thing that had been denied him ever since he fled Venus. If he used a console in any way that required retina scans, they would track him down immediately.

What was he to do now? He still had the urge to find Marea and, if she was still alive, to make amends to her in whatever way he could.

Cori was showing him a picture of the last of the Seventy Wonders, the Leaning Tower of Babylos. A huge screw-ridged stone needle, it swayed in the wind as an electric storm raged around it, its tiers crammed with humans who were crying out in a multitude of discordant tongues.

'Do you think it was anything really like that, Father?' she asked.

'Do you?'

She sighed. 'I hate it when adults turn your questions around.'

The tower launched itself towards the heavens on a column of flame, the people aboard it wailing in misery and fear.

'Something like that could never fly,' Cori said dismissively, 'let alone take our ancestors to new worlds.'

'It's symbolic. Mythical. The essence of the truth is probably in there somewhere.'

Across the atrium there was a small shrine, little more than a brief stopping-off point for weary shoppers.

'Did your mother ever let you go inside the garden shrine?' he asked Cori.

Cori snapped her book shut. 'She always said I was too young.'

In most societies, children did not commune with the No-osphere at least until puberty; but it was only tradition.

'Would you like to come inside with me now?'

'Yes, please!'

She loved anything new. He took her hand and led her into the place.

It was as small inside as out, holding no more than thirty cubicles arranged on two levels. There was only one interces-sor, a rather tired looking woman in a crumpled plaid body-wrap who eyed Cori suspiciously.

'Will you need a booth for two?' she asked.

'Yes,' Tunde said.

'Is this her first time?'

'No,' said Cori.

The woman seemed unconvinced but she did not demur, leading them to a cubicle in a shadowy corner that had two seats. As soon as they were alone, Tunde said, 'You told a fib!'

'I didn't.' She nibbled her lip: guilty secret time. 'Me, Es and Maxim sneaked into Mother's shrine last year. We spoke to Grandma Karin and Great-Uncle Orvalle.'

He put a finger under her chin. 'Is this the truth?'

She nodded seriously.

'What happened?'

'I think they were both annoyed with us for using the shrine without permission. They were grumpy, scolding.'

This sounded like Orvalle, at least, a gruff customer who would brook no nonsense. Karin was, he assumed, one of Yolande's ancestors; she had never spoken to him about the deceased in her family.

The cubicle held two hoods and a joint input glove for their clasped hands. Tunde fitted the hoods over their heads, checked that they were on-line, then directed Cori to focus on the icon of a constantly blossoming sapphire rose.

'Try to think of nothing,' he told her, 'or concentrate on yourself and your family. Don't be afraid.'

'I'm not!' she said eagerly.

They put their free hands into the prayer terminals, and immediately he could feel the tingle radiating up his brainstem.

It was well over a year since he had last communed with the Noosphere. Most of his ancestors were fisherfolk of limited intellect and interests with whom he had little in common; it was snobbish, perhaps, but he always felt that they resented him. Yet he needed them now, needed some contact, some sense that he was not alone.

There was always a sensation, when you first entered the Noosphere, of a vast populated darkness, huge in size and teeming with mentalities, only the tiniest fraction of whom were accessible. He felt like a blind man in an immense dark hall filled with strangers, his senses pricked for the presence of someone he knew. This time it was a little different because Cori was with him, her smaller, untutored mind drawn next to his, a little fearful yet avid for experience.

He fully anticipated that his first contact would be with Orvalle, a boisterous spirit who had known him as a small child before he entered the Noosphere. But what he encountered instead was a profound sense of strangeness and dislocation, a single mentality which he did not recognize, a presence quite distinct and unfamiliar. His own surprise was echoed by that of Cori, who was undergoing a similar experience.

Both mind and emotion formed the question: 'Who are you?', but he was shocked when after a brief silence the reply came in an actual word, as if someone had spoken inside his head:

'Nathan.'

I surfaced as if catapulted out of a fever dream. My whole body was drenched with sweat, the memory of the cubicle, the infinite swarming darkness, still vivid. It was my own voice, speaking back to me. I had told him the name they had given me. I had spoken, and he had heard me.

Nina was also awake. She looked as fraught as me.

'Did you dream it?'

'I was there with you. I heard you speak. I was with Cori.'

It took a moment for this to register. 'You were with the daughter? In her head?'

'Only when they were on-line in the shrine. I went into her. Then I heard your voice.'

The room began to lighten. The door opened. Chloe and Lucian came in.

They were dressed as before and were as imperturbable as ever. Nina and I were holding one another, and I realized she was naked under the sheets. Had we made love? I had no memory of it.

'I want to know what's going on,' I said. 'What are you doing to us?'

They took two chairs from beside the bed and sat down, almost demurely. They were unremarkable white chairs, but I had never noticed them before. I kept expecting them to stretch their arms or start hopping around the room, but to all appearances they were inert.

'We haven't deliberately been keeping things from you,' Chloe said. 'There's much you have to know, but it's only been possible to tell you a little at a time.'

'I want to know about the dreams,' I said. 'I want to know what they are.'

'Your dreams are real,' Lucian said. 'At least, they represent events that have actually occurred in the recent past.'

'As we explained,' said Chloe, 'it's a useful way for you to experience the world into which you've been reborn. But there's more than that. The story that's been unfolding isn't yet finished.'

'Are these dead people?' Nina asked.

'No, no,' said Chloe. 'Indeed not. We know their stories through their various communions with the Noosphere.'

'They are the most private and sacred transactions,' Lucian added. 'But since you aren't truly of our world, we didn't hesitate to pass them on. Their tale lies at the centre of the great crisis which faces the whole of humanity.'

I laughed out loud at this. It was as much an angry laugh as an incredulous one.

'Are you going to insult us with clichés?' I said. The two of them looked like a pair of precocious, self-satisfied, overgrown children. I wanted to shake them out of their smugness.

'Lucian isn't exaggerating,' Chloe said. 'The Dementia is spreading, and there are other dangers. We've fed you the story so far for two reasons – first to inform, second to ask for your help.'

I expected more, but they simply sat there, hands in their laps. They had none of the mannerisms of ordinary people, no tics or twitches or signs of self-consciousness.

'*Our* help?' said Nina.

Lucian gave a solemn nod. 'You two are apart from things, of ancient genetic stock, uncontaminated. You are unique.'

I snorted my scepticism. 'I don't feel unique. I feel like some sort of . . . victim. An experimental subject.'

Chloe frowned. 'We understand. We honestly do. But how else could we have revived you? How else could we have brought you gently to an understanding and acceptance of a world so very different from anything you remember?'

'I remember nothing, that's the problem!'

'Nevertheless,' said Lucian, 'you're aware of what is strange and what is familiar, aren't you? Had we brought you into this world without any mental preparation whatsoever, then it's more than likely your minds would have ceased to function in any sane way.'

'*This* is insane!'

'From your perspective, of course it is. Yet there's no choice but to accept it because it is real. We are real.'

'It will be even easier to accept,' Chloe added, 'when you can participate in it.'

Nina found my hand under the bedsheets. She held on tight.

'Are you going to release us?' I said. 'To send us out there?' I pointed towards the window. The lunar day.

'We have a different sort of participation in mind,' Lucian said. 'There's still more than we've revealed to you so far, but I would ask you to be patient, to let the story unfold in its proper course.'

'To do that,' Chloe said, 'it will be necessary for you both to dream again.'

They appeared so perfect, and that in itself was irritating. There was nothing at all intimidating in their manner, just the constant voice of sweet reason. But their world was a world where nothing could be taken for granted, where the bizarre was commonplace.

'And if we say no?' I said.

'There's no compulsion. But you two are perhaps the only ones who can help us.'

'Why?' I said. 'How? What do you want from us?'

'We want you to dream again,' said Chloe. 'To see what is possible. To understand as much as you can. And then, we hope, to assist us.'

'And if we don't?'

Chloe smiled. 'You're almost fully recovered. You can be free agents, go out into the Noospace to make what lives you wish.'

The Noospace. I understood it as the physical counterpart of the Noosphere, every place in the Solar System where humans lived. I understood it, but I had only experienced its reality by proxy.

'Just like that?' I said.

'Of course.'

I didn't believe it would be that simple. Even if they were prepared to let us walk out, it obviously wouldn't be that simple.

'You'll never let us go.'

'Naturally we hope you'll stay,' Lucian said. 'At least for a while. But it's your choice. What we want most is your trust and cooperation.'

I felt Nina's grip on me relaxing a little.

'You're asking a lot of us,' she said.

'We realize that,' Chloe responded. 'Though in a way we're asking nothing of you except that you allow us to continue the story.'

There was a long silence.

'Can I see your hand?' I said to Chloe.

She was surprised, but rose and came forward, holding it out, palm downward.

I grasped it, then pinched a fold of skin on its back. Chloe flinched, mouth opening in surprise.

They were flesh and blood. No different in make-up from Nina and myself.

'I need to speak to Nina,' I said. 'Alone.'

Lucian got up. Without another word, he and Chloe withdrew.

I waited until the door closed behind them, listened for the sound of their footsteps. I heard nothing. Was the room monitored? Could they hear and see everything anyway? The question was academic. If they could infiltrate our dreams at will, then it was unlikely even our thoughts could be kept secret from them.

'What do you want to do?' I asked Nina.

'What can we do?'

'We could walk out of here. See what happens.'

She looked askance at me. 'Are you serious?'

'It's an option.'

'And go where?'

I said the first thing that came into my head: 'Maybe they'd give us passage to Earth. We must have come from there originally.'

It was an assumption: I had no evidence.

Nina wasn't taken by the suggestion. 'We'd be like innocents abroad.' She was perfectly at ease in her nakedness beside me. 'Doesn't the idea scare you? It scares me. Even more than staying here.'

It hadn't been a serious proposal. Apart from anything else, I knew I was too weak to go walkabout.

'So what are you saying? We go along with what they want?'

'Do we have any other choice?'

She was calm, matter-of-fact. And of course she was right. But I didn't like it one bit.

'Whoever I was before,' I said, 'I'm not used to taking things lying down.'

'I know what you mean,' she said, and then she gave me a conspiratorial grin. 'Although a *few* things are better that way.'

I had no memory of any intimacy we had shared. And I wanted it – as I knew I would have wanted her.

'I must be on the mend,' I said. 'Something's stirring down there.'

She laughed.

But we both knew that now was not the time. We knew that we were going to have to find out how the story ended.

Eight

Nina and I stood with Chloe and Lucian in a bright tunnel that was somewhere below ground. I knew this without being able to remember how we had got there.

'We were born here,' Chloe was saying as if in answer to a question, 'paired off together at birth.'

'You're brother and sister?' Nina asked.

She shook her head. 'Every year foetuses melded from promising gene lines are brought to term here on the No-osphere. The children are raised and trained by those in the service of everyone in the Settled Worlds.'

As my eyes adjusted to the bright light, I could see figures, men and women, some sitting at consoles that resembled prayer terminals, others moving down umbilical corridors that fed into a huge central chamber. We ourselves were approaching the end of one such corridor, though we were not walking and nor did our feet appear to be touching anything palpable. It was as if we were slowly gliding down a tunnel of light.

I accepted this, as I had accepted everything in my dreams. It was so strange and unreal that I had no reaction to it at all.

'In our case,' Lucian was saying, 'we were tutored in the many special duties which it is necessary for the Advocates to perform.'

This brought me up short, and to my surprise we seemed to stop moving.

'You mean you two are going to replace Julius and Orela?'

'If only it were that simple,' Lucian replied. 'The mental capacities demanded of the Advocates can't be bred, nor can they always be brought to fruition even when carefully nurtured.'

We began moving on again. The corridor opened up, and we were looking down on something vast and incredibly intricate. It was impossible to say whether it was animal, vegetable or mineral because it seemed to combine aspects of all three. It resembled a globular many-spiked crystal which shone gold and silver, yet it also had the aspect of an enormous flower, and again of an undersea creature whose petalled spines were responsive to unseen currents. Around it, swarming like slow-moving insects, were men and women, some tending peripheral organics, others engaged in tasks I could not even guess at.

Nina was looking down with a wonderment that I must have shown as well.

'Many of us were born here,' Chloe was saying, 'and most remain to serve the Noosphere in whatever capacity they can. But to become an Advocate – that's beyond the capabilities of any but the most gifted and mentally resilient.'

'The training is arduous,' Lucian continued. 'The Advocates must possess the capacity to enter into the Noosphere and partake of the millions of minds who may be using shrines on every habitation of the Noospace. They must be able to comprehend and empathize with their fears and desires. They must be able to communicate those desires so that the will of the people prevails.'

'Most will fail the test ultimately,' said Chloe. 'As we did. But that doesn't mean we can't be of use. We, and many others like us, remain servants in less elevated but no less important capacities. We monitor and process information from the constant communion of souls within the Noosphere, whether through private prayers or public votes.'

Lucian indicated the radiant thing at the centre of the chamber: now it was like a golden sun bursting with innumerable spears of light.

'This is the heart of the Noosphere – the central coordinating matrix which stores communions and holds the psyches of the departed.'

'Let me get this clear,' I said. 'Whenever someone uses a shrine, their *prayers* are recorded here?'

'Better to say that they are *processed*. In absolute confidence, of course. But how else could it be? How else can the Advocates learn what the people want? How else could we act on their wishes?'

'I thought they were communing with their ancestors.'

'And so they are. But they expect practical results from their prayers, and these we endeavour to provide.'

We spiralled slowly down and around the golden heart of the Noosphere, its radiance bright but undazzling. It was hard to imagine that billions of departed souls were contained within it. None of the workers who attended it paid us any heed. They were reduced to silhouettes by its light.

'If the people express their wishes through the shrines,' said Nina, 'then why do you need Advocates?'

'Because they are the human faces of the Noosphere,' Chloe said. 'No community can survive without personifications of leadership. They are meant to represent the pinnacle of mortality, the embodiment of all that is best and wise in the human species.'

We were gliding slowly away now, another corridor closing around us. Nina slipped her hand into mine.

'Are Julius and Orela mortal?' she asked.

The corridor was growing dimmer, narrower. Ahead of us it curved away into darkness.

'In theory,' Lucian said, 'their life terms are the same as everyone else's. One hundred years.'

'But Julius and Orela are older than that, aren't they?'

'Indeed,' Chloe said pointedly. 'And therein lies our dilemma.'

Without any obvious transition, we were suddenly back inside my room. As if we had never left. I had already witnessed too many wonders even to question it.

'Julius and Orela,' Chloe was saying, 'are unfortunately a central complication in the urgent matters which concern us.'

'A complication?'

'You mustn't think us disloyal. You have to understand that our prime concern is with the Noosphere and those who use it – the vast communality of the human race. Julius and Orela are representatives, not rulers.'

'And you're unhappy with them?'

'We're concerned that their interests are no longer the same as those they serve.'

I remembered something from one of my dreams.

'Are they *unstable*?'

'They're serving beyond their time,' Lucian said. 'That fact creates many imponderables.'

'There are sound reasons for having a fixed span of mortality,' Chloe said. 'It's not simply, as you might suppose, a question of population limitation. Though we can halt the decay of flesh, we can't prevent the mind from eventually beginning to wither through sheer weight of experience. Beyond a hundred years, there is the increasing risk of dislocation, imbalance and even insanity.'

'Julius and Orela are now twenty years beyond their allotted span,' Lucian said. 'They've held their positions for more than sixty. In the past, most Advocates served little longer than twenty-five years. Then they would either pass on or retire to live out their lives in private.'

'You saw the shrine of Oldengland,' Chloe said. 'He was one of the first Advocates.'

'The tradition is that the Advocates choose their successors during their terms,' Lucian continued. 'Unfortunately, Julius and Orela have consistently rejected the candidates which the Noosphere has produced over the past half-century. Successors in waiting should have been adopted many years ago, but none has been.'

'They rejected you two?'

'You must understand,' said Lucian, 'this isn't a matter of personal grievance. To become Advocate is to surrender your own life entirely to the service of humanity. At least, that was formerly the case. For us personally there was some relief in being spared this sacrifice. Nevertheless we, and others like us, have come to believe that Julius and Orela are deliberately obstructing the appointment of their successors.'

'Do they have children of their own?' Nina asked.

Chloe shook her head. 'It's a condition that they accept sterility, and that any children previously sired are ineligible for the position. There's no dynastic component. The appointments are made purely on individual merit.'

'It sounds to me as if they just want to cling to their status.'

'That's what we fear,' Chloe agreed. 'We certainly believe

that their judgement had become increasingly clouded the longer they've remained in office.'

'Apart from anything else,' said Lucian, 'it sets a very bad example. How long will the people continue to accept the wisdom of a hundred-year span if their representatives are blatantly living on beyond their terms?'

'Of course,' Chloe said, 'Julius and Orela insist publicly that they're merely holding their offices in trust until suitable successors are found.'

'And the people believe this?'

'The Advocates are popular. They've always travelled widely among the worlds of the Noospace. Both have the common touch, and both have increasingly used their positions blatantly to court popularity. That's why we can't enforce the appointment of successors against their wishes. Yet the need is very pressing, especially now that the Dementia is beginning to spread unchecked.'

'Just what is this sickness?' I said. 'It's hard to believe that no one has any idea what causes it.'

'You've seen its effects,' said Chloe. 'It's a form of mental derangement characterized by violent mania and a complete loss of social control. Until we isolate the infective agent, we can do nothing except attempt to contain it. Unfortunately the Advocates don't seem to appreciate the extent of the danger. They make public shows of concern to appease the people, but little beyond that.'

'I thought they'd established the Sanctuary and organized the plagueships.'

'That's true,' Lucian conceded. 'But it was done without consulting the Noocracy or the people at large. We know nothing of what treatment is being carried out. The biotecs assembled there are answerable only to Orela and Julius themselves.'

'We're convinced,' said Chloe, 'that they've both forgotten that they're servants rather than leaders. They've become secretive and exclusive. That is why it's vital we appoint successors.'

'Somehow,' Nina said, 'this is connected with the womb, isn't it?'

'The womb was grown here,' Chloe replied. 'It was the latest of many, but this time it was done without the Advocates' knowledge using the most advanced techniques available. It was designed to be self-sufficient, because there were rumours that the Advocates would no longer countenance the production of potential successors and might actually have it destroyed should they find out.'

'Destroyed?' said Nina. 'I thought you valued the preservation of life above everything.'

'It's one of our fundamental precepts,' Lucian said. 'It was only then that many of us here began to accept the true extent of Julius and Orela's derangement.'

'We worked in great secrecy,' Chloe said. 'Even here the Advocates have many partisans who might have betrayed us. In the event, we were only partially successful. By the time we had developed the womb, there were already whisperings that our scheme was known by those loyal to Julius and Orela. There was no alternative but to fly the womb to a place of safety where it could be nurtured and brought to maturity without threat. We chose Mars, where a community sympathetic to our aims existed. But the ship was sabotaged in flight, the womb itself barely escaping destruction. The rest of the story you know.'

I thought about it. 'Julius and Orela ordered the ship destroyed?'

'They'll stop at nothing to maintain their positions,' said Lucian.

'And they had Marea's husbands killed?'

'At the very least, their agents interpreted their orders in the most brutal way. We know they would do anything to gain possession of the womb in order to destroy it. It represents the most direct threat to their power.'

'We, too, would like to recover the womb,' Chloe said, 'but we can only work secretly within the Noocracy, or through unofficial agents. Most arbiters remain faithful servants of the Advocates, despite their misgivings. They follow their instructions implicitly, as they've always done.'

'So Bezile was also following orders?'

'She was acting as a high official of the Noocracy, whose

power is ultimately symbolized by the Advocates. Julius and Orela seldom show their hands directly, but there are many ways in which they can make their will known.'

'And the Augmenters?' I said. 'What's their place in this?'

For the first time, neither Chloe nor Lucian was immediately forthcoming.

'They have their own agenda,' Lucian said at last, 'which is neither ours nor the Advocates'. They wish to supplant what we have now, to change the very human fabric, alter our whole relationship with the Noospace.'

'By redesigning the human race?'

'The people have always rejected the idea of radical physical changes. The Augmenters represent a minority view.'

'So you disapprove of them?'

'I hope we'll be able to show you just how *undesirable* their programme would be.'

A silence fell. Outside the window a sequence of lights pulsed along a golden band, then was gone. Traffic? I knew nothing, could not even begin to imagine how this place, the moral and spiritual centre of the species, functioned.

'We're asking for your help,' Chloe said, 'because you're in a position to intervene in our favour.'

'Intervene?' I said. 'What do you mean?'

'In your last dream you were able to communicate with your host, the man called Tunde. This is as we intended. We've forged a link between you and certain others whose lives you've experienced. Their minds are accessible to you through the Noospace. Not only can you speak to them, you may also be able to influence their actions.'

This was new. I looked at her with outright disbelief.

'The best way for you to understand is to experience it yourself. To dream a dream in which you can participate.'

'We will also be able to assist you if you require it,' said Lucian, 'by providing you with information and knowledge which is available to us here.'

Nina said, 'What are you suggesting?'

'That you make your next dream an adventure,' said Chloe, 'so we can prove to you that what we say is true. I'm sure you'd consider it a virtuous thing to help the man called Tunde rescue the woman Marea from Io.'

'Much of the story you've dreamt so far had unfolded before you were fully reborn,' said Lucian. 'You've merely been witnessing its consequences. As have we. The woman Marea in particular deserves a better fate.'

'Then why don't you intervene directly?'

'And openly act against the Advocates? What would we gain but the saving of an admittedly innocent life? There are thousands of millions of lives at stake here. If you acted as our agents, you would protect those of us who are trying to save them. And you would also know that what we've told you is true.'

'There would be no danger to you,' said Chloe. 'Even if your enterprise ended in disaster, if, say, the man called Tunde died, you would be quite unharmed. We can withdraw you at any time, and you can be sure we'd do so the instant we felt it necessary. Having invested so much effort in bringing you back to life, we have no intention of losing you.'

'I don't understand how this is possible,' Nina said.

'It's possible,' said Lucian, 'because we're here, and we have direct access to the Noosphere. And because we already know that your minds have the capacity for the vicarious experience of other lives.'

'We'd both go together?' said Nina.

'In a sense you wouldn't go anywhere,' said Chloe. 'You would remain here, under our supervision. But your minds – your spirits, if you will – they would travel with your host.'

'Together?'

'Together.'

'And we'd be able to communicate with one another?'

Chloe nodded. 'You may discover other capacities, too, but it is best that you experience them yourselves.'

'This is insane,' I said.

'I think you know that it isn't.'

'And if we refuse?'

'Then nothing will happen. Events will take their course for better or worse.'

'I have to tell you,' Lucian said, 'it will be for the worse.'

*

'Who are you?'

'*My name is Nathan.*'

'I can hear your voice so clearly. Are you an ancestor?'

'*I'm not a relative. I'm alive.*'

I was powerfully aware of Tunde's fear and incomprehension. Beside me I felt Nina's presence, an echo of my own. I sensed Tunde's daughter withdrawing her hands in shock from the prayer terminal. Nina seemed to have gone with her.

'What are you?' Tunde said.

'*A human being, just like you. I'm communicating with you through the Noosphere. That's where I am.*'

'Mortal?'

'*Second time around.*'

This naturally puzzled Tunde, but he did not question it.

'*You remember Marea?*'

'What?'

'*We know she passed on the womb to you. She's in a labour camp on Io, due for blanking.*'

Tunde didn't even ask how I knew this: the superstitious awe surrounding the shrines and the Noosphere made anything possible.

'They imprisoned her?'

'*She's lucky she wasn't killed. Did you never stop to think that if they were pursuing you they would also want her?*'

Tunde's shame was profound; but it was also very belated.

'I didn't intend any harm to come to her.'

'*It's time you made amends.*'

'How?'

'*By rescuing her.*'

Surprise and confusion. A wash of apprehension and fear.

'*I'll help you. There's a lot I know.*'

'I can't do this!'

'*You must!*'

'My daughter. She's only a child.'

'*No harm will come to her, I promise you.*'

'I've got somebody with me,' Cori announced. 'She says she'll look after me.'

Tunde opened his eyes and stared at her. She sounded quite calm and unfrightened.

Tunde was a little panicked. 'What's happening?' he demanded.

'*We're here to help you,*' I assured him. '*You must trust us implicitly, follow our instructions exactly. Now leave here and make your way to the terminus.*'

'What?'

'*We're going to find you a ship for the flight to Io.*'

The man was in awe of me, I knew, as if he were speaking to a ghost or an angel. For a while he sat rooted in indecision, but I did everything I could to instil confidence and trust. Disengaging himself and his daughter from the terminal, he grasped Cori's hand and stumbled out of the booth.

The contact was not broken; I was firmly lodged in his startled mind.

As they were making their way out of the shrine, the intercessor who had admitted them approached.

'Was your communion satisfactory?' she asked by rote.

Tunde paused. For a moment I thought he was going to blurt out everything.

'Yes,' he replied at last, before pushing past her and hurrying Cori out into the street.

There were crowds everywhere. Some sort of carnival was in progress, naked dancers disporting themselves on young serpentines, hatchling blimps floating overhead festooned with holograms advertising stimstore specials and the latest in optic interactives. We pushed through the jostling throng, and I heard Cori say, 'Yes, I understand.'

Tunde had not spoken to her, so it had to be Nina. The child remained calm, unlike her agitated father. I lacked the patience to soothe him; I sat back, somewhat exhilarated that I was there. This was as real as my previous dreams, yet now I was, as Chloe and Lucian had promised, actually taking part in it.

We boarded a centipede crammed with home-going commuters, Tunde dropping coins into its cashmaw. The 'pede squirmed out through the traffic, presently entering a long tunnel whose mirrored surfaces reflected its segmented black flanks with their ranks of glazed faces framed at its oval portals. And then out again, the city already behind us, the 'pede halting to excrete passengers, now clattering across a bowled brasswood bridge. A big sailship was passing by below, its voluminous white fins rippling as it propelled itself along, several young surrounding it, learning from their parent the arts of flight. I was seeing this for the first time, and yet I had the vocabulary to comprehend it, just as I had done when my dreams were unwilled.

The 'pede stopped at an outlying settlement to disgorge even more passengers. Tunde remained nervous, cowed. He cast a glance at Cori, who seemed to be murmuring to herself.

'*Your daughter's fine,*' I said. '*My companion is with her, and she'll be safe.*'

'Is that who she's talking to?'

'*Yes.*'

'What do you want with us?'

'*I've told you. You have a debt to repay.*'

'I'm an ordinary man.'

'*All you have to do is trust me. Trust me, and do exactly as I say.*'

I felt such a sense of power, generated as much by Tunde's awe of me as anything else. Of course I was conscious that it was the same sort of power wielded over Nina and myself by Chloe and Lucian. I was aware of them as distant presences in the background. And now, as the 'pede wove out of a stormtree forest and the terminus came in sight, they began to feed me information so that I could instruct Tunde on how to find the ship to take him to Io. It came in an inchoate way, mixing information with mental imagery showing the geography of the place and the siting of the ship we were going to take. Through the Noosphere Chloe and Lucian had detailed knowledge of flight schedules throughout the Settled Worlds, and I understood how they intended I should make use of it.

We disembarked at the main entrance but, under my instructions, followed a gravity trail that led us away from the passenger terminals. Cloudscrub and the hulking backs of loading bays screened us from sight as we skirted the perimeter wall until we approached the very edge of the terminus, where the runways jutted out over the Hercules Sea itself. And here we came upon an aquavine that had found purchase in the rocky earth; it had coiled up, clinging to the wall, its uppermost tendrils gripping the top like splayed fingers.

'Here?' Tunde said. He already knew.

'*We climb over,*' I said.

Something occurred to him. 'I've left our baggage in the shrine!'

'*It's too late to go back for it now.*'

'It's all we had!'

'*Tunde, you've got to help us. Marea's going to die if you don't.*'

'I'm afraid.'

'*Trust me. We'll be fine.*'

This was easy to say when I was sure that I was in no physical danger myself; but I was so glad to be doing something active, even through someone else, that I scarcely gave it a thought.

Dusk was falling, the banded sky lavender and gold. We helped Cori up first; she showed no fear, and scrambled to the top in a few instants. More gingerly, Tunde followed. He was a big man, and the vine stems began to buckle under his weight as he ascended. Then he put his hand around a ripe pod, which promptly burst with a crack, showering him with water. He almost lost his purchase, and it was only the sound of Cori's laughter that made him hang on. He hauled himself up, joining Cori at the top.

We looked down on a compound set aside from the rest of the terminus. The ships in the numbered docking spaces resembled armoured beetles, built for speed and robustness. They bristled with antennae and complex proboscises.

Tunde froze. 'This is a politia dock,' he said.

'*That's correct.*'

'Those are interdictors. They're *armed*.'

'*We won't be taking any of them. That's the one we're going to be flying.*'

One ship stood alone in the shadows of the control tower. It was a squat crab-like craft, smaller than the others but fast and manoeuvrable. A scuttle, used for rapid deployment of politia in both suborbital and interworld flights. The sight of them alone was often enough to quell a disturbance or send rioters darting for cover.

'This is madness,' Tunde said. 'What am I supposed to do? Walk in there and take it? Through a razorthorn hedge?'

Beyond the parapet wall the compound was surrounded by tall, tangled razorthorn, its ciliated foliage responsive to the slightest touch, launching clusters of barbed seeds that could kill the incautious intruder. It was such an effective barrier that the compound had no other guard; the ships were unattended, asleep, the only evidence of occupancy being the pale light leaking through a faulty lid on a control tower window.

At this point I heard a distant flapping and a great rustling breath which rapidly grew louder. Tunde spun around as a cargo blimp rose up from the ravine, gulping in air, pendulous wattles dangling over us. I knew from Chloe and Lucian that it was an unmanned craft and that they had diverted it for us.

The hollow sacs at the end of each wattle were packed with vegetables and fruit for the morning market in Antaeus. But the one that hung closest was empty.

Before I could tell Tunde what to do, Cori had hoisted herself into the sac. Seeing this, Tunde immediately followed.

The sac was leathery and elastic, redolent of roseplums. It enfolded us snugly, Tunde putting an arm around his daughter for extra security. Its new cargo aboard, the blimp drifted down in utter silence over the compound. It slowed and descended close to the scuttle. When it was low enough, Cori jumped down.

Tunde jumped after her, landing awkwardly and muffling a groan. He had jarred his ankle: I felt the pain. But it was nothing serious. He straightened. The blimp was already rising, exhaling gases from its capacious rear end so that a ripe wind blew over us as it headed away towards the city, resuming its original journey.

The scuttle had opened one eye and was peering down at us. Beyond it the compound remained deserted, quiet.

'What do you want?' it said in an irritable voice.

I told Tunde to say: 'Access.' Then I gave him a string of words and digits which meant nothing to me. He repeated them faithfully.

'This is really most inconvenient,' the ship said. 'I wasn't due out for another twelve hours.' But a door opened in its midriff, and down came a ramp flap.

Again Tunde hesitated, and again it was Cori who led the way. I was grateful for the daughter's presence, for Nina's influence. Where she went, he followed.

We hurried down a corridor to the bridgehead. The ship was slowly awakening, turning on its lights, powering up its propulsion systems.

'You aren't even in uniform,' I heard it grumbling. 'This is an emergency, you say.'

We had said nothing of the sort, but the code that Chloe and Lucian had given me instructed the ship to reverse its original flight plan and follow Tunde's instructions. Irritability was evidently inbred into it, but it would have to obey its human operator.

'There's a spare uniform in the closet,' the ship said briskly. 'Perhaps you'd like to put it on.'

It was clear the ship felt Tunde to be improperly dressed. A phosphor dot was winking over one of the closets at the rear of the bridgehead. I told Tunde to open it. Inside hung the uniform of a politia officer.

'*Put it on,*' I instructed him.

'I can't—'

'*Don't argue. We don't want the ship becoming suspicious, do we?*'

He did as he was bid. The jet fabric was self-fitting, extending itself to cover his large frame, braided collar and cuffs adjusting to the correct length. Tunde regarded himself in the closet mirror.

'*You look the part,*' I told him.

'What are we supposed to be doing?'

This time he did not speak aloud, but addressed me internally.

'*Take control of the ship. Let's get out of here.*'

The ship had raised two seats, one smaller than the other to accommodate Cori.

'I don't usually carry minors,' it complained. 'It's quite irregular.'

It had a man's voice, and I wondered whether it had been deliberately designed to be finicky. Ships' characters were largely bioengineered depending on their function, but their overall personalities were never entirely predictable.

'I presume she's your daughter,' the ship was saying.

Tunde didn't reply.

'This is an official flight. I hardly think we should have a child aboard.'

I felt the slow burn of Tunde's irritation.

'Listen,' he told the ship, 'if you don't shut it right now, I'm going to close you down and pilot on manual.'

There was a moment's pause, and then the ship said, in a more tentative tone: '*Is* she your daughter?'

'None of your business. Initiate launch.'

The ship immediately obeyed, activating its vertical thrusters.

'*Good for you,*' I told Tunde. '*It's time you started asserting yourself.*'

'You all right?' he asked Cori as the seat webbing enfolded them.

She nodded; she was fine.

The ship began to lift, rapidly picking up speed. The console optic winked on: the control tower was querying authorization for the flight. From Chloe and Lucian I conveyed another code, which Tunde transmitted. Presently the optic indicated clearance, by which time the terminus was rapidly dwindling beneath us.

'This is really exciting!' Cori remarked.

'I'm glad you think so,' Tunde said drily.

The bridgehead was filled with the thrusters' roaring, and the acceleration pressed us back in our seats. Beyond the eye sockets, the sky rapidly faded to black.

'Maximum speed for Io?' the ship queried.

'Yes,' Tunde replied.

Fear was welling in him, and he did not want to contemplate the idea of having only the scuttle between himself and empty space.

'Shall I cocoon you for the duration?'

Tunde didn't hesitate: 'Do so. Close your eyes, Cori.'

The seat webbing began to exude a foam, which rapidly enveloped us.

'I estimate the flight time as five hours thirty-five minutes,' was the last thing I heard before the foam blotted out everything and we slept.

I drifted in darkness, and I thought I sensed Chloe and Lucian's presence in the background. They did not speak, but it was comforting to feel them there, to know there was a link with the conscious world.

'Nathan?'

It was Nina. Her voice was disembodied but she spoke normally, as if she were close.

'I'm here,' I said.

'Where do you imagine we are?'

'Still in their heads, I suppose. But they're sleeping, so there's only this.'

'It should be frightening. We're just pure mentalities. Yet I feel calm.'

'Is the girl all right?'

'She's loving every minute of it.'

'She wasn't afraid of you being in her head?'

'I explained as much as I could, and she accepted it. She's bright, and she likes the idea of being important. All children do.'

'That sounds like the voice of experience.'

'Does it?'

There was a long pause, and I could almost sense her discomfort.

'Anything?' I asked.

She gave the mental equivalent of a sigh. 'Perhaps it's better that I'll never know.'

Her presence was strong, even though I could see nothing. At that moment I think we both had a powerful sense of our missing lives, and of a certitude that we would not know them again.

'Can you believe this?' I said.

'It's like a dream within a dream. Is Tunde coping?'

'He's scared to his boots. But as long as you keep the girl happy, he'll cooperate.'

Another silence, then: 'I'm not sure this is right. We're using them.'

'Maybe so,' I conceded. 'But I know deep down he wants to do the decent thing and rescue Marea. He owes her. We're acting as his conscience.'

Before she could say anything further, I felt the presence of Chloe and Lucian growing stronger. They began to communicate, instructing us on what we were to do next.

When Tunde woke he was disorientated for a moment, and he stared uncomprehendingly at the hazy umber panorama that filled the eye sockets.

'Beginning descent,' the ship informed him. 'Touchdown in approximately thirty minutes, Haemus Base.'

'*Wakey wakey,*' I said, to remind him I was there.

He jolted at this, compelling me to say, '*Keep calm. Everything's going to be fine. Follow my instructions and we'll have Marea out of there in no time.*'

He focused his concern on Cori, who was beginning to stir as the last of the cocoon shrivelled away. She gave a big yawn, opened her eyes and grinned at him.

Io was leprous, its tawny surface blotched and pockmarked like a bruised and bloodied skin. Cori announced that she wanted to explore the scuttle before we landed. Tunde and the ship were against it, but Nina and I overruled them, leading her aft.

The scuttle was compact, its passenger section divided into two broad but low-ceilinged chambers, designed for the transportation of politia squadrons. Beyond this the central corridor led to the ship's shrine, a hermetic room whose curving walls and ceiling focused on a prayer terminal with a pair of seats. Unlike most ship shrines, it looked pristine, its chrome and ivorine surfaces framing a steel-grey optic.

'*Austere,*' I remarked inwardly to Tunde.

'It's spooky,' Cori said gleefully. 'I like it!'

I was about to suggest she sit at the terminal when Chloe

and Lucian communicated something that made me stop. And made the pliable Tunde agitated again.

'Let's get out of here,' he said, taking Cori by the arm.

At this point we felt a buffeting, and the ship announced that we should hasten to secure ourselves.

We hurried back to the bridgehead and got webbed in. As the scuttle decelerated with great hissing of its retros, the pressure rose and Cori exclaimed that her ears had popped.

'Do you want me to land?' the ship enquired. 'Or will you bring me down yourself?'

Tunde stared as if hypnotized by the rush of the ground towards us.

'You do it,' he said urgently.

'I'm hungry,' Cori announced.

'You can't possibly be!' said Tunde. 'Not now.'

She was scrolling through the armrest menu, eyes widening at the displays of desserts.

'I wouldn't eat anything until we're down,' the ship advised her in the manner of an exasperated parent.

Dark blotches became craters and lakes and lava flows as we closed on the surface. Lateral lids began clearing the eye sockets of fine dust.

Cori selected a bananamint spiral drenched in toffice syrup and dusted with rainbow sherbet. The ship grumpily extruded a feedline to deliver into her hands, complaining that it had never before been required to serve *confectioneries*.

I could feel Tunde's rising fear, and I seized hold of his mind, telling him to let me take control, let me do all the talking. Part of that fear was caused by my presence in his mind, and only his concern for Cori prevented him from relinquishing complete control to me so that he could hide like a passenger in his own body. The base veered into view, a ragged dark cross. Orange dust blossomed, obscuring it.

The ship bucked, tilted, manoeuvring for the best position. We dropped, and an instant later there was a lurch, then a recoil which flung Tunde tight against the webbing. Cori gave a squeak comprising fright and delight in equal measure.

'We're down,' the ship announced.

I was sure it had been trying to teach us a lesson by a

deliberately heavy-handed landing. And it had worked: Cori's bananamint spiral was sitting in her lap.

The ship retracted the webbing, and I let Tunde occupy himself with cleaning his daughter. By the time this was done, the dust was settling outside.

'Listen,' I said to Cori, 'you're not supposed to be here, so you're going to have to hide.'

She stared at me, wide-eyed. 'Are you Nathan?'

The name still did not seem mine, but I had no other. I nodded.

'Is my father there?'

'Yes. He's fine.' Tunde seemed content to let me take over whenever I pleased. 'You have to help us. I want you to hide. Do you know where?'

She thought about it. 'The shrine.'

'*No!*' Tunde cried, but I was ready and stopped him from saying it aloud.

'You'll be safe there,' I told her. 'But on no account are you to try to use the prayer terminal, understand?'

Tunde was aghast, but Cori looked at me as if I was stating the obvious.

'Nina's already explained it,' she said.

I could almost see a hint of Nina's smile on her lips. I wondered exactly how much she had explained.

Tunde remained tense, but I assured him that Nina wouldn't let his daughter come to any harm.

'Does Father love this woman Marea?'

I stepped aside to let him answer; but all I experienced was the confusion of his emotions – emotions in which the fear for Cori's safety was paramount.

'He obviously cares a great deal for her,' I said.

'Call us if you need us,' she said in Nina's inflection. Then she went off down the corridor.

I had to quell Tunde again, but his resistance was brittle: I think he was still frightened of me. Through the socket I could see a small procession approaching from the base. At its head was, I knew, Governor Andreas. A cordon of armed guards flanked him, enclosing two figures. I zoomed one of the optics.

Both were suited, but it was obvious they were Marea and Vargo.

'Right,' I told the ship, 'get ready to open up.'

I donned a suit and visored helmet while one of the orifices on the control ridge ejected an imprimatur shard. Then I went down to the airvalve, surprised that I felt no fear.

Andreas and his escort had halted a respectful distance from the ship. I saluted him as I approached, palming my comlink.

'We weren't expecting you until tomorrow,' Andreas said.

'Change of orders,' I told him. 'She's being taken back to Mars.'

'What?'

I handed him the imprimatur that Chloe and Lucian had fabricated while we were in transit. He slotted the shard into a compad, scrutinized it, did not seem pleased.

'This is irregular. I was told the sentence was to be carried out here.'

'High Arbiter Miushme-Adewoyin sends her most personal apologies.' I was reciting what Chloe and Lucian had instructed me to say. 'It is an urgent and sensitive matter. She greatly appreciates your cooperation and discretion.'

He eyed me. 'We came here expecting to see a sentence carried out.'

I did not budge. 'I'm merely following orders.'

He was a hard man, naturally suspicious. But I wore the uniform of the politia and had come in the ship he was expecting.

He turned to the guards. 'Bring her forward.'

Marea approached, Vargo at her side. My visor was mirrored, so she could not see my face. But I could see hers: it was blank with terror.

I switched to an open channel. 'You will come with me,' I said.

It was Vargo who spoke: 'She wants me with her.'

I knew this was traditional: the condemned were always allowed the company of one other person before the execution.

'There's no need,' I said. 'She's being shipped to Mars.'

This threw him for a moment. 'She's asked me to be her mentor, give her a proper farewell.'

'The arrangements have been changed.'

'It's her final request,' he insisted. 'You can't deny her.'

Given the circumstances, it was brave of him to speak up. Andreas reacted angrily, telling him to mind his mouth or he'd be sent back to the rockface. Then I sensed Chloe and Lucian telling me that I was to let Vargo aboard, take him with me as well. It seemed to be a spur-of-the-moment decision.

I didn't like this sudden change of plan, but Marea's patent terror swayed it.

'That's all right,' I said. 'It's permitted. He can come aboard for a few minutes.'

Andreas was not happy. He directed two guards to accompany us, but I told him this wasn't necessary.

'These are two dangerous criminals,' he insisted.

There was a pistol in my suit holster. I unsheathed it. 'There won't be any problems.'

Marea was regarding me with a strange expression. Though distorted and muffled by the suitcoms, it was Tunde's voice. I wondered if she had recognized it.

Andreas bristled: he had obviously wanted to be there at the end; but the new orders took precedence.

'He can have ten minutes,' he said. 'Then I want him back.'

I didn't like his manner, and I decided to make a point. 'The prisoner is under my jurisdiction now, Governor. Your man will be returned to you when I'm ready.'

I marched Marea and Vargo up the ramp into the ship, holding the pistol at their backs. Neither spoke. I directed them to the bridgehead. As soon as we had reached it, I told them, 'Get webbed in.'

'What?' This was Vargo.

'We're getting out of here. Move it!'

I waved the pistol, urging them into the seats.

'Ship,' I said, 'initiate emergency launch.'

The ship made a sound as if it was clearing its throat. 'Are we in danger?'

'Just do it! And give me another seat!'

The ship went into action immediately, retracting its ramp and powering its engines. It extruded another seat beside

Marea, and I sat down hastily; Marea and Vargo were already webbed.

'Keep an eye on the governor and his party,' I told the ship.

One of its optics focused in on the governor's party. Andreas had already realized what was happening. He and his guards had begun to retreat.

The ship lurched, and began to lift. I felt Tunde's anxiety rising.

'Is Cori secure?' I asked the ship.

'Quite,' it snapped back. 'The shrine is the safest place inside me. Do you want maximum acceleration?'

'No.' I wanted to remain conscious. 'Optimum speed and flightpath at normal tolerance.'

'I thought you said this was an emergency.'

'Dammit, do it!'

Through one of the ship's sockets, I saw Andreas looking up at us. Then he was swallowed by the blossoming dust cloud as we sped away.

Though at tolerance, the acceleration was fierce without protection, and I was pressed back in my seat. Long minutes passed. Then the ship said:

'Three craft, probably interceptors, closing fast.'

I struggled to look at the displays.

'One G,' I said to the ship. Immediately it began to slow.

An optic gave the local topography and the likely origin of the craft: Haemus Base itself. So Andreas had moved swiftly to summon back-up; he intended to hunt us down.

I sensed guidance from Chloe and Lucian. We were within a few minutes' flight time of Loki, one of the moon's major volcanoes and currently active.

'I want you to fly into the Loki plume,' I told the ship.

'What?' It sounded outraged. 'Do you realize the danger? The debris could clog my respiratory system, bring on a seizure.'

A pointed silence was my only reply. Marea and Vargo watched me, saying nothing, wondering no doubt what the hell was going on.

'Very well,' the ship said with great forbearance. 'On your own head be it.'

I watched the tracker optic. The three ships continued to close. Then suddenly a grey fog enveloped us, a fog which rapidly darkened to black.

We were high above the peak itself, but the plume was extensive, molten rock and sulphur ejected explosively from below the moon's crust, a massive cloud fountaining out over hundreds of kilometres of Io's surface, dampening down Jupiter's light in the region for months, coating everything below it in black snow, making life even more miserable than ever for the unwilling benighted inhabitants of the moon.

For a long while there was only the roar of the drive cells, a roar increasingly accompanied by the crepitation of dust particles. Presently I ordered the ship to exit the plume. Minutes later we broke free, and the ship was flooded with amber light as Jupiter hung, huge and gibbous, in the darkness of interplanetary space.

I waited a few moments, then said to the ship: 'Have we lost them?'

It made a throaty sound. 'There is no pursuit.'

Its voice was hoarse, though I was sure it was only for effect. The bridgehead began to fill with grinding and hissing sounds as the ship announced that it was conducting a pneumatic evacuation of its entire propulsion system 'to expel particulate matter of volcanic origin'.

I told the ship to relax the webbing across Marea and Vargo's chests so that they were able to free their arms. For a few moments nothing happened. Then the webbing partially withdrew, stopped, then finally retracted fully.

Marea and Vargo removed their visors and masks. Marea was thin and pale, but it was her hairless head that shocked Tunde. Vargo was also bald.

'Who the hell are you?' Vargo said.

I took my own helmet off. Tunde was recovering from his initial surprise, and I let him come more to the fore.

Marea looked astounded, then delighted, to see him.

'Tunde,' she said at last.

He grinned at her.

'I can't believe it's you. How did you come to be here? You knew where I was?'

He nodded, his grin hiding the fact that he was taken aback by the sight of her.

'You've joined the politia?'

An echo of his old charm reasserted itself. He winked at her. 'After a fashion.'

Cori appeared, safe and smiling. She ran to her father's side.

'This is one of my daughters,' he told Marea. He introduced her.

Marea was still staring at him as if he were unreal. 'How did you find us?' she wanted to know.

There was nothing for it but to tell her the truth. I did my best to hold back and let Tunde explain in his own words. He gave his account of what had happened to the womb, of his flight to Titan, his year spent hiding there. And then he told of his encounter with myself and Nina in the shrine, of how I had 'inhabited' him, helped him steal the ship and ultimately rescue her.

When he had finished talking, Marea and Vargo exchanged incredulous glances. Then the ship began a high-pitched warbling, and I saw that some of the status displays were flashing alarms.

'Ship,' I said, 'what's happening?'

'Vent strunt treckle,' the ship responded. 'Central rampt tessiflera. Ick.'

'What?'

More gibberish followed. Vargo scrutinized the sensitories on the flight ridge.

'We're drifting back towards Io,' he announced. 'There's cortical interruptions, short-circuiting by the look of it. Most likely ash blockages in the central controlling system from the plume.'

I sought Chloe and Lucian's guidance. They could do nothing except confirm what Vargo had said.

Vargo himself was waiting. 'Well?'

'What do you suggest?' I asked.

He could not believe that the answer wasn't obvious to me. 'You'll have to override the ship's neural network and fly it yourself.'

He said it as a statement, but neither Tunde nor I had ever piloted a ship. Neither had Chloe and Lucian.

'You *do* know how to fly it?' Vargo said.

I shook my head.

Vargo made a contemptuous noise. He sat down in the pilot's seat and reached for navigation sensitory.

'Pleag releag,' said the ship. 'Nip spung.'

Marea stood there in silence, gazing at Tunde with a strange expression while Tunde watched Vargo wrestle for control of the ship. Once again, the sight of empty space – the thought that we were marooned in it – was beginning to make a cold panic trickle through him.

Then the star-field swayed and shifted. Presently Vargo said: 'We're getting there.'

The ship was pulling out of Io's gravitational field and resuming its outward-bound course.

'I think this is in all our best interests,' the ship announced at great volume. 'Whenfh mimm undranglar—'

Vargo shut down its vocals.

'Is this true?' Marea said. 'Is that really how it happened?'

She was addressing Tunde. It was hard for him to look at her without feeling uncomfortable.

'It's quite true,' Cori said; she spoke with Nina's intonation. 'We were revived on the Noosphere, and we can gain access to certain minds through the shrines.'

Marea's eyes did not move from Tunde.

'Let me get this clear,' she said. 'You *sold* the womb on, then went into hiding before finally this Nathan person came into your head and helped you fly the scuttle to Io?'

'I know it's hard to credit, but it's true.' He essayed a grin, realizing he had every reason to feel delighted since we had actually pulled it off.

'You bastard!' she said, and slapped him hard across the face.

Nine

I was in darkness again. I could feel Tunde's cheek tingling, see the rage on Marea's face, but the pain was receding, the scuttle gone, leaving me adrift in a featureless blackness.

'Nina?'

A silence. Then: 'Nathan?'

I felt her approach – or rather it was as if her mind swam closer to me.

'I thought you might have stayed with Cori,' I said.

'We withdrew you both,' came the voice of Chloe. 'It seemed prudent.'

'I don't understand,' said Nina. 'Weren't we in real time with them?'

'Of course,' said Chloe.

'And now we're back – where?'

'In the Noosphere. Or rather its Noospace.'

'How is this possible?'

It was Lucian who spoke: 'Once you're embedded in a mind through a prayer terminal, a permanent link is forged through the Noosphere. We can return you here at any time, and you'll also be able to revisit Tunde or Cori because an imprint of your consciousness remains with them.'

'We can go back to them at any time?'

'With our help, yes.'

'We could return right now?'

'If it was necessary.'

This only served to deepen my suspicion. The darkness, the bodilessness, was infuriating. I wanted to be able to see them, to make my presence felt in every way I could.

'You didn't tell us this before,' I said.

'We explained the necessity of proceeding slowly,' Chloe replied. 'Isn't it better that you gradually discover these capacities for yourself?'

'Why did you withdraw us?' Nina asked.

'Tunde and the others are safe for the time—'

'What about Vargo?' I interrupted. 'You didn't tell me he would be coming along with us until the last moment.'

Part of my anger rose from the feeling that we were being manipulated, part of it from the abrupt withdrawal. I had enjoyed participating in Tunde's adventure; I had enjoyed my capacity to influence it.

Lucian said, 'We only learned at the last moment that Marea had requested he be her mentor at the end. It would have been difficult to refuse her this final consolation. And, as it turned out, his presence is invaluable. The others will need his piloting skills now that the ship is crippled.'

'I don't like this. How's Tunde going to explain our sudden disappearance?'

'Tunde must wait. There have been new developments.'

Nina was close to me; had we been physical we would have held one another.

'Where are our bodies?' I demanded.

'They remain where they are,' said Chloe. 'On the Noosphere. With us.'

It was hard to retain a proper sense of orientation, to decide where Nina and I truly 'were'. This was not made any easier by Chloe and Lucian's constant talk of 'the Noosphere' and 'Noospace' in different contexts. Sometimes they seemed to mean actual physical locations – the Moon and all the Settled Worlds – sometimes they obviously meant the transubstantial realm through which communions were conducted with ancestors, the dark void which we presently inhabited. It was empty to us, I assumed, because our ancestors had died long before the Noosphere was established.

'Can we return to them?' Nina was asking.

'If you wish,' said Chloe. 'But we'd prefer it if you would allow us to let you dream again.'

'Bezile?' said Nina.

'She's just left communion. The Advocates have held a

council, and there were many revelations. It's vital to us that you experience what she did. There's little time.'

For once I could sense their urgency beneath the measured tones. Whatever else was going on, they were definitely eager for us to cooperate.

'Are we going to be *inhabiting* her?' I asked.

'Not as with Tunde,' Lucian answered. 'You'll be a spectator only. Bezile is no longer in the shrine, but her communion has been recorded and you'll experience what she did. As if it were happening for the first time.'

I let a silence extend, wondering if Nina would speak. She was a calmer presence than I, more accepting of our situation yet far from passive. I knew she was intrigued and wanted to experience the dream.

'You'd see the Advocates in the flesh,' said Chloe. 'You must be curious about them.'

'We urge you to help us,' added Lucian.

'We'd go together?' I said. 'Nina and I?'

'You would dream the same reality,' Chloe said.

'We're late. We'll be lucky if we arrive on time.'

Even by his usual nervy standards, Luis was fretful. He kept fussing with Bezile's robes, primping and smoothing and straightening folds as her processional wound its way along the sinuous gravity trail of the twilight zone towards Icarus.

'For heaven's sake,' Bezile said, slapping his hands away. 'Do calm down! We haven't been summoned to an execution.'

'You have the text of your deliverance fully memorized?'

'Every single word,' Bezile told him with great forbearance. 'Every pause, emphasis, every metaphor and oxymoron. It is burned into my brain as if it had been branded there with microsurgery. You're acting as if this is our first time.'

'It's twelve years since the Advocates last summoned us all. And these are difficult days. Much is afoot, and the stakes are high.'

She gave a patient sigh. 'Do you intend to assail me with platitudes, Luis? Fetch some ice delights. I'm in need of a little refreshment.'

Grateful to have something practical to do, Luis scuttled

away down the long coiling corridor of their train, rocked and swayed by the weaving lateral movements of the beast, bumping blithely as he passed into the sub-arbiters, intercessors, mediators, the household stewards and the other members of the office who sat demurely in their narrow seats. The younger members of Bezile's retinue in particular would be thinking themselves fortunate to accompany her: it was not often that one got an invitation to the presence of the Advocates, rarer still that one attended in a council at their 'summer house', as they so coyly termed it.

Absently gnawing her thumbnail, Bezile gazed out through the wide-angle orb as her train began to climb the crater wall. Little did Luis know that there was a very real reason to be concerned: she might well be in disgrace following the debacle with the womb. Nothing official had been said ever since Shivaun's escape a year ago, but the announcement of the council on Mercury had been abrupt, her summons peremptory.

Well, she would bluff it out. If she couldn't trust one of her own daughters, then who could she trust? Still, it was disappointing: all those years of having your scions trained to be the perfect expressions of your wishes. And Shivaun had been the best of them, the one that had risen furthest. Bezile had even contemplated revealing her true maternity to her had the womb been successfully delivered and the Advocates suitably gratified; instead Shivaun had gone scurrying off to the ends of the Solar System, vanishing among the corpses on that tomb moon. The very thought of it was enough to make her shudder, especially since the place was crawling with Augmenters.

The processional sidewinded higher towards the crater lip. Bezile gazed back along the gravity trail with its ragged canyons dropping on either side where the bedrock had been quarried to provide landmasses for the Outer Worlds. It was almost twenty years since her last visit to Mercury, and its surface looked as bleak as ever, the riven heat-blasted rock, the inordinately long shadows at this latitude, the sheer apparent absence of life on its gouged surface. In fact several million lived here, snugly hidden away on fertile canyon faces and clustered around the polar regions, but it always seemed unutterably bleak to her eyes, cratered dust and crags, the sun, that ultimate swallower, a bloated arc looming over the ragged horizon, too fierce to acknowledge with the eye.

Luis returned with her ice delights, frozen creamed juices in pretzel wafers. Her mood mellowed when the first one she tried proved to be an astringent limecurrant. Luis sat down beside the driver, anxiously awaiting the moment when they crested the ridge so that he could convey their greetings to the palace. At fifty-two he was a stripling really, but he fussed like a dodderer in his death throes.

Peppermeat next. Then peanut fudge. A little too bland for her tastes, but she had no intention of wasting it. The crater lip loomed, and as the train surmounted it even she could not resist a certain feeling of ... well, perhaps *awe* was not quite the right word.

She'd heard that the Advocates had had their palace re-designed; in fact, it must have been reduced to protoplasm and entirely regrown. In place of the old and rather stately quin-cunx of tessellated domes, there rose a tower that had obviously been modelled after a strand of DNA, a double helix of constantly shifting rainbow colours, topped by a blob of flashing golden light that might have been contrived by putting a hyperactive photoplasm in a transparent bowl.

'Magnificent,' Luis began to burble. 'Wondrous.'

They were not words she herself would have chosen, but she kept her counsel. As the train began to descend into the crater, the rest of her retinue peered eagerly from their portholes and made obeisances to the sight. The craterscape had also been extensively remodelled: gone were the sleeping willows, the tranquil grassy spaces where one could rest while the trees wafted fragrant nepenthe; in their place were angular pools sporting corkscrew fountains and chevroned flamingoes, ge-ometrees with foliage like green ice crystals. Apparently arti-ficiality was the latest vogue in architecture and landscape design, and this was as blatant an expression of it as any.

The processional was forced to straighten down the linear road leading to the palace gates; it was the beast's least favourite mode of motion, and the least comfortable for its passengers with its jerky compression and expansion of musculature. Its hood parted, admitting the garden air. There were more murmurs of delight at the scents, but to Bezile it was redolent of nothing more than a sanitized latheratory.

Finally they docked at the palace gate. Bezile stood stately and ample in front of the gilded portal while everyone around her scurried and arranged themselves into ceremonial order. She stifled a yawn; she had found the flight from Venus tiresome and did not travel well these days.

Palace functionaries ushered them inside while Luis jabbered apologies for their lateness. Did she wish to go to her rooms and refresh herself beforehand? This was quite permissible, though time was pressing and the Advocates were eager for the council to commence. No, she told them with weary politeness, she was at their disposal – a phrase she considered rather unfortunate as soon as it was out.

An ectoplasmic levelator spiralled them up and up before finally depositing them at the mouth of a large glistening chamber full of ruddy arching surfaces and pendulous lights. It was rather like being inside the belly of a behemoth. Other parties were arranged around the chamber: she nodded to Lasantha of Terremon on Callisto, acknowledged Geordano of Titania Prime, pointedly ignored Bettwys, her sometime rival from Ishtar, a poisonous woman with a devious nature and the personal morals of the most unprincipled whore.

Her retinue spread itself around the alcove which had been set aside for them. It was close to the sweeping platform of the oratory from where she and her peers would give their deliverances, and from where Julius and Orela would in turn address them all. She chose to see this as a sign of status. Close by was the alcove reserved for Venzano's party. It had not yet arrived.

'You see?' she said to Luis. 'We're not the last.'

Luis merely became even more anxious. 'Perhaps something's happened. He's due to give the first address.'

'What is the matter with you?' Bezile said irritably.

'It's not like him to be late.'

'As you well know, he was on a courtesy visit to Despina when the summons went out. He has further to come than the rest of us.'

'Depton's here, all the way from Pluto.'

'Depton's probably been here for days. You know how punctilious he is.'

'I don't like it. There's been no news from Venzano's office in the last twenty-four hours.'

She sighed. 'How many years have we been doing this, Luis? Security is always tight when there's an attendance council. Should we advertise our travelling arrangements on public channels so that every lunatic in the Noospace has a chance to sabotage our flights?'

Luis was not mollified; he kept pursing his lips, a mannerism she had always found extremely irritating.

'Do calm down. You're already on your second heart, at your age! You overwork and worry too much.' She reached across to one of the laden dispensaries on the table. 'Here, have a tranquince.'

Luis declined the fruit. Bezile was tempted to take a bite herself, but she needed to keep her wits sharp. She and the Prime Arbiter had done as much as possible to try to track down the womb over the past year. Agents of the Noocracy had been infiltrating Charon, but so far they had no leads. Charon was a tight, enclosed community, suspicious of outsiders, a den of Augmenter sympathizers. It didn't help that not even Venzano had been able to ascertain precisely what the womb contained and what its value to the Noosphere was: every enquiry in that direction had drawn a blank. There were obviously things that even a Prime Arbiter was not meant to know. If she allowed herself to think about it, this was worrying; but it was better not to dwell on such matters. Confidence was everything; confidence from without and within.

Really, what more could she have done? She had been diligent in communing with the Noosphere, spending at least an hour a day in her private shrine doing her utmost to purify her thoughts and give a sympathetic response to the mood of her ancestors, whom she often found trite and over-excitable. And, to be fair, there had been no comeback, neither praise nor criticism, from the living or the departed. If Julius and Orela had intended to censure her for handing over the womb to a daughter who had proved to be a traitor, then surely they would have done so by now?

The disembodied voice of the Advocates, speaking as one, filled the chamber, welcoming them and requesting their attentiveness during the introductory display; they were free to help themselves to the food and drink on their tables; the Advocates would join them in person a little later.

Lids parted on the chamber wall behind the oratory, revealing a large optic. For the next hour they were treated to displays and commentaries on the current status of the worlds of the Noosphere. Much of it was bland in the extreme, mere public fodder – the council proceedings would be transmitted live throughout the Noospace – and most of those assembled in the chamber were more interested in eating their way through the positively delicious selection of comestibles that had been provided: everything from Martian candysteaks to ripplerunners, a new concoction from Oberon which left explosions of fragrant sweetness as they wriggled down your throat. Bezile tried everything, listening all the while to the talk of improving percentages in interworld votes, the crucial role of mediators in consoling relatives of Dementia victims, a claim that the Augmenter presence had now been effectively stamped out as far as the Neptunian moons.

This last one she severely doubted. No doubt officially it was the case, but she was certain pockets of Augmenters still existed in murky corners everywhere. The attractions of physicality – of constantly *ongoing* physicality, no matter how warped – would always outweigh the slightly more nebulous consolations of the Noosphere for a small minority. Weren't Julius and Orela themselves living proof of that fact?

She quashed the thought immediately, knowing it to be heretical. She was a practical woman, little interested in matters of individual philosophy, more concerned with consolidating the appeal of the Noosphere so that everyone would ultimately know that their lives were lived towards the goal of pure spirituality. Privately she did consider it time that new Advocates were found, if only to have fresh faces and fresh ideas, and to stifle the complaints of those within the Noocracy who had long been arguing that Julius and Orela should have passed on at their centenary. It was hard to deny any longer the view that both were growing increasingly eccentric and blind to the needs of the people. The new palace was a sheer extravagance when more resources were needed to combat poverty and the spread of the Dementia. It was also in appallingly bad taste.

Luis was tugging at her arm. The delegation from Ganymede had arrived.

She saw that Venzano was not at their head; they were led by his deputy, Salvadorian. The entire retinue was solemn, subdued. They settled into their alcove, leaving the Prime Arbiter's place conspicuously vacant.

'Something's up,' Luis remarked.

That much was evident. A few of the delegation raised wine goblins and picked at morsels, but their extreme decorum was obvious. Meanwhile the optic was concluding with a stirring feature on the pious Phoebans, who were so devoted to their ancestors that they eschewed child-bearing and communed thrice daily with the Noosphere. No one in the chamber was paying attention; everyone was watching Venzano's table. Bezile sucked a flamesnow sherbet through a liquorice straw.

The optic dimmed, and presently the oratory flushed with opalescent light. Without ceremony or introduction, Julius and Orela rose through a floor valve.

Both were dressed in their official robes of dove-grey and scarlet. A long murmur of recognition and fealty came from the audience, tradition permitting no stronger response. Julius and Orela acknowledged it by raising their hands, palms outward, at once a wave and a plea for silence. The Advocates looked both serene and serious, Julius wearing a grey skullcap, Orela's hair silvered and demurely pleated at her nape. A zeegee monitor drifted down and dilated to close-up.

'Welcome,' Orela said finally. 'We are pleased so many of you could come, grateful to you for making the long journey here.'

'It's been twelve years since we last met together,' Julius continued. 'Could the time have passed that swiftly? It's a genuine pleasure to see so many familiar and faithful faces.'

'As always,' Orela went on, 'there have been many changes since we last convened. As always, we confront new challenges.

We've convened this council in great haste because we believe that all of us in the Noospace face a danger graver than any the human race has experienced since we left our homeworld.'

Her voice was as soothing as nepenthe, but Bezile was inured to that and was rather insulted by what she was actually saying. Were the Advocates now adding hyperbole to the usual introductory pleasantries?

'A severe crisis confronts us,' Julius said, 'and concerted action will be vital. Some of you, we know, have been concerned that we have rather neglected you in recent years. We admit that fault, though it was an error of omission rather than intent. An error which today we shall correct.'

'However,' said Orela, 'we're quite aware that many of you have been in transit for several days, and perhaps you would appreciate a little diversion first. An entertainment of sorts.' She gave a strange smile. 'An entertainment that is also designed to *educate*.'

Everyone had been expecting the Advocates to explain Venzano's absence, and the sudden switch of emphasis was rather disconcerting. Julius and Orela withdrew to the edge of the oratory. And then on to it stumbled a troupe of . . . Bezile could only think of them as *manimals*, versions of the brutish precursors of true human beings who had inhabited Earth millennia ago and whose exaggerated adventures on the juvenile channels continued to thrill children throughout the Settled Worlds.

But these were not plasticated holos: these were the real thing. There were eight of them, naked except for grubby loin-rags, their bodies hairy and grotesque, with sagging bellies, slobbering gap-toothed mouths and yellow-toenailed naked feet. Age hung on them in folds of wrinkled skin, blotches, bulging veins and tufts of hair where none should have been.

The assembly was uniformly shocked by the sight. The change in mood had been so abrupt and unexpected, the sight of the creatures so revolting that people could not hide their disgust. Luis snatched up the tranquince as two of the creatures – a male and a female – capered forward and began to perform a clumsy dance that would have been embarrassing had it not been such an awesome demonstration of bad taste.

Everyone sat rooted, unable to look away, as the manimals performed. While the two at the front spiralled clumsily around one another like two drunken beasts, the remaining six joined their hands together and conducted lumpen communal leaps into the air. Their naked feet crashed to the floor as they came down. They gave out barking howls of laughter and slapped one another's flanks in mutual amusement. Spittle lathered their lips and chins. They had missing teeth, crooked limbs, elephantine thighs; their movements were the lumberings of the most brutish beasts. Meanwhile Julius and Orela looked on like doting parents.

Bezile scrutinized the other tables. Without exception, no one had been prepared for this, not even Modramistra, High Arbiter of the asteroid communes, an intelligent and diligent woman popularly felt to be Venzano's successor in waiting. She was seated with her vast retinue at the centre of the chamber, and she was as agog as anyone else.

Now the creatures began to execute – or attempt to execute – a series of sequential leaps over one another's backs. Once again, they tripped, stumbled, slobbered. Bettwys, who had no sense of decorum whatsoever, began to chuckle, and then others joined her, a timid, uncertain laughter spreading from table to table, growing in force as everyone released their unease the only way permissible. Soon the antics of the creatures were being greeted with outright laughter, the more so since Julius and Orela did not appear to object. They continued to watch the performance, paying no apparent heed to the reaction of their audience, smiles of patient amusement on their lips.

Now one of the male creatures had sprouted an erection through the filthy swaddling at its groin. It mounted a stooping female, clutched her by the shoulders and began thrusting madly. Within seconds it was over, the male pulling free and shambling away in a crouch, the female maintaining her pose as if nothing had happened; her inane smile revealed gapped yellowed teeth. Even Luis was now joining in the laughter, hiccuping his mirth like a regurgitating digester.

Bezile was repulsed: this was true vileness, and a studied insult to every one of them. They were complicit by default, by the sheer fact of their presence. How would the thousands of millions of ordinary citizens who would eventually see the transmission feel? How would they react to this disgraceful spectacle?

She saw that one of the few people apart from herself who still sat straight-faced and immobile was Modramistra herself. Well, at least she was in good company. Mercifully, the manimals were coming to the end of their performance, having clambered over one another in a shambolic attempt at a human pyramid which swiftly collapsed into a sprawling heap of grunts and tangled limbs. Finally they scampered off the oratory, disappearing down a side artery.

It occurred to Bezile that the creatures had never given any real indication of being aware of their audience, even at the very end. Their entire performance – if you could dignify it with such a word – had been done in the manner of trained beasts, operating on automatic. Even now the stench of them, the sour miasma of sweat and mortification, fouled the air. They were creatures from the murkiest depths of the human past, from the times when the human form was determined by the blind whims of evolution, when you could not alter so much as the colour of your eyes, let alone have a body in its perfect prime throughout a lifetime. She shivered at the thought, at the fact. The question was: why were the Advocates parading the degeneracy of their origins before them?

The obvious answer was that they were truly mad. Unlike many others, Bezile had resisted this conclusion despite growing evidence, preferring to concentrate on the fact that the Noocracy continued to function reasonably efficiently, despite the Advocates' occasional excesses. And she, having spent most of her lifetime in its service, had persevered and reserved judgement. But this was such an outrageous lapse in good taste she was at a loss to imagine how Julius and Orela could begin to justify it.

The Advocates had now returned to the centre of the oratory. The laughter had died quickly, leaving a nervous whispering. Luis nibbled furiously on the tranquince, golden fruit-flesh lathering his lips.

Julius and Orela were smiling at them.

'A shocking display, yes?' said Julius. 'You were generous in your response, courteous and forbearing. Would anyone care to venture as to the origin of our performers?'

There was silence, and then a brave soul towards the rear of the hall shouted, 'Protohumans!'

Julius nodded gravely. 'A reasonable assumption,' he said. 'But not, in fact, the case. Shall we try again?'

A longer pause, then a woman's voice: 'Spawn of the Augmenters!'

A nervous scattering of laughter.

'One would scarcely say they were Augmented,' said Orela.

'A failed experiment,' someone else said.

Julius shook his head. 'These are no products of the Augmenters, or even true primitives. At least, they were not born that way.'

He waited for further suggestions, but none came.

'They are gymnasts,' Orela announced.

Everyone was perplexed at this.

'Those eight were once individuals like you or me,' Orela explained. 'They were truly gymnasts, one of the nullgrav teams from Hristobel on Callisto who performed spectacularly during the PanWorld Games on Ariel two years ago.'

'A devout and dedicated team who lived blameless lives,' Julius added. 'Alas, they were also among the first to fall victims of the Dementia.'

The optic behind them was showing the team in action at the games, gracile athletes negotiating floating platforms as part of their routine. All were perfectly made, perfectly handsome; it was impossible to reconcile them with the brutes that had cavorted on the oratory.

'By sheer good fortune,' Julius said, 'a medical team was on hand when they first began to exhibit symptoms of the Dementia. They were sedated and eventually brought to our Sanctuary. There their conditions were stabilized and they were given the best care we could provide. We hoped to find clues to the nature of the sickness by monitoring them. What we actually saw, however, was their slow degeneration into the primitives you saw before you.'

There was shocked silence at this. Most victims of the

Dementia that were actually subdued before they killed them-selves either became catatonic or had to be permanently sedated to control their aggression. But until now there had been no suggestion that there was a physical component to the disease.

'The mortal decay begins gradually,' Julius told them, 'but soon progresses swiftly according to the actual biological age of the victim.'

'All the members of the team,' said Orela, 'were aged between thirty-nine and sixty-one standard years. During the past year of their confinement, they underwent the degenera-tion appropriate to their ages. Our attempts to reverse the ageing proved ineffective.'

Julius allowed a pause before continuing: 'Their mental processes also decayed, as you have seen. We were able to tame the grosser aspects of their madness by psychochemical inter-vention, but it's plain that the manic and destructive phases merely mask an inexorable mental and physical decline. Organ-ically, their brains do not appear to have suffered damage, but the higher cognitive functions have been lost. The pitiable end result is what you saw today.'

Bezile realized that Luis was offering her a napkin. She slapped his hand away, blinking the blurriness from her eyes. On the screen the athletes were still performing, weaving effortlessly through a series of free-floating obstacles like swimmers in a sea of air.

'What we are seeing,' said Orela, 'is a reversion to an untutored and unmodified type. In other words, to the primi-tive in us all.'

Now the manimals were back on screen, captured in their performance, drooling and wrinkled. It was just possible to see a resemblance in certain cases between the former athlete and the hulking subhuman.

'As you know,' said Julius, 'the Dementia usually results in death – an end that is perhaps preferable to what we see here.'

'We still have no antidote to it,' Orela continued, 'and yet we are confident that at last we have identified its source.'

A wave of excitement swept through the chamber. Julius motioned for quiet.

'At the Sanctuary we began to explore the possibility that someone may have been tampering with the human genome. We began to suspect some kind of biological detonator that, under the right conditions, triggers the Dementia.'

It was Yuang of Titan who spoke up, rising from his seat:

'With respect,' he said, 'I don't see how that's possible. One of the very first suggestions as to the origin of the Dementia was that it might be some kind of Augmenter slow-burn virus. I've had a team of biotecs exploring that very possibility. There's simply no evidence of unusual proteins or any other biochemical agents in the tissue of the afflicted. We've seen similar senescence in some of our patients, but in our opinion the decay is simply a by-product of overwhelming *mental* changes.' He waited. Julius and Orela said nothing. 'All our studies continue to suggest that if there is an infective agent, then it is of a type quite unknown to us. In fact, we believe it doesn't exist. We tend increasingly to the view that the basis of the syndrome is psychological.'

Bravely spoken! thought Bezile, and not simply because Yuang had had the courage publicly to debate a point with the Advocates. Neither of his possibilities – a wholly new disease or an infective psychosis – was comforting, but that was no reason to reject them, or to pander to the desire for a tangible enemy that people always felt when they were under threat.

'We welcome your views,' Julius said. 'Everyone knows that Titan is renowned as one of the highest centres of biological and medical excellence among the Settled Worlds, sometimes on a par with the Noosphere itself.'

He stopped to allow the mild rebuke to register. 'Nevertheless,' he went on 'the indicators point to Augmenter subversion of the Noosphere itself.'

'We intend to present proof of this to you quite shortly,' Orela said. 'Proof that the Augmenters may in fact be planning a major assault against the Noosphere.'

There were startled murmurings at this, much muttered discussion. Bezile would have no part of it. She was tired of the flummery, and her impatience got the better of her. She hauled herself to her feet.

'According to the commentary, the Augmenter heresy has more or less been eradicated.'

'Among the worlds of the Noospace,' agreed Orela. 'But, as you know, sympathizers remain, and many Augmented took refuge far beyond the human pale. There is every reason to believe that they are now mobilizing.'

'Mobilizing?'

'Indeed.'

But she did not immediately elaborate, even though Bezile waited. So, on an instinct – and because she wanted the issue aired – she said: 'Is this in any way connected with the Prime Arbiter's absence?'

The Advocates came to the edge of the oratory and looked down on her with their oceanic gazes. Bezile had to resist the powerful urge to sit down.

'Very perceptive of you, Bezile of Melisande,' said Julius. 'You will, of course, be aware that Prime Arbiter Venzano is not with us. It is our sad duty to report that he was assassinated in his private quarters on board the ship carrying him here. All attempts to revive him or translate his psyche to the Noosphere failed.'

This time the shock was profound, and some of Venzano's retinue, as though finally released from the constraints of the occasion, began openly to weep.

For several minutes the chamber was a pandemonium of distress and outrage. Who had done such a thing? And to the Prime Arbiter himself! How had the deed been accomplished? How could anyone be so vile as to deprive the highest official of the Noocracy of his right to a life in the hereafter? Even the soberest of their number was shocked by the depravity. Bezile realized that she had sat down willy-nilly. Luis, who had eaten three tranquince, was slouched in his seat like a drunkard, blubbering.

A figure came on to the oratory. It was Salvadorian, Venzano's long-serving deputy, a hard-working man of good reputation. He told how he had found Venzano in his private shrine, a pulse-pistol hole in his temple. An immediate search of the ship had uncovered an intruder hiding in a vent duct. A pistol that had recently been fired was in his possession, and when confronted he had readily admitted the crime.

Palace guards now appeared, escorting a lanky figure with faceted eyes. Clothed in a crude leatherene bodysuit, he was improbably tall and long-limbed, his skin as pale as milk. An Augmenter, fashioned to survive in low-gravity environments distant from the sun.

Orela approached him. 'Do you admit that you are responsible for the death of Prime Arbiter Venzano?'

'I admit it.'

'You killed him?'

'I fired the gun at his face.'

There were gasps of revulsion, cries of anger. Narrow-chested, the Augmenter spoke in a reedy yet harsh voice. He spoke without remorse or fear.

'Tell us why,' Orela demanded.

The Augmenter looked over the assembly with his inhuman eyes. He said nothing.

'Is it not true,' said Orela, 'that the Prime Arbiter had discovered the origin of the Dementia? Had he not discovered the fact that it was an Augmenter plot to destabilize the Noosphere?'

The Augmenter folded his spindly arms together. He remained defiantly silent.

'Is this not why you were sent to kill him?' Orela persisted. 'So that the peoples of the Settled Worlds would not know of your kind's treachery?'

Bettwys and a few of the others were already exclaiming their outrage. The Augmenter refused to speak.

'It's true,' Salvadorian said. 'We found among the Prime Arbiter's files an intercepted message from an unidentified source which is nevertheless of obvious Augmenter origin. The Dementia is a genetic trigger, activated at random by their agents.'

Now half the assembly was on its feet. Bezile saw that Yuang was shaking his head vigorously, attempting to protest. But his words were drowned by the increasingly heated cries of others.

The Augmenter was led away, and the Advocates brought a measure of calm to bear simply by standing still and waiting.

'You see the danger we ordinary humans now face,' Julius said at last. 'On the one hand a descent into degeneracy, and on the other a war with a species who wish to transform us into beings repellent to the vast majority of those we serve.'

To emphasize and dramatize the point, the optic behind them had come to life again, showing both the manimals and the Augmenter assassin in close-up.

'It is hard to believe,' said Orela, 'that they would stoop to the killing of the Prime Arbiter. Perhaps it's a measure of their desperation. Or perhaps it's merely a prelude to a far more serious onslaught. Our evidence suggests the latter.'

'That is why,' said Julius, 'it is essential we respond swiftly and with the utmost fortitude. We must immediately appoint a new Prime Arbiter.'

More reaction: initial surprise, earnest discussions, then overtones of assent.

Bezile urged herself to remain calm, to maintain a clear head. Of course it made perfect sense: the arbiters were assembled in one place so that votes could be cast and the result announced without delay. Normally a new Prime Arbiter was only appointed after extensive private communion with the No-osphere, but the circumstances *were* exceptional. It would be a prudent and emphatic demonstration of their unity. Yet she disliked the blatant stage-managing of the whole affair. It was crude in the extreme, and dismaying to see how easily those who should have known better had been carried along.

Consoles appeared at each table, with privacy hoods so that the arbiters could make their choice free from prying eyes. Apart from the Advocates, only High Arbiters, those with bailiwicks of ten million souls or more, could participate in the vote. There were forty-three of them, covering every major world in the Noospace from Mercury to Pluto. Their selection would ultimately have to be ratified by the people in a compulsory vote, but that was a mere formality.

Luis had stirred somewhat from his soft-boned daze, but not sufficiently that he was capable of saying anything coherent. She turned her back on him, letting the hood envelop her. As soon as it had done so, she cast her vote without hesitation for

Modramistra, who in her opinion should have been appointed to the position over the unfortunate Venzano in the first place.

She was among the first to complete her vote, and she sat back and waited, refusing to meet Luis's swampy eyes. There was muted excitement at the tables, much private speculation on the outcome. Bezile took a mouthful of wine. She was certain Modramistra would carry the day.

The Advocates stood before their own console, placidly awaiting the result. The consoles retracted their hoods, indicating that the votes had been cast. Then the results were displayed, firstly a list of those with no votes, then one name at a time with the number of votes cast.

Bezile was gratified to note that her name was not among the majority of zeros and she could not resist a glance at Bettwys, whose was. There was one vote for Faustine of Europa, one for Depton, three each for Geordano and Lasantha. Yuang had garnered six. And there was Modramistra – but with only a dozen votes. Bezile stared with amazement. Her own name was last, and against it was the number nineteen.

No one was more surprised than she. She had never remotely imagined she would be a frontrunner, let alone win. Usually someone from the Outer Worlds was appointed to the position, if only because they had the majority of votes and tended to resent the Inner Planets' closer physical links with the Noosphere. She hadn't even considered herself especially popular with her peers: there were some, she knew, who considered her arrogant.

Everyone had risen and was applauding politely – everyone, that is, except for Yuang and his retinue, who were walking out. No one else appeared to notice.

Luis and the rest of her table were urging her up while the Advocates beckoned her forward on to the oratory.

'By a clear majority,' she heard one of them saying, 'Her Graciousness Bezile Reeta Miushme-Adewoyin of Melisande and the continent of Aphrodite is appointed the new Prime Arbiter of the Noosphere.'

*

Darkness again. The transition had been smooth, instantaneous. I felt Nina close at hand.

'Were you there?' I asked.

'Right to the end,' she replied.

Lucian and Chloe manifested their presences.

'That's merely a part of it,' Lucian said. 'There's more.'

I rounded on him. 'What next? More manoeuvrings? More revelations? Everything we see only brings more unanswered questions.'

'We're merely showing you what's been happening,' said Chloe. 'With all its uncertainties and ambiguities. If we had simply told you, would you have believed us?'

I didn't answer.

'Was it the Advocates who ordered Venzano's killing?' Nina asked.

'You must make up your own minds,' said Chloe. 'When you've seen everything.'

'Bezile doesn't trust them,' I pointed out.

'To us,' said Lucian, 'that means she's finally come to her senses.'

'Why did Orela and Julius appoint her to succeed Venzano?'

'We have no proof that the voting was anything but fair.'

'It was a fix. Even Bezile didn't expect it.'

'That may be true,' Chloe agreed, 'but nothing is certain. We can tell you little about the Advocates' motives. Or their private activities. They're secretive. They keep their own counsel.'

'But can't you access their minds through the Noosphere?'

'The Advocates have not partaken of communion in the past year.'

I was incredulous at this, but both Chloe and Lucian insisted it was true.

'They neglect their proper duties,' Lucian said. 'Of course, they would claim they're concentrating their energies on combating the Dementia. We think otherwise.'

'And the Augmenters?' said Nina. 'Are the Advocates using them as a cover?'

'It's better to show than tell,' Chloe said.

We both knew what she meant. Nina said, 'You want us to dream again.'

'To experience. In that way, you can make your own judgements without our bias.'

'Imrani?'

'You must have been wondering what happened to him.'

Ten

Imrani was restless. He sat at the organ in the navel of the cathedral, trying to coax a suitable dirge from the reluctant creature. Its fluted tubes pulsed at his command, but only whispery sighs issued. The status displays indicated that the organ was slightly feverish, the diagnostic window suggesting the possibility of a mild viral infection. But Imrani knew better: the organ was constipated, and the problem was probably emotional rather than physical. The creature had lain unused for several years before his arrival, and then he had played it regularly for congregations of visiting pilgrims; but in recent months there had been few pilgrim ships and the ribbed aisles of the cathedral lay empty. He was sure the organ was sulking as a result.

Once again he tried to clear the blockage by sending pulses of compressed air through the pipes. The resulting cannonade of farts would have raised chuckles in even the most solemn of congregations, but there was no one here but himself and Felix. Felix of the automatic smile and relentless companionship. Imrani could see him in the organ mirror, sitting directly behind in the front aisle, patient and pleasant. His ever-present shadow.

Imrani stared at his own face, looking at a stranger. After he had been rescued from the ice, he'd awoken to find that his facial features had been remodelled. It was nothing too drastic – a slight flattening of the nose, lowering of cheekbones, smoothing of jaw line – yet the overall effect, with lightened restyled hair, was to make him look quite unlike his old self. But it was the eyes that bothered him most: they were now blue rather than brown. Elydia had told him that his originals were frost-damaged and that it was in any case an essential precaution as part of his new disguise. He was a hunted man. He still hadn't got used to the idea that he might be perceiving the world with someone else's visual apparatus. He'd never had the courage to ask where the eyes had come from; he liked to think that they'd been grown from his own tissue, but this was unlikely given the prevalence of corpses on Charon.

As always, it was chilly in the navel, the arching vaulted spaces rising high and silent above him, galleries, pews and corridors hewn from the ice, ghostly in the flickering light of candlemasses. The cathedral was an extensive complex, most of it lying underground, with only the spired towers and central dome jutting above the surface, dominating the settlement of Acheron. He had spent most of the past year here, only being allowed out in the company of Felix and Elydia to sightsee or visit Shivaun's corpse. They daren't take risks, Elydia always insisted; if he fell into the hands of the politia or some minion of the Noosphere they would whisk him away and suck his brain dry in order to find out what he knew.

His fingers were growing numb with cold. He sighed and got up from the organ, abandoning his attempt to ventilate it. What was the point when he had no one to play for anyway?

Felix also stirred. He was a large, leonine type with shoulder-length brown hair. Well-muscled, upright, always sporting that bright-eyed look Imrani had often observed in fitness zealots. He rose early each morning and spent a hour exercising and weight-training. It was practically the only time Imrani was free of him.

'I want to *do* something,' Imrani announced. 'Something *active*. How about a walk outside?'

Felix's smile remained fixed. 'I don't think that would be prudent at the moment.'

It was the answer he had expected. 'Why not? It's quiet.'

'That is when we have to be most careful. There's safety in crowds.'

'I remember you telling me I had to beware of large groups.'

The smile did not relent. 'You've been very patient in accepting these restrictions on your movement. Believe me,

Elydia and I appreciate your cooperation. It will not be for much longer.'

Felix's tone was always one of perfect reasonableness, but Imrani had begun to think of him as a warden rather than a companion.

'How much longer?' he asked.

Felix put an arm around his shoulder. Imrani felt constricted rather than comforted.

'Soon,' Felix said. 'Soon you'll have complete freedom of movement, I promise you.'

'It's been over a month since I was allowed outside. I'm getting claustrophobia stuck in here!'

At present, they were even denying him access to Shivaun's tomb. Until recently he had visited her twice a month, standing before her ice-locked body on one of the nearby ridges, always with tears in his eyes. He missed her beyond expression. She had been entombed in her expediter's uniform on a ridge where the ice itself shone rather than the corpses. She stood alone, hands on hips, head held high, gazing out along the Valley of the Dead with her sightless eyes. Imrani had given her the simple valediction: WE LOVED YOU. There were no attending holos or mementoes; she was alone on the ridge, alone in her severe beauty and fortitude, even in death. They had been too late to save her, though Elydia assured him they had tried. He'd often wondered whether they might have been able to revive her if he hadn't opened her up to rescue the womb. Maybe it was he who was ultimately responsible for her death.

No. The suit light had been red, she was already gone.

On an impulse, Imrani strode briskly away, heading towards the rear of the navel then climbing the spiralway which coiled around the inside of the dome. Previously he was at least able to peer out through the cathedral's crystalline windows over Acheron and the valley beyond, but even this was no longer allowed; for days the windows had been blinded, their orbs white as milk. According to Felix, there was an as yet untraced leakage of air from the cathedral, and every orifice was to remain sealed until its source was discovered.

He heard Felix's footsteps behind him. He increased his pace, climbing higher until he reached the upper balcony, his breaths pluming in the chill air. On the curving ceiling above were moving holograms that showed an idealized vision of the afterlife, naked humans walking through verdant meadows, lying on golden beaches, swimming in turquoise seas. There were children, tame animals, a benign sun in an azure sky.

'Beautiful, isn't it?'

Felix had come up beside him, as silent and swift as death itself.

'It was done by Rodric, Elydia's husband.'

Imrani watched a man and woman pick a greenish fruit from a tree. He knew the story: how Rodric the famous artist had met Elydia the famous biotec and how they had been together for forty years of monogamous marriage before Rodric died in a freak accident when a faulty warmsuit electrocuted him while skiing Pluto's methane snows. He had heard it many times before. Everything had begun to pall, despite his attempts to keep himself occupied by visiting different parts of the subterranean complex. He had spent hours as a spectator in the disembowelling and demortification rooms; he had sat with congregations listening to sermons on the evanescence of human life and the calamity of truedeath; he had been given a tour of the fabricatory that manufactured miniature replics of the dead for grieving relatives; he had browsed through the dispensaries that sold souvenirs of the valley; negotiated the map room with its colour-coded zonal displays; attended the nerve centre where up to five hundred pilgrims could call home on their own console at standard rates. He was bored, bored, bored.

'Perhaps you'd like to wrestle?' Felix said. 'Or something more *cerebral*, like tesseract?'

Imrani stared at him. The one and only time he'd agreed to wrestle with Felix he'd had the feeling the big man was holding back, and even then he was hopelessly outclassed and had retired with limbs that ached like knotted rope for days afterwards, despite the attentions of the massager.

'I hate tesseract,' he told Felix. 'I'm going to my chamber.'

For once, he did not attempt to hide his irritability. He stumped off, heading down the spiralway then taking branch arteries towards his quarters.

There was no one about, either on the stairways or in the cavernous rooms that gave off them. This was unusual. Even without attending pilgrims, the cathedral was usually busy; if its dark-apparelled mediators and solicitors were not engaged in processing corpses or counselling the bereaved, they would be occupied in dusting its ornate surfaces or feeding candle-masses so that it remained atmospherically lit and tolerably warm.

Imrani paused, silencing his own footsteps. Nothing. No sound or movement. Then, in the distance, he heard Felix's familiar tread. He hastened on again, calling to his doormouth to open, hurrying inside and closing it after him.

His chamber was windowless but well-appointed, with a large console and a private shrine. Bright Martian spotterfish swam in a ceiling globe, splashing the walls with spectral washes of colour. He waited a little while, heard Felix's footsteps approach, pause, then move on. Felix's own quarters – and those of Elydia – were next door, and Imrani heard him go inside. He was Elydia's partner – lover, presumably. Well, it took all sorts.

Something about Felix's remarks on the balcony had pricked his curiosity. He wasn't normally inquisitive, but he activated the console and asked for a resume on Rodric – he couldn't remember his surname.

'The artist,' he told the console. 'The one that was married to Elydia Chan-Vetterlein.'

The optic winked into action with a picture of the man.

Imrani immediately told it to halt.

It was as he had somehow suspected. Felix was the living image of Rodric.

'I hope you don't mind.'

Imrani spun around. Without him hearing, Elydia had come into the room.

'Your doorvalve wasn't sealed, so I thought I'd look in on you. Felix told me you were a little out of sorts.'

She was a tall, handsome woman, her dark hair liberally streaked with grey, her face lined – physical features which he continued to find slightly shocking. Of course arbiters and other high officials often sported cosmetic wrinkles as signs of their status, but this was extreme, the real thing. She had once told him that she had deliberately let herself be elderized so that she looked as a late middle-aged woman might have done in the days when humans were subject to ongoing physical decay. It was hard to imagine such times, and he preferred not to.

Elydia's gaze had gone to the optic. She gave a slow smile.

'Rodric,' she said. It sounded like a sigh. 'Even now I miss him, you know.'

Imrani was embarrassed; he didn't know what to say.

'I always felt responsible for his death. You see, it was I who grew the suit. The suit that killed him. The malfunction was a result of faulty design, too high a potential in the neural network. Purely my fault.' Her gaze moved from the optic to his face. 'You're shocked.'

'It isn't that.' He had to come out with it. 'Felix . . .'

Realization dawned on her face, and she practically laughed. 'Oh, *that*. Yes, he's the very picture of him, isn't he?'

Again Imrani didn't know quite how to put it. 'Is he real?'

Elydia was genuinely surprised. 'Why, of course! What on earth do you mean?'

'I mean, is he Rodric?'

'Oh, I see. You're asking if he was cloned? No, no. He's his own person, a lover I found some years afterwards.'

Imrani was puzzled. 'But he looks exactly like him.'

She nodded. 'Felix voluntarily had himself remodelled, body and soul – insofar as that is possible – so that he would resemble Rodric as closely as possible.'

'Body *and* soul?'

'Psycosmetic surgery. As a recuperatory worker, you can't be unaware of it.'

'It's illegal unless it's remedial.'

'Yes,' she said with the weary dismissiveness of someone who had often debated the issue and no longer intended to. 'It was his own choice. I put no pressure to bear on him whatsoever. You never end up with an exact double in any case, but then no one could ever have exactly replaced Rodric. In fact, when I realized that Felix was determined to go through with it, I insisted that he be given none of my former husband's artistic tendencies. A *reflection* is sufficient; a copy would have been just that – a poor imitation.'

Imrani was finding it hard to take this on board. 'He *chose* to have himself remodelled?'

'Yes.'

'But why?'

Elydia sat down on the couch opposite, picking up a small lump of tomb crystal that stood as a centrepiece on the occasional table beside it.

'I think perhaps he understood the depth of my love for Rodric. I think perhaps he loved me so much he was prepared to make himself into something as close to Rodric as possible.'

Imrani wondered if he was expected to find this noble: to him it was distinctly creepy.

'And did it work?' he asked.

'In what way?'

'Do you love him like you loved Rodric?'

'He's not the same man. But he's a perfect substitute. I love him well enough.'

Imrani frowned. 'I don't see how you could recapture what you had.'

Elydia gave a short laugh. 'That's not it. You young always have quaint, romantic notions of what constitutes love of another person. You love an *image* of the thing, not the thing itself. You project your own notions of identity on to it. It becomes the mirror of your desires.'

'So you *pretend*.'

'No, no, you misunderstand me. The physical resemblance was the least important part of it. Before he was rather too gauche, too gushing—'

'What was he? What did he look like before the change?'

She shook her head, as if she could scarcely remember. 'That's not important. He's achieved his desires. To be with me. To have what he wants from me – love, companionship, fulfilment. What more are our lives for?'

Imrani found it too outlandish to contemplate. His love for Shivaun had been something totally unexpected, totally beyond his control. In some ways he hadn't even *liked* her, yet when they were together he'd never felt more alive.

Elydia was giving him a grandmotherly look. He finally voiced the question he had been wanting to ask ever since his recovery:

'Are you an Augmenter?'

'I am. Augmented, too.'

She raised the crystal so that it glittered with the fishes' rainbow hues.

'You're surprised.'

He could only nod.

'That's because people are led to believe that the Augmented are distortions, freaks. That's not the case.'

His disbelief must have shown, because she said, 'Would you like to see some?'

It was the last thing he wanted. Did she intend to summon a parade of them from somewhere?

To his vast relief, she simply spoke to the console: 'We'd like to see some library images of humans who underwent physiological modification. Pre-purge, if you will.'

The console optic blinked. 'Do you require a commentary?'

'A brief one will suffice.'

The optic blinked again, and Imrani was looking at the head of a man who appeared ordinary except for the absence of hair, flattened ears and lateral slits where his nostrils should have been. The console told him that the man was an aquatic, with nasal gills that enabled him to remain underwater for an hour or more. Another holo replaced it, this one showing a very squat figure with sunken slitted eyes, adapted for high-gravity environments. A third was of a carbon monoxide breather who looked ordinary except for her ruddy skin and bloodshot eyes.

'This is routine,' Elydia interrupted somewhat peevishly. 'Show us the Synthivores and related groups.'

The scene shifted again to an interior with a group of diners around a table. Imrani saw nothing unusual apart from the quaint bodywear until he realized that the table was serving what looked like coloured fibres in an oily black gravy. The commentary informed him that the diners called themselves the Inorganicists. They were a group who refused to eat anything animal or vegetable and had had their alimentary

canals redesigned so that they could subsist off plastics, pow-
dered minerals and rocks.

Now a view of the Martian Badlands appeared, and another
group were shown being showered by slops of refuse that a
garbage train was jetting into a crater sump. Naked and
hairless, they were laughing and falling about, licking the mess
from one another's bodies, delirious with the fun of it. Their
skins had a greenish hue, held chloroplasts that enabled them
to photosynthesize; but their most useful trick was the ability
to respire anaerobically so that their blood sugars could be
converted directly to alcohol, enabling a permanent drunken
high.

This was too much for Imrani, and his face must have shown
it because Elydia told the console to pause.

'Do they revolt you?' she asked.

'No. It isn't that. Well, not exactly. They just look a little
. . . well, *weird*, I suppose.'

'Weird enough so that they should have been exterminated?'

'No. I didn't mean that.'

'They were. Every one of them.'

To emphasize the point, she instructed the console to give
details of the fate of each of the 'variants' shown. All had lived
for a time in various habitats throughout the Settled Worlds –
the aquatics had swum the Venusian seas – and all had been
eliminated during what Elydia called the purges, either by
direct genocide or by deliberate incarceration.

'Those that weren't killed were sterilized,' Elydia informed
him. 'When they died, they were the last of their kind.'

It was a slightly different version of events from the one he
had been brought up with. The networks always portrayed the
Augmenter Wars as a reaction of ordinary men and women
against creatures who were intent on supplanting *Homo sapiens sapiens*.

'Do you think they deserved that?' Elydia was asking him.
'They only wanted to live peacefully in their places. A lot of
them were designed for work that no *ordinary* human would
do. But people are easily stirred against others who seem *weird*
to them.' She used the word in the same tone he had. 'No
doubt you were taught that they were easy to hunt down

because they looked so blatantly different and set themselves apart. But many were forced to live in ghettos, while others showed no obvious changes to the casual eye and lived peacefully alongside other humans. They were especially persecuted when the purges started. Augmentation need not mean noticeable changes to the human physique. I, for example, have merely had my skeletal, muscular and cardiovascular systems enhanced for improved stamina and strength.'

Again his disbelief must have shown. Elydia smiled, then held the crystal out and closed her fist around it. Slowly she crushed it over the table, letting the glittering white granules cascade down on to the whorlwood surface, stirring the table to shake its back and fold itself up before stalking off into a corner to sulk.

Elydia brushed her hands clean, as if she had completed a purely routine task.

Tomb crystal was as hard any rock. Imrani thought about it.

'Can Felix do that, too?'

'Indeed. I wanted him to be as strong as me.'

He thought of Felix's arm around his shoulders, of bones that might have been built of plasticeramic, muscles of high-density fibrils . . .

'The Augmented came in many shapes and forms,' Elydia said. 'Some were designed purely for sport or idleness – or pleasure.'

At her instructions, the console now showed an impossibly voluptuous woman and an impossibly well-endowed man. To Imrani's eyes, both looked grotesque, a view unmodified by Elydia's information that both had enhanced nerve-endings in their sexual organs and were capable of extended multiple orgasms.

'In the early days there was a yearning to experiment with the body, to see how far the human form could be stretched, as it were. Much of it promised to open up fruitful new avenues of physicality for the human race. Then the puritans of the Noocracy engineered public opinion to reject human variation. The Augmented were either exterminated or forced to flee.'

She was awaiting some response. Again, he was lost for one.

'It was not the war of liberation now portrayed for public

consumption,' she said. 'The Augmented were victims, not victimizers. They have no desire to rule, or dominate. They merely wish to take their proper places – their proper places as gaily coloured threads, if you like, in the varied tapestry that is our human destiny.'

He had heard her preach sermons to bereaved congregations, and the phrase had a similar sort of manufactured air. Not that Elydia had ever publicly expressed her Augmenter sympathies to outsiders, let alone revealed that she was in fact herself Augmented. Surely the Noocracy must have had some inkling of it? Charon was obviously a bolthole for changelings, and only his naivety had prevented him from seeing it until now. No doubt it was an Augmenter that had rescued him from the ice. He'd never quite had the courage to ask.

'So you see,' she said, 'we're not so very different from you, not so different at all. Haven't we done our utmost to protect you during your confinement here? We are no one's enemies except those that wish to destroy us.'

And then, as if she had satisfactorily completed her business, she rose.

'What about the womb?' he said.

'The womb?'

'Shivaun died to deliver it to you. You've never told me why.'

'There are reasons. Good reasons.'

'What reasons?'

'Your curiosity is understandable, but I'm afraid I can't satisfy it – at least, not yet.'

'You owe me an explanation. I nearly died out there as well.'

'I know.' She sounded contrite. 'Believe me, your bravery is appreciated, it really is. I realize that my silence on the matter is a terrible discourtesy, but I can only ask you to bear with us. Soon you'll understand everything.'

It was always the same answer – no answer whatsoever. They told him nothing, kept him here like a prisoner.

'Was Shivaun Augmented?'

'Not as such.'

'Then why did she bring you the womb?'

'She didn't tell you?'

'She never got the chance. Was it because of what happened to her husband and sons?'

Elydia scrutinized him, as if deliberating.

'Their deaths distressed her greatly,' she said. 'I felt obliged to explain that simple gill implants could have saved them.'

'You converted her? Just by saying that?'

'No, no, dear boy. It was far more complicated than that.'

She sat down again, putting her hands together as if in prayer, making a big show of collecting her thoughts. Everything she did struck him as a little contrived, over-practised. He didn't trust her in the slightest.

'In my earlier years,' she said at last, 'long before I came here, I once helped a newly appointed arbiter on Venus produce a batch of daughters by parthenogenesis. Nothing illegal in that, except that she was an ambitious woman and wanted her offspring to be reflections of herself. She wanted them to become faithful servants of the Noosphere, as she herself was. So I helped her – we were friends then. I helped her design them so that they would have a healthy interest in spiritual matters, a keen interest in the afterlife. There were seven of them.'

'You used psycosmetics?'

'And more. I was ambitious myself, keen to try everything I could. Perhaps it was against my better judgement, even then, but which of us is free of indiscretions?' She shrugged. 'As you know, the results are always unpredictable in any case. This particular mother-to-be didn't want the distraction of raising her brood herself, so they were farmed out to fosters and raised without knowledge of their true lineage.'

Elydia paused, almost as if expecting him to guess the rest. When he remained silent, she went on:

'I followed their progress intermittently over the years, even after I had fallen out with their mother. Differences in philosophy, you understand. One of the children eventually became an intercessor in a minor shrine, another turned rather mindlessly Devout, while a third departed the Noospace to proselytize among the Oort communes and was never heard of again. Three failed signally in their calling – they were solid citizens, but no more. The last of them was Shivaun.'

He stared at her in astonishment.

'I never forget a tissue sample,' she told him, 'or a retina scan. As soon as she turned up here, I knew who she was. My files confirmed it. She was that arbiter's daughter. And acolyte, as it transpired.'

Imrani made the connection. 'Miushme-Adewoyin?'

'None other. Shivaun was less than delighted when I revealed this to her. You see, she'd set her heart on becoming an expediter and was already under Miushme-Adewoyin's tutelage at one of the seminaries in Melisande.'

He didn't see, quite. 'What's so wrong in that?'

'The urge had been *designed* into her. By me, at her mother's behest. Shivaun took it badly. She felt as if she had been robbed of her free will. As if her life-path had been preordained. Understandable, don't you think?'

Imrani thought about this. Shivaun would have shared the same ancestors as Bezile when communing in a shrine, but there was no way she would have known this since the dead could not speak of the living, only respond to the needs of the communicant. Not that Shivaun had ever used a shrine in all the time he had known her. No wonder she'd been such an angry person. No wonder she'd betrayed Bezile at the end.

'I know what you're thinking,' Elydia said to him. 'Why, in that case, did she proceed to become an expediter? Did she ever tell you?'

'Why?'

'I surmise it was so that she could get close to Bezile, be her faithful servant until such a time that she could exact her revenge. We can't be sure about these matters, but how else could it be explained? When the womb fortuitously came into her hands, it was the perfect opportunity to act in the most brazen defiance of her calling.'

Imrani was tired of the sound of her voice, the crafted words that spewed effortlessly out of her mouth. They were drowning him.

'I also believe she came here because she herself then intended to be Augmented. Alas, we reached her too late.'

Imrani fell into contemplation. Shivaun had never revealed any of this to him. He tried to comfort himself with the thought that at least she had brought him with her, at least he had been with her at the end. It didn't help in the slightest.

'No doubt,' Elydia said, 'she would have hoped you would join her. In Augmentation, I mean.' She rose, walked to the doormouth. 'You should consider it, you know, consider the physical enhancements you might desire. There's no compulsion, naturally, none whatsoever. But think about it, don't dismiss it out of hand.' She winked at him. 'There are quite a few advantages.'

And then she was gone, the door puckering shut behind her.

Imrani stood there for a while before flopping into his slouch. He had to admit he was dismayed and disappointed by the revelations. True, he'd always wondered about Shivaun, wondered about her rage; but the mystery had been preferable to the facts. Sometimes it was better not to know.

He blanked the optic and studied the dusting of tomb crystal on the rug. Elydia's presence had filled his chamber like something stifling. Did she truly think he might consider becoming Augmented himself? It went against everything he believed in. At the recuperatory he was used to *restoring* the human body after injury or illness, and that meant remaining as true to the existing phenotype as possible. That was where the skill lay. Not that he had anything personal against the Augmenters: in his view, people should be free to lead the lives they chose, as long as they didn't interfere with others. But he wasn't about to start having fins or fabricated innards added to *his* physique, thank you.

He watched the fish orbit relentlessly in their bowl. Finally he went over to the doormouth and quietly asked it to open.

'Sorry,' it replied. 'I'm shut for the night.'

Only Elydia and Felix could open it. He was a prisoner until morning. He gazed around the chamber, his cell for the past year, a place where he had never felt at home. It was an hour past midnight, the depths of the night, but he knew he wouldn't be able to sleep. In a corner alcove, screened by a curtain, was a small shrine. He hesitated, then ordered the curtain to scroll up.

The shrine was old, its optic veined, chrome-plated prayer terminals worn smooth to the white plastic below by the passage of many hands. For the past month he'd used it every day, sometimes twice a day. He'd grown Devout by necessity, because the companionship it offered was his only comfort now that Shivaun was gone. He sat down and reached for the hood.

Yet again the darkness. This time I did not wait.

'Is this true about the Augmenter purges?'

I was directly addressing Chloe and Lucian.

'It's Elydia Chan-Vetterlein's version of the truth,' Lucian replied.

'We don't subscribe to it,' Chloe added, 'but we want you to hear all sides. In the end, you must make up your own minds. When as many facts are available to you as we can supply.'

Nina said, 'Is Imrani in danger?'

'His position is far from secure, especially now he's begun to question his confinement.'

'He's been shabbily treated,' said Lucian. 'You may both be in a position to help him.'

'Through the Noosphere?'

'He's about to begin communion.'

'We can occupy him?' I said. 'Now? In real time?'

Chloe said, 'You can help him act in the best way possible with the advice and information we can supply, as you did with Tunde. If you offer him the chance to escape, he'll most likely grasp at it.'

'Escape?' said Nina. 'How?'

'With our help, it should be possible.'

In their own way, they were as evasive with us as Elydia and Felix were with Imrani. On this occasion I didn't let it concern me: I was eager to play my part.

They must have intuited this, because I sensed them withdrawing, I sensed another consciousness pressing in, expectant at first, then uncertain when he did not find what he had been anticipating.

'*Imrani?*' I said.

He froze at the intensity of the contact.

'*It's all right,*' I said, as gently as I could. '*We're here to help you.*'

A frightened pause. Then:

'Who are you?'

I told him my name, and then Nina spoke hers, my first awareness that she had accompanied me. Imrani shrunk back, fearful and suspicious.

'*There's no need to be afraid*–' I began, but Nina interrupted with a calm: '*Let me.*'

Her placid voice was a counter to my urgency, and she explained as briefly as she could how we had come to occupy the Noosphere.

To my surprise, I felt his fear quite quickly giving way to curiosity. He had the flexibility of youth, and our sudden manifestation was something new and exciting in what had become a restricted life of tedium. His acceptance of us had the swiftness of someone who desperately *wants* to believe, and his response to Nina was guilelessly enthusiastic. I think it was helped by the fact that our contact through the Noosphere was so immediate and intimate. He *knew* we were who we said we were, preposterous though it seemed; and because he had been lacking comradeship, he showed no hesitation when Nina revealed that we intended to help him escape.

I could see his face reflected in the mirrored lids on either side of the optic. He was bursting with relief and gratitude, tears trickling down his cheeks. Nina soothed him, assuring him everything would be fine.

'How?' he said at last. 'How are we going to get out of here?'

'*Through the door,*' Nina replied. '*We'll tell you what words to say to get it to open.*'

Against my instinct, Nina advised him to wait for an hour before making his move. This seemed to me like an inordinate delay when we could leave immediately, but Imrani agreed with her, saying that Elydia and Felix often stayed up into the small hours; he wanted to be sure they were sleeping when he left.

So we waited, while I began to bristle with impatience. Presently Imrani began pressing his ear to the chamber wall, checking to see if Elydia and Felix were asleep.

'*Walls are sound-proofed,*' I reminded him. '*This is wasting time.*'

'That's what you think,' he said. 'There's a quirk in the respiration ducts that carries sounds right through from their bedchamber. You won't believe what I've heard some nights. Felix might be Augmented, but he snores like a rhinocerhorse!'

Nina joined in with his amusement, while I, for want of anything better to do, simply listened through his ears.

There was nothing. No sound whatsoever.

'*It's quiet,*' I said. '*They must be asleep. Let's go.*'

But he still delayed, insisting we should wait a little longer. Nina agreed with him, much to my irritation.

Imrani was naturally curious to know more about us. I was reluctant to tell him anything not connected with our immediate mission, but Nina patiently answered all his avid questions about the other lives we had experienced during our various transitions. He was both awed by and envious of our capacities, even though Nina stressed that we could only act through our hosts.

'*Listen,*' I said eventually, '*we have to move.*'

At last Nina agreed with me.

'Should I pack a bag?' Imrani asked, almost teasingly.

'*Let's just get out of here,*' I said with great restraint.

A whispered code supplied by Chloe and Lucian caused the doormouth to open in silence. Imrani stepped outside. There was no one about.

We went down stairways and along gloomy corridors lit only by the occasional candlemass which made Imrani's shadow loom large on the ice walls. His initial excitement and sense of adventure began to give way to apprehension as we descended a spiralway to one of the side exits.

There was a wardrobe of warmsuits beside the door. It opened up, asking Imrani what colour suit he wanted.

He eyed the array, which ranged from scarlet to gold.

'Pink!' he said with provocative glee.

'*White,*' I insisted. '*You want minimum visibility.*'

He took the pink one anyway, suiting up speedily.

'It's thirty-two days since I've been out there,' he told us. 'I counted every one. Thirty-two days stuck in this mausoleum.'

'*Let's move!*' I urged him.

We entered the doorvalve. Imrani fitted his mask and checked the suit's homeostatics. The outer envelope parted. We stepped outside. And stopped, startled by what we saw.

It was obvious why Imrani had been kept inside, why the windows had been sealed. Immediately beyond Acheron, the entire valley floor was filled with ships. They were as many and as varied as we had ever seen, ranging from elephantine long-haul voyagers to bulbous ferries and ancient scouters, their patched metal hulls pitted and streaked after centuries of flight.

There were warmsuited figures everywhere, too, checking vent ducts and folded sails, manoeuvring bloated wagon-fliers over holds. The fleet was preparing for take-off.

Under my urging, Imrani strode forward, crossing the deserted square of the settlement, not looking back. The squat domes and bunkers of Acheron were shuttered, dark; all the activity was focused around the ships.

As we approached, I said, '*Don't hesitate. Act as if you belong.*'

'I wish you'd be quiet!' Imrani said irritably. 'You're making me nervous.'

'*Calm down!*' Nina whispered soothingly. '*Let's all relax. The last thing we need is an argument.*'

'*You* tell me what to do then,' he said to her. 'He puts me on edge.'

I didn't like the idea of being rebuffed, but Nina was right: this was no time for an argument.

In fact, we needn't have worried. Imrani walked past a group of figures who were doing some repair work on the guidance systems in the nose of one ship, plasm-torches flaring as they welded new connections. No one paid us special attention. The suited figures were of every size and shape.

'You see?' Imrani remarked, gesturing to a sylph-like figure in lilac. 'Pink's fine. No one's turned a hair.'

I resisted the urge to point out that they were as varied in physique as they were in colour. I did not want to add to his anxiety.

We continued on through the centre of the fleet. On one side of us a transplanetary sailship was unfurling its enormous silver wings, while on the other a swollen tanker extruded transfusion lines into the belly of a spirogyrator. Beyond rose the tiers of the valley sides with their ranks of corpses, insensate witnesses to the spectacle.

Chloe and Lucian were directing us towards a customized phoenix, a popular class of ship used for both civilian and politia flights. Extra vent sacs had been grown on the undersides of its wings, its head was enveloped in a radiation hood, and a plated exoskeleton covered its entire body, gleaming gunmetal in the interstellar night.

No one was attending the ship, and a forward portal was open.

'We're going on board?' Imrani enquired.

'*Yes*,' said Nina.

Imrani went up the ramp. I could hardly believe it had been so easy. But as soon as we were inside, a security monitor dropped down from the corridor ceiling, halting us.

'Welcome aboard,' the ship said. 'Please identify yourself.'

It spoke in Elydia's voice. The monitor was peering closely at Imrani, its optic almost touching his visor. I realized that it could not have been Elydia herself because she would have recognized Imrani.

Chloe and Lucian immediately supplied us with another coded sequence which compelled the ship to accept our presence as motile cargo. The monitor withdrew into the ceiling.

Imrani watched it go, amazed at the effect of the code.

'It's letting us in?' he said.

'*We've just become a part of the manifest*,' Nina told him.

'Wow!'

'*Are we going to stand here?*' I said.

'Where to?' Imrani asked, and I had the distinct impression he was addressing Nina rather than me.

'*The cargo holds*,' she said. '*We're going to hide there.*'

The holds were located in the main body of the ship, a series of interconnecting chambers, all of which were empty apart from one which held provision dispensaries networked to the ship's galley. Imrani settled down beneath a tangle of alimentaries, fashioning a grain-sac into a recliner.

'What now?' he said.

'*Now,*' Nina said, '*we wait.*'

I was not good at waiting, and in the interval I tried to get Chloe and Lucian to reveal why we had boarded the ship. But they had withdrawn: for the moment we were alone.

It was not long before Imrani's eyes closed. I tried to stir him but Nina placated me, insisting that he needed his rest. Soon he was asleep, and then there were just the two of us, presences only in the darkness of his mind.

'Nathan?'

I still felt as if the name didn't belong to me.

'We're being used,' I said. 'I don't like it. They're only feeding us what suits them. They knew about these ships, but they haven't explained *why* they're here.'

'Perhaps they need us to find out.'

I was dubious it was so straightforward.

'It could be some kind of task force,' Nina said. 'Or an evacuation fleet. Maybe Charon's been put under martial law or something. Maybe they're going to have to defend themselves.'

I thought about the figures we had seen outside. Augmenters many of them. It was possible that the Noocracy had finally decided on a show of force to root them out. But to me the ships assembled here looked more like an *attacking* force. I said as much.

'You may be right,' Nina conceded. 'But even Chloe and Lucian might not be sure. They might want us to have the freedom to use our own judgement, depending on the circumstances.'

'*Very* considerate of them.'

'You're all I have, you know.'

This was said with such simplicity and sincerity that I felt chastened. Though I could not see her, I could picture her face, conjure the smell of her warmth, her touch.

'Do you trust them?' I asked.

'Lucian and Chloe?'

'I like people to show a bit of emotion. Those two are just a pair of talking heads.'

It was good to have a sense of my own personality, of something that was independent of the world into which I had been born. I could survive without knowing my past, I was certain, as long as I was sure of myself in the present.

'I don't think they intend us any harm,' Nina said.

'That's a tremendous relief. So there's nothing to worry about?'

'I really believe they do need us to help them.'

'You haven't answered the question.'

She was silent for a while. Then she said, 'I don't trust anyone, Nathan. Not even you.'

I wasn't prepared for this. 'What do you mean?'

'You're impulsive, intolerant of others' weaknesses. We have to move carefully here, especially when, as you've said yourself, we know so little.'

I wondered if she meant more than this, but decided to make light of it. 'But apart from that,' I said, 'you think I'm wonderful.'

'I didn't say I didn't like you. We *need* one another. There's no one else.'

She had come 'closer'. I pictured her face, imagined embracing her.

I had a sensation of time passing. Because I wanted to show Nina that I could be patient, I simply waited in the silence and the dark, aware of her presence close by but not attempting to communicate. I focused instead on my own thoughts, searching through what I knew, being as fully aware of myself as was possible in the hope that perhaps some elusive memories of my past might surface. None did. I knew only that I existed now; I remembered only my awakenings and the dreams. My life was the story which had still not reached its end.

It was Nina who finally stirred my from my introspection.

'Did you hear something?' she asked.

I listened, and there it was: muffled voices and footfalls. Presently they came closer. We heard movement, conversation in adjoining chambers, the sound of large masses being shifted.

'They're loading,' I said.

No one entered our own chamber, where Imrani slept blissfully on. The loading continued for perhaps two hours, then everything went silent for a while. Presently we heard more conversation and the ship began to talk, responding to a systems check.

Imrani did not stir even when I tried to wake him by 'shouting'.

'Leave him,' Nina urged me.

In the darkness we waited, listening while the systems check was completed. Then, after a long delay, we heard a low vibration, sensed it in Imrani's body as the ship powered up.

It was only when the ship lifted off with a peremptory lurch that he woke.

Imrani blinked away his sleep in the feeble light of the chamber glownodes, taking a few moments to orientate himself, to remember that we were with him.

'What's happening?' he said.

The tug of the ship's acceleration gave him his answer.

'Do you know where we're headed?' he asked.

Chloe and Lucian manifested themselves again, telling us that it was important we investigated the other cargo chambers as soon as the ship was fully on its way. I had a sense that they were preoccupied, engaged in other matters; they left us as swiftly as they had come, much to my frustration.

Nina conveyed their instructions to Imrani. We waited a further hour, until the ship had reached a constant acceleration. Each of the holds, including ours, was secured, but once again Chloe and Lucian had provided us with access codes.

'Is it safe to go out?' Imrani wanted to be assured.

'*We have to risk it*,' Nina told him simply.

Was that what Chloe and Lucian intended? Only to give us the barest information or instructions so that we would have to rely on our own wits? Well, damn them, we'd do exactly that.

Imrani slipped out into the corridor. It was quiet. One by one, we began checking the other chambers.

The first few we entered contained only extra provisions and vat-sacs holding spare biomechanicals. Eventually we came to a smaller chamber and I sensed Chloe and Lucian's distant presence again, their expectancy growing even from afar. They knew there was something special inside it.

'*Take it easy*,' I whispered to Imrani as he instructed the valve to give us access. '*Take your time*.'

'Now who's cautious?' he retorted.

It was plain he didn't like me, and that I couldn't expect the cooperation I had received from Tunde. In that case, Nina would have to do the reassuring and cajoling.

The valve opened. The hold chamber was dark: we could see nothing without stepping inside.

At first I thought the chamber was empty, but the glownodes brightened in response to our entry and I saw it.

Against the far wall, safely ensconced in the slender webbing of a packing threader, was a bulging sac taller than any human and twice as wide. An oval sac with veins and arteries standing out on its surface. Inside could be discerned the shape of two human figures, fully adult.

We only had a few instants to register it, but the three of us knew what it was. Screeching with alarm, the threader itself came scuttling out of the shadows, an arachnid the size of a scroungedog intent on defending its charge.

We had no time to react. The creature pounced, closing its fangs around Imrani's thigh. I felt the venom go into the muscle like a flood of iced water, and then we were falling, the threader scuttling back out of reach with a rasp of chitin.

Imrani fell backwards, and the paralysis spread swiftly up his body. Dimly I was aware of the threader continuing to screech, and presently a face loomed over us.

It was Elydia. She smiled.

'So here you are! We thought you had managed to sneak on board one of the ships, but I didn't quite expect to find you here. How enterprising of you!'

I tried to speak, but Imrani couldn't have used his voice even if he had wanted to: his vocal cords were frozen.

'Hasn't the womb grown?' she said, and it was the last thing I heard or saw as a tide of blackness washed over us.

Part Three

THE OORT CROWD

Eleven

'What is this?' Marea was asking.

'It's a null-shrine,' Vargo said, 'though they never tell you that. You can use it in the ordinary way, but there's a special override. They let you plug in, commune with your ancestors, and then, when you're not expecting it – zap! – they extinguish your consciousness, and that's the end of you.'

Marea had her hands in the prayer gloves, though the shrine was not activated.

'Is that what you used to do?' she asked.

'It was one of my duties,' he told her.

'You were an executioner?' Cori said, wide-eyed.

He shook his head. 'It's the shrine that does the executing. I was the pilot.'

'How many times?' Cori wanted to know.

Vargo looked down at her. 'Six,' he said.

'Exactly six?' said Marea.

'You never forget one.'

'You saw it happen?' Cori asked.

Vargo didn't reply directly. He addressed the ship: 'Show us the freezer compartment.'

Lidded flaps on the wall opened, revealing a low but wide horizontal chamber bathed in a frosty light. There was room for several bodies.

'Do they put you in there?' said Marea.

'It's a corpse hold. For storage until the ship reaches its destination.'

'And then what?'

'Who knows? Maybe they'd have used you for spare parts,

or biowired your cortex into a ship's control system. Ship, does your consciousness derive from a crim?'

'Certainly not!' the ship replied huffily. 'I was grown on Iapetus, Dhall Transfigurations, politia craft a speciality. My cognitive functions were developed by a specialized team.'

'Any information on the potential usage of the corpse of Marea Elodaris, Bellona Environs, Mars?'

The ship made a burbling noise, then a chirrup. 'There's nix on my mangofeast. Poot.'

'Sometimes they install you in a pleasure centre as a piece of erotica,' Vargo said. 'Or maybe—'

'You knew,' Marea interrupted.

'Yes, I knew.'

'Is that why you agreed to come with me?'

'Dying's a lonely business. It's even worse when it's an execution. When there's no one there who knows you or cares a damn.'

Marea gazed at him for long moments without speaking. She was dark-eyed, haggard.

'Did they choose you because of your religion?'

'Maybe they did. I never asked.'

She withdrew her hands from the gloves and rose from the terminal, wrapping her cloak tight around her.

'Didn't you ever feel any qualms?'

'You know the kinds of people who get blanked? Child murderers. Multiple killers. Individuals who refuse corrective psychosurgery, who relish their crimes. Those are the ones I saw off.'

'I didn't do any of those things.'

'It was hard to imagine you did.'

'Was this the ship they were going to send?'

'The very same.'

'Why didn't you say anything? You knew it had a null-shrine.'

'What difference would it have made? They'd have had to web you in if you'd known. I've seen it happen. Not a pretty sight.'

Marea looked again at the twin seats, the spaces in the corpse hold. 'Do they do them in batches?'

'It's happened,' Vargo said. 'Not in my time. I only ever carried singletons.'

'Did they know?' Cori asked.

'Sometimes.'

'Were they scared?'

'To their souls.'

She was full of ghoulish interest. 'So who did the executing?'

'Usually it would be an expediter or a judicator. No flashing lights or melting flesh or screams of torment. One minute you were alive, the next you were dead.'

But he said it dramatically, peering close at Cori. She drank his words in and then, as if she had weighed it up and finally reached her conclusion, announced: 'Well I think it's perfectly horrible.'

She went over to Marea and hugged her.

'You shouldn't have made her hide in there.'

This was Tunde, speaking to me. Only now did I fully realize that I was inhabiting him again. There had been a period of complete darkness and blankness immediately following Imrani's collapse. I had no idea how long it had lasted.

Tunde must have spoken aloud, because Cori said, 'I was safe. I had Nina with me. She's back.'

Vargo gazed at her, then at Tunde. 'You, too?'

Tunde nodded.

'What do they want?'

Tunde waited for me to answer, but it was Cori who spoke:

'All we know is that we're being guided by servants of the Noosphere.'

It was Nina speaking through her. Vargo didn't try to hide the fact that he was less than delighted by our return.

'What is it this time?' he asked.

'We want to help,' I said through Tunde.

'We don't need you,' he said. 'Or the ones you claim are directing you.'

'Really?' I said acidly. 'Without our help, you'd have never got off Io.'

Marea stalked past us and went down the gangway.

Tunde made to follow her, but Vargo blocked the way, holding Cori back too.

'Listen to me,' he said. 'I don't trust either of you. You let anything nasty happen to her and I'll kill you.'

Cori gave a little squeak of terror. Vargo swept her up into his arms. "'Course I'd have to do it without hurting *you*,' he said to her.

'Orbituary,' the ship blurted. 'Loop-de-loop. No villains please.'

I understood from Tunde that Vargo had only been able partially to restore the ship's cortex; it phased in and out of lucidity.

We joined Marea in the bridgehead. Hours must have passed since I last inhabited Tunde because we were in orbit around Europa, a cloud-streaked water world not unlike Earth, except that it lacked significant landmasses. Europans lived on floating plantations, harvesting various crops for export to other worlds.

'I suppose I should thank you,' Marea said to Tunde.

I decided to take a backseat. Tunde said, 'Will you marry me, Marea?'

Her expression didn't alter. She went to a dispensary and punched up a tube of vine-milk.

'You like your women without hair?' she said.

'It'll grow back. I'm serious.'

She sucked the milk through a straw, draining it avidly, eyes on him. But she said nothing further.

I had the impression that he had done much more explaining during my absence, telling her the truth about his life, or at least the truth as he saw it.

'Will you?'

'You can certainly pick your moment. This is hardly the time, is it?'

'I love you.'

She shook her head.

'I do.' He said it as if it were a statement of principle.

'That's easy to say. How do I know I can trust you?'

Cori had been listening with absorbed curiosity. 'She's quite right, Father,' she remarked. 'I think you're lucky you got away with a smack on the cheek.'

Marea laughed. 'Is that you speaking, or the other one?'

'Me, of course!' Cori said indignantly. 'He's *my* father.'

Without a further word, Marea walked off, heading towards the rear of the ship. Tunde made to follow, but Vargo said, 'Leave her.'

I agreed with him, and told Tunde as much. He stood rooted with indecision. After a minute or so the shrine sensory on the flight ridge winked on.

Marea was communing with her ancestors.

In our absence, Vargo had suggested making for Europa. It was the closest settled world to Io, and he had friends in a small Deist community on one of the equatorial plantations who might be prepared to shelter them. But there was to be no opportunity to test this.

'Hectic,' the ship burbled. 'Meddlesummer.' Then it announced in more normal fashion that another craft was in the vicinity and on an interception course.

The longsight showed it to be a heavily armed interdictor, the mainstay of the politia fleet that patrolled the interworld flight paths to discourage smuggling and piracy. It was already asking us to identify ourselves.

The ship was big and fearsome-looking, its armoured hull and barbed wings sprouting pulse-cannons, scorpion tail packed with plasma borbs.

'It's decision time,' Vargo said to Tunde. 'Do we stay and chat, or run for it?'

Tunde didn't like the idea of having to decide. I wanted to see how he would react without my intervention.

'Can we get away?' he asked.

'In theory,' Vargo said. 'Interdictors are fast, but the scuttle could probably outpace it on a short run. That's assuming they don't decide to fire on us.'

A single direct hit from a pulse-cannon would be enough to disable the ship, while a plasma borb, a sphere of incandescent antimatter, would annihilate it in a flash.

'I thought your friends are supposed to know the answers,' Vargo was saying. 'What do they tell you?'

I hadn't been aware of Chloe and Lucian until now; they manifested themselves, telling me what to do.

Through Tunde I spoke another code to the ship, which promptly acknowledged and transmitted it.

Vargo looked suspicious. 'What was that about?'

'I suggest we swap clothes,' I said. 'You've just been reinstated to the politia at your former rank, your criminal records erased.'

He simply stood there.

'I'm not joking,' I said. 'This is straight from the Noosphere. How'd you think we got control of this ship in the first place?'

Vargo was a pragmatic man, as evidenced by the fact that he had accommodated himself to the presence of Nina and myself within Cori and Tunde, despite his misgivings. While we changed clothes, the scuttle broadcast the information that it was transporting a blanked prisoner from Io under the command of Varentinian Goboruwulan Peichnek.

'Is that your full name?' I couldn't resist asking.

The ship's mobile console weaved up to him, gurgitating an irised lens which I instructed him to put in his blind eye. With some reluctance, he did so. It had the effect of making the eye appear normal.

The interdictor confirmed that the flight was authorized, but requested person-to-person communication. This was a surprise; even Chloe and Lucian seemed to believe that we would have been allowed to fly on without further inquiry.

Vargo climbed into the pilot's seat while the rest of us hid out of the comlink's line of sight.

The optic opened, showing a woman pilot at the controls of the interdictor.

'Your ship is armed,' she said; it was a statement rather than a question: all scuttles were fitted with pulse-cannons as a minimum. 'You're needed for other duties. Proceed immediately to Callisto orbit and await further instructions.'

Vargo was taken by surprise at this, and he almost glanced back to where Tunde was hiding.

'What is this?' he said angrily. 'I've got a corpse to deliver. It can't wait.'

'These are emergency orders,' the woman said. 'They override your previous instructions.'

Vargo held his ground. 'This is judicial business. You're executive. Back off.'

The woman didn't even blink. 'You have two minutes to comply, Commander Peichnek. If you don't, and attempt to resist or escape, we'll disable your craft – even if that means you die as a result.'

The optic blanked.

Vargo jumped up as the rest of us came out of hiding.

'I thought we were supposed to be in the clear!' he said.

I had a sense that Chloe and Lucian had been referring back, presumbly to some source in the Noosphere. They conveyed what was apparently unanticipated information to me. I passed it on through Tunde:

'The order is new, and there's no way of countermanding it. It's come direct from the Advocates themselves.'

Twelve

The Advocates' ship was like a pearl-white bird with arching wings and a forked tail. Yet this was no decorative ceremonial craft but a powerful and agile flyer, heavily armed in case of unwarranted attack, its crew hand-picked by Orela and Julius themselves. There was talk that the Advocates had named it *The Glory Rode*.

The ship was on full propulsion, six hours out from Mercury. Bezile had tried to nap in the interim, but sleep eluded her. The summons to accompany the Advocates had been another bolt from the blue.

Leanderic, the Advocates' chief steward, escorted Bezile and Luis from their quarters to the bridgehead, a study in poise with his delicate movements and impeccable manners. The bridgehead itself was spacious enough to hold an entire convocation of arbiters, tiered skulldecks rising from the navigation pit where both crew and palace minions attended the sensitories. Banks of optics on the flight ridges fed in a constant welter of information from the Settled Worlds so that the Advocates were kept informed of the current status of the Noosphere, wherever they were. Julius and Orela always had been an itinerant pair, never dwelling long in one place. They also travelled light: the entire ship's complement numbered no more than two dozen souls.

Bezile was irritable from lack of sleep, and when Luis wondered aloud, and with his usual trepidation, where they were heading, she simply told him to shut up. The council had been adjourned abruptly soon after her appointment as Venzano's successor, Julius and Orela telling everyone to return posthaste to their Arbitrations to await further important instructions. She had no idea what was afoot, but the Advocates plainly enjoyed mystery. She only hoped that none of it was connected with the loss of the womb. Even before Shivaun had betrayed her calling, she had received a personal communication from Leanderic directing her to say nothing of the affair to anyone. Absolutely nothing. Well, she'd abided by that. Even Luis hadn't got the slightest hint. *Especially* Luis.

They were led down a spiralway into the big hospitality chamber in the belly of the ship. The plass floor gave a dizzying perspective of space, the star-mottled darkness stretching downwards for ever. Bezile raised her gaze, breathing steadily to control herself, surprised to see that the entire chamber was empty except for the small conical cloud of a privacy screen at its furthest end. As they approached it, Luis stumbled and almost fell face down, but Leanderic grasped his arm in one effortless movement and steadied him. Bezile resisted the urge to chuckle. Luis looked quite uncoordinated with fear, his mouth soundlessly opening and closing in thanks.

They faced the screen.

'Step through,' they were told.

Bezile did not hesitate: it was better to get it done. Taking Luis's elbow, she passed through the veil.

Julius and Orela sat together among a nest of white sofa snakes. Bezile was startled to see that both of them were quite naked, only the padded coils of the snakes preserving a certain modesty. She had to admit she was shocked. Though nudity was in no sense disreputable in many societies of the Noospace, Julius and Orela had never been seen publicly – or privately, insofar as she knew – without some vestment of their office. Apart from anything else, the people expected their Advocates to maintain a proper sense of their status. Bezile felt as if she and Luis had stumbled unwittingly on a private moment.

But both Julius and Orela seemed perfectly at ease with themselves, indicating stools in front of them. Stools! And inorganic at that, bare ribbed metal with a kind of grating on top, like cast-offs from some ancient vintage ship. Bezile had never put her ample bottom on anything more uncomfortable.

'We're so pleased you were able to accompany us,' Orela said, as if there had been a real choice in the matter. 'We felt a private audience was most appropriate, given everything that's happened. Once again, our heartfelt congratulations on your worthy appointment as Prime Arbiter.'

'Such a refreshingly *unexpected* outcome,' Julius added with apparent enthusiasm. 'We're quite confident you will serve us most successfully.'

Bezile didn't like the tenor of this. She noticed that Luis's hands were clasped together as if in prayer, the fingerjoints bloodless. He was staring at the Advocates' feet.

She decided to take the initiative.

'It was indeed unexpected,' she agreed. 'I truly did not aspire to the post but I will serve to the best of my capacities.'

'Naturally you will,' said Julius. 'We expect nothing less.'

'I'm grateful for the opportunity to express my regrets directly to you over the episode with the womb. The woman was a clone-daughter, a perfectly trustworthy servant of the Noosphere in the past. I had no reason to think that she would betray us.'

Julius waved her apology aside. 'We've no desire to rake over the past. What's done is done. You were less culpable than others, though it might have been wiser to have contacted the Noosphere directly you acquired the womb rather than Prime Arbiter Venzano. He is – *was* – not perhaps as *diligent* a servant as yourself, and certainly not as efficient, given that he allowed himself to be fooled by a crude simulacrum. And let the woman escape into the bargain.'

It sounded like they had no regrets about Venzano's passing. Bezile stopped this line of thought immediately.

'He was also rather tardy in informing us that it was in his possession,' Orela said. 'It's essential that the Prime Arbiter maintains an *intimate* degree of communication with our offices.'

Bezile managed to swallow. 'Of course,' she said briskly.

'No matter,' said Julius. 'And yet you must have been curious.'

'Curious?'

'About the womb itself. Its very nature.'

'I made some investigations,' she admitted. 'Consulted an

old and trusted friend who has now passed on. He was able to tell me very little.'

Orela stroked her cheek against one of the snakes. 'We know you to be a loyal servant after your own fashion, and we feel it only proper that we tell you the secret of the womb.'

It was a qualified compliment, and for an instant Julius's eyes had gone to Luis. In that microsecond, Bezile understood that Luis was an agent of the Advocates, doubtless reporting everything she did to them. She quelled the flash of anger she felt, used every iota of self-control to keep herself focused on what was being said.

'The womb was made by Augmenter sympathizers within the Noosphere itself,' Orela said. 'It contains two foetuses, a male and a female. They are intended to be our heirs.'

She could tell that even Luis had not known this.

'The Augmenters have infiltrated the Noosphere?'

'They have followers everywhere,' Orela said. 'Small in number, but they nevertheless exist.'

'Who are they?'

'At present we only know them by their actions. They hide their tracks well, but we're taking steps to root them out.'

'What is not clear,' said Julius, 'is precisely what sort of human creatures are inside the womb.'

To Bezile's astonishment, Orela had allowed a snake to slip its tail between her legs. She was moving against it, pressing its coils against her belly.

'We're aware,' Julius was saying, 'that there is a small body of opinion within the Noocracy itself that has a certain sympathy with the Augmenters, that might like to readmit them to full citizenship. Perhaps you yourself might be inclined to show, let us say, a degree of charity towards them?'

This was too much. 'With great respect, I find it remarkable that you should consider that. I've never had any truck with Augmenters.'

'Good,' Orela said. It was like a moan of pleasure. Her eyes were half-closed, the snake slithering at her groin ... Bezile had to force herself not to look.

'It was not a serious suggestion,' Julius said, 'but there's no harm in clarifying such matters. These days many loyalties are ambiguous.'

Bezile nodded, said, 'Indeed,' and was unable to resist glancing at Luis. He still sat with his eyes downcast, not daring to look at anyone.

To her relief, Orela appeared to have exhausted her diversion with the snake, though one of her breasts was quite bared. At least Julius was maintaining a degree of proper dignity. But then he thrust a finger up one nostril and began rummaging around. She couldn't help her astonished stare. He quite ignored her.

'We were concerned to clarify your position,' Orela said, 'because an Augmenter assault is imminent.'

This was merely repeating their rhetoric at the council. They had not actually specified the exact nature of the threat.

'It's important we show you the extent of the danger,' Julius remarked. 'To that end, we've arranged a little diversion.'

Bezile had already noticed that the light coming through the portals beyond the privacy veil had begun to turn blue. Orela nulled the veil.

The entire hospitality chamber was flooded with azure light. Directly below them was Earth.

Julius smiled at her surprise.

'The home of our species,' he said. 'Birthplace of us all.'

Bezile had never been this close to the planet. No doubt the flier was using it as a gravity slingshot for the final short hop to the Noosphere. Yet even as she thought this, she saw from the expressions on the Advocates' faces that this was not the case.

'We're landing there?'

'A brief sojourn,' Julius informed her. 'As Prime Arbiter it's important you understand what the Augmenters are capable of.'

She did her best to sound composed. 'There are Augmented there? On Earth?'

Julius wafted a hand, as if it were a moot point. 'Of a sort. Contained, naturally, so no mischief is possible. You and your secretary will be quite protected.'

The revelation made sense, in a horrible sort of way. Earth, the very source of the human race and the place where many of its bioforms were first fashioned, had been irreparably contaminated by them and had been abandoned once the other worlds of the Noosphere were settled. It had long been used as a dumping ground for failed or maverick species: unruly houseplants, rogue vehicles, degenerate strains of everything from bacteria to behemoths had been sent there, along with shiploads of plasma slurry doubtless containing every manner of microorganisms that might by now have metamorphosed into heaven knew what.

The planet had long been uninhabitable in the normal human sense of the word with that sort of mess lying around. Generations before Bezile's time there had been a great debate throughout the Inner Planets as to whether the dumping should be stopped, the unwanted strains destroyed at source or sent into the sun as a matter of permanent policy; Earth could then be cleansed and resettled. Ultimately, though, this was deemed impossible to carry out. Firstly, there was the widespread aversion to the wilful destruction of protoplasm, especially on a planetary scale. And consider the cost, let alone the practicality, of sterilizing a whole world! Secondly, there had always been independent operators who were ready to evacuate cargos of any kind practically anywhere as long as no one was looking: an official dumping ground would marginalize that sort of illicit activity. And finally, it was suggested that a useful if chaotic gene pool would always be present on Earth should it be needed in the future.

But no one landed on Earth, had not done, as far as Bezile was aware, for centuries. Junks skirted its atmosphere, launching their waste from high orbit or, better still, during distant flybys. If any fugitives had attempted to hide there, they had never been heard of again. Earth had long been the pariah planet of the Noospace.

It filled the entire chamber now, bathing the four of them in its light. It made Julius and Orela appear even stranger than usual, shadows pooling under their eyes, giving them a demonic air. The snakes were writhing again, baring their fangs then jetting out a gauzy substance which formed veils over the Advocates' bodies, covering the more blatant features of their physicality. A novel way of donning undergarments, Bezile thought, trying to see the ludicrous, stage-managed side of it. The trouble was, it was no longer simply theatre. They were going down to the planet of the damned under the guidance of lunatics.

Leanderic appeared with the dove and scarlet vestments of their office. Grey was supposed to represent mentality, scarlet the emotional heart of humanity. Brain and blood. Bezile could not shake a graphic image of both. Suitably clothed, Julius and Orela managed to restore a certain sense of their proper status. But Bezile would not easily forget the snake at Orela's groin, the nostril bulging with Julius's finger.

Then a wardrobe waddled in, opening its midriff to reveal black leatherene bodysuits. The five of them – Leanderic included – were made to suit up so that another transformation took place: they looked like absurd stormtroopers out of *Augmenter Alert!* Bezile felt especially ridiculous, a lump in black plasticized armour.

Leanderic led them down to the bay in the underside of the ship. Luis would not meet her eye, and as much as Bezile would have welcomed the familiar routines of his company she could not think of him as anything other than a worm.

A scarab scouter sat in the main bay, its emerald flanks ornately filigreed with gold. Bulbous antennae sprouted from its head like reeds frozen with dew. The image surprised her: it had come from Mars, from a chill lakeside morning during one of her courtesy visits many years before. Terror made you sentimental.

They were taken on board and seated behind the Advocates in the control dome. Besides the four of them and Leanderic, there was a crew of only three. This was another departure: normally the Advocates were surrounded by a host of attendants and guards. The bulging eye blisters gave them an ample view of their destination.

Julius turned and laid a hand on Bezile's arm; she almost flinched at the contact. The scouter gave a slight lurch, and it was moments before Bezile realized that they had already launched, were dropping down towards the blue planet.

Julius began talking about the thunderstorms he had experienced on Earth, fierce torrents of water falling from enormous dark clouds, lightning splitting the sky, winds churning the sea into a frenzy of white-capped motion. He spoke of the fragrant air, the myriad ever-changing cloud-forms, the impenetrable green forests clamorous with life.

'Do you go there often?' Bezile asked, incredulous.

'Not as often as we would like,' Orela interjected. 'There's always so much else to do.'

She joined in, extolling the virtues of Earth's polar regions with their crags of floating ice and ultramarine waters in which she liked to swim naked, despite the chill and the strange organisms in the waters that sometimes caressed her flesh. Bezile was sure this was a joke. There was no reason to smile, either way. To her enormous surprise, Luis actually spoke:

'You have no fear of the . . . creatures there?'

Orela's smile was so lofty it was beyond patronizing.

'We take precautions,' she said. 'As you will see. Consider it a little adventure.'

Earlier there had been a buffeting, swiftly damped: they had obviously entered the atmosphere. Now the eyelids closed, blotting out the cloud-pocked oceans and the blotches of tawny-green land. The pale surfaces of the control dome shone instead, an eerie, doleful light.

Orela took Luis's palm and proceeded to study it, tracing its lines with the nail of her index finger. Luis froze like a marmosite in thrall to a jackadder. It was clear that, although he may have been their spy, he knew no more than Bezile about what was going to happen. Orela began to babble that palmistry was an ancient art, that much could be gleaned from the intimate details of the skin, its folds and lines, the spirals and arches on the fingertips.

'You have no children,' she announced. 'No wife.'

Luis nodded mechanically, in awe.

'You are an extremely diligent servant of the Noosphere. Sometimes you work too hard.'

Luis did not contradict this.

'To you, loyalty and industry are the prime personal virtues. You believe in decency, dignity and honour.'

'I do,' he managed to say.

And so it went on: a facile and factitious character portrait that merely reiterated common knowledge. How much longer would Bezile have to suffer this? Here she was, in the presence of the two humans who were the vessels through which the people expressed their wishes, the symbols of their governance and spiritual guidance: self-absorbed and spouting banalities.

One of the crew announced that they would soon be at sea level.

'You must excuse us,' Julius said. 'We shall not be long.'

He and Orela rose and departed down a corridor.

Bezile decided to ignore Luis, turning instead to Leanderic.

'Is there anything we should know?' she asked. 'So that we can be prepared?'

Leanderic hesitated for an instant, and Bezile thought that for once he might set his dutiful aplomb aside. But the moment passed.

'There's nothing I can tell you,' he said.

Something in his tone made Bezile say, 'Is this the first time you've accompanied the Advocates here?'

'Yes.'

'What's it all about?'

'I know no more than you.'

Bezile was sure it was the truth. Leanderic, though a faithful servant of Orela and Julius, was not renowned for guile or dissembling.

He rose and went to attend the Advocates, as if he risked disloyalty should he stay. As soon as he was gone, Bezile turned on Luis:

'Do *you* have any idea?'

He stared at her as if astonished.

'No,' he spluttered. 'None, I promise you. I'm as much in the dark as anyone.'

She gave him her evil eye, and he withered.

'You know I never trusted you,' she said.

This was not true; what irked her most was that she had. But it was easy to induce a sense of guilt in someone as conscientious as Luis: excessive diligence was always a mask for deep feelings of personal inadequacy.

'How long have you been their spy?'

He didn't like the word, but she knew he wouldn't be able to deny it. He looked away.

'I was simply asked to report confidentially on the running of your Arbitration direct to the Advocates' office. I assumed it was common practice. I did not consider I was being disloyal.'

She gazed long at him and sighed. 'No. I don't suppose you did. That's why people like you are so invaluable to people like them.'

It was the closest she had ever come to speaking with outright disloyalty; but Luis was too wrapped up in his own anxieties to notice.

'You knew I had acquired the womb?' she asked.

He couldn't resist a certain smugness. 'That was obvious.'

'Did you think I couldn't be trusted?'

'It wasn't a question of that. It was felt – I was led to believe – that you might not always be in full possession of the facts that would allow you to work in the best interests of the Noosphere.'

She made a scornful sound. 'That's mealy-mouthed!'

He kept his head lowered. 'I only did as I saw best. For the interests of us all.'

She had no desire to berate him further. He was simply an efficient functionary, one of the many dutiful and unimaginative types whom those in power could always make use of. She had done so herself on endless occasions.

Julius and Orela returned. They were wearing black helmets with viewfinders and flared gauntlets. As if to complete the transformation into toy soldiers, Orela was shouldering a squat rifle with a dark hole at its bulbous end. Julius had belted a holster on to his armour. It held a long-barrelled pistol.

Leanderic settled them in their seats, still treating them like icons even though they looked like thugs. Their seats span webbing around them as the ship began to decelerate.

'Do you always arm yourselves on these visits?' Bezile asked with what she hoped was conversational innocence.

'There's nothing to fear,' Orela said. 'You're under our protection.'

Presently the eyelids opened, and Bezile saw that they were flying over a vast expanse of ocean. The sky above was bluer

than she could have imagined, an infinite depthless blue. There
was no land in sight, nothing but water. But as she stared she
could see swirling patches of colour in the aquamarine, like
clouds of animate mud. As the ship slowed, she glimpsed a
pale shape snaking through the water, then a mass of tendrilled
jelly that seemed to squirm and pulse as they flew by low and
slow, too close to the waves for her comfort. Something
erupted from the water, splattering the blister with blood-
brown effusions. The lids blinked it away. There were things
like knotted green ribbons coiling in the air surrounded by
darting curlicued creatures that were attacking and perhaps
eating them, Bezile didn't care to know precisely. They flew
through a swarm of insectoids that clung briefly to the blisters
like small black sunbursts, then were gone.

'Interesting, isn't it?' said Orela.

What was one to say? 'I presume Luis and I will also need
protection when we go outside.'

'That won't be necessary, I assure you. We'll be landing
somewhere a little less . . . active. There's no reason for you to
be concerned.'

In fact it was all designed precisely with that purpose in
mind. And it was working, most demonstrably on Luis, who
had the frozen stare and the twitching hands of the thoroughly
mortified.

In the near distance was a smear of land. The shuttle
accelerated again, and they approached it rapidly, flying in
over a littoral that looked clogged with dense pink and crimson
foam. Trees reared up, branches bent and corkscrewed, leaves
like flaps of rotting hide. Then they were crossing clearer
ground punctuated everywhere with pools and small lakes,
now climbing again, up the flanks of a low mountain whose
dimpled top held a small greenish lake. The scarab ship banked,
circled, hovered. Descended.

The landing was faultless: they settled as if the scouter had
been laid to rest on a pillow. The engine pulse dimmed, died.
As the dust cleared, Bezile saw that they were perched on the
ledge of the crater rim overlooking the lake.

The Advocates were already released from their webbing.

Leanderic helped Bezile out of her seat. Luis asked again if they were to be given helmets, gloves, more protection.

'Not necessary,' Julius assured him. 'This is merely a stop-over. We simply want you to see the sights.'

'What about masks, air filters?' he persisted, his fear quite overcoming his normal sense of decorum.

'And miss the smells of Earth?' said Orela blithely. 'Its tastes and textures? You'll be fully scanned when we return. We'll put you in a purger and have your bodily fluids replaced if necessary. Don't be alarmed, it's quite a stimulating experience. We've undergone it several times and it's hardly damaged us, has it?'

In that jaunty moment, Bezile knew that they were truly mad. Fluid exchange was standard medical intervention when systemic infection was suspected, but a mask would have obviated the need for such protracted treatment. It was clear that the Advocates *enjoyed* this sort of indignity. It was part of their patent urge to court danger and discomfort.

The main airvalve was already open, waiting for them.

'Are we walking?' Bezile said, still not quite able to believe it.

'A leisurely stroll on the mother of worlds,' said Julius. 'Think of yourself as a sightseer.'

Only the five of them descended the ramp; the crew remained with the ship. Orela toted her rifle and Julius commented soothingly that their 'excursion' would be constantly monitored from the scouter: it could come instantly to their rescue in the unlikely event that they got into difficulties. Luis was already huddling as close to Bezile as her disapproval would allow.

The air was warm, redolent of sickly blossoms and rank vegetation. Overhead the sun shone down dazzlingly from the serene white-streaked blue. They descended a gradual slope towards the lake, rock giving way to patchy vegetation, spiked and flapped, hung with mortifying bruised white flowers. Spinning things rasped past them and veils of amber vapour drifted by – pollen, Bezile supposed, unable to prevent herself from inhaling it. They were still walking on bare rock, follow-ing a rough path that kept them clear of vegetation; but tiny creatures were skittering around her booted feet. She did not glance down.

After a short while they approached the margins of the lake. The stench of aquatic decay was overpowering now, the tangled vegetation alive with clouds of insects.

'Here we need to be a little more circumspect,' Orela said conversationally, leading them forward. 'It's important to look before you tread.'

But then, to Bezile's complete surprise, she levelled her rifle and unleashed a torrent of fire.

Both Bezile and Luis leapt back in alarm, and even Leanderic was startled. The rifle gave off a hoarse roar, and the flame kept jetting out of its end as Orela swung it back and forth in an arc, smothering everything in the vicinity of the lake. Above the roar, Bezile heard a terrified animal shriek, and something large, like a many-winged bat, whirled up into the air, its leathery limbs blazing. It tried to flee across the water, but Julius, who had been clapping with delight while Orela doused the ground with fire, unholstered his pistol. The viewfinders dropped down over his eyes and he took careful aim.

The bolt hit the creature in one of its wings. It did a kind of feeble somersault in the air, then crashed down to the charred earth. Julius did not pause. He spun around and fired at another creature, an inverted coronet of pink jelly that had come scuttling out of the inferno. The bolt vaporized it.

There was more – more slaughter and mayhem. Bezile closed her eyes to it, hearing only the roar of the flame and the cries of the Advocates, cries of delighted bloodlust as they employed their weapons punctuated by shrieks and squeals from the things they were dispatching. It went on and on. Bezile tried to think of her ancestors, of the tranquillity of a shrine, private moments of peace and companionship with the immortal afterlife. This was worse than she had dared imagine.

A silence fell, and Bezile realized that Orela had finally switched off the flame. The air was thick with poisonous smoke. Then a breeze came up like a balm, washing it away.

Around them nothing moved and nothing could be heard. High in the air dark shapes were hovering – twisted bird-like things, circling, keeping their distance. All that remained of the vegetation in front of them was black ash, fires still flickering around its edges, tufts of smoke trickling up into the boundless sky.

Bezile's eyes stung. Luis and Leanderic stood rooted like herself. The Advocates had removed their helmets and were inhaling deeply, their weapons lowered; they seemed sated. Bezile didn't dare meet Luis's gaze; he was swaying slightly, as if he might faint. Leanderic was blank with shock.

Presently Julius turned to them and said, 'A rather violent outburst, I'll grant you, but things are different here. Sterilization procedures are absolutely vital.'

There was a light, almost cheerful note in his voice. Bezile was devoid of any response. *Sterilization procedures.* So that was what they called it. She was startled to hear Luis say: 'What are we going to do now?'

'Now?' said Julius. He pointed the barrel of his pistol towards a nearby outcrop. 'Now perhaps we'll sit on that rock for a while, in the sunshine. We have to wait until the ground has cooled before we can go down to the water.'

It was almost like a non sequitur, the latest of many. There were beetles and spidery things regularly traversing the bare rock, and although most must have been incinerated or frightened into hiding by the fire, Bezile did not care to sit upon it. But there was no alternative.

The five of them proceeded to perch themselves on the outcrop, Julius and Orela sitting cross-legged on its flat top while Bezile merely leant against a shaded incline, keeping a careful watch for any scuttling creatures. Luis and Leanderic sat on either side of her, not speaking, eyes glazed. Above them the bird things spiralled while ahead of them the ash smouldered and the air held the stenches of destruction. Not since her days as a novice had Bezile contemplated the ancient idea of Hell. It existed, and she was here.

She could see the Advocates from her position. They had raised their bare faces to the sun and were holding hands – a gesture which Bezile found sickening under the circumstances. She felt suffocated by the body armour, suffocated and defiled.

'No doubt you are shocked,' Orela said out of the blue.

Bezile wondered what to say that wouldn't sound banal.

'Such wanton destruction of life,' Orela went on. 'It's against all our principles, the more so because Julius and I represent the conscience of the Noosphere. No doubt that is what you are thinking, yes?'

There was no spit in Bezile's mouth: no words to say.

'And yet have you never felt the urge to vent such violence? Truly? If only as a fleeting thought?'

Now Orela was peering down at her with her mad black eyes.

'Well?' she insisted.

There was nothing for it but to humour her.

'There have been occasions,' she confessed, 'when I could have cheerfully wrung a few necks.' She made a point of glancing at Luis, and he visibly winced.

'Precisely,' said Orela. 'But we control such urges in civilized society unless we're criminals or insane. Here, however, normal civilized standards don't apply because there *is* no civilization, nothing that gives evidence of human shaping and organization. It is merely biological chaos.'

Sunlight was gleaming gold on the scarab's closed eyelids, up there on the rim, too far away.

'But is not all life sacred' – Bezile couldn't believe she was actually saying this – 'and to be preserved for its own sake wherever possible?'

'Indeed,' Orela said emphatically. 'But it's the human purpose, the very future of us, that we are concerned with here. That's why it was necessary for me to clear a path to the water. The lifeforms are riotous here – riotous and destructive. We might have been attacked had we let any survive.'

The bird things were closer now, hovering silently as if awaiting their moment of revenge.

'What about those?' Bezile said, pointing.

It was Julius who leapt to his feet and unleashed a bolt from the pistol. It exploded wide of the birds, but they scattered with rasping shrieks and furiously fled in every direction.

'You see?' Orela said. 'These weapons are merely protective.'

Bezile was tired of words; they could be made to say anything.

'Perhaps you would welcome a drink?' Julius said, producing a water goblin from his belt.

Bezile shook her head.

He squeezed the goblin and its mouth opened. He put it to his lips and drained it, water running down his chin. Then he tossed the creature into the ashes, watching where it fell. It twitched, but did not flee.

'I think,' Julius said, rising, 'we can proceed.'

They walked down through the ash. The dark cinders crunched under their feet and dusted the uppers of their boots. Bezile could feel the warmth percolating through. Nothing living moved in it.

The pool was not large, but it appeared deep, its dirty greenish surface reflecting the scattered cloud. As they reached the water's edge, Bezile saw a movement in the water, something that seemed to be shifting and changing shape, something that looked like large starry cells, interconnected with long branching threads, a network spreading the entire extent of the pool.

'Don't go too close,' Orela said, with the whispered mischief of a child.

The cells, like spiked amoebae, were milky white to pinkish, their circular nuclei blood-black. The nuclei appeared to blink as the cells reorientated themselves, making new connections, others withering, even as she stared.

'What is it?' she asked.

'A suprahuman,' Orela informed her.

'A what?'

'We thought of giving it a name,' Julius said. 'But it seemed rather inappropriate to something that is not truly human, not in the traditional sense, at least.'

He was enjoying himself, toying with their curiosity and alarm.

'What is it?' Bezile said again.

'It's an Augmenter creation,' Orela said. 'An aquatic life-form. A development of *Homo sapiens*.'

Bezile didn't believe this for a moment. But the thing in the water had begun to stir at the sound of their voices. The water roiled, and suddenly a shape rose up out of it, a shape made of that very water, the interconnecting cells threaded through it. The shape it took on was that of a human.

She, Luis and Leanderic backed away instinctively. The water creature 'stood' near the shore, perfectly sized, and it spoke:

'Welcome.'

Its 'voice' was like a gargle. Julius and Orela looked delighted.

'Did you have this made?' Bezile said.

'Certainly not,' said Julius. 'It was confiscated and "exiled" here.'

'Is it intelligent?' said Luis.

'Very much so,' said Julius. 'Go to the edge. It will communicate with you.'

Plainly Luis was petrified at the idea.

'Go,' said Orela. 'Speak to it.'

They used the full persuasive power of their voices, but Bezile suspected it was the way in which both were holding their weapons that made Luis shuffle forward a little.

'Go closer,' Orela said with a smile. 'It's from human stock, just like you.'

He did as he was asked, moving right to the edge of the shoreline. The water thing continued burbling, though its words were not quite recognizable.

'Is this close enough?' said Luis, voice squeaky with terror.

And then the thing reached out and took him.

It happened so quickly that Bezile, though on her guard, was completely shocked. The edge of the water suddenly flowed forward, lapping over Luis's feet then rising up his body to cover him completely. At the same time he was pitched forward into the water, dragged below it so that he vanished. Then the human shape dropped down and water began roiling again. Bezile could see the branches and cells of it flashing through changes in size and orientation. This went on for long seconds, perhaps even minutes, as Bezile stood aghast. Then the human thing rose up again.

'Bezile,' it said.

Bezile fled, back through the cinders towards the track. She expected that Julius and Orela would try to stop her, perhaps by shooting her down; but they did not.

She huddled under the outcrop. Leanderic was also retreating in some haste. The Advocates turned and slowly followed.

Bezile's heart was rampant in her chest, her throat hot with her flight. Leanderic joined her, his composure quite gone. Bezile felt light-headed, unreal.

The thing was still 'standing' in the water, 'facing' towards her. The Advocates approached.

'He's not dead,' Orela said. And smiled. 'He's merely been absorbed into its being.'

Bezile could see no trace of terror or disgust in her eyes. They were dead, the deadness that comes when one is sated with experience, when one has lived too long, witnessed or participated in everything from the sublime to the terrible and has lost the normal human capacities of response.

'Each node acts as a centre of intelligence,' Julius was saying. 'There is instant communication between them, great cohesiveness of form and mind.'

'You sacrificed him!' she bellowed. 'You let him be swallowed up!'

They both remained unmoved. Orela said, 'It was necessary.'

'Necessary! Why? He didn't deserve that!'

'He's not dead,' Orela said again. 'He now forms part of the whole organism. As far as we know, he is still intact within the greater body.'

'I'm sure that's a huge consolation to him! Is it my turn next?'

They shook their heads, suddenly serious.

'We had to show you,' Julius said. 'This is what the Augmenters want us to become.'

Bezile forced herself to stand upright. The water thing was gone, vanished back down. But only gone from sight.

'That is the future they ultimately intend for the human race,' Orela said. 'A suprahuman, many minds existing as one in a physical form.'

'The organism would be self-repairing,' Julius added. 'Potentially immortal.'

'At present it can only exist in water,' Orela said, 'which is

why we are able to contain it here. But the Augmenters'
ultimate aim is to create a racial organism that could survive
anywhere. A biological equivalent of the Noosphere.'

Was this merely more of their madness? Yet Bezile had seen
the creature herself, seen what it could do.

'It's repulsive,' she said. 'How would they ever muster
sufficient popular support for *that*?'

'They wouldn't need to,' said Julius, 'if force of arms gave
them control of the centres of power. They could then subvert
the Noosphere to achieve their aims.'

'What? And how would they do that?'

'They have a fleet of ships already on its way.'

Bezile glanced at Leanderic. He knew nothing, it was clear;
he was rigid with horror.

'Which is why we must make haste,' Orela said. 'Our own
defences have been summoned to combat the threat. We must
join them.'

Both she and Julius made to move away. Bezile said, 'You're
going to leave that . . . *thing* in there?'

They paused. Julius said, 'We wanted you to see it. The
decision on its future is yours.'

'Mine?'

'You're still within your lifespan,' Orela said. 'Your concerns
are more mortal than ours. Perhaps you have a better appreciation of what such a being would mean to the great mass of
humanity. You decide its fate.'

With this, she ceremonially handed over her rifle to Leanderic, who accepted it as if it were a sac full of poison. Then
she and Julius walked away along the track towards the ship.

Bezile stared after them, wondering if they did indeed, after
all, have some appreciation of their own madness. It occurred
to her that she might take the rifle from Leanderic and turn it
on them, put paid to their insanity for ever. But she was not
one to deny any human being the transition to the afterlife, let
alone the two who were supposed to be its archetypes, dangerously mad though they were.

Leanderic was standing stock-still, the rifle cradled in his
arms. As if he were holding an infant.

Bezile spoke his name, as gently as she could. 'We must act,' she said.

Leanderic nodded like an automaton. The lake was flat, featureless, giving no hint of the loathesomeness it contained.

'Come with me,' she told Leanderic.

The steward followed her back through the ash towards the lake shore. They did not go too close. The water thing rose up on their approach. Again it had the outline of a human, though whether man or woman it was impossible to say; impossible and irrelevant: it was just a parody of the real thing. Certainly there were no discernible features on its 'face'. Scant enough comfort in that.

'Bezile,' it said, voice like the rush of water.

Leanderic raised the rifle as if to ward it off. The display on the side of the barrel told Bezile the charge was set to maximum.

'You cannot kill me,' the thing seemed to be saying in a rather agitated yet doleful tone. Was this a declaration or a plea? Under the water, its cells were changing pattern frantically, as if to find some last-ditch counter to the threat it faced. Leanderic stood motionless.

'Let me,' Bezile said softly, offering to take the gun.

'Pleasshh . . .' said the thing in the water.

Leanderic fired.

The power of the blast made Bezile step back, but Leanderic did not move. He continued to direct the flame at the centre of the lake, and the nuclear roaring went on and on while the water seethed and steam billowed into the air. Soon they were entirely clouded, but Leanderic kept firing, holding the rifle steady, feet planted apart. Nothing could be heard above the roar of the flame, no cries, shrieks, nothing except the sound of annihilation. Bezile's throat was sore, she was nauseous, but she couldn't allow herself to faint.

Then, finally, it was ended. The rifle made a sound like a huge cough, and spat a final gout of flame before the roaring ceased.

Leanderic scarcely seemed to notice. The rifle dipped, then fell from his hands. Bezile saw that his palms were blistered from its heat. There were tear tracks down his sooty cheeks.

Bezile approached, drew the steward to her ample bosom. And waited while he trembled without tears against her breast.

After a time the air cleared. Every molecule in the lake had been vaporized and the silt at its bottom was hard and cracked with the heat. There was not a trace of the creature.

Bezile's head swam, and she had to blink hard to focus. She saw that the Advocates were waiting some way up the track. Overhead the bird things were circling again.

'Come,' she said to Leanderic, leading him away.

Thirteen

Again I woke to darkness. I had dreamt Bezile without volition; without volition I had left her.

Nina came close. I could tell she had been disturbed by the dream even before she spoke.

'Nathan?'

'I'm here.'

'It was horrible.'

And then she touched me.

I started, only realizing at her touch that we were both 'physical' once more.

I sat up, becoming aware that we were back in my room. I knew this because we were lying in my bed: there was no light; but I could smell Nina's warmth, feel her hand on my arm.

We hugged one another. Both of us were naked, and I breathed her in deeply, touched my lips to her shoulder blade to taste her. Her hair brushed my cheek, and her arms were tight across my back.

We didn't speak; both of us were so shocked by what we had experienced we had no words for it. I also felt an acute sense of loss in the knowledge that the Earth had become a world more alien than any of the others we had visited. I had no memories of how it had once been, but I still believed it was the place where Nina and I had been born, that it had once been our home. More than ever we were stripped of our birthrights, and we could make no accommodation with that fact except to cling on to one another in silence.

Presently the ceiling slowly began to suffuse with a pearly light. There were plain white bodysuits draped across the foot of the bed. We put them on.

The door opened. Chloe and Lucian entered.

They looked exactly the same as before, perfect composed youths. Imperturbably awaiting our questions.

'It really happened?' I asked. 'What we saw?'

'Yes,' Chloe assured me.

'That creature was fashioned by the Augmenters?'

'So we believe.'

'The womb, too?'

'No,' said Lucian. 'That is merely another of the Advocates' deceptions. You experienced what Bezile witnessed and heard. That experience was true. The facts may be otherwise.'

'I'm tired of this!' I shouted. 'I want to know exactly what's happening! Whose side are you on?'

'Our duty is to preserve the integrity of the Noosphere,' Chloe said calmly. 'It's now in crisis – that much must be obvious to you.'

'When did this happen?' Nina asked.

'You mean the episode on Earth?' said Lucian.

'Of course she means that!'

I stood a little taller than both of them, was larger built. But they were not intimidated.

'Most recently,' Lucian said. 'A matter of hours ago. Prime Arbiter Miushme-Adewoyin has only recently emerged from communion. That's how we have knowledge of it.'

I no longer felt any physical weakness, and I had an urge to grab the two of them and demand they tell us exactly what they wanted of us.

Chloe simply raised a hand and said, 'Come.'

And then, without apparent transition, we were moving along another tunnel of light which rose and opened out until we were looking down on a vast oval concourse, bone-white, surrounded by banded tiers of silver and gold that were obviously buildings or habitations for those who lived on the Noosphere. Overhead in the black sky hung the luminous Earth, clouds shrouding its vast oceans and sweeping landmasses.

I could no longer see it without thinking of the warped lifeforms that scuttled on its surfaces and swarmed in its oceans and atmosphere. I could not stop thinking about the thing in the lake.

Nina was clinging on to my arm. We stood on a sweeping platform overlooking the concourse. This, Chloe began to tell us, was the ceremonial heart of the Noosphere, where the people would gather for the public appearances of the Advocates on celebratory occasions or whenever significant pronouncements were made. Stalked optics loomed like pendulous flowers above us, ready to transmit such occasions to the inhabitants of the Settled Worlds. And behind us was the Shrine of Shrines itself.

We turned. A white dome arched upwards, its central spire a fluted ivory spear rising impossibly high. A portal in the dome pulsed open, a dark oval in the eggshell surface. Chloe and Lucian led us towards it.

Everything was vivid yet a little unreal. My dislocation was profound and I could not speak. The air hung motionless and sterile around us, nothing moving apart from ourselves. I caught a scent of Nina's femaleness and wanted to bury myself in her there and then.

Chloe and Lucian led us into the dome. There was a warm, almost reddish darkness, and again we seemed to glide along. Then everything brightened and we were standing at the centre of the dome, its entire vast surface blistered with countless multifaceted optics displaying an enormous variety of images. Some showed the faces of the Noocracy in ceremonial or public duties; others displayed panoramic views of thronged city streets, meremeadows, crater plantations, wheeled habitations moving as one across a storm-racked plain; yet others held single individuals seated before prayer terminals, communing with the afterlife.

There were thousands upon thousands of them, the images shifting and changing even as I stared. These were living pictures of the multitudes of the Settled Worlds in their multifarious guises, everyone from the elevated and protected in the most favoured circumstances to the debased and desperate in neglected corners of every inhabited surface throughout the physical realm of Noospace.

And there was more. I had a sense of the babble of their voices, the pleas, demands, fears, longings – the entire spectrum of human emotion was there, mute, on the screens, those in shrines urgent for comfort and guidance. Immediately before us was something that looked like a translucent sphere, holding at its centre something resembling a dual prayer terminal. And yet I knew, perhaps because Chloe and Lucian were telling me, that it was quite the reverse – a receptacle rather than a transmitter for the receiving of the prayers of those multitudes on the optics. This was the Shrine of Shrines.

Nina seemed as overwhelmed as I. We were dwarfed by the optics, by the sheer *population* they displayed and the enormity of their needs.

'This is where the Advocates receive the communions of the people,' Chloe told us. 'Here they can be directly aware of the true feelings and wishes of those they serve at any given time.'

'They *receive* the prayers?' Nina said.

'They act as a filter,' Lucian replied. 'Only humans can truly comprehend the desires of other humans. The Noosphere itself will ultimately make decisions according to those desires, but the Advocates are an essential personal element, the bridge between the individual and the communality.'

'And of course,' Chloe added, 'the personal outweighs the public for most people at any given time. The Advocates are better able to advise us of particular cases that may merit urgent attention.'

'I want to be sure I understand this,' Nina said. 'The Advocates can take in *all* that up there?' She pointed to the optics. 'Every bit of it?'

'It's *channelled* through them to the Noosphere itself,' Lucian said. 'So they obtain a fleeting sense of it. Even when they aren't here the Noosphere continues to function efficiently, but there's no longer any personal element to the communion. And the Advocates may not be as intimately informed of the needs of the people as their position would dictate.'

The images were innumerable, too much to absorb with the eye alone. I wondered exactly how the Advocates received individual communions through their shrine. Did they dip into particular prayers at random or let the whole panoply wash through them, bursting with desires and urgencies? If so, no wonder they had eventually gone mad.

'In previous times,' Chloe was saying, 'the Advocates came

here regularly, often daily, never less than once a full blue moon. Julius and Orela followed this tradition at the start of their tenure. They were devout in the pursuit of their duties. But later they began to falter, spending more time in travel, in the pursuit of their own preoccupations.'

'Naturally,' said Lucian, 'it's important that the Advocates *do* visit the worlds of the Noospace, making their physical presence manifest. No one would deny them that. But in recent decades Julius and Orela gradually began to dispense even with ceremonial visits and now spend all their time either travelling privately – often in secret – or in retreat at Icarus. They haven't been here in a quarter of a century. As a result the Shrine of Shrines has lain empty.'

'I don't understand,' said Nina. 'If this is true, then surely the people would have noticed or known, wouldn't they?'

Chloe shook her head. 'We've endeavoured to ensure that the Noosphere continues to fulfil the needs of the people. And the Advocates are adept at *implying* that they are still carrying out their duties.'

I could not take my eyes off the shrine within the sphere. Its surfaces were pearly, pristine, folded and arched and curlicued like some impossibly complex flower. The Advocates would sit at its very centre, living things within its petals.

'Perhaps they've simply had enough of serving others,' I remarked.

'That may well be so,' replied Lucian. 'In which case, why did they not retire years ago? The Advocacy is a burden few can bear for more than half a lifespan. But Julius and Orela will not relinquish their positions. At the same time, their private conduct shows increasing degeneracy.'

'It's a consequence of their age,' Chloe said. 'Advocates are no more proof against the inexorability of physical and mental decline than any of us.'

It seemed to me that they were being far too blithe about the voracious mental demands of the office itself. Though I was sure that none of the thousands of faces on the screens – and they kept changing even as I stared – could see or hear us, it was hard to hold on to the conviction that the four of us were alone in the dome. How would it have been if we were *inside* the shrine, directly connected to every one of them?

'We believe,' Lucian was saying, 'that their instability represents perhaps a fatal danger to the Noosphere. But you must decide for yourselves.'

'What about the Augmenters?' I said. 'Are they really about to attack the Noosphere?'

'Their fleet is on its way,' Chloe said, 'as you've seen. We don't approve of their philosophy – especially in such extremities as the suprahuman abomination – but it may be necessary to reach an accommodation with them. For the good of the human race at large.'

These were weasel words. There was nothing on her face to indicate that this had been a difficult decision. She looked like a child mouthing adult words whose significance she did not really understand. But I knew better than to be fooled by appearances.

'Are they planning on attacking the Noosphere?' I asked again.

'It's better you discover their purpose from their own words and actions.'

'Wait a minute,' I said swiftly, fearful that they might switch us there and then back into Bezile or Tunde or Imrani. 'Why should we trust you? We only know what you've chosen to let us experience.'

'What you've dreamt has actually happened,' Chloe said. 'Can you deny that you know it to be true?'

I couldn't, but I wasn't ready to give in that easily. 'How do we know that this isn't just a scheme to allow *you* two to take over as Advocates?'

Chloe laughed, the first time I had witnessed a spontaneous display of emotion from either of them.

'The new Advocates already exist,' she told me. 'In more than embryo.'

'On Elydia's ship?' said Nina.

Chloe nodded. 'Julius and Orela did not lie about that. They're in the womb. Waiting to be born.'

*

Imrani surfaced from unconsciousness. It took a moment for him to orientate himself: he was webbed into a seat in one of the skulldecks of the phoenix. Beside him sat Felix, who was staring out through the observation lens. In the near distance, straight ahead, Jupiter shone bronze in the darkness of space.

His limbs were stiff from the effects of the toxin, his head fuzzy. He closed his eyes again, and I made my presence felt:

'*Are you all right?*'

He was surprised by my intervention, but his grogginess blunted his reaction. I had the sense that there was no lasting damage: the threader's venom had been designed to paralyse rather than kill.

Nina was present, too, and I allowed her to take the lead in calming him. Gradually Imrani rose to some semblance of normal alertness. The skulldeck console showed a close-up of the cloud-streaked disc of Callisto. There was a fleet in orbit around it. It was far smaller than the Augmenter armada we had seen in the Valley of the Dead.

'So,' said Felix, 'you're awake at last.'

The smile was as broad as ever, but it never showed in his eyes.

'Comfortable enough?' he said, using his hands to adjust the webbing around Imrani's chest.

'Where are we headed?' Imrani asked, at Nina's urging.

'In good time,' Felix said softly, the big fingers of his hands paused near Imrani's throat. 'Are you thirsty? Threader venom sometimes has that effect. Would you like some water?'

He spoke without emotion, without concern. Imrani shook his head.

The lens showed several of the armada's ships, the closest a big black bell that wafted silvery fronds as it kept pace with the phoenix. Felix murmured something to the console, then turned back to Imrani.

'You've slept through most of the voyage,' he remarked. A studied sigh. 'I rather envy you that. Interplanetary travel is really rather tiresome.'

Imrani did his best to indicate the other ships of the armada.

'Where did they come from?' he asked.

Felix refocused the lens so that we could see a swathe of the ships. There were hundreds of them, more even than we had seen at Acheron.

'From the Outer Reaches,' he replied. 'From the many small worlds and habitats far beyond the Noosphere where the persecuted found sanctuary after the purges.'

'Are you going to wage war?'

He made a sound like a laugh. 'Let's hope that won't be necessary. Elydia can explain better than I. I think it's time we joined her.'

He retracted the webbing and helped Imrani to his feet. Though Imrani's haziness had largely cleared, he moved stiffly and Felix had to help him along. His big hand fitted almost entirely around Imrani's bicep, and it was as if we were being marched rather than led to the doorvalve.

A spiralway glided us down to the bridgehead. Elydia stood in front of the pilot's station. There were two Augmenters with her, one a bulky figure standing at her side, the other oddly perched in the co-pilot's seat.

The seated man was spindly, almost skeletal, his hands splayed across the control nodules, long flexible fingers effortlessly accessing information from the optics and sensitories. He had a narrow pale face with a protuberant nose and mouth that gave him a fish-like appearance. He wore a smaller version of the pilot's neural hood.

The other Augmenter was amply folded in shimmering silver robes, skin gleaming with a purplish sheen. The woman – it was clear at proximity that she was indeed female – appeared pregnant in the ancient human sense, but the umbilical curved up into a face-mask, and a pungent reek emanated from her.

Elydia smiled warmly as Imrani was led forward, and she provided the introductions. The co-pilot was called Jagdavido, a 'Mentalent' whose enhanced nervous system enabled him to process data with a speed and efficiency far beyond any mere biomechanical. Jagdavido, engrossed in his task, eyes rolled in his head like a Devout drunk on communion, did not acknowledge them. The woman was an ammonia-breather who had once inhabited the Vaporous Swamps of Titan's North Pole. Her name was Addomatis, and she was two hundred and forty years old, Elydia told us, the oldest survivor of the Augmenter purges. She had undergone four 'bodily restructurings' during her long lifetime.

Addomatis made no sound except for slow snuffling intakes and exhalations of breath; the sharp odour of ammonia only partially masked a ranker smell. Imrani involuntarily took a step back from her. The bruised lids on her lozenge eyes opened and closed slowly; it was hard to tell whether she was listening or dozing. Jagdavido, by contrast, was a bustle of contained energy, fingers constantly twitching at their tasks. Beside him the pilot sat rigid, head enveloped in a hood so big it hid her face, its filaments directly connected to the ship's control cortex.

Elydia was pleasantness personified. She wore a dark green robe of some rough material, and her hair was done up in a topknot. She resembled a warrior queen from the distant past of Earth.

Imrani was unnerved by his proximity to the two Augmenters, and I took the opportunity to speak through him:

'What do you want with me?'

'What?' Elydia's tone implied that the answer should have been obvious. 'I want you to witness our return to the fold of humanity.'

'Are you going to attack?'

She feigned shock at the suggestion.

'Your ships are armed. I know that.'

'A prudent protective measure,' she said. 'We come to offer peace and harmonious coexistence. I detect a new steeliness in you. Perhaps you continue to doubt us. But we're bringing the people their new Advocates.'

She indicated the rear of the bridgehead. The spiralway had blocked sight of it on our descent, but now I saw that the womb had been installed there.

It stood upright, supported by a descending tangle of fibres from the ship's control system. Its swollen surface was now stretched so thin that it was possible to make out the vague contours of the faces within it. A man and a woman, naked but with hair already on their heads. Though their eyes were almost certainly closed, they seemed to strain against the sac that contained them, as if eager to burst into life.

'Are you teaching them how to fly the ship?' I said acidly.

Elydia laughed. 'They aren't sentient. Not yet. It's merely a means by which we can continuously monitor their status. They're almost at the end of their term.'

'And then what?'

It was Nina who asked the question through Imrani. Elydia gave him a thoughtful stare, then seemed to shrug away her curiosity.

'They're our peace offering to the peoples of the Noosphere. A token of good faith.'

'They don't belong to you,' I said.

This surprised her. 'How would you know that? They couldn't have been created in the first place without our assistance.'

I sensed Chloe and Lucian's presence in the background, and I immediately asked them: Is this true? There was a silence, and then Lucian confirmed that 'Augmenter methods' had been used to make the womb self-sustaining. He conveyed the impression that it was a necessary bargain against the threat of Julius and Orela's insanity. Both he and Chloe were adamant that the man and woman inside it were not in any way Augmented themselves. There was an unaccustomed insistence and urgency to their presences that spoke of sincerity – or at least a sincere desire that Nina and I should believe them.

At this point Jagdavido began a strange bleating noise that was like a high-pitched purring.

'Contact from the Jovian fleet,' he said. 'High Arbiter Salvadorian wishes to communicate.'

He spoke rapidly in a piping voice that lacked nuance and emphasis.

'Put him on,' Elydia said, thumbing a large optic on the control ridge. It opened, showing Salvadorian and several others. He wore his arbiter's robes but he was obviously on the bridgehead of a ship.

'Greetings,' said Elydia lightly. She told him her name, then announced: 'We come in peace.'

I wondered if she was mocking him, a mockery that came from the knowledge that her ships outnumbered his tenfold.

Salvadorian's grave face did not alter. 'Your fleet is armed,' he said. 'You're here without our consent.'

Elydia maintained a cheerful expression, an almost jaunty tone. 'We're carrying the new Advocates. We intend only to deliver them safely to the Noosphere.'

Salvadorian and those around him did not noticeably react to this.

'Julius and Orela are our Advocates,' Salvadorian said. 'This is an unwarranted intrusion into Jove-space.'

Elydia settled herself in the optic seat, leaning forward as if she was conducting a casual conversation with an old acquaintance.

'They no longer serve you in that capacity,' she said. 'They have lied and murdered to protect their positions. You, Arbiter Salvadorian, are as much a victim as anyone else.'

Salvadorian's face remained implacable. 'We ask you to reverse your course and leave the Noospace.'

'Prime Arbiter Venzano was murdered on their orders,' Elydia said. 'The Augmenter assassin was merely their tool. A renegade. We reject his actions utterly.'

'That is a lie.'

'Is it? What if I tell you I can present you with proof that they, the Advocates, actually initiated the Dementia and have been using it to manipulate public opinion in their favour?'

Salvadorian waved a dismissive hand. 'Do you imagine I would countenance such a slur for even a nanosecond? If you continue on your present course, we will be obliged to defend Jove-space with all the force we can muster.'

Elydia shook her head. 'It's not necessary for you to believe me. Others in whom you might have greater trust can confirm that what I say is true.'

She turned away from the optic and motioned to one of the crew who was standing near a corridor valve. The valve opened, and through it stepped High Arbiter Yuang.

Like Salvadorian he wore his robes of office, and he was accompanied by several of his retinue. He strode across to the optic, letting Salvadorian see him.

'It's true what she says,' he began without preamble. 'We are now convinced that Orela and Julius are the originators of the Dementia.'

Salvadorian didn't hide his incredulity. 'We? What is this heresy? Are you a prisoner?'

'I'm here of my own free will,' Yuang told him. 'I believe that the Noosphere is best served by the truth, no matter how unpalatable. I could no longer give the Advocates my support after the travesty of the council on Mercury. Both are dangerously out of control, without scruples. They *used* you – unless, of course, you were also party to their plot.'

The suggestion clearly outraged Salvadorian. It was only with great restraint that he managed to control himself.

'I suggest you explain that insinuation,' he said. 'To me, you're the one that's acting like a traitor.'

Yuang remained calm. 'Venzano was not carrying evidence of Augmenter involvement in the Dementia. If anything, his researchers had reached the same conclusion as ours on Titan, and that was doubtless why the Advocates had him killed.'

'These are just words.'

'Consider,' said Yuang. 'Only adults or those who have reached majority succumb to the sickness—'

'Not so,' interrupted one of Salvadorian's group. 'We've had victims as young as six.'

'As have we. And it was these cases we investigated most thoroughly. The minors concerned had had access to a shrine, either illicitly or through parental collusion, in the immediate period before their affliction.'

It was clear that this was news to Salvadorian and the others around him. There was a brief discussion among them, nothing clearly carrying across the optic.

Yuang turned to a woman in his retinue, introducing her to Salvadorian: 'This is Rowenna Nyari, the chief coordinator of our research efforts. Perhaps she can explain better than I.'

Nyari was tall, dark hair chain-coiled in the Titanian style. She had strong features, a forthright air.

'Everyone who has succumbed to the Dementia has had recent previous access to a shrine,' she said. 'In every single case we've investigated in sufficient detail this has proved to be true, and there's no doubt in my mind that you'll find the same on your own worlds should you choose to check. The shrine is plainly the vector for the Dementia. Victims are "infected" during communion. The pattern is more or less random, and it may be days or simply hours before the condition manifests itself. Nevertheless, we believe that actual shrines are specifically targeted.'

'This is preposterous!' another of Salvadorian's group blurted. '*Everyone* uses shrines. If this were true, we'd all be mad.'

'It may only be a matter of time,' Nyari said. 'A matter of time, or of chance. We believe that the infections are directed and localized to spread panic, but not to the extent that the entire fabric of communities or worlds is destroyed.'

Salvadorian consulted further with his colleagues. I watched through Imrani's eyes, trying to gauge their reactions. No one had expected this. The shrines were the most sacred and private of places. If Nyari was right, then it was monstrous.

Finally Salvadorian turned back to the optic.

'I still consider this dubious,' he announced. 'If the Dementia is targeted as you claim, then why have there been no cases on the Inner Planets? Shrines are even more commonplace on Venus or Mars than on Miranda or Nereid.'

'There are no Augmenters on the Inner Planets,' said Yuang. 'Or at least so few that inflicting the Dementia there would merely muddy the issue. The Outer Worlds were targeted precisely because the Advocates intended to make the people believe that Augmenters were behind it.'

Further consultations. Salvadorian had cloaked the sound, but this time the debate seemed more heated.

'I never thought,' Elydia remarked, intent on the optic, 'that the ability to lip-read would ever prove so useful.'

The boast was redundant since it was obvious that Salvadorian's associates were now divided between those who accepted Yuang's evidence and those who did not.

At length Salvadorian addressed the optic again: 'Nothing you've said presents proof that the Advocates engineered this crisis. You're asking us to accept a heresy on the basis of circumstantial evidence.'

'The onset of the Dementia coincided with the opening of

the Advocates' new palace at Icarus,' Yuang said. 'Rumours are rife that Orela and Julius have had a new Shrine of Shrines created there. Outbreaks of the Dementia can be matched either to the Advocates' known presence on Mercury or to periods when their whereabouts was unrecorded.'

This time the hubbub from Salvadorian's ship carried across the optic. Among his group were arbiters from Callisto and Europa as well as senior commanders of the Gallilean politia. I knew this, I realized, because Chloe and Lucian had conveyed it to me. I tried to communicate with them, but already they were retreating, leaving me with the sense that they wanted Nina and me to witness the drama as it unfolded without any interference from them.

Salvadorian spoke to Yuang again: 'If what you say is true, then what exactly is the Dementia? Exactly how is it contracted?'

It was Nyari who answered.

'We can only speculate on that,' she said. 'We know two things – one, there is no infective agent in any physical sense; two, the Advocates are deranged. Just as they receive the communion of others, so they may have used some means of transmitting their own presence – their own madness – back.'

'The Advocates aren't allowed reciprocal contact through communion!' someone – I recognized him as Lasantha from the Icarus council – shouted.

Nyari actually smiled, though it was a smile full of fatalism. 'I think we are dealing with representatives who have long ceased to be bound by such scruples,' she replied calmly. 'Imagine it. Imagine yourself as an ordinary communicant. Imagine having your mind suddenly filled with the freight of the Advocates' lives, the full tenor of their madness. That would surely be enough to induce an overwhelming mental derangement of the type so classically exhibited by Dementia victims.'

There was a long silence. Then once again Salvadorian began conferring with his colleagues. Now the debate was sober, grave, voices lowered, faces sombre. I saw Addomatis apparently watching through half-open eyes, breaths like slow snores, her odour filling the entire bridgehead; I saw Jagdavido apparently oblivious, digits twitching at the nodes and polyps of the control ridge. It was impossible to imagine what thoughts were passing through their minds. Imrani stared at the motionless pilot, still immobile, enveloped by the hood, hands deep in armrest sockets, brain at one with the ship. Did she imagine she was the phoenix itself, I wondered, leading the Augmenter armada out of deep interplanetary space – they had arrived here direct from Charon – into their first contact with the peoples of the Noospace? Or was her consciousness entirely subsumed to the workings of the ship?

There was no answer to this from Chloe or Lucian, no sense of their presence whatsoever.

Salvadorian spoke to Yuang again: 'If the facts are as you suggest, then why wasn't this revealed at the Icarus council?'

Yuang looked rueful. 'Because I hadn't even contemplated it until then. We had arrived at the conclusion that the shrines were the source of the Dementia – something which I intended to announce during my deliverance – but it never occurred to me that the Advocates were actively involved – not until I saw how shamelessly they manipulated all of us. I am a representative of the Noosphere as much as you, Arbiter Salvadorian. There are times when dutifulness and loyalty blinds us to the patent facts. But no longer. It is time we had new Advocates. Whatever else the cost.'

Everyone on the ship waited. Elydia began to drum her fingers on the arm of her seat. The ammoniacal odour grew stronger, and I saw that Addomatis was leaking fluid from flaps behind her ears. It coursed down the silvery garment she wore and began to pool on the floor. Most of Yuang's retinue reacted with outright distaste. Felix and one of the crew led her away while another arrived with a scroungedog which promptly slavered up the spillage. Imrani kept glancing at the pilot, and it was only Nina's gentle persuasion that kept him focused on the wider picture.

Meanwhile Salvadorian and his colleagues were conferring. When he finally addressed the optic again, his face was no less grave than it had been at the start.

'What do you want of us?' he asked.

'Nothing,' Elydia told him. 'We simply wish for unhindered passage to the Noosphere.'

'That could have been achieved without the necessity for entering Jove-space.'

'We wanted to convince you of the justice of our cause. To enlist your sympathy if not your cooperation. We wanted to show you our faces, to show you that they are not evil.'

Salvadorian seemed unimpressed by this. 'You intend to deliver new Advocates to the Noosphere?'

'Indeed.'

It was plain he didn't believe this. 'And then what?

'We intend to ask only that we be allowed back into the commonality of the human race. We would like to live in peace with others – apart, if necessary, but without conflict. We have no desire to usurp the governance of those who are not like us. Like any other human being, we merely ask for a place in the sun.'

Again it had the flavour of a rehearsed speech. Salvadorian sighed. 'Are you expecting us to join you?'

'Only you can decide that.'

He shook his head slowly. 'We will take no direct action against the present Advocates until matters are clearer. However, we are prepared to disperse our fleet if you immediately vacate Jove-space.'

'Done!' Elydia agreed, in a clear note of triumph.

The optic blanked. Straight away, Elydia gave instructions for the armada to make full speed for the Noosphere. Jagdavido responded instantly, fingers writhing across the sensitories.

Elydia rose and turned to Yuang. 'We value your assistance,' she said.

'I merely spoke the truth,' he replied stiffly.

'Will you accompany us?'

'I have duties in my own Arbitration. The people are restive, frightened. Don't forget your presence will terrify most of them, whether you wish it or not. I must go where I can do best.'

'So you shall. We readied your carrier, just in case.'

'Don't think,' he said, 'because I spoke in your favour I share your cause.'

Then he turned and led his retinue away.

As soon as he was gone, Elydia came smiling towards Imrani. He had not moved throughout the entire negotiations. I had scarcely paid him any attention myself, simply using his senses for my own purposes. But now Elydia, in her triumph, was solicitude itself.

'This has been a terrible shock to you,' she said, leading him by the arm towards a seat. 'We have no wish to harm you, I assure you, especially since without you we would never have acquired the womb.'

'What if the Inner Planets decide to resist you?'

Imrani was still somewhat dazed, and I knew it was Nina speaking through him. Elydia said, 'Let's hope it doesn't come to that, shall we? Surely they would want their new Advocates delivered safely.'

I could see that inside the womb the chests of the man and woman were gently rising and falling: they were breathing. But Imrani's attention was drawn again to the pilot. Uncertainly he pointed a finger.

'Who is that?'

Elydia gave a sympathetic smile. 'I think you know already.'

Imrani pushed past her and walked right up to the pilot so that he had a full view of her face. Under her hood, her skin was bone-white, her eyes glassy, staring straight ahead. Seeing nothing.

'Hello, Imrani,' she said. 'I hope you are well.'

She spoke rapidly, without expression. Though it was Shivaun's vocal cords, the three of us knew that it was Jagdavido speaking through her.

'I'm afraid she's quite dead,' Elydia was saying. 'There was nothing we could do about that. But we are few in number, and short of good pilots. Her autonomic nervous system and some cerebral functions have been directly wired into the ship. Jagdavido is linked to her so that he can immediately access—'

Imrani flung himself on her, screaming with rage and attempting to throttle her. She swiped him away, sending him reeling to the deck. Then Felix was hauling him up, pinioning his arms, holding him effortlessly despite his rage and writhing.

Elydia composed herself. 'I understand your anger. It's

painful to have to relive our grief over again. I'm sorry it was necessary. Shivaun isn't the only one of the dead we were compelled to use as crew for our fleet. I didn't intend you to see her, but it was your choice to steal aboard this ship. Consider it this way: she's continuing to serve the human race.'

Imrani spat in her face.

Elydia stepped back, and I could feel Felix's hands tightening on Imrani's arms, squeezing hard.

'It's all right,' Elydia told him. 'It's to be expected. I think perhaps you'd better take him back to his quarters.'

Imrani did not resist as Felix led him away. His tears came freely, out of a chaotic mixture of grief, anger and memories of Shivaun in her prime, of the two of them together sharing intimate moments, Imrani forever enthralled by her forbidding beauty, by his sheer good fortune in finding her. The memories washed through me, too, so powerfully it was almost as if I had lived them myself; and because I had none of my own, I took them to myself, swallowed them whole.

Felix was hurrying him up the spiralway to the skulldeck. As soon as we were inside, he pushed Imrani roughly down into one of the seats.

'You shouldn't have done that,' he said. 'There was no need.'

He spoke with the chilling evenness of contained anger. Imrani was scarcely listening, but Nina suddenly said through him:

'I loved Shivaun as much as you love Elydia. How would you have felt if it had been her?'

Felix had already activated the webbing on the seat. He wasn't even listening.

'We've tried to treat you decently,' he said, making sure the webbing was as tight as possible. 'You defiled her, spat in her face.'

He loomed over Imrani, taking hold of his hands.

'I can't forgive you for that,' he said, and then he squeezed and twisted.

There was a cracking sound as Imrani's fingers erupted with white-hot pain.

Fourteen

'. . . services are no longer required,' the woman was saying. 'You may resume your authorized journey.'

I was back in Tunde, watching Vargo at the controls.

'Thanks for nothing,' he said to the interdictor commander; but she had already blanked the optic.

Tunde, Marea and Cori came out of hiding. Marea was preoccupied, distant. I caught Cori's eye, mouthed the word 'Nina?'. She winked at me.

On the longsight we could see the Augmenter armada already beginning to bypass Callisto. It was relatively close, an absurd array of improbable craft; yet its sheer numbers would have been sufficient to scatter Salvadorian's fleet. I was full of Imrani's pain, but I couldn't afford to dwell on it.

'Marea,' I said, directing her attention to the leading craft in the armada. 'Remember the womb?'

She gave me a scathing look. 'The one you sold to free yourself from Yolande?'

'It's fully grown now. And it's on board that ship.'

She was dubious. 'Fully grown? It's only been a year.'

'You knew it was no ordinary womb. It contains the new Advocates.'

Marea obviously realized that I was inhabiting Tunde again. Tunde himself seemed more subdued than ever, drawn in on himself. I scarcely gave it a thought; I was more concerned with telling them what I knew.

Marea took a seat beside Vargo. From the longsight perspective, it seemed as if the phoenix was heading straight towards us, though Vargo was already peeling away from Salvadorian's fleet, intent on using Callisto's gravity as a slingshot for resuming course to Europa. Even so, the Augmenter armada would pass by at relatively close range.

Once again the transition from Imrani to Tunde had been instant. Chloe and Lucian were in the background, but they would not answer my questions. Instead they began urging a new course of action on me. I felt as though we had abandoned Imrani to Felix, but they insisted that, in order to help him, I would need to act through Tunde.

There was nothing else I could do. Chloe and Lucian were obviously able to switch me effortlessly from one host to another, and I didn't want to take the risk that they might withdraw me altogether, return me to the dark limbo or the white room. I wanted to play my part in whatever way I could.

'There's been a change of plan,' I said to Vargo.

He eyed me, knowing I was back in Tunde.

'We need to match course with the Augmenter fleet,' I said.

'What?'

'I'm only telling you what I've been advised.'

'Forget it!'

'He's right,' said Marea.

'What do you mean? We need to get the hell out of this! This is our chance to escape.'

Marea shook her head. 'If the womb's there, then I want to know what's going to happen to it.'

'This is crazy!'

'I lost everything because of it – my husbands, our child. I nearly lost my own life as well.'

Vargo hadn't expected this. Neither Nina nor I had actually told the others Marea's story; during our absence, Tunde had explained for Vargo's benefit how he had acquired the womb, but Marea herself had continued to be unable to say anything about what had happened after he left Mars. Until now. Something, perhaps her escape from Io, had breached the block, and she related how she had found Yuri and Salih murdered, then was arrested and deported to Io on a fabricated charge of murder.

Vargo listened without interrupting; Cori was also agog. When Marea had finished, she went to her side and patted her hand, the child comforting the woman.

Vargo gave a slow, exasperated growl. 'You're out of your mind,' he said to me. 'In more ways than one. You want us to get *involved*?'

'We tail them,' I said. 'At a safe distance.'

'And then what?'

I had no answer to that. Chloe and Lucian would give me none.

'Don't deny me this,' Marea said to him. 'We're here because of the womb. I ended up on Io because of it. They were going to blank me. I can't let it go when it's so close.'

Vargo sat back in his seat. He unfastened his tunic at the neck, contemplated the armada ships.

'You want my opinion,' he said to Marea. 'We can't trust them.'

I knew he was referring to myself and Nina.

'You have to let her,' Cori said urgently. 'Without her, *you* wouldn't be free.'

'You keep out of it!'

'I've got as much right to say what I think as you!'

'Is that you speaking? The kid?'

'Of course it is!'

Only then did I realize how Marea had been able to breach her block. Nina was in her.

Bezile rose from the prayer terminal, bereft of the usual comforts of communion. Her ancestors – tradesfolk and petty civic functionaries, most of them – had proved woefully unequal to the task of providing emotional solace after she had conveyed the abominations she had witnessed on Earth. Their responses had ranged from abject revulsion to outright incredulity – *as if she had actually invented it!* Most had been so distraught that they had fled from her mindset entirely, shrivelling into the infinite dark. To think that the afterlife was populated with such spineless souls – and every one of them of her own bloodline. It was far worse to have your ancestors fail you than your children. The enormity of it was quite beyond their squeamishness.

Intriguingly, just at the moment when she was withdrawing from her communion, she had felt the immanence of a more robust and unfamiliar spirit, perhaps an ancestor she had never known before; but she was too far gone in exiting to entertain it, too disgruntled with the paltry response from everyone else. Besides, an extended communion was a luxury she could ill-afford while the mad Advocates were clearly intent on further insanity.

She paused at the threshold of the shrine, stiff and weary, every orifice sore after a total fluid exchange. Of course she'd requested nepenthe and had drowsed blissfully through much of it, but the enforced *intrusion* was something she would not readily forgive. Though she had no evidence, she suspected that the Advocates had been secret spectators to the whole procedure, relishing every moment of her evacuation as she lay spreadeagled and naked, catheters snaking from her nostrils to her—

No. It did no good to think about it, though even her eyeballs ached. The doormouth opened. She exited.

Two of the Advocates' functionaries were waiting for her outside. They led her along the corridor, matching her doddery pace, until they came to a slideway that, to her vast relief, began to whisk them along.

They traversed the long neck of the ship in silence. Bezile had never felt more wretched. Doubtless that was what the Advocates had intended: weak, she was more prey to their manipulations.

The slideway delivered them to the bridgehead of the ship. Julius and Orela sat alone with Leanderic on the topmost skulldeck. The armoured suits were gone and they again wore the Advocates' robes. Both of them greeted her with ostentatious consideration.

'We trust your prayers have been comforting,' Julius said. 'It's a pleasure to have a Prime Arbiter who is diligent in her observances even under great duress.'

'You look pale,' Orela said. She patted the seat between them. 'Sit with us.'

With some reluctance, and even greater delicacy, Bezile lowered herself into it. They were facing the forward eye blister. Directly ahead of them lay the gleaming spiral of the

Sanctuary. It was surrounded by hundreds of small craft, as if every plagueship in the Noospace had descended on it.

'Are we going there?' she asked. 'To the Sanctuary?'

'It is our destination,' Julius confirmed. He gave an exaggerated sigh. 'These are trying times. More than ever we need brave spirits.'

What was this supposed to mean? On the other side of Julius Leanderic sat straight-backed in his seat, his expression blank. He, too, had undergone fluid exchange. They had had no opportunity to speak since their return to the Advocates' ship.

Bezile felt tired and spirit-sick. Is this what despair feels like? she wondered. Then shook herself mentally. She could not afford such an indulgence. Especially not now.

She tried to keep the weariness out of her voice, saying, 'I'd like to know what you intend next.'

'Intend?' Julius turned a solemn gaze on her. 'We intend nothing more than the very salvation of the Noosphere.'

'Hundreds of Augmenter ships are even now approaching Earth-orbit,' Orela informed her. 'The Gallileans mustered a defensive fleet, but then gave way to the intruders.'

The Sanctuary spun slowly in the blackness. 'Gave way?'

'They betrayed us. Allowed the Augmenters unhindered passage.'

'To think that we would face such treachery,' Julius said. 'Even Modramistra has failed to rally to the people's cause, even the arbiters of Mars. All declared their neutrality and refused to dispatch any ships to intercept them. The Augmenters have continued their approach without opposition. There has been no response from Mercury or Venus to our pleas for assistance.'

Despite his words, he sounded quite sanguine. Orela activated one of the optics on the control ridge. The Augmenter ships formed a compact sphere just beyond the gibbous Earth. They were a ramshackle assemblage of vintage and cannibalized craft, but Bezile had never seen so many.

'They're going to attack?'

'Why else would they have come?' said Julius.

Between themselves and the Augmenters lay only the Sanctuary and its attendant flotilla.

'Was no one prepared to defend the Noosphere?' Bezile asked incredulously.

'Not one,' Orela answered. And immediately brightened. 'Yet we have our Prime Arbiter here as our faithful servant, do we not? We are resourceful, steadfast, and we know our cause is righteous. Let's not be faint-hearted. We shall defend the Noosphere to our very last breath.'

It was plain they were serious. Bezile was compelled to ask: 'How? Is the Noosphere mustering a fleet?'

Julius pointed through the blister towards the Sanctuary. '*That* is our fleet.'

It was a moment before Bezile understood what he meant. The plagueships.

Most were converted cargo vessels or refurbished derelicts. None carried any weaponry.

'You're going to send the plagueships against the Augmenters?'

Orela activated several more of the optics. They showed Dementia victims strapped into pilots' seats, heads encased in neural hoods.

'They will be our final defence,' she said. 'Fearless pilots who will guide their ships straight at the heart of the intruders—'

'Fearless?' Bezile couldn't contain herself. 'They're mad. Oblivious.'

'We've done everything we can for them,' Julius said. 'Far better they die a glorious death in the service of the Noosphere than a miserable protracted extinction in a sickbed.'

'They're diseased! Gibbering travesties of their former selves!'

Julius shook his head patiently, as if she were a stupid child failing to grasp an obvious point. 'They're sedated, stabilized. The ships will be able to access their higher cortical functions without difficulty.'

'Each of their holds is packed with an infant photoplasm,' Orela said in a gleeful manner. 'The explosions should make quite a display.'

And she and Julius giggled at the prospect.

Photoplasms were seething blobs of incandescent gas, perhaps the most remarkable products of human bioingenuity.

They were regularly harvested from the stellar photosphere, Bezile knew, and transported in magnetic chambers to sustain the radiant envelopes of the gas giants.

'Are you saying this was *planned*?' she shouted. 'You arranged it in advance?'

'A prudent precaution,' Julius told her. 'In case the loyalty of our subjects proved uncertain.'

Our subjects. Bezile longed for Luis's pedantic presence, useless though he would have been in such a situation. He had been sacrificed. As a demonstration. An entertainment, even.

Leanderic would be no help to her. Bezile saw with renewed amazement that he had not even had his scorched hands repaired: they were upturned, charred and festering, in his lap. His face was as still as a corpse's.

'This is madness,' she said. 'You are mad.'

The Advocates were intent on their 'fleet'.

'Of course we are,' Orela said conversationally. 'Who would not be when they know what we know? When they've experienced what we have experienced?'

'Then let go,' Bezile said. 'Give way to successors. You can be cured of your sickness, given an honourable translation to the Noosphere.'

Julius laughed and leaned close. 'Shall I tell you the greatest heresy of all?' he whispered. 'A heresy, and yet a truth. A great and terrifying truth.'

'Better she doesn't know,' Orela interjected.

'What heresy?'

'You'll regret it if you ask,' Orela said. 'Remain in blissful ignorance.'

Bezile was weary of their blatant theatricals. 'What heresy?' she said again.

Julius glanced at Leanderic, as if to check whether he was listening. He did not appear to be aware of any of them. Bezile could feel the heat of Julius's breath as he whispered straight into her ear:

'There is no afterlife. No real translation to the Noosphere.' He drew back. 'Shocking, yes?'

His eyes were like black voids, empty of humanity. Bezile

breathed slowly; she could not take much more of this. How was one to respond to such an outrage?

'It's true,' Orela said brightly. 'A truth which every Advocate must carry like a lump of bile which cannot be swallowed or spat out.'

Bezile shook her head. 'I will not hear any more!'

'Believe me,' Orela said, 'we share your desolation. But we have long been inured to it.'

'Our ancestors were clever,' Julius went on. 'They designed the Noosphere to provide universal yet particular comfort by making it a spiritual mirror that would reflect back the secret urgings of the soul in the guise of an individual's ancestors.'

This was mere babble. How much longer would her punishment continue? Would it never end?

'Do you expect me to swallow this?' she said.

'There is no afterlife,' Julius repeated. 'There is no Noosphere – at least not in the sense of an extended realm which the passed-on inhabit. It is merely created, brought into transient life, by each communicant. It takes its particular form from their existing mind state.'

'When you die, you die,' Orela said. 'It's an end of things, just as it was for our primitive ancestors. We know this as a truth, a certitude. Is it any wonder, then, that we should choose to cling to life, to wrest every experience from it while we may?'

There had been Advocates who had retired well before their lifespans, who had lived out their retirements in contented quietude. None had ever even hinted at such an abomination. This was the lie of all lies, an apostasy from which there could be no recovery, no forgiveness.

She made to rise.

'Are you leaving us?' Orela said with apparent surprise.

'Your steward needs attention. I shall take him to the recuperatory.'

'You'll miss the fun!'

Bezile heaved herself upright. Neither of the Advocates even looked at Leanderic. It was almost as if he was not there.

'It's a terrifying thing,' Julius said, 'to be stripped of one's most cherished beliefs. It's a terrifying thing to discover that you are indeed truly mortal, the afterlife a mere chimera. Feel free to cry. Don't restrain your grief on our account.'

Bezile hauled Leanderic from his seat. His lips parted, but he didn't speak.

'You must rejoin us before the battle commences,' Orela said as Bezile led the steward away. 'And don't worry – we intend to preserve the people's illusions, whatever the outcome. Anything is better than a truth without solace.'

None of the crew accompanied Bezile as she joined the glideway to the recuperatory. She was grateful for that. It was hard to tell whether Leanderic was leaning against her for support, or quite the reverse. This, then, was her punishment for failing to deliver the womb to the Advocates. To be trapped with them, their insanity displayed in full bloom, a diseased fleet under their command to defend a people whose entire existences, they claimed, were based on the greatest of deceits. It would have been absurd beyond belief were she not actually living it.

The recuperatory was unattended, and Bezile helped Leanderic undress, ordering his drapery to slide very carefully over his damaged hands. Leanderic responded to instructions but did not react in any other way.

Bezile laid him between the open folds of a sickbed, then told the bed to undertake a full therapeutic session to restore him, body and soul. The bed's optic blinked on, and then it enfolded itself about its patient, flaps suffusing with a reddish glow.

Bezile perched herself in a recliner and gazed idly at the optic as it began the diagnostic examination. The bed commenced a commentary, but she told it to be quiet and simply do whatever was necessary. She closed her eyes, then said:

'Who are you?'

I jumped at this, only at that moment becoming fully aware that I was actually lodged there in her mind. I had been crouched at the back of her consciousness until now, not realizing that I was living out her experiences as they actually happened.

I knew she was addressing me because the question was directed inwards.

'Speak,' she said. 'Are you some spy the Advocates have put inside me?'

I realized she hadn't spoken aloud on either occasion; but her thoughts were clearly and directly articulated at me.

I hesitated, then said, '*I came through the shrine. Through the Noosphere.*'

She contemplated this for a moment. 'You were the presence I felt on exiting?'

'*I must have been.*' Once again the transition had been instantaneous, unwilled.

'Who are you and what do you want?'

She had absolutely no fear of me – indeed, her prevailing reaction was one of irritation at my uninvited presence.

There was nothing for it but to tell her everything. And tell her I did, in as much detail as I could recall. It took a considerable time, but Bezile was patient, the needful patience that comes from a surfeit of horror and physical discomfort. She kept her eyes closed, lay perfectly relaxed, concentrating utterly on everything I told her. I did my best to put everything I had experienced in order while recounting it with as much brevity as I could muster.

Bezile did not once interrupt me. With her eyes closed, I could see nothing, but I was powerfully aware of her presence. Bezile was an altogether different character from Tunde or Imrani or even Marea, a woman of power and influence who was used to wielding her authority. A woman seldom awed and daunted. She had seen the thing in the lake on Earth, and my manifestation must have seemed nothing remarkable by comparison.

'And where is your companion now?'

'*Nina?*' I realized for the first time that she was not with me. '*I don't know*,' I confessed. '*She must still be with the others.*'

Again Bezile fell into contemplation. She was adept at guarding her thoughts, and I found it hard to read them.

'This is quite a little tale,' she said at last.

'*Chloe and Lucian,*' I said. '*Do you know of them?*'

The names meant nothing to her.

'The Noosphere has tens of thousands of servants,' she said. 'Are they with you now?'

I searched, but there was nothing. '*No.*' Then I asked: '*Is it true that pairs are bred for the Advocacy?*'

'In a manner of speaking,' Bezile said. 'But it is seldom that simple.'

'*I don't trust them.*'

'Trust is a commodity at present in short order. What do they want from me?'

'*I don't know. I don't even know why I'm here with you at this moment. They fling us from one place to another with few explanations.*'

'Consider yourself fortunate. Many would relish the opportunity to sample the lives of others.'

'*Without real control?*'

Bezile was interested in my dilemma only insofar as it related to hers. Her thoughts remained elusive, but I sensed her contemplating her daughter's fate as a drone pilot aboard Elydia's ship: there was anger mixed with genuine sadness that she had died without translation to the Noosphere. But Bezile was not one to dwell on personal misfortune.

'The new Advocates are aboard the Augmenter ship, you say.'

'*Not yet born.*'

'This is something of a break with tradition. Normally new Advocates are only appointed after a long and rigorous period of training, usually under the tutelage of the existing incumbents. Does the Noocracy intend them to begin their duties fresh from the womb?'

I had no answer to this.

'A question of rather vital importance, wouldn't you say?'

'*I've told you everything I know.*'

'I wonder if the Advocates are aware that their successors in waiting are so close. These are murky waters we are plumbing.'

'*What do you intend to do?*'

Bezile didn't answer, though I knew she was contemplating the possibilities. She had continued to speak inwardly to me throughout. Physically she remained in some discomfort, but she had a robustness of spirit which made me realize that I could not act through her in the way I had done with Tunde or

Imrani. There was no way in which she would allow her own mind to be usurped.

'*Do you think it's true what Julius and Orela said about the Noosphere being an illusion?*' I asked.

She snorted her dismissal. 'Could a creature such as you infiltrate my consciousness if it was merely the mirror of my soul?'

This time I experienced the translation as a flight into a deeper blackness. I called out for Chloe and Lucian, but they did not manifest themselves.

Time passed, and I had the strange sensation of it both rushing and crawling: there, alone in the blackness, I had nothing to measure it against. I could only endure it, let it pass without protest or expectation.

When I surfaced I was back in Tunde again. He was stirring from sleep, stretched out on a foldbunk with Cori cradled in his arms. I sensed the echo of a dream in which he and Adele were doing a zeegee dance in a cavernous silver floatdome, a dream which my sudden return had unwillingly forced him to leave.

He sat up slowly, laying Cori back down on the pillow. As before he was subdued, even morose. The bunk relaxed its lip and he swung his feet down.

Marea lay asleep in another bunk opposite. Tunde stared at her as if he were looking at a stranger. There was a confusion of emotions within him, but guilt and unease predominated.

He knew I was back, but it hardly registered on his consciousness.

'*Is everything all right?*' I asked him.

He said nothing. I could tell that he was already weary of the whole enterprise. For him the wider drama meant little, the issues were remote. He did not want to be out here pursuing the armada; he wanted only to be somewhere safe and comfortable with his daughter.

'She looks so changed,' he said with reference to Marea.

'*She's been through a lot,*' I replied.

'Are we going to die?'

To his credit, he was thinking more of his daughter and

Marea than himself. I couldn't offer him any certainties, but I said: '*Would I be here if I thought that?*'

'Do what you want through me. Just keep us safe.'

Then he sank down mentally, as if temporarily ceding his body entirely to my uses.

Across the bridgehead, Vargo was intent on the controls. Had he slept himself? It seemed unlikely, given that the ship was giving out a soft unintelligible murmuring; he could not have trusted it to fly itself.

Ahead of us was the Augmenter armada, filling the entire space of the eyesockets. We were following them, keeping a prudent distance but matching velocity. Beyond the sphere of ships hung the silver spiral of the Sanctuary, its attendant craft a diffuse halo around it.

Marea began to stir, much to Tunde's discomfort. I took over, rising and going across to Vargo.

'Enjoy your nap?' he said, eyeing me with his usual suspicion.

'Julius and Orela are going to attack the Augmenter fleet,' I told him. 'They're using Dementia victims as drone-pilots in the plagueships. Each ship is carrying a newborn photoplasm as payload.'

He had removed the cosmetic lens, and he squinted through his blind eye at me.

'That's a good one,' he said. 'Mad pilots and plasma balls.'

'It's true.'

'Bull.'

'I promise you.'

'How do you know?'

I told him, while in the background the ship started to regale us with a faint but falsetto version of the theme song from *Augmenter Alert!*

Marea was also listening, standing framed against one of the eyesockets, her cloak wrapped tight around her. She was feeding it crumbs from a meal cracker. Judging by her face, it did not appear that Nina was present in her. I knew I was expecting a great deal of them simply in accepting my presence and my various comings and goings. They would have to take my story on trust, in much the same way as Nina and I had had to accept everything that Chloe and Lucian had shown us.

Everything was conditional. Yet none of us had any choice but to act on the basis of what we believed to be true.

'So what are you telling me we should do?' Vargo was asking, a clear edge of impatience in his voice.

I had no answer from Chloe and Lucian, but I said, 'We maintain our course. Wait and see what happens.'

Vargo switched off the ship's vocal. 'Marea?'

She didn't speak; her attention was on Tunde.

Vargo made an exasperated noise. 'I say we head for Europa like we originally planned.'

Marea fed the cloak another morsel. She shook her head.

'He could be leading us into anything,' Vargo said.

Marea kept staring at me. 'Is Tunde there?'

I waited for Tunde himself to reply, but when he remained silent, I said: 'Yes.'

'I need to talk to you. In private.'

She walked off towards the rear of the ship. I shrugged at the scowling Vargo, then followed her down the corridor.

Marea didn't stop until she reached the shrine. She stepped through the doormouth. I went in after her.

'Tunde?'

She stood at the centre of the chamber, her cloak still drawn tight around her. Tunde remained reticent, more than ever reluctant to communicate.

'He won't talk,' I said.

'Why not?'

'I don't know. I think he's feeling guilty.'

This had the effect I intended, Tunde coming to the fore, determined not to let me explain for him. He took her by the arms, said, 'I'm here, Marea.'

Gently she pulled herself free of him. I wanted to retreat as much as possible, to leave them to have this private moment alone. But my curiosity, my very presence, wouldn't allow it.

'I can't marry you, Tunde,' she said. 'Not ever.'

'Marea—'

'Once upon a time I thought of asking you myself. It was only the perfect picture you painted of life with Yolande that stopped me.'

'That wasn't true.'

'I know that now. I know a lot more. Things have changed. They can never be like they were.'

Tunde's disappointment was more a matter of pride than desire; underneath it was a barely acknowledged relief.

'Can you forgive me, Marea?'

She gave a brief laugh. 'What did you do? You took the womb off my hands. They'd have tried to kill me for it anyway. I was only angry because you profited from it, whereas I ended up marooned on a hellhole. That was hardly your fault.'

'I feel as if I used you.'

'Maybe you did. Maybe you didn't prove to be the man I thought you were. So what? There's worse things.'

'I lied to you.'

'You rescued me.'

'Only with Nathan and Nina's help. At their urging.'

There was a dark mist of hair on her scalp: it was growing back. On Io they'd been forced to use depilants to keep leechflies at bay.

'They couldn't have done it without you, could they? You must have consented to it.'

I tried to echo that fact within him, but he told me to be silent.

'We're quits, Tunde,' Marea said. 'You don't have to marry me to make amends.'

'We could try a short-term contract.'

'Is that what you really want?'

And I saw that the honest answer was 'no'. I urged him to say it. He couldn't bring himself to speak, but at last he shook his head.

Marea smiled. 'Thank heaven for that!'

Despite himself, Tunde was hurt. 'Am I that bad?'

She put a hand to his cheek. 'It isn't that. We missed our time, Tunde. It's no one's fault. But we can't go back.'

There was an awkward moment. Then a voice said, 'So there you are!', and Cori walked in, full of juvenile bustle.

She saw the rather solemn looks on both their faces and stopped.

'Oops,' she said. 'Did I interrupt something?'

Tunde smiled and swept her up in his arms.

'I think,' he said, 'your timing was perfect.'

Imrani surfaced to intense pain.

'Try playing the organ now,' Felix said, like someone reciting a joke he didn't quite understand.

I felt the pain almost as much as Imrani; but because I was not totally *him* I was able to help him withdraw a little from it, put up barriers with his mind to blunt some of its fierceness.

He looked down at his hands; some of the fingers were twisted out of shape. All of them had been broken.

'You moron!' he yelled at Felix in rage.

Felix took hold of his hands again. There was another crack, another blaze of pain.

Imrani's anger enabled him to ride it, to swallow it down. Felix had snapped both his thumbs, but he hadn't cried out and did not lose consciousness. He was in danger of hyperventilating with the effort of controlling himself. This time it was I who had to try to calm him. I urged him against provoking Felix to unrestrained violence. Imrani grudgingly subsided. I searched his mind. There was no sense of Nina's presence.

The ship gave a slight lurch. Moments later the skulldeck optic began blinking. Felix opened it.

'We need you down here,' Elydia said.

'What about this one?'

'Make sure he's secure, then get down here. Quickly.'

Felix took something from a pouch and pressed it against Imrani's face. It was a fragrant pad, and Imrani's head filled with the overpowering aroma of nepenthe. We swam away, not losing consciousness entirely but stupefied by the drug. Felix departed without another word, leaving the optic on in his haste.

For a while we drifted in a haze. It might have been pleasant had we not been trapped and in pain. Imrani began to blubber. He was ashamed of himself for doing so, especially in my presence, but I assured him I didn't think the worse of him.

'Where's Nina?' he wanted to know.

Her absence bothered me as much as him. She did not appear to have been inhabiting Marea during my brief visit to the scuttleship. Why was I back here, as much a prisoner as Imrani?

'*I don't know*,' I told him. '*This time there's only me.*'

'You got me into this!'

He tried to thrash out in sheer anger and frustration, but the webbing held us tight.

I searched for Chloe and Lucian, for a magic code to set him free. There was nothing, not the merest hint of their presence.

The skulldeck suddenly flared with light, then dimmed just as abruptly. Seconds later, we felt a buffeting.

'What's happening?' Imrani asked.

I hesitated, then said, '*I think Orela and Julius have launched their fleet.*'

I explained about my visit to Bezile and about the Advocates' plagueships. Imrani was woozy and might have easily slipped down into sleep had I not kept rousing him. There was another flash of light, and on the optic I could make out figures scurrying on the ship's bridgehead. Felix had turned off the sound, but there was no mistaking the urgency. The armada was under attack.

Again I searched for Chloe and Lucian. There was no response. Imrani kept closing his eyes, wanting to blank everything out, and I was just as adamant he stay awake. The ship gave a powerful lurch, then started ululating an alarm.

The nepenthe had blunted our senses, but now a sharper odour began to clear them. A figure was looming over us.

Addomatis.

She was alone, breathing heavily through her mask, the reek of ammonia stronger than ever. Both Imrani and I inwardly recoiled at her proximity.

Laboriously she reached down, and instants later the seat webbing retracted, freeing us.

She stood before us, not speaking, regarding us with her strange bruised eyes. Her hands were outstretched, lilac-skinned blotched with purple, hands like those of a festering corpse.

'Nina?' I said through Imrani.

There was only the heavy intake and exhalations of her

breathing, the acrid miasma that clung to her. I thought I saw her nod, but I couldn't be sure. Imrani was immobile, terrified. I lifted up his arms.

Addomatis's fingers coiled around his wrists. With surprising strength, she lifted us up.

Fifteen

Bezile stood over the unconscious form of Leanderic. He lay on the open sickbed, hands resting at his sides. The regrown skin showed no hint of the former burns, and even his fingernails were a healthy pink. His face was tranquil at last, as if the pain and anguish had been washed away. Yet Bezile was troubled.

'*What's up?*' I asked immediately.

She accepted my return with all the equanimity of her calling. I was also surprised at my own calmness in the face of my abrupt transitions. There was little time to question anything when events themselves were moving so rapidly.

'He's been infected,' she said.

'*What?*'

'Tell us, bed.'

The sickbed spoke in a feminine monotone: 'Diagnostic analysis suggests the subject is experiencing the incipient mental traumas associated with the early stages of the Dementia. Synaptic firing is abnormal—'

'Enough,' said Bezile.

Leanderic continued to breathe gently in sleep.

'It's recent,' Bezile said. 'Since our return to the ship. We both undertook communion the moment we were back.'

She spoke with the careful calm of someone who had considered the worst and found it possible. I understood what she was saying.

'*Has the bed tested you?*'

'No point, my boy. What purpose would it serve?'

She was matter-of-fact, as if nothing could be achieved by fretting about it.

'*They would hardly have done that to you. You're their new Prime Arbiter.*'

A mirthless laugh at this. 'Leanderic has served them loyally for many years. He has far more claim on their affections.'

'*But they're risking themselves.*'

'Of course. Why else do you think they've contrived all this?'

Nearby stood the wardrobe which Orela and Julius had used for their visit to Earth. It lay open, the black suits and Julius's pistol inside. Bezile had summoned it before my return. She went across and took the gun out. It was surprisingly light for its size. Bezile set the charge to maximum, then slipped it into one of the inner pockets of her robe.

She sighed. 'How absurd that I should have to descend to this.'

She made for the doormouth. On the sickbed Leanderic gave a faint moan.

'*Is he sedated?*' I asked.

'Postrecuperative sleep, my boy.'

'*He might wake.*'

'Indeed he might.'

The doormouth opened.

'*You're going to leave him here? Unattended?*'

'What do your advisors advise?'

I confessed that I had had no recent contact with Chloe or Lucian. It hardly seemed to concern her.

'Our Advocates must be aware of the possibilities, don't you think?'

Then she stepped outside and began heading briskly down the corridor.

As before, there was none of the crew about. Bezile joined the slideway, gripping the handrib with some fierceness, mustering all her considerable mental resources. I could detect no signs of madness within her, yet I did not truly know what it was like to experience the Dementia. I had only seen its effects.

The crew were busy in the navigation pit, and no one paid Bezile special attention as we made our way up to the skull-deck. Explosions of light intermittently filled the eye blisters, flooding the entire bridgehead.

Orela and Julius were sitting where Bezile had left them,

watching the clash between the fleets with outright glee. The Augmenter armada was attempting to counterattack, white plasma tracers flashing, antimatter borbs whirling through space, bursting like miniature novas. But the resistance to the plagueship assault appeared sporadic and uncoordinated, the armada already scattered, clearly unprepared for the direct and suicidal attack from a lesser fleet they had believed to be unarmed. The motley plagueships were flying straight at their enemy, blind to any defensive fire. I watched two Augmenter sicklewings desperately targeting a bulbous drone with twin fusillades of plasma-pulses. The drone burst apart in a golden inferno, but both sicklewings were caught in the blast, one spinning wildly out of control, the other fountaining luminous secretions from its ruptured carapace as it spiralled towards Earth. Orela enthusiastically informed Bezile that an exploding photoplasm radiated electromagnetic pulses that could destroy or disrupt the control cortex of any ship that was close.

Various optics below the blister were on longsight, and I could see the phoenix framed in one of them. It seemed to be swaying like a bird riding a thermal, though it was difficult to be certain since most of the remaining ships were now swamped by the blue glare of Earth, which hung so close it was as if they were fighting for possession of the planet itself.

Bezile gripped the pistol handle, determined not to let the savagery of the battle deflect her from her task. But if I thought that she would immediately pull out the pistol and shoot the Advocates I was wrong.

'Your steward is sick,' she announced. 'He has the Dementia.'

Neither of the Advocates took their eyes off the battle. I thought of the diseased pilots aboard their ships, consumed in nuclear infernos. I tried to imagine the variety of Augmenters, the wretched variety of their deaths. I urged Bezile to draw the pistol and shoot Orela and Julius. She would not. I offered to do so myself. She refused me point blank.

'We're glad you could rejoin us,' Julius said at last. 'The battle has taken an interesting turn.'

He motioned to a seat. Bezile remained standing.

'We had the advantage of surprise,' Orela said. 'We

destroyed many of the Augmenter ships in our first onslaught, while many others have simply fled. Their fleet no longer poses a threat to the Noosphere. But soon we will have exhausted our own ships. Perhaps now is the time for us to join the battle.'

Julius indicated the optic that was showing Elydia's phoenix.

'We believe this to be their flagship,' he said. 'It's mortally damaged. Should we be magnanimous in victory and go to its rescue? What do you think, Prime Arbiter Adewoyin?'

Bezile's hand tightened around the pistol handgrip.

Shoot them! I urged her.

She angrily warned me to keep my peace.

The Advocates began relaying instructions to the crew to intercept the phoenix. I felt the tug as the flier accelerated, heading towards the battlezone. On another optic I glimpsed the scuttle, right out at the edge of the fray. Privately I prayed that Orela and Julius were not aware of it: their flier carried enough weaponry to annihilate a ship ten times its size.

Shoot them! I said again. *End it now!*

Bezile cursed me for my impertinence, remained unbudging. Her reluctance to use the pistol was partly due to her very status as Prime Arbiter and her inbred abhorrence of killing any living creature, let alone the Advocates; but it was also influenced by an uncertainty as to whether such an act would be rational and volitional or merely the first demonstrable symptom of the Dementia.

We closed rapidly on the phoenix. A pair of escape pods issued from its flanks at high speed. Julius and Orela each framed one in a viewfinder on the targeting optics.

'No!' said Bezile.

They fired.

Twin pulses of light sped from the flier. There were two brief sunbursts. The pods vanished from the optics.

Bezile pulled out the pistol and levelled it at the Advocates.

'Stop,' she shouted. 'Stop I say!'

Julius and Orela turned. And smiled at her.

'Up,' she said. 'Up, or I'll shoot you both.'

They rose from their seats.

Bezile had used the full power of her voice, and now the crew began to take notice.

Bezile marched the Advocates to the edge of the ribbed walkway, where the three of them could be clearly seen from below.

'We have an outbreak of the Dementia on board the ship,' she informed them. 'You are to evacuate it immediately.'

A few of the crew slowly began to rise from their positions; most did not move.

'The Dementia victim is the Advocates' steward,' Bezile went on. 'It is likely that I, too, am afflicted. The Advocates deliberately infected both of us. They have lost their sanity and are no longer fit to lead you.'

Bezile kept the pistol trained on Julius and Orela. They were simply smiling beatifically. Neither spoke. There was no movement, no obvious reaction, from the crew below. They looked guarded, uncertain. Some had served the Advocates all their adult lives.

'If you continue to follow them,' Bezile said, 'they will almost certainly lead you to your deaths. Take the scarab scouter and go!'

Again she used the full strength of her voice. Most of the crew had risen, and it was plain their loyalties were divided. No doubt the normal human urge to escape the tyranny of the Advocates' command was in conflict with their sense of duty.

Then a figure burst into the bridgehead – Leanderic, naked, fevered, plainly in the first throes of the Dementia. He paused at the threshold, trembling, then mounted the walkway towards the skulldeck, moving with great leaping strides that were animal-like. Then he paused, as if uncertain, gazing down into the pit with wild eyes.

Almost as one, the crew began to hurry towards the levelator valves. The valves puckered open. Some of the crew hesitated. The steward gave a feral roar. Swiftly they piled in. The valves folded shut; their descent nodules blinked on.

Leanderic slowly turned his head. Again he began to climb the walkway towards us. He looked feral, a predator stalking its victims. Julius and Orela clasped one another in glee.

'You'd better shoot him,' Orela said.

'Before he does us an injury,' Julius added.

Then Leanderic's face changed, as if a wave of calm had gushed through him. He stopped moving, took a long inhalation of breath.

'There's little time,' he said.

It had to be Nina who had somehow occupied him. I intuited this to Bezile. She reacted promptly, ordering the Advocates down the walkway.

'Is this how it ends?' Orela remarked as we descended towards the bridgehead proper. 'In one last betrayal?'

'Don't talk to me about betrayal,' Bezile said. 'You inflicted the Dementia on your own steward.'

We moved with great caution down towards the pit, Leanderic preceding us. Nina was barely holding him together; he was quivering, his face slick with sweat.

'Will you execute us yourself?' Julius said. 'After all, we provided you with the weapon.'

'We've been longing for death,' Orela went on. 'But it must be a glorious death, a death of drama and revenge. We deserve at least that.'

We saw the scarab ship veer away past the eye blister, narrowly avoiding a crippled Augmenter wagon-flier that was cartwheeling towards Earth.

Bezile ordered the Advocates into two seats beside the pilots' stations. They sat almost demurely, studiously contrite. Very carefully she webbed them tightly in.

'Take the co-pilot's seat,' she told Leanderic.

The steward obeyed. I could almost see the battle raging within him. Bezile ensured he was equally secure before webbing herself into the pilot's seat.

She pulled down the neural hood and told the ship she was taking control.

'Set course for Earth,' she informed it. 'Atmospheric entry at maximum speed.'

The ship absorbed this, then said, 'Are you aware of the consequences of such a trajectory?'

It spoke in a perfect blend of Orela and Julius's voices, though its tone was quite impersonal.

'Maximum speed,' Bezile repeated. 'This order is not to be countermanded.'

'The integrity of my structure will not survive the passage. Friction heat will—'

'I'm aware of that! Do as you're ordered.'

It paused. 'We will all be consumed.'

Bezile merely waited for the flier to carry out her instructions. Julius and Orela started ostentatiously to whisper to one another.

'It's a mortal sin to destroy life wilfully,' the ship told Bezile.

Bezile depressed its vocals and took over manual control, sliding both hands into the navigation sensory.

Presently the ship began to accelerate towards Earth.

Orela gave a hoot of delight. 'Splendid! A fiery death on the birthworld!'

'A glorious end indeed,' echoed Julius. 'And no more than we deserve.'

Leanderic managed to turn his head towards Bezile.

'Take a life craft,' he said. 'Leave us. There's no need for you to sacrifice yourself.'

'My dear man,' Bezile said to him, 'it's far too late for that. We're all diseased here.'

'You can't be sure you're infected.'

'Look at them. Look at them!'

She was indicating the Advocates. Orela and Julius were laughing outright at us, like children enjoying a spiteful revenge.

Beyond the eye blisters, there was only the Earth.

Imrani teetered across the skulldeck as the ship lurched again. I could hardly credit that I was back in him, but there was no time to question it. Holding his damaged hands up, he headed out towards the spiralway.

The ship's alarm was frantic, the air filled with the stink of organic fluids and charred tissue. There was no sign of Addomatis.

Imrani scrambled unsteadily down the stairway as greasy smoke snaked from doormouths and vent ducts. Though the corridor surface was level, I had the sensation that we were walking over a rolling sea; the ship's gravity stabilizers were beginning to fail.

Imrani careered on, finally bursting into the bridgehead. Jagdavido lay slumped across the sensitories, his hands fused into them, dead eyes open, black blood from his nostrils bearding his narrow face. The status display showed that one emergency pod remained on board; it was ready for launch. In their haste to escape, Elydia and the others had abandoned not only Shivaun, who sat rigid at the controls, but also the womb.

It was free of its tangle of filaments but otherwise undisturbed except that a vertical indentation had appeared down its centre. I was certain it was pulsing. I wanted to go over and examine it, but instead Imrani rushed across to Shivaun. His immediate urge was to free her from the neural helmet, but even as he raised his hands his broken fingers reminded him that he would not be able to.

Then Shivaun lifted her own hands from the controls. She began unfastening the helmet. Her movements were swift, purposeful, just as swift and purposeful as he remembered them. She pushed the helmet up. Shook out her hair. Unstrapped herself from the seat. Rose and turned to him.

Her eyes were alive, a shine in their arctic blue. She smiled warmly at him. Came forward and enfolded him in her arms. He felt her mouth on his and responded wholeheartedly to the kiss, scarcely conscious that her lips were ice-cold.

When finally the kiss ended, Imrani stared at her in astonishment. Only slowly did the realization begin to dawn that it could not possibly *be* her. She was dead, truly dead.

'Goodbye, Imrani,' she said fondly, and the light fled from her eyes. At the same instant I felt Nina joining us, flooding out of Shivaun and into Imrani while Shivaun's body slumped to the deck.

The ship made a noise like a great bursting cough, and its entire innards heaved. Imrani was flung to the deck, the womb toppled over and the ship's alarm announced: 'Loss of atmospheric and gravitational integrity imminent! Manual exit escape pod primed essential urgent!'

It fell silent: the control cortex had failed.

The pod bay was at the rear of the bridgehead. We could only get through it by manipulating the pressurepad controls on the airvalve ourself. But Imrani's hands were ruined. He was crouched over Shivaun's corpse, blubbering. The womb lay on its back, pulsing, splitting slowly apart. The new Advocates were being born.

Imrani jammed his hands under Shivaun's body, yelling with the pain. He lifted her up, began staggering towards the pod bay.

'What are you doing?' I cried out to him, but he wouldn't listen to me. He carried her across the bridgehead, then lost his grip, slumping down next to the womb, Shivaun spilling out of his arms.

The womb had split open, and the Advocates' bodies lay perfect within, their faces obscured by a milky mucus which coated them from head to toe. Their eyes remained closed.

And then Chloe and Lucian swamped our minds with their presence, telling us that they did not yet have any mentality and that we would have to inhabit them if we were to save our own lives and Imrani's.

'What?' I said. 'Inhabit them? How is this possible? They've only just been born.'

'Believe us,' Chloe said. 'You can do it. You *must* save them!' The ship shrieked, and the deck began to ripple again. The urgency of the situation galvanized us. Imrani, weeping, stretched out his broken hands, laying his palms on the Advocates' foreheads.

He seemed to fall forward—

—and then I was looking out through a cloudy fluid.

It took a moment to orientate myself. I was lying on my back in one of the new-born bodies.

I could sense its physicality very powerfully: it enveloped me with its strength. I blinked and raised a hand, wiping the back of it across my eyes to try to clear the mucus. Imrani was peering down at me, sobbing.

I sat up, feeling the tenor of every muscle in the body, the rough touch of my tongue in my mouth, a taste of salt, the musky smell of the womb fluid. I was perfectly functional. Beside me Nina was also rising in the female form.

My vision would not clear, but I knew we had no time for contemplation. We raised one another up, then helped Imrani hoist Shivaun's body into his arms again. He teetered across to the pod bay.

It was Nina who manipulated the valve pad. The pod sat open in the bay, and the instant the three of us clambered inside it announced that it was initiating maximum velocity launch. Something closed in rapidly around us and everything went dark. There was an explosive burst, and the acceleration swamped my consciousness.

Waking was a slow process, and I knew some time had passed. I had the sensation of something soft and wet being stroked all over my body, and there was a fragrant smell. I was being lathered, washed.

Then I woke and saw Marea, Tunde, Vargo and Cori gazing down at me. It was Marea and Tunde who had bathed me, I knew, before laying me on one of the bunks.

I sat up slowly. Nina lay on one side of me, Imrani on the other. Both began to stir, Imrani groaning, Nina opening her eyes. She stared at me with astonishment.

'Nathan?'

It was at once a query and a recognition. She looked exactly as she had done on the Noosphere, in the white room. As I knew I also did. Yet we now inhabited the new Advocates' bodies.

I breathed in slowly, deeply. There was no trace of any other psyche apart from my own within the body, and I knew why.

I was its owner. The bodies were ours.

I searched for Chloe and Lucian, but was not surprised to find no hint of their presence. They had accomplished their task with the utmost cleverness, gradually leading us to this consummation. I could tell that Nina finally understood it as well as I. It was perfectly obvious that they had intended us to inhabit the bodies in the womb from the outset. The whole story had been a means to that end.

It was also obvious that Marea and the others had had no conscious part in it. They were staring at us with a mixture of awe, puzzlement and even impatience. Wrenched from the safety of their former lives to serve the purposes of the tale, they had been used just as much as Nina and I.

I rose, the bunk snuggle wrapping itself around me; I was naked beneath it. Nina did likewise, though Imrani, his broken hands swathed in orthopaedic mittens, merely lay there.

'Is it over?' he asked tremulously.

'Almost,' I told him.

'You're the new Advocates?'

It was Nina who nodded.

I felt quite calm and lucid. Vargo had returned to the controls of the scuttle. I walked over to him.

'The Advocates' ship?' I asked. In my own voice.

Vargo indicated one of the optics. It showed the nose of the flier flaring as it ploughed into the Earth's atmosphere.

I had imagined it would have been over by now. Perhaps we had not been unconscious that long.

'We have to try to save them.'

This was Nina. I knew she meant Bezile and Leanderic.

'No chance,' Vargo was saying. 'They're well out of range. Nothing's going to stop that ship burning.'

'There's only one way to be sure,' Nina said.

I understood what she intended: that we attempt to transfer ourselves into them once again.

There was no question but that we had to try. To let them die now would make us complicit in their murder. Had the entire drama been contrived merely to bring us to life? Had it been necessary? Should the blame for all the horrors rest alone with Julius and Orela, or might there have been a better way to have brought us to our new status, one that could have avoided the suffering of others?

Neither Nina nor I knew whether it would be possible to transfer ourselves without Chloe and Lucian's help: and they were resolutely absent. It might also be dangerous, given that we would be entering minds afflicted with the Dementia.

It occurred to me that Bezile and Leanderic might prefer to die with Orela and Julius. I said as much.

'Perhaps they would,' Nina agreed. 'But they deserve salvation, if possible. It would be our first official act of charity.'

She said this as a simple statement of fact. Already she

seemed to have accommodated herself to our new roles. In many ways she was stronger than I, and yet we complemented one another perfectly. As the Noocracy had intended, no doubt.

Marea and the others kept their distance and said nothing; even Cori was respectful. Already they were treating us as if we were no longer ordinary mortals like themselves. Only Vargo maintained his customary air of scepticism; no doubt our latest incarnation as the new Advocates was no more welcome to him than our previous manifestations. As a Deist, he might even consider us abominations.

Nina offered her hand; I took it. Together we stared at Julius and Orela's ship, concentrating on it, unspeaking, yet as one.

I imagined myself in the navigation pit, inhabiting Bezile again. I closed my eyes and conjured up the image of her in the pilot's seat as vividly as possible. But though I tried, no transition occurred. We were firmly rooted aboard the scuttle. In our newly acquired bodies.

There was only one thing for it. Without speaking, Nina and I left the bridgehead and went down the corridor to the shrine.

It seemed more forbidding than ever now that we knew its true purpose. But if we were the new Advocates, then it should hold no terrors for us.

Nina and I approached the prayer seats. I had an urge to take her in my arms and kiss her, if not out of love then as an ordinary mortal demonstration of deep affection; but there was no time for such a nicety. We sat down, lowered our hoods, slipped our hands into the prayer terminals and activated the icon. It was a small pulsing black star on a field of white. I focused on it, let it draw me in. At the last moment I thought I heard somebody enter the shrine behind us, and I was certain it was Vargo. Then the icon swallowed me whole—

—and I was in Bezile again.

I could feel her webbed into the pilot's station, but although she was conscious her eyes were firmly closed and I could see nothing.

The bridgehead was filled with the laughter of Julius and Orela – mad, uninhibited laughter, as if they were celebrating their imminent deaths.

Bezile, meanwhile, was completely focused on fighting down a terror which threatened to overwhelm her. It was not simply the prospect of her own extinction but the vivid and gruesome images of physical decay which were erupting in her mind: visions of unhinged Dementia victims running amuck, of rotting corpses, maggot-infested skulls – endless mortifications of the flesh. They were the products of Julius and Orela's diseased imaginations, the distillation of a million nightmares wrought from a lifetime of overwhelming experiences.

So absorbed was Bezile in the battle to keep these visions at bay that she scarcely registered my manifestation. I flooded myself through her mind, telling her that we had come to save her, to rescue her from her madness.

There was no response. Amid the relentless cackling of Julius and Orela, I could hear an animalistic whimpering coming from Leanderic. Nina had evidently entered him, and I imagined her struggling with his unleashed madness. She had already achieved greater feats than I, entering the mind of the Augmenter Addomatis, the dead brain of Shivaun. And now she was struggling with a mental frenzy. Leanderic had suffered even more than Bezile and did not possess her resilience. For Nina it must have been like entering a maelstrom of horror.

Yet again I tried to seize control of Bezile's mind, telling her to unweb, to rise. I tried to fill her with the reassurance that even truedeath held no terror. I had only the remotest fear of such an end myself, and perhaps this was proof that Nina and I were indeed of the past and had been raised in a world where death was a fact of existence, the silence that greets the end of every human drama.

But Bezile was wrestling with horrors, and I could not impinge on her.

And still I could hear the Advocates' laughter. Suddenly it came closer.

I focused on attempting one small action, pouring every effort into getting Bezile to open her eyes.

She did so.

And I saw Orela and Julius standing there before us.

They were free of their webbing. Entirely free. On their faces were gleeful smiles.

'Did you really think,' Julius said, 'you could seize control of *our* ship?'

He came forward and put a sculpted fingernail to Bezile's chin. For a moment Bezile's horrors had subsided; for a moment she was painfully lucid. Julius stroked his finger sharply downwards, slicing into the skin.

'It's designed to respond to *our* command,' Orela said. 'At a word from us, it would perform somersaults.' She rolled her eyes as if in demonstration, straddling the quivering Leanderic, stroking his cheek. 'I don't think we are truly ready for death,' she said. 'Not just yet. There are more experiences to be wrested from life.'

'Always more,' Julius agreed eagerly. 'Did you know that some of the Augmenter ships have made planetfall on Earth? Rather enterprising of them, under the circumstances. I think perhaps we will seek them out and join them. Perhaps we'll even be able to forge a new community there. A challenging prospect, wouldn't you agree?'

The grisly death visions were seeping back again, threatening to swamp Bezile's mind once more. And I, too, had begun to feel afraid – afraid that Nina and I were also going to die, our lives ending before they had truly begun. My growing terror also encompassed Julius and Orela: I wanted only to escape from their malignant presence.

'How unfortunate,' said Orela, 'that neither of you will be able to join us. But that, alas, is the nature of mortality. Shall we end it with a kiss?'

Orela wrapped her lips around Leanderic's mouth, while Julius came forward to cup Bezile's face in his hands.

I tried to reach out and grasp Leanderic's hand. Tried and failed. Julius's mouth opened, and he pressed it to Bezile's. I felt the rank heat and the wetness, felt the teeth being bared as if he intended to bite us to death.

Then Chloe and Lucian manifested themselves in full force. Like a great liberating tide, they rushed in and through us, into the Advocates themselves, washing away our terror and madness in an instant.

Julius and Orela broke contact, the two of them staggering

back. A flood of calm suffused them, their wild eyes closing. For a moment they teetered like drunkards, then straightened.

When their eyes opened again, they gazed at us in perfect calm. The flame of their madness had been doused in the instant that Chloe and Lucian entered them, and now I saw them as they must have been in the first days of their Advocacy, as if the good intentions and the proper appetites of their calling had been restored to them. Then I knew nothing.

There was a black star on a white field. Hands were gently raising us from the prayer terminals – the hands of Marea and Tunde and even Vargo. They were gentle, kindly.

They led us away from the terminal but did not take us out of the shrine. Bezile and Leanderic were there, Imrani and Cori, too.

And Julius and Orela.

I drifted away, and when I came back again Julius and Orela were seated, hooded. Leanderic had taken their robes and they wore humble white bodysuits. Bezile was asking them if they were certain they wanted truedeath rather than translation to the Noosphere. Both nodded solemnly, lucidly.

The ship's console had been brought in and was recording the scene. Orela and Julius closed their eyes. Bezile began to deliver a eulogy of their tenure. Her exhaustion barely showed through her determination to carry it through. I couldn't focus on her words; it was as if I were drugged with nepenthe. Nina, too. She was swaying slightly beside me.

Cori came between us, taking our hands in hers. I smiled down at her, heard Bezile say, 'May your souls rest for ever in oblivion.'

The black star blossomed, consuming everything.

Epilogue

The great concourse was thronged with the multitudes of the Noosphere. Nina and I stood, already robed, on the wide platform which overlooked it, the dome of the Shrine of Shrines rising at our backs.

Before us, suspended vertically in a zeegee ceremonial bier, hung Julius and Orela. Their bodies were draped only in the sheerest white wraprounds, their faces composed at last in death. An optic focused on them as Bezile, at the edge of the platform, recounted how they had finally met their end with due dignity in the death-shrine of the scuttle.

It seemed to me as if Nina and I had come here direct from Julius and Orela's death ceremony. In possessing the Advocates, Chloe and Lucian had restored their sanity sufficiently to turn their flier around and rendezvous with the scuttle. They had been taken on board along with Bezile and Leanderic, whose sickness had been cured with the swamping of the Advocates' madness. I had a memory of Julius and Orela declining the option of translation to the Noosphere in the calm and reasoned tones of Chloe and Lucian themselves, who for all I knew were the very embodiment of the Advocates' youth and sanity and had never existed as anything more than that. They had formally accepted Nina and me as their successors, the scuttle's console recording everything. Then they had seated themselves at the shrine and embraced their dying without a murmur.

I recalled this, but it was as though I had lived it through a dream. Afterwards Nina and I had said our farewells to Marea and the others, who now had the freedom to return to their former lives. Then we had accompanied Bezile and Leanderic back to the flier with the Advocates' corpses, setting a course for the Noosphere itself.

I had no memory of the intervening period. Was this how it was for the Advocates, that they were only truly conscious when they had a part to play?

Strangely, I felt no sense of outrage at having been so completely manipulated by Chloe and Lucian – or whatever it was they represented. Yet perhaps it wasn't so strange, because the truth was that I had suspected their final purpose long before this, before even they first showed us the Shrine of Shrines and gave us a hint of what it might be like to be the Advocates, to dip into the billions of other lives throughout the Noospace. I think I understood what they ultimately intended when they revealed that we could inhabit other minds without using a shrine, that the minds of those whose stories we had lived were accessible to us. I knew then that we were central to the outcome of the tale, that we would be the movers and shapers at the end. And what better role for a man and woman who were empty vessels themselves than to become the new Advocates?

I thought of myself awakening, amnesiac, in the white room. I saw again the view from the window, the first of many illusions. Perhaps it had all been a sleight of mind; perhaps we had never truly existed there except as mentalities which had to be trained and shaped before they could be 'born' into this world. Was even the story of our origin merely a convenient fiction, our subsequent involvement in the lives of others the labour pains of our deliverance?

And yet Marea and Tunde and Imrani existed. They had suffered heartbreak and hardship and irrecoverable loss. Shivaun had died as a result of the tale. Already it was like a distant thing, driven and improbable. Did I even, even now, truly exist as a living person? Did Nina? She stood close, beautiful and composed in her splendour. I could smell her fragrance, touch her robes, yet it was possible that even she was a figment, a mirror for my own soul. Would it one day dissolve and would I find myself truly a primitive, surrounded by the dust and ashes of my own creation? Or deeper still, vanishing away entirely so that I, too, would cease to exist?

I stopped myself. Perhaps this was how Julius and Orela's insanity had first begun. Was this the ultimate fate of the Advocates? Or were they driven to madness because it *was* really true that there was no afterlife, the Noosphere merely a sop to the unbearable truth that the fate of every one of us remained extinction? The dome, with its multitude of optics, awaited us. For better or worse, Nina and I would soon know.

The crowd below were eager for a better view of us. Nina and I clasped hands while Leanderic approached to lead us forward to the edge of the platform. Had it not been for Bezile and Leanderic's presence there before us, it would have been easy to imagine that *everything* had been an illusion and that the stories Nina and I had dreamt were mere fictions, Marea and the others existing only within them.

The idea was intolerable to me. I imagined Marea in a pastoral idyll on Europa with Vargo, pet cloak enfolding the newly restored daughter Rashmi while her husband regarded her with bluff fondness, through two good eyes. I could smell the swampmat habitation, feel the heat haze rising. And Tunde, remarried to Adele, taking their children on a blimp tour of Titan's hatchling canyons, Cori studiously chaperoning her step-siblings as they watched the dashing courtship of jewelled darters over twilit crags and canyons. And Imrani, returning Shivaun's corpse to its resting place on Charon, discovering that her daughter Niome is the living image of her, the perfect replacement who laughs with delight as he serenades with a new set of pipes and an improbable moustache. It would be the least any one of them deserved.

I knew – without knowing how – that several days had passed since the battle between the Augmenter armada and the plagueships. None of the latter had survived, but many of the Augmenter ships had indeed made planetfall on Earth. There was to be a public vote on whether they should be allowed to remain there permanently – if indeed they could survive the hostile environment. Nina and I were to give a deliverance on that very subject as one of our first official acts following our investiture. I knew that we would speak in their favour, arguing that diversity has always been a characteristic of our species and that there must be accommodation. We intended our

Advocacy to be marked by tolerance and acceptance of the Augmenters, though urgent and covert steps would have to be taken to ensure that no more entities like the thing in the lake existed, and to eradicate them if they did.

With the deaths of Julius and Orela, the Dementia had also died. There had been no more reported cases, and a mob had reduced the palace at Icarus with plasm-torches. There was general outrage when the worst of the former Advocates' excesses had been revealed, but now the crisis had passed and Bezile was assuring everyone that a new era was about to begin and that Nina and I would serve no more than a fifty-year term. I had no recollection of us discussing this, let alone agreeing it, but fifty years seemed long enough, a daunting prospect indeed. What would become of us when our term was ended, if we survived it with our minds intact?

Bezile came between us and formally introduced us to the crowd. She had made a swift recovery and seemed perfectly at ease in her role as Prime Arbiter. I felt confident that Nina and I would be able to work closely with her for the good of the peoples of the Noospace: after all, we knew her intimately.

Optics closed in around us as we were vested in our scarlet and grey robes. Thousands of millions would ultimately watch the occasion throughout the Settled Worlds. They would be looking to us for guidance and solace after the upheavals of the past year. To some we would become like gods.

My head filled with the roar of the people. It was a terrifying and exhilarating moment. The Shrine of Shrines beckoned, the Dome of Uncountable Eyes. Bezile was telling us that it was time we began our duties by taking our place within it.

I hesitated at the brink of the platform, and was suddenly seized with the notion of hurling myself and Nina off. The moment passed, and instead Nina and I embraced.

Our kiss was formal, ceremonial; it was almost as if we were each in awe of the other. I understood that whatever private moments we had once shared would no longer be possible: now we belonged to everyone. Nina's eyes reflected my own inconsolable sense of personal loss; but any words I might have spoken were drowned by the acclamation of the crowd.

Forthcoming Vista paperback
SF and Fantasy titles

The Difference Engine William Gibson & Bruce
Sterling 0 575 60029 2

A Land Fit for Heroes vol 3: The Dragon Wakes
Phillip Mann 0 575 60012 8

Terry Pratchett's Discworld Quizbook David Langford
0 575 60000 4

Eric Terry Pratchett 0 575 60001 2

Lethe Tricia Sullivan 0 575 60039 X

Golden Witchbreed Mary Gentle 0 575 60033 0

Sailing Bright Eternity Gregory Benford 0 575 60047 0

The Knights of the Black Earth Margaret Weis &
Don Perrin 0 575 60037 3

Fairyland Paul J. McAuley 0 575 60031 4

Timescape Gregory Benford 0 575 60050 0

Reach for Tomorrow Arthur C. Clarke 0 575 60046 2

The Wind from the Sun Arthur C. Clarke 0 575 60052 7

Hawkwood's Voyage Paul Kearney 0 575 60034 9

Chaga Ian McDonald 0 575 60022 5

VISTA books are available from all good bookshops or from:
Cassell C.S.
Book Service By Post
PO Box 29, Douglas I-O-M
IM99 1BQ
telephone: 01624 675137, fax: 01624 670923